AFTERMATH

STAR WARS™
AFTERMATH

Book One of The Aftermath Trilogy

CHUCK WENDIG

arrow books

12

Arrow Books
20 Vauxhall Bridge Road
London SW1V 2SA

Arrow Books is part of the Penguin Random House group
of companies whose addresses can be found at global.
penguinrandomhouse.com.

Penguin
Random House
UK

First published in Great Britain by Century in 2015

www.randomhouse.co.uk

A CIP catalogue record for this book is available from
the British Library.

ISBN 9781784750039

Printed and bound by Clays Ltd, Elcograf S.p.A

MIX
Paper from
responsible sources
FSC® C018179

Penguin Random House is committed to a
sustainable future for our business, our readers
and our planet. This book is made from Forest
Stewardship Council® certified paper.

To Tracy
for taking me to see my first Star Wars *movie*
(The Empire Strikes Back *at a drive-in theater!).*

To Mom for buying me all those sweet Kenner toys.

To Michelle and to Ben for going along on this
crazy speeder ride with me and making it ten
times as awesome as it already is.

STAR WARS™

TIMELINE

TIMELINE

ACKNOWLEDGMENTS

The writer is like Han Solo: captain of the ship but lost without a crew to man it. And so I must acknowledge those folks who have helped make this book happen: Shelly Shapiro, Jen Heddle, Gary Whitta, Jason Fry, David Keck, Pablo Hidalgo, and my agent, Stacia Decker. Thanks, too, to some of my writer pals who keep me sane: folks like Kevin Hearne, Delilah S. Dawson, Stephen Blackmoore, Ty Franck, Adam Christopher, Julie Hutchings, Mur Lafferty, J. C. Hutchins, and Sam Sykes. Thanks finally to the *Star Wars* fan community for having fun with me on Twitter (GeekGirlDiva, I'm lookin' at you).

Thanks, in fact, to all of Twitter because without social media, I don't think I would have ever gotten to write this book.

clinks my glass of blue milk against yours

A long time ago in a galaxy far, far away. . . .

The second Death Star is destroyed. The Emperor and his powerful enforcer, Darth Vader, are rumored to be dead. The Galactic Empire is in chaos.

Across the galaxy, some systems celebrate, while in others Imperial factions tighten their grip. Optimism and fear reign side by side.

And while the Rebel Alliance engages the fractured forces of the Empire, a lone rebel scout uncovers a secret Imperial meeting . . .

PRELUDE:

Today is a day of celebration. We have triumphed over villainy and oppression and have given our Alliance—and the galaxy beyond it—a chance to breathe and cheer for the progress in reclaiming our freedom from an Empire that robbed us of it. We have reports from Commander Skywalker that Emperor Palpatine is dead, and his enforcer, Darth Vader, with him.

But though we may celebrate, we should not consider this our time to rest. We struck a major blow against the Empire, and now will be the time to seize on the opening we have created. The Empire's weapon may be destroyed, but the Empire itself lives on. Its oppressive hand closes around the throats of good, free-thinking people across the galaxy, from the Coruscant Core to the farthest systems in the Outer Rim. We must remember that our fight continues. Our rebellion is over. But the war . . . the war is just beginning.

—Admiral Ackbar

CORUSCANT

THEN:

Monument Plaza.

Chains rattle as they lash the neck of Emperor Palpatine. Ropes follow suit—lassos looping around the statue's middle. The mad cheers of the crowd as they pull, and pull, and pull. Disappointed groans as the stone fixture refuses to budge. But then someone whips the chains around the back ends of a couple of heavy-gauge speeders, and then engines warble and hum to life—the speeders gun it and again the crowd pulls—

The sound like a giant bone breaking.

A fracture appears at the base of the statue.

More cheering. Yelling. And—

Applause as it comes crashing down.

The head of the statue snaps off, goes rolling and crashing into a fountain. Dark water splashes. The crowd laughs.

And then: The whooping of klaxons. Red lights strobe. Three airspeeders swoop down from the traffic lanes above—Imperial police. Red-and-black helmets. The glow of their lights reflected back in their helmets.

There comes no warning. No demand to stand down.

The laser cannons at the fore of each airspeeder open fire. Red bolts sear the air. The crowd is cut apart. Bodies dropped and stitched with fire.

But still, those gathered are not cowed. They are no longer a crowd. Now they are a mob. They start picking up hunks of the Palpatine statue and lobbing them up at the airspeeders. One of the speeders swings to the side to avoid an incoming chunk of stone—and it bumps another speeder, interrupting its fire. Coruscanti citizens climb up the stone spire behind both speeders—a spire on which are written the Imperial values of order, control, and the rule of law—and begin jumping onto the police cruisers. One helmeted cop is flung from his vehicle. The other crawls out onto the hood of his speeder, opening fire with a pair of blasters—just as a hunk of stone cracks him in the helmet, knocking him to the ground.

The other two airspeeders lift higher and keep firing.

Screams and fire and smoke.

Two of those gathered—a father and son, Rorak and Jak—quick-duck behind the collapsed statue. The sounds of the battle unfolding right here in Monument Plaza don't end. In the distance, the sound of more fighting, a plume of flames, flashes of blaster fire. A billboard high up in the sky among the traffic lanes suddenly goes to static.

The boy is young, only twelve standard years, not old enough to fight. Not yet. He looks to his father with pleading eyes. Over the din he yells: "But the battle station was destroyed, Dad! The battle is over!" They just watched it only an hour before. The supposed end of the Empire. The start of something better.

The confusion in the boy's shining eyes is clear: He doesn't understand what's happening.

But Rorak does. He's heard tales of the Clone Wars—tales spoken by his own father. He knows how war goes. It's not many wars, but just one, drawn out again and again, cut up into slices so it seems more manageable.

For a long time he's told his son not the truth but the idealized hope: *One day the Empire will fall and things will be different for when you have children.* And that may still come to pass. But now a stronger, sharper truth is required: "Jak—the battle isn't over. The battle is just starting."

He holds his son close.

Then he puts a hunk of statue in the boy's hand.

And he picks one up himself.

PART ONE

PART ONE

CHAPTER ONE

NOW:

Starlines streak across the bright black.

A ship drops out of hyperspace: a little Starhopper. A one-person ship. Favored by many of the *less desirable* factions out here in the Outer Rim—the pirates, the bookies, the bounty hunters and those with bounties on their heads to hunt. This particular ship has seen action: plasma scarring across the wings and up its tail fins; a crumpled dent in the front end as if it was kicked by an Imperial walker. All the better for the ship to blend in.

Ahead: the planet Akiva. A small planet—from here, striations of brown and green. Thick white clouds swirling over its surface.

The pilot, Wedge Antilles, once Red Leader and now—well, now something else, a role without a formal title, as yet, because things are so new, so different, so wildly up in the air—sits there and takes a moment.

It's nice up here. Quiet.

No TIE fighters. No blasts across the bow of his X-wing. No X-wing, in fact, and though he loves flying one, it's nice to be out. No Death Star—and here, Wedge shudders, because he helped take down two of those things. Some days that fills him with pride.

Other days it's something else, something worse. Like he's drawn back to it. The fight still going on all around him. But that isn't today.

Today, it's quiet.

Wedge likes the quiet.

He pulls up his datapad. Scrolls through the list with a tap of the button on the side. (He has to hit it a few extra times just to get it to go—if there's one thing he looks forward to when all this is over, it's that maybe they'll start to get new tech. Somehow, this datapad had actual *sand* in it, and that's why the buttons stick.) The list of planets clicks past.

He's been to, let's see, five so far. Florrum. Ryloth. Hinari. Abafar. Raydonia. This planet, Akiva, is the sixth on the list of many, too many.

It was his idea, this run. Somehow, the remaining factions of the Empire are still fueling their war effort even months after the destruction of their second battle station. Wedge had the notion that they must've moved out to the Outer Rim—study your history and it's easy to see that the seeds of the Empire grew first out here, away from the Core systems, away from the prying eyes of the Republic.

Wedge told Ackbar, Mon Mothma: "Could be that's where they are again. Hiding out there." Ackbar said that it made some sense. After all, didn't Mustafar hold some importance to the Imperial leadership? Rumors said that's where Vader took some of the Jedi long ago. Torturing them for information before their execution.

And now Vader's gone. Palpatine, too.

Almost there, Wedge thinks—once they find the supply lines that are bolstering the Imperials, he'll feel a whole lot better.

He pulls up the comm. Tries to open a channel to command and—

Nothing.

Maybe it's broken. It's an old ship.

Wedge fidgets at his side, pulls up the personal comm relay that hangs there at his belt—he taps the side of it, tries to get a signal.

Once more: nothing.

His heart drops into his belly. Feels a moment like he's falling. Because what all of this adds up to is:

The signal's blocked. Some of the criminal syndicates still operating out here have technology to do that *locally*—but in the space above the planet, no, no way. Only one group has that tech.

His jaw tightens. The bad feeling in the well of his gut is swiftly justified, as ahead a Star Destroyer punctures space like a knife-tip as it drops out of hyperspace. Wedge fires up the engines. *I have to get out of here.*

A second Star Destroyer slides in next to the first.

The panels across the Starhopper's dash begin blinking red.

They see him. What to do?

What did Han always say? *Just fly casual.* The ship is disguised as it is for a reason: It looks like it could belong to any two-bit smuggler out here on the fringe. Akiva's a hotbed of criminal activity. Corrupt satrap governors. Various syndicates competing for resources and opportunities. A well-known black market—once, decades ago, the Trade Federation had a droid manufacturing facility here. Which means, if you want some off-the-books droid, you can come here to buy one. The Rebel Alliance procured many of its droids right here, as a matter of fact.

New dilemma, though: What now?

Fly down to the planet to do aerial recon, as was the original plan—or plot a course back to Chandrila? Something's up. Two Star Destroyers appearing out of nowhere? Blocked comms? That's not nothing. *It means I've found what I'm looking for.*

Maybe even something much better.

That means: Time to plot a course out of here.

That'll take a few minutes, though—heading inward from the Outer Rim isn't as easy as taking a long stride from here to there. It's a dangerous jump. Endless variables await: nebula clouds, asteroid fields, floating bands of star-junk from various skirmishes and battles. Last thing Wedge wants to do is pilot around the edge of a black hole or through the center of a star going supernova.

The comm crackles.

They're hailing him.

A crisp Imperial voice comes across the channel.

"This is the Star Destroyer *Vigilance.* You have entered Imperial space." To which Wedge thinks: *This isn't Imperial space. What's going on here?* "Identify yourself."

Fear lances through him, sharp and bright as an electric shock. This isn't his realm. Talking. Lying. A scoundrel like Solo could convince a Jawa to buy a bag of sand. Wedge is a pilot. But it's not like they didn't plan for this. Calrissian worked on the story. He clears his throat, hits the button—

"This is Gev Hessan. Piloting an HH-87 Starhopper: the *Rover.*" He transmits his datacard. "Sending over credentials."

A pause. "Identify the nature of your visit."

"Light cargo."

"What cargo?"

The stock answer is: droid components. But that may not fly here. He thinks quickly—Akiva. Hot. Wet. Mostly jungle. "Dehumidifier parts."

Pause. An excruciating one.

The nav computer runs through its calculations.

Almost there . . .

A different voice comes through the tinny speaker. A woman's voice. Got some steel in it. Less crisp. Nothing lilting. This is someone with some authority—or, at least, someone who thinks she possesses it.

She says, "Gev Hessan. Pilot number 45236. Devaronian. Yes?"

That checks out. Calrissian knows Hessan. The smuggler—sorry, "legitimate pilot and businessman"—did work smuggling goods to help Lando build Cloud City. And he is indeed Devaronian.

"You got it," Wedge says.

Another pause.

The computer is almost done with its calculations. Another ten seconds at most. Numbers crunching, flickering on the screen . . .

"Funny," the woman says. "Our records indicate that Gev Hessan died in Imperial custody. Please let us correct our records."

The hyperspace computer finishes its calculations.

He pushes the thruster forward with the heel of his hand—

But the ship only shudders. Then the Starhopper trembles again, and begins to drift forward. Toward the pair of Star Destroyers. It means they've engaged the tractor beams.

He turns to the weapon controls.

If he's going to get out of this, it's now or never.

Admiral Rae Sloane stares down at the console and out the window. The black void. The white stars. Like pinpricks in a blanket. And out there, like a child's toy on the blanket: a little long-range fighter.

"Scan them," she says. Lieutenant Nils Tothwin looks up, offers her an obsequious smile.

"Of course," he says, his jaundiced face tight with that grin. Tothwin is an emblem of what's wrong with the Imperial forces now: Many of their best are gone. What's left is, in part, the dregs. The leaves and twigs at the bottom of a cup of spice tea. Still, he does what he's told, which is something—Sloane wonders when the Empire will truly begin to fracture. Forces doing what they want, when they want it. Chaos and anarchy. The moment that happens, the moment someone of some prominence breaks from the fold to go his own way, they are all truly doomed.

Tothwin scans the Starhopper as the tractor beam brings it slowly, but inevitably, closer. The screen beneath him glimmers, and a holographic image of the ship rises before him, constructed as if by invisible hands. The image flashes red along the bottom. Nils, panic in his voice, says: "Hessan is charging his weapons systems."

She scowls. "Calm down, Lieutenant. The weapons on a Starhopper aren't enough to—" Wait. She squints. "Is that what I think it is?"

"What?" Tothwin asks. "I don't—"

Her finger drifts to the front end of the holograph—circling the fighter's broad, curved nose. "Here. Ordnance launcher. Proton torpedo."

"But the Starhopper wouldn't be equipped—oh. *Oh.*"

"Someone has come prepared for a fight." She reaches down, flips on the comm again. "This is Admiral Rae Sloane. I see you there, little pilot. Readying a pair of torpedoes. Let me guess: You think a proton torpedo will disrupt our tractor beam long enough to afford you your escape. That may be accurate. But let me also remind you that we have enough ordnance on the *Vigilance* to turn you not only to scrap but rather, to a *fine particulate matter.*

Like dust, cast across the dark. The timing doesn't work. You'll fire your torpedo. We'll fire ours. Even *if* by the time your weapons strike us our beam is disengaged . . ." She clucks her tongue. "Well. If you feel you must try, then try."

She tells Nils to target the Starhopper.

Just in case.

But she hopes the pilot is wise. Not some fool. Probably some rebel scout, some spy, which is foolish on its own—though less foolish now, with the newly built second Death Star destroyed like its predecessor.

All the more reason for her to remain vigilant, as the name of this ship suggests. The meeting on Akiva cannot misfire. It must take place. It must have a *result*. Everything feels on the edge, the entire Empire standing on the lip of the pit, the ledge crumbling away to scree and stone.

The pressure is on. An almost literal pressure—like a fist pressing against her back, pushing the air out of her lungs.

Her chance to excel.

Her chance to change Imperial fortune.

Forget the old way.

Indeed.

Wedge winces, heart racing in his chest like an ion pulse. He knows she's right. The timing doesn't favor him. He's a good pilot, maybe one of the best, but he doesn't have the Force on his side. If Wedge launches those two torpedoes, they'll give him everything they have. And then it won't matter if he breaks free from the tractor beam. He won't have but a second to get away from whatever fusillade they send his way.

Something is happening. Here, in the space above Akiva. Or maybe down there on the planet's surface.

If he dies here—nobody will know what it is.

Which means he has to play this right.

He powers down the torpedoes.

He has another idea.

Docking Bay 42.

Rae Sloane stands in the glass-encased balcony, overlooking the gathered battalion of stormtroopers. This lot, like Nils, are imperfect. Those who received top marks at the Academy went on to serve on the Death Star, or on Vader's command ship, the *Executor*. Half of them didn't even complete the Academy—they were pulled out of training early.

These will do, though. For now. Ahead is the Starhopper—drifting in through the void of space, cradled by the invisible grip of the tractor beam. Down past the lineup of TIE fighters (half of what they need, a third of what she'd prefer), drifting slowly toward the gathered stormtroopers.

They have the numbers. The Starhopper will have one pilot, most likely. Perhaps a second or third crewmember.

It drifts closer and closer.

She wonders: *Who are you?* Who is inside that little tin can?

Then: A bright flash and a shudder—the Starhopper suddenly glows blue from the nose end forward.

It explodes in a rain of fire and scrap.

"Whoever it was," Lieutenant Tothwin says, "they did not wish to be discovered. I suppose they favored a quick way out."

Sloane stands amid the smoldering wreckage of the long-range fighter. It stinks of ozone and fire. A pair of gleaming black astromechs whir, firing extinguishing foam to put out the last of the flames. They have to navigate around the half dozen or so stormtrooper bodies that lie about, still. Helmets cracked. Chest plates charred. Blaster rifles scattered and broken.

"Don't be a naïve calf," she says, scowling. "*No*, the pilot didn't want to be discovered. But he's still here. If he didn't want us to blast him out of the sky out *there*, you really think he'd be eager to die in *here*?"

"Could be a suicide attack. Maximize the damage—"

"No. He's here. And he can't be far. Find him."

Nils gives a sharp, nervous nod. "Yes, Admiral. Right away."

CHAPTER TWO

"WE HAVE TO TURN AROUND," Norra says. "Plot another course—"

"Whoa, whoa, no," Owerto says, half laughing. He looks up at her—one half of his dark face burned underneath a mottled carpet of scars, scars he claims to have earned with a different story each time he tells it: lava, wampa, blaster fire, got blitzed on Corellian rum and fell down on a hot camping stove. "Miss Susser—"

"Now that I'm home, I'm going by my married name again. Wexley."

"*Norra*. You paid me to get you onto the surface of *that* planet." He points out the window. There: home. Or was, once. The planet Akiva. Clouds swirling in lazy spirals over the jungles and mountains. Above it: Two Star Destroyers hang there like swords above the surface. "More important, you ain't the only cargo I'm bringing in. I'm finishing this job."

"They told us to turn around. This is a blockade—"

"And smugglers like me are very good at getting around those."

"We need to get back to the Alliance—" She corrects herself. That's old thinking. "The *New Republic*. They need to know."

A third Star Destroyer suddenly cuts through space, appearing in line with the others.

"You got family down there?"

She offers a stiff nod. "That's why I'm here." *That's why I'm home.*

"This was always a risk. The Empire's been here on Akiva for years. Not like *this*, but . . . they're here, and we're gonna have to deal with it." He leans in and says: "You know why I call this ship the *Moth*?"

"I don't."

"You ever try to catch a moth? Cup your hands, chase after it, catch it? White moth, brown moth, any moth at all? You can't do it. They always get away. Herky-jerky up-and-down left-and-right. Like a puppet dancing on somebody's strings. That's me. That's this ship."

"I still don't like it."

"I don't like it, either, but life is full of unlikable things. You wanna see your family again? Then we're doing this. Now's the time, too. Looks like they're just getting set up. Might be more on the way."

A half-mad gleam in his one good eye. His other: an implacable red lens framed in an ill-fitting O-ring bolted to the scarred skin. He grins, then: crooked teeth stretched wide. He actually likes this.

Smugglers, she thinks.

Well, she paid for the ticket.

Time to take the ride.

The long black table gleams with light shining up from it—a holographic schematic of the *Vigilance*'s docking bay and surrounding environs. It incorporates a fresh droid scan and shows damage to two of the TIE fighters, not to mention the bodies of the stormtroopers—those left there as a reminder to others what can happen when you tussle with rebels.

The pilot of the Starhopper? Most definitely a rebel. Now the question: Was this an attack? Did he know they were here? Or is this some confluence of events, some crass coincidence that led to this intersection?

That, a problem for later. The problem now is figuring out just where he went. Because as she thought, the ship contained no body.

Best she can figure, he rigged the proton torpedoes to blow. Before they did, however, he . . . what? She taps a button, goes back to the Starhopper schematic she pulled off the Imperial databases. There. A stern-side door. Small, but enough to load small parcels of cargo in and out.

Her new pilot friend ducked out the back. Would've been a considerable jump. *Jedi?* No. Couldn't be. Only one of those out there—and zero chance the rebels would send their golden boy, Skywalker.

Back to the bay schematic—

She spins it. Highlights the access ducts.

That's it. She pulls her comm. "Tothwin. Our pilot is in the ducts. I'll bet all my credits you'll find an open vent—"

"We have a problem."

The problem is that you interrupted me, she thinks but does not say. "What is it?"

"We have a blockade-runner."

"Another terrorist?"

"Could be. Looks like a bog-standard smuggler, though. Flying a small Corellian freighter—an, ahh, let's see, an MK-4."

"Dispatch the TIEs. Let them deal with it."

"Of course, Admiral."

*   *   *

Everything feels like it's in slow motion. Norra sits, frozen in the navigator's chair next to Owerto Naiucho, the scar-faced smuggler—flashes of light on his face, green light from the incoming lasers, orange light blooming from a TIE fighter meeting its untimely end. Outside, ahead of them, a swarm of TIEs like a cloud of insects—the horrible scream as they pass, vibrating the chair beneath her and the console gripped in her white-knuckled hands. In the moments when she blinks, she doesn't see darkness. She sees another battle unfolding—

"It's a trap!" comes Ackbar's voice over the comm. The dread feeling as Imperial TIEs descend upon them like redjacket wasps from a rock-struck nest. The dark of space lighting up with a crackling beam of viridian light—that coming from the half-constructed Death Star, just one more shovelful of dirt on the Alliance's grave as one of their own capital ships is gone, erased in a pulse of light, lightning, and fire—

The freighter dives toward the planet's surface. Turning like a screw. The ship shuddering as laser-fire scores its side. The shields won't hold forever. Owerto's yelling at her: "You need to handle the guns! Norra! *The guns*." But she can't get up out of that chair. Her bloodless hands won't even leave the console. Her mouth is dry. Her underarms wet. Her heart is beating like a pulsar star before it goes dark.

"We want you to fly with us," Captain Antilles says. She objects, of course—she's been working for the rebels for years now, since before the destruction of the first Death Star, but as a freighter pilot. Carrying message droids, or smuggling weapons, or just shuttling people from planet to planet and base to base. "And that doesn't change the kind of pilot you are," he says. "You outran a Star Destroyer. You

forced two TIE interceptors to crash into each other. You've always been a great pilot. And we need you now for when General Solo gets those shield genera- tors down." He asks her again: Is she in? Will she fly with the red and the gold? Yes. She says yes. Because of course she does—how could she say otherwise?

Everything, gone dizzy. Lights inside the cabin flash- ing. A rain of sparks from somewhere behind their chairs. Here in the *Moth*, everything feels balanced on the head of a pin. Through the glass, the planet. The clouds, coming closer. TIE fighters punching holes through them, vapor swirling behind them. She stands up, hands shaking.

Inside the bowels of the beast. Pipes and hissing steam. Skeletal beams and bundles of cord and con- duit. The guts of the resurrected Death Star. The shields are down. This is their one chance. But the TIE fighters are everywhere. Coming up behind them, hawks nipping at their tail feathers. She knows where this goes: It means she's going to die. But that's how things get done. Gold Leader comms in—Lando's voice in her ear, and his Sullustan copilot's just behind it. They tell her what to do. And again she thinks: This is it, this is how I die. *She accelerates her fighter. The heat signature of the core goes left. She pulls her Y-wing right—and a handful of the TIEs break off and follow her deeper. Away from the* Millennium Falcon. *Away from the X-wings. Laserfire frying her engines. Popping the top off her astromech. Smoke filling the cabin. The smell of ozone—*

"I'm not a gunner," she says. "I'm a pilot."

Then she pulls Owerto out of his pilot's chair. He protests, but she gives him a look—a look she's prac- ticed, a look where her face hardens like cooling steel, the look of a raptor before it takes your eyes. The smuggler gives a barely perceptible nod, and it's good that he does. Because as soon as she's down in the chair and grabbing the stick and throttle, she sees a pair of TIE fighters coming up fast from the front—

Her teeth clamp down so hard she thinks her jaw might break. Lasers like demon fire score the sky ahead, coming right for them.

She pulls back on the stick. The *Moth* ceases its dive toward the planet's surface—the lasers just miss, passing under the hind end of the freighter, continuing on—

Boom.

They take out two of the TIE fighters that had been following close behind. And even as she continues hauling back on the stick, her stomach and heart trading places, the blood roaring in her ears, she loopty-loops the ship just in time to see the remaining two TIEs clip each other. Vertical wing panels smashing together, prying apart—each of the short-range Imperial fighters suddenly spinning away, pirouetting wildly through space like a pair of Republic Day firecracker pinwheels.

"We got more incoming!" Owerto hollers from somewhere behind her—and then she hears the gears of the *Moth*'s twin cannons grinding as the turret spins into place and begins barking fire.

Clouds whip past.

The ship bangs and judders as it kicks a hole in the atmosphere.

This is my home, she thinks. Or was. She grew up on Akiva. More important, Norra then was like Norra now: She doesn't much care for people. She went off on her own a lot. Explored the wilds outside the capital city of Myrra—the old temples, the cave systems, the rivers, the canyons.

She knows those places. Every switchback, every bend, every nook and cranny. Again she thinks, *This is my home,* and with that mantra set to repeat, she stills her shaking hands and banks hard to starboard, corkscrewing the ship as laserfire blasts past.

The planet's surface comes up fast. Too fast, but she tells herself that she knows what she's doing. Down there, the rise of lush hills and slick-faced cliffs give way to the Canyon of Akar—a winding serpentine valley, and it's there she takes the *Moth*. Into the rainforested channel. Drizzle speckling her view, streaking away. The wings of the freighter clip branches, tearing up a flurry of leaves as she jukes left and jerks right, making the *Moth* one helluva hard target to hit.

Laserfire sears the canopy ahead.

Then: a bank of fog.

She pushes down on the stick, takes the freighter even lower. Here, the canyon is tighter. Trees stretching out like selfish hands, thrust up from rocky outcroppings. Norra deliberately clips these—again on the left, then on the right. The *Moth*'s turrets belt out cannon fire and suddenly a TIE comes tumbling end-over-end like a flung boulder—she has to bank the ship hard to dodge it. It smashes into a tree. A belching fireball.

The freighter shudders.

More sparks. The cabin goes dark. Owerto: "We've lost the turrets!"

Norra thinks: *We don't need them.*

Because she knows what's coming. One of the oldest temple complexes—abandoned, an artifact of architecture from a time long, long ago, when the Ahia-Ko people dwelled here still. But before that: a cascading waterfall, a silver churn of water leaping over a cliff's edge. A cliff they call the Witch's Finger for the way it looks like a bent and accusing digit. There's a space underneath that bridge of stone, a narrow channel. *Too narrow,* she thinks. But maybe not. Especially not with the turret gone. Too late to do differently now—

She turns the freighter to its side—

Ahead, the gap under the rock. Waterfall on one side. Jagged cliff face on the other. Norra stills her breathing. Opens her eyes wide.

That mantra comes one last time, spoken aloud:

"This is my home."

The freighter passes through the channel.

It shakes like an old drunk—what's left of the turret shears off. Clangs away, spinning into the waterfall spray—

But they're out. Clean. Alive.

On the console, two blinking red blips.

TIE fighters. Behind them.

Wait for it.

Wait . . . for it . . .

The air claps with a pair of explosions.

The two blips flicker and are gone.

Owerto hoots and claps his hands. "We're clear!"

Damn right we are.

She turns the freighter and sets a course for the out-skirts of Myrra.

Nils Tothwin swallows hard and steps over the shattered glass and puddle of fizzing liquor—that from a ceremonial bottle of Lothalian currant wine, a wine so purple it's almost black. The puddle on the floor could at first be confused for a hole in the floor, in fact.

Tothwin rubs his hands together. He's nervous.

"You haven't found him," Rae Sloane says.

"No."

"And I saw that the smuggler's ship is gone."

"Gone as in, escaped."

She narrows her eyes. "I know what I meant."

"Of course, Admiral."

The puddle bubbles. That bottle, given to her to celebrate her rise to the role of admiral. Appropriate then that it was ceremonial, because that's what became of her role, too—her leadership was purely ceremony. For years she'd been sidelined. Yes, given command of the *Vigilance*. But the *Vigilance* was itself given nothing close to a major role in the struggle against the rising Rebellion. Paltry work. Patrols in the Outer Rim, mostly. Defense and escort of bureaucrats, moffs, dignitaries, ambassadors.

It's what she gets. She made too many enemies early on. Sloane was always one to speak her mind. She didn't know her place. And it hurt her.

But now: This is the time for second chances.

She cuts the silence: "This is a bad time for chaos, Lieutenant. Out there, already two of our esteemed guests have arrived." Moff Valco Pandion in the Star Destroyer *Vanquish,* and in the *Ascent,* one of the Galactic Empire's oldest strategists and tacticians: General Jylia Shale. "Soon, the others will arrive. I cannot have this be a time that demonstrates my weakness. We cannot reveal an inability to control our own environment, because if that happens, it will prove— particularly to Pandion—that we cannot even control this meeting. And this meeting? *Must* be controlled."

"Absolutely, Admiral. We will find the interloper—"

"No. *I* will lead the charge to find our unanticipated guest. *You* assemble a team. Go to the surface in advance of the meeting. Track the smuggler and freighter that evaded us. Just to be sure it's not part of something bigger. This must go right, and if it goes wrong? I will hold you personally accountable."

What little color he has in his face drains.

"As you wish, Admiral."

* * *

Steam rises like stirred specters off the surface of the *Moth*—the rain has stopped and now the sun is out. Bright and hot. The air thick with humidity. Already Norra feels her hair—normally straight and silver as the waterfall they just passed under only an hour before—starting to curl at the edges, the hairs snarling together. An odd thought: *Have I brought a brush? Did she even bring the right clothes? What will Temmin think of her?*

She hasn't seen her son in . . . too long now. Three standard years? At that, she winces.

"You are one wild pilot," Owerto says, coming around the side. He slaps the ship: *whong, whong, whong.* "I'm man enough to admit that you maybe saved the *Moth*'s bacon out there."

She offers a terse smile. "Well. I had a good moment."

"Flying like that isn't luck. It's skill. You're a rebel pilot, right?"

"Right."

"Seems you're on the winning team, then."

Not yet, she thinks. But all she says is, "One hopes."

"They really gone? The Emperor? That machine-man, Vader? Whole Death Star blown to little bitty bits all over again?"

"It was. I was there. I was . . . inside it, actually."

He whistles low and slow. "That explains the fancy flying."

"Maybe."

"Congratulations. You're a hero. Must've been something."

"It was something, all right." Even now, thinking of it, a cold shiver ratchets up her spine despite the oppressive heat. Others may have felt exhilarated

during that battle. But for her: It lives on in her nightmares. Watching good pilots spiral into the surface of
that massive base. Hearing their screams over the
comm. "Your money," she says, abruptly. She pulls a
small sack out of her duffel. Tosses it to him. "Ten K
on arrival, as promised. Thanks. Sorry about your
ship."

"I'll get it fixed up. Good luck with your family."

"My son, mostly. I'm here to get him and get back
out."

He arches an eyebrow over his one good eye.
"That's gonna be some tricky business what with the
blockade. You figured a way offplanet yet?"

"No. Are you offering?"

"Pay me the same and promise to fly the ship again
if the chips are down, and you got yourself a deal."

She offers a hand. They shake on it.

"Oh," he adds as he walks away. "Welcome home,
Norra *Wexley*."

CHAPTER THREE

AKIVA HAS ALWAYS had Imperials. Just not occupying ones. As with many of the worlds on the Outer Rim—wheeling on their axes at the edges of known space—Imperials used the planet but could never, or perhaps *would* never, stake an official claim. These exoplanets were beasts too rough, too wild, too strange to ever be brought under the Galactic Empire's yoke. When the Imperials came here, it was for reasons often personal: the drink, the spice, the smoke, the gambling, the black-market goods. Or maybe just to sightsee the wild faces and unmet aliens that cross paths at this outpost of miscreants and deviants.

That, *all* of that, is what brought him here.

Sinjir Rath Velus. Imperial loyalty officer.

Well. *Ex*-Imperial loyalty officer.

The galactic tides swept him here and washed him up on this planet of wild jungles and jagged mountains, this place of black volcanoes and glass-sand beaches. Here he sits. Same seat at the same bar, in the same back-alley quadrant of Myrra, with the same Mon Calamari bartender pushing drinks across the oka-wood bar top.

Nursing a sashin-leaf mead—golden, sweet, tastes like a cross between a jybbuk-fruit and oi-ois, those little red berries his mother used to pick. This is his third of the day, and the sun's only been up a few hours. Already his head is like a fly in a sticky spider's web, struggling and trying to fly free before ultimately failing and giving in to fatal torpor.

His head feels gummy, swimmy, boggy.

Sinjir holds up the drink and regards it the way one might regard a lover. With passion and fervor he says to it, "You can count on me. I'm all in." Then he quits nursing it and slams it back. It goes down easy. He shudders with pleasure. Then he taps the bottom of the glass on the wood. "Bartender. Drink-keeper. Peddler of strange liqueurs! Another, please."

The Mon Calamari, named Pok, trundles up. He's old, this Mon Cal—his *chin tentacles,* or whatever they are, have grown long and thick, a fringed beard of red skin, twitching suckers, and glistening barnacles. His one arm is gone, replaced instead with the gleaming silver limb of a protocol droid. A hasty, ill-fitting job—the wires plugged unceremoniously into the blistering flesh of his red shoulder. An unappetizing thing to look at, but Sinjir cares little at this point. He deserves nothing better than this.

Pok gurgles and grunts at him in whatever tongue the Mon Cals speak. They have the same conversation every time:

Pok makes his *sounds.*

Sinjir asks, then demands, that the bartender speak Basic.

Pok says, in Basic, "I don't speak Basic," before going back to gabbling in his alien way.

And then Sinjir makes his request and Pok fills the glass.

At the end of that exchange, Sinjir makes a new request: "I'll take . . . by all the stars in all the skies it's hot, isn't it? I'll take something refreshing? What's refreshing, my squid-faced friend? Give me that."

The bartender shrugs, his gelatinous frog-egg eyes quivering, before fetching a wooden cup with a couple of ice cubes rattling around in the bottom. Pok grabs a dingy bottle from the shelf: something with a non-Basic script scrawled across it. Just as he cannot understand the Mon Cal's words, Sinjir cannot translate the language on the bottle. The Empire had little interest in learning the ways and tongues of other cultures. They didn't even want their people to learn on their own time.

(Sinjir is reminded of the time he found the young officer studying *Ithorese,* of all things. That young, fresh-faced fellow, sitting cross-legged on his cot, a long index finger scanning lines of the alien script. Sinjir broke that finger for him. Said it was better than any administrative punishment—and faster, too.)

(Sinjir is also reminded: *I am a terrible person.* Guilt and shame duel in his gut like a pair of hissing Loth-cats.)

Pok pours from the bottle.

Sinjir gives it a swirl. The smell coming off it could strip the black from a TIE pilot's helmet. He tastes it, expecting it to set his tongue and throat on fire, but it's quite the opposite. Not sweet. Floral. A taste that fails to match the smell. Fascinating.

He sighs.

"Hey," someone next to him whispers.

Sinjir ignores it. Takes a long, noisy sip of his strange brew.

"Hey."

They're speaking to him, aren't they? Ugh. He tilts his head and arches both eyebrows expectantly, only to see some Twi'lek sitting there. Skin pink like a newborn baby's. One of the tail-head's head-tails comes off the top of his too-tall forehead and winds around his shoulder and underarm the way a worker might carry a coil of rope or hose.

"Buddy," the Twi'lek says. "Hey."

"No," Sinjir says quite crisply. "That's not—no. I don't talk to people. I'm not here to talk. I'm here for this." He holds up the wooden cup, gives it a little swirl so that the ice makes noise. "Not for *this*." He gesticulates, waggling fingers in the general area of the Twi'lek.

"You seen the holovid?" the Twi'lek asks, indicating that he's one of those brash, belligerent types who only understand social cues when they're delivered at the end of a fist or at the tip of a blaster rifle.

Still. Holovid? He's curious. "No. What is it?"

The Twi'lek looks left, looks right, then pulls out a little disk—bigger than his palm, smaller than a proper dinner plate. Metal ring. Blue glass center. The alien licks his sharp little teeth then hits a button.

An image appears hovering over the disk.

A woman. Regal bearing. Chin lifted high and even in the fuzzy hologram, he can tell her eyes are bright, flickering with keen intelligence. Of course, maybe it's because he already knows who she is:

Princess Leia Organa. Once of Alderaan. Now: one of the heroes and leaders of the Rebel Alliance.

The recorded image of the princess speaks:

"*This is Leia Organa, last princess of Alderaan, former member of the Galactic Senate, and a leader in the Alliance to Restore the Republic. I have a message for the galaxy. The grip of the Galactic Empire on our galaxy and its citizens is relinquished. The Death Star outside the forest moon of Endor is gone, and with it the Imperial leadership.*"

Here the hologram changes to a sight all too familiar to Sinjir:

The Death Star exploding in the sky above Endor.

He knows because he was there. He saw the great flash, the pulse of fire, the bulging clouds like brains knocked out of some fool's cracked head. All the bits of it up there, still, floating like so much detritus. The image flickers. Then it's back to Leia.

"The tyrant Palpatine is dead. But the fight isn't over. The war goes on even as the Empire's power diminishes. But we are here for you. Know that wherever you are, no matter how far out into the Outer Rim you dwell, the New Republic is coming to help. Already we've captured dozens of Imperial capital ships and Destroyers—" Now the image becomes three-dimensional footage of Imperials being led off a ship's ramp in cuffs. *"And in the months since the destruction of the Empire's dread battle station, we have already liberated countless planets in the name of the Alliance."* A new image: rebels being greeted as saviors and liberators by a cheering crowd of—where is that? Naboo? Could be Naboo. Back to Leia: *"Be patient. Be strong. Fight back where you can. The Imperial war machine falls apart one gear, one gun, one stormtrooper at a time. The New Republic is coming. And we want your help to finish the fight."*

One last flickering image:

Alliance fighters with fireworks exploding in their wake.

Another sight familiar to him—he watched the victorious rebels shooting off their fireworks far above the tops of the massive Endorian trees. Those strange rat-bear creatures cheering and hooting and chirping in the distance as Sinjir hunkered down, cold and alone and cowardly, in the brush.

"It's a new day," the Twi'lek says, smiling big and

broad with those tiny pointy teeth lined up in crooked, serrated rows.

"One conqueror replaces another," Sinjir says, lip tugged up in a characteristic sneer. But the look on his face fails to match the feeling in his heart, much the way the drink in front of him has a smell that doesn't jive with its taste. In his heart, he feels a swell of . . . hope? Really? Hope and happiness and new promise? How disgusting. He licks his lips and says, "Still, let's see it again, shall we?"

The Twi'lek gives a giddy nod and goes to tap the button.

A scuff of boots behind them. Pok, the bartender, grunts in alarm.

A creaky black glove falls on Sinjir's shoulder. Another lands on the Twi'lek's shoulder, giving it a painful squeeze.

Sinjir smells the oiled leather, the crisp linen, the official-issue detergent. The smell of Imperial *cleanliness*.

"What have we here?" comes a brutish growl of a voice—a guttural-tongued officer that Sinjir turns to find looks rather *sloppy*. Got a gut pushing out the belly of his gray uniform, so far out that one of the buttons has gone undone. His face is unshorn. Hair a bit of a muss.

The other one next to him is considerably better kept—firm jaw, clear eyes, uniform pressed and washed. Smug grin—a smugness that isn't practiced but (as Sinjir knows well) comes naturally.

Behind them, a pair of stormtroopers.

Now, that's something. Stormtroopers. Here, on Akiva?

Akiva has always had its Imperials, yes, but never stormtroopers. Those white-armored soldiers are for

war and occupation. They don't come here to drink
and dance and disappear.

Something has changed. Sinjir doesn't yet know
what. But curiosity scratches at the back of his head
like a mole looking for grubs.

"Me and my tail-headed friend here are just watching a little propaganda," Sinjir says. "Nothing to
cause anyone any alarm at all."

The Twi'lek sticks out his chin. Fear shines in his
eyes, but something else, too—something Sinjir has
seen in those he has tormented and tortured, those
who think they won't break: *courage.*

Courage. What a foolish thing.

"Your time is *done,*" the Twi'lek growls in a shaky
voice. "The Empire is over. The New Republic is
coming and—"

The oafish officer gives a hard, straight punch to
the Twi'lek's throat—the tail-head gurgles, clutching
at his windpipe. The other one, the smug one, puts a
steadying hand on Sinjir's shoulder. A warning, un-
spoken but clear just the same: *Move and you join
your friend.*

Someone barks—behind the bar, Pok grumbles and
makes some mushy-mouthed warning of his own
while pointing to a sign above his head. That sign, in
Basic, reads: NO IMPERIALS.

It's actually that sign that has kept Sinjir here day
and night for the last week. First because it means no
one from the Empire will come here—which means
no one will recognize him. Second, he just likes the
irony of it.

The oaf grins at the Mon Calamari bartender.
"Times are changing, squid-beard. You might want
to reconsider that sign." He gives a sharp nod to the
stormtroopers and the pair of them step forward,

blasters raised and pointed right at Pok. "We're here to stay."

With that, the big oaf starts whaling away on the tail-head again.

The Twi'lek man bleats in pain.

This is not how it's all supposed to go. Not at all. Sinjir makes a decision, then, and it's a decision to simply stand up and walk out, putting all of this behind him. No need to make trouble. No need to become a blip on anybody's radar screen. Walk off. Find another watering hole.

That's what he decides to do.

It is, quite puzzlingly, not what he actually does.

What he *does,* instead, is stand up hard and fast. And when Officer Smugface tries to push him back to his chair, Sinjir reaches back, grabs the man's hand, and pries two fingers up with a sharp motion. He goes the distance, ratcheting them back so far that they snap—

The man screams. As he should. Sinjir knows how to deliver pain.

This causes some concern among the officer's cohorts, of course. The oaf flings the tail-head to the ground and goes for his pistol. The two stormtroopers pivot on their heels, swinging their rifles around to him—

Sinjir's drunk. Or, drunk-*ish.* That should be a problem but to his surprise, it really isn't—it's as if the warm wash of strange liqueur has worn away any second thoughts, any pesky *critical analysis* that might give him pause, and instead he moves swiftly and without hesitation. (If a bit inelegantly.)

He spins behind the wailing, smug-faced officer. Lifts his arm like the lever on a Corellian slot machine, and with his other hand stabs out and plucks the officer's pistol from his holster.

Already, the oaf is firing his blaster. His own blaster (well, the smug one's blaster) spins out of his hand, sparking. *Damnit.*

Sinjir tightens his profile and turns the smug one to meet the attack—lasers sear holes in his chest and he screams before going limp. Then, with a quick plant of his foot and hard throw, he launches the slack body toward the pair of stormtroopers—neither of whom is ready for the attack.

And both of whom fall backward, crashing into tables.

The oaf cries out, lifts his pistol again—

Sinjir dissects the man's defenses. Hand under wrist. Pistol launches up, fires toward the ceiling—dust streaming down on their heads. He stabs out with a boot, catching the man in the shin, knee, upper thigh. The Imperial's thick body crumples like a table with its leg broken, but Sinjir won't let him fall—he holds him up by the wrist, and with his free hand strikes at vulnerable points. Nose. Eye. Windpipe. Breadbasket. Then back to the nose, where he hooks the oaf's nostrils with a pair of cruel fingers, forcing him to the ground. The man weeps and blubbers and bleeds.

The stormtroopers are not down for the count.

They scramble to stand. Blasters again up—

Someone rises up next to the trooper on the right and swings a chair upward in a hard, merciless arc. The chair gets right under the soldier's white helmet and spins it around. That trooper flails just as a bottle of liquor spirals through the air, cracking the second one in the helmet. A bottle flung from the droid arm of the Mon Cal behind the bar.

For good measure, Sinjir twists the oaf's wrist so that the pistol drops from the Imperial's grip and into his own. Then he twirls it and fires two shots. One in the center of each of their helmets.

The stormtroopers fall. This time, they won't be getting back up.

Sinjir plants himself over the oaf. He again grabs the man's nose and gives it a twist. "Wonderful thing about the nose is how it's tied to all these sensitive nerve endings behind the face. This fleshy protuberance—yours like a hog's snout, if I'm being honest—is why, right now, your head is filling with mucus and your eyes are filling with tears."

"You rebel scum," the oaf gargles.

"That's funny. Really, very funny." *You idiot. You think I'm one of them when really, I'm one of you.* "I want to know what's going on."

"What's going on is that the Empire is here and you're—"

He twists. The man screams. "Spare me the sales pitch. Details. Why are you here? With stormtroopers, no less."

"I don't know—"

Another twist. Another scream.

"*I swear I don't know!* Something's going on, though. It's ramped up fast. I . . . we came down off of the *Vigilance* and then the comms blackout and the blockade—"

Sinjir gives a look to Pok. "You know anything about comms being out? Or a blockade?"

The bartender shrugs.

Sinjir sighs, then jams a fist in the oaf's face.

The sloppy officer's head racks back and consciousness leaves him. Sinjir lets him drop. Then, to Pok: "Somebody's going to want to clean this up. Ah. Good luck with that?"

And then, whistling, he traipses out the front of the cantina.

INTERLUDE:

CHANDRILA

A BLURRY IMAGE.

A sound: *whap, whap, whap.*

The blurry image shakes. It gets blurrier for a second, and then focuses the other way, lurching inelegantly toward clarity.

The image resolves. Standing there are two women. One, a human. Tall, thin, professional. Dark hair coiffed up like a wave about to break. A necklace around her neck that looks like a flock of birds chained together—it catches the light of the sun. Her smile is big, broad, practiced.

The other woman is smaller. Pantoran. Blue skin. Golden hair pulled back in a simple, practical braid. She wears a dress to match: Some might call it practical and unpretentious, others might say it is drab, dull, or even unsophisticated. Her only jewelry is a pair of silver bracelets. Her smile is also practiced, but nervous, too.

Behind them: the humble skyline of the capital, Hanna City.

The first woman, Tracene Kane, says to the Trandoshan behind the camera: "How's it look, Lug?"

A growl-hiss from behind the camera. "It looked bad. I hit it. Now it looks good."

Tracene gives the other woman—Olia Choko—an apologetic shrug. "Old tech. Doesn't always comply."

"It's your first broadcast," Olia says. "It's understandable."

"This day is a first for both of us, I think." Tracene laughs—it's a laugh that sounds almost too big to be real. Maybe it's who she is. Or maybe it, like her smile, is born of effort and orchestration. "So here's how this is going to go. I'll begin the interview, and I'll do a brief intro—blah blah blah, first day of the new Galactic Senate, it's a new dawn for the galaxy, and then right to you: Olia Choko, public relations representative for Mon Mothma and the new Senate. We'll get right into it."

"Great," Olia says. She takes a deep breath. "Just great."

"You look nervous."

"I'm . . . a little nervous."

"You'll be fine. You're pretty. You're alien. You'll trend well."

"Oh!" Olia says, thrusting up a finger. "You're going to get a shot of what's behind us, right? Hanna City reflects the Senate's humble new beginnings—we're here for the people of the galaxy, all the hardworking people. And Mon Mothma is from here, so—"

Tracene puts a hand on Olia's shoulder. "We got this."

"Oh! But, uh. Don't forget, too, to get a shot of the art installation in the city circle—it's a bunch of stormtrooper helmets painted different colors, marked with different symbols like flowers and starbursts and Alliance sigils. It's by the artist—"

Tracene gives Olia's arm a squeeze. "I said *we got this*. We have the footage. You're the last link in the chain. We talk to you. Then the Senate walks in. Nothing will go wrong. You good?"

Olia hesitates. The smile on her face is strained. She looks like a panicked squark-bat frozen in the beam of a miner's headlamp. But she nods. "Yes. I'm good. I'm fine. I can do this."

To the camera, Tracene points. "We're on in three, Lug. Three. Two—" She mouths the word *One*—

"This is Tracene Kane broadcasting on the first day of the Queen of the Core Network. I'm standing here with Olia Choko, public relations representative of Chancellor Mon Mothma and the new Galactic Senate here on Chandrila . . ."

CHAPTER FOUR

THE INTERROGATOR DROID HOVERS. A small panel along its bottom slides open with a *whir* and a *click*. An extensor arm unfolds—an arm that ends in a pair of cruel-looking pincers. So precise and so sharp they look like they could pluck a man's eye clean from his head. (A performance this droid has likely performed once upon a time.) The arm reaches down toward its target.

It grabs the ten-sided die, lifts it, drops it.

The die clatters. Face up: a 7.

The droid exclaims in a loud, digitized monotone: "AH. I AM AFFORDED THE CHANCE TO PRO-CURE A NEW RESOURCE. I WILL BUY A SPICE LANE. THAT CONNECTS TO MY FOUR OTHER SPICE LANES. THAT GIVES ME FIVE TOTAL, WHICH GRANTS ME ONE VICTORY POINT. I AM NOW WINNING. THE SCORE IS SIX TO FIVE."

Temmin's lips curl into a frustrated frown. The board beneath the two of them consists of a map of countless hexagonal territories. Some of the hexes contain planets. Others: stars, or asteroid belts, or nebulae.

He has never won a game of Galactic Expansion

against the repurposed interrogator droid. But he's close now. It's never been this close.

"Ease off the throttle, you overconfident borgle-ball. One point does not make you a conqueror." He rolls the die. A 5. Not enough to earn him a new resource, but he can place a new shipping lane or smuggler route. He has to think about this. He leans back on the chair. Lets his eyes gaze over the workshop and market—all around, shelves and tables mounded with what looks to be junk. And a lot of it is. Astromech parts. Starship scrap. Disassembled blasters. Over in the corner is a WED repair droid—long defunct, wound up with blinking, twinkling lights. Hanging above his head from a set of braided cables is a speeder bike scored with laser marks.

And there, against the far wall, is an old Trade Federation battle droid, scrunched down into its folded-up form and wrapped up in a ratty blanket.

It's not one of the B2s—the war droids with the cannons on the forearms and the hard chest plating.

It's not one of the droidekas, either—those roly-poly death machines, as if a jungle scorpion had a baby with a rolling thermal detonator.

It's just an old B1. A clanker.

Everything here is, or looks like, a clanker.

Temmin picks up a smuggler route tile, marked with a red dotted line, and he's about to place it when the interrogator droid suddenly turns.

As if to face somebody.

"YOU-HAVE CUSTOMERS," the droid intones.

Temmin cracks his knuckles and stands up, plastering on his best salesman smile. The young teen kicks his rolling chair away and turns to face—a trio of thugs. His smile wavers, but only for a second.

"A Koorivar, an Ithorian, and an Abednedo enter a junk shop," he says, cracking wise. They don't seem amused. "It's like the start of a joke," Temmin says, then adds: "But if you have to explain it, it sorta stops being funny." He claps his hands. "What can I do for you, gents?"

"I am a *lady*," the Koorivar snaps, stepping forward. She adjusts her crimson cloak and lifts her chin. The spiraling horn atop her head is twisted and bent. A pale tongue flicks the air and licks craggy, scaled lips.

She has a long, serrated knife hanging at her hip.

Temmin knows who she is. Who all three of them are.

The Abednedo with the fleshy nose slits and the skin tendrils around that scowling, puckered mouth: Toomata Wree. Known usually as "Tooms."

The Ithorian with the sleepy eyes, the threadbare coat, the cannon slung over his tree-branch-looking shoulder: Herf.

And the Koorivar: Makarial Gravin. (Though, truth be told, Temmin really thought she was a he. The Koorivar don't make it easy to tell.)

All three work for—or, rather, belong to—Surat Nuat. They are the Sullustan's property.

"Ma'am," Temmin says, spreading his arms wide. "What can I do you for, today? What junkyard delights can I offer you—"

"Cut the rancor spit, you little puke," the Abednedo says.

In the alien's tongue, the Ithorian adds: *"You have stolen from the goodly savior of Myrra, Surat Nuat."*

"Hey, no," Temmin says, holding up his hands. "We're all friends here. I would never, *ever* steal from Surat. We're buddies. It's all good."

"You stole from Surat," the Koorivar hisses. "Worse, you have offended him with grave insult by taking what is rightfully his."

Temmin knew this day would come. Just not so soon.

A nervous feeling rises in his belly. "The last thing I would want to do is insult Surat—we all could only *wish* we were as savvy and as slick as he is. I don't know what you think I stole from him, but—"

Makarial the Koorivar takes another assertive step forward. "Think hard about what happened on the Trabzon Road. Does *that* tickle your brain stem?"

Temmin snaps his fingers—a nervous habit he picked up from his father. "You mean the transport that crashed out there? No, no—I mean, yeah, yes, I *definitely* scavenged what was left there. I own that. That one's on me. But I had no idea that was Surat's ship—"

"It had his guild sigil all over it!" Tooms, the Abednedo, seethes. The ringlets of skin hanging from his face twitch and tremble as he speaks.

"Not that I could see—the transport was attacked by the Uugteen. Such primitives, you know? They burned that thing good on the outside. Roasted it like a florakeet before plucking its feathers."

"And yet, the insides were ripe for your plunder," Makarial accuses.

"They couldn't crack that nut. The Uugteen, I mean. Their crude knives couldn't pop the latch, but I had a torch and—" He fake-laughs. "I beseech you, friends. I didn't know who I was taking from."

He knew. Of course he knew. And he knew one day this would catch up to him. But the potential payout . . .

If ever he hopes to unseat Surat, he has to play the game with big moves. No weak-kneed bowing and scraping, no soft touches, no hesitant plays. Everything: big, bold, smart as a whip, strong as a bull.

"You still have the weapon?" Tooms asks.

"Ahhh, heh-heh, ahhh." Temmin clears his throat and then lies through clenched teeth: "Not so much."

The Koorivar's eyes go wide. With rage and indignation, if Temmin has to guess. Makarial moves fast. The knife is off the alien's belt and, in the span of a flash of lightning, against Temmin's throat.

Outside, the weather complies, adding its own threat: a rumbling boom of thunder. A hard rain falls against the roof of Temmin's shop, only serving to accentuate the silence. Behind Temmin, the interrogator droid hovers near the table where the Galactic Expansion board sits.

The boy swallows. "I'll make it up to you. I've got lots on offer here. Hey. Look. Speeder bike. Or I can scrounge up a couple of droids—"

"This is all junk," Makarial says. "Surat knows your trick. And so we know your trick. This—" With her free hand, the Koorivar makes a move similar to (and maybe mocking of) Temmin's own gesture when they got here. "—*all* of this is a front. You are no junk merchant."

"One man's trash is another man's treasure—"

The knife presses harder against his exposed throat. "We care nothing for trash. We care everything for treasure."

"So, let's talk treasure, then."

"Surat has a price."

He feels something wet drip down his throat. *Blood or sweat?* He's honestly not sure. "Everybody does. Name the price."

Makarial smiles. A terrible sight to behold, for the Koorivar are, to Temmin's mind, uglier than a happabore walking backward. All those lumps and scales. A nose like a fat, segmented grub. Bone spurs above the eyes. The breath doesn't help, either—it stinks of rotting meat.

The Koorivar says with a flick of her tongue: "Your shop."

"The shop. Like—the building?"

"And everything in it. And everything *below* it."

Now: real panic. A cold saline rush through his blood. They know. They know where he keeps some—*most*—of his best goods.

That is not ideal.

"I have something!" he blurts. "Something big. Something . . . Surat wants. Okay? *Okay?* Just, can I show you? Please? *Please.*"

The three alien thugs give one another looks. The Ithorian, Herf, gives a noncommittal shrug. In Ithorese: *"We might as well see."*

Makarial removes the knife from his throat. He gasps, rubs his neck—his hand comes away wet with sweat, not with blood. He claps his hands. "It's right over there. See that ratty blanket? It's uhh. It's under there."

Makarial nods to Herf. The Ithorian unslings the cannon—it's a custom mod job, that gun, based off a DLT body but jacked up for bigger firepower. The barrel is long—so long it's probably as tall as Temmin.

The stoop-necked Ithorian blinks his hammerhead eyes, then uses the barrel of the gun to lift up the blanket. Thus exposing the first-generation battle droid: the B1.

It stands up. Its bones rattle as it does. Literal bones—the bones of beasts, fish, birds. Bound to its metal limbs with twine and wire. Those aren't the only modifications to the droid's appearance, either. Half its head is missing: replaced with a telescoping red eye. The front of its nose has been sharpened and curved—less the bill of some plucky waterfowl, more the beak of a bird of prey. All of it: painted black and red.

Meant to strike a note of fear.

The alien thugs all laugh. The Abednedo laughs so hard he stoops over, slapping a knee, little green mushroom ears twitching with delight.

"A battle droid?" Makarial asks. More laughter. "You wanted to show us . . . a battle droid? The most incompetent droid soldier in the history of both the Republic and the Empire. A mechanical comedy of errors." The way the alien enunciates that last bit: *a meh-CAN-ee-kall CO-mee-dee of err-ORs*. "And you believe that Surat Nuat wants a meager, worthless B1 droid?"

"I call him Mister Bones," Temmin says.

Upon saying the droid's name, its eye glows a sinister red.

"MISTER BONES IS ONLINE," the droid says: Its voice is a grinding distortion interrupted by bursts of static. Words speed up and then slow down again, mangled by what seems a faulty vocoder. "HELLO, EVERYONE."

The Abednedo shakes his head. "An idiotic name for an idiotic droid."

"I think you've insulted him," Temmin says.

The laughing stops. For just a moment, as they try to figure out what that even means, or what game Temmin is even playing.

Their hesitation is not wise.

Mister Bones cackles—a scratchy, warped laugh from his speakers—as his one hand swings free on a hinge. From the hole springs a sparking, vibrating blade. The Ithorian is slow to react, and by the time Herf is bringing up his DLT cannon, Bones has whipped his arm back three times already—and the cannon is whittled down, three smoldering bits clattering to the floor.

The Abednedo draws a blaster—

Bones tackles Herf, and slams him straight into Tooms. The Abednedo flails and falls, with the Ithorian landing on top of him, and Bones on top of him. Temmin's B1 bodyguard begins pounding both fists down, punching the Ithor's oddly shaped head hard enough that each hit ratchets it back into Tooms's noseless face. *Whap! Whap! Whap!*

Mister Bones gabbles and laughs.

Makarial's maw stretches wide, hissing a gassy exhortation of distress and rage. The Koorivar reaches behind, under her cloak, and draws a blaster—pointing it right at Temmin's head. Temmin, who is now frozen, reaching for his own blaster—stuck in a leather holster bolted to the underside of a nearby table.

"Do not pick that up," Makarial whispers.

Temmin calculates his odds.

They're not good.

He withdraws his hand. Smiles. Nods. "Sure, sure."

"Tell your *droid* to back off."

"Now, hold on—"

"*Tell him.*"

Temmin grins. "Which droid are we talking about here?"

Makarial's pale, ghostly eyes focus, then narrow in bewilderment—just as the interrogator droid floats up behind her, a syringe fixed to the end of its second extensor arm. Temmin chuckles.

The floating droid stabs down with the needle. A needle filled with a toxic narcotic—locally sourced, locally brewed, and with enough stopping power to put a Gamorrean to sleep for the better part of a week.

The needle snaps off, and clicks as it hits the ground. Never actually *delivering* its toxic payload.

Right, right. Temmin thinks, with no small disappointment: *The Koorivar have really hard skin, don't they?*

Temmin runs. He leaps up over a table, then to another table, then across a trio of metal stools—blaster fire sizzles in the air behind him, knocking junk off shelves. An oil can hops off the corner of a table ahead of him. Temmin yells as he bolts for the door—

There. Ahead. The door is open. Someone is standing there.

Someone new. Long dark cloak.

Someone with a blaster all his own.

The new figure raises the blaster. Temmin drops his weight, letting his legs skid out from under him—laserfire trades above his head, and somewhere behind him Makarial yelps in pain. There comes a crash.

Temmin leaps to his feet, presses himself flat against the textured wall of his junk shop. Makarial's down, writhing and howling. Mister Bones has lifted his head like a curious, startled hound. The new visitor regards the situation, then peels back his hood.

It's not a him at all. It's a *her.*

Temmin's eyes go wide.

"Mom?"

CHAPTER FIVE

"ADMIRAL SLOANE, the shuttle is ready."

She stands. Hands behind her back. Staring down a long hallway. At the end of the hallway: a vent cut free with a micro-torch. Ahead of her, stormtroopers go in and out of doors—cabins, sleeping quarters. No sign of the interloper anywhere. She bites down on her teeth to suppress anger.

Lieutenant Tothwin says again: "Admiral, I said—"

"I heard what you said," she snaps.

"The others. They're already heading to the planet's surface."

"Everyone is accounted for, then."

"Yes. Pandion. Shale. Arsin Crassus's yacht showed up on screen a short while ago and is now descending to Akiva."

"And Yupe Tashu?"

"Adviser Tashu's shuttle is on screen as well. We directed him to continue on toward the meeting site. They're expecting you to be there ahead of them—"

"They can wait."

"Of course. It's just that—Moff Pandion is already—"

"Tell me," she says. "This deck. Nothing of import here, is there?"

"Admiral?" he asks, not understanding her.

She wheels on him, impatient. "I mean, this is just empty guest rooms here, and at the other end, kitchens, sanitation, a game room." Sloane chews on that. Could he be using the sanitation chute? The stormtroopers have already checked it out, and didn't find anything.

"Perhaps he thought to steal a bit of food—"

"*No,*" she says, suddenly figuring it out. "It's a ruse. It's always a ruse with the rebels, isn't it? Always some trick, some game. He didn't stop here, he just wants us to think he did so we waste time. That ventilation shaft. Where does it go? Show me the schematic."

Tothwin fumbles with the holodisk, snaps it on. There, the schematic for the *Vigilance*. She scrolls through it, moving the image about, highlighting the shaft and following it to its logical conclusion—

Oh, no.

She growls: "I know where he's going."

Or where he's already gone.

Damnit!

His leg isn't broken, he doesn't think. But it's jammed up pretty good. Once upon a time, he crashed an A-wing at the lip of a volcano—one of his first runs out as a pilot for the then-burgeoning Rebel Alliance, at the urging of a friend—a rebel agent known only as Fulcrum. That crash left him limping for months, and there? His leg was broken. In three places, no less. Almost cut short any career he hoped to have as a pilot, but he convinced the rebels to let him work a freighter manning the guns and as occasional navigator, so.

Whatever the case, he's pretty sure the leg isn't busted.

But it sure hurts from his jump out of the back of that Starhopper—moments before he set the torpedoes to blow.

Clambering through ventilation ducts didn't help the pain. But getting away from Imperial eyes was key. Since then, he's been sneaking around, doubling back, covering his tracks—dropping in and out of vents. At first he was guideless, without a plan, but it didn't take long to realize what he had to do—and better yet, being here on this Star Destroyer offered him something of a real opportunity.

Communications are blocked to all traffic in the space above Akiva and, he's betting, to all on the ground, too.

But if anybody has the channels still open?

It's the Empire.

And so now, he stands in the communications room. The bodies of three comm officers lie nearby. One slumped over her station, another two dropped on the floor. Stunned, not dead. Wedge isn't a killer. He's a pilot, and taking down other pilots means ending the lives of combatants. Comm officers aren't soldiers, aren't pilots. They're just people. Wedge thinks: *That's a lesson we could stand to learn. Imperials are just like us.* Some of them, at least. It's easy to label those who serve the Galactic Empire as pure evil, all enemy, but truth is, a lot of those who do so were either sold a bill of lies, or forced to by threat of pain or death. Already the New Republic has seen defectors. Men and women who have seen a chance for escape, for a new life . . .

That means getting the message out. That means running the comms now and bringing in the troops.

Two holoscreens rise up. On the one side he tries to aim a subspace frequency toward New Republic space—but all those frequencies remain blocked.

That presents a short-term problem and a long-term one: Right now, it means he can't send a message to where it needs to go. In the long term, it means the Empire knows their frequencies. Suggesting that somewhere, there's a mole in the halls of the New Republic—maybe unsurprising, but all the more reason he has to get a message out somehow.

He flips over to local channel traffic.

There, none of the known Republic channels is blocked.

That means he can get a message out to those loyal—but they *must* be local. What are the chances? That here, at the precipice of colonized space, he'll find someone listening, someone loyal to the New Republic?

It's the only shot he has.

He dials it up. Wedge zeros in on the emergency channel, then draws the mike out of the console, the metal cold in his hand. Into it he starts to speak: "This is Captain Wedge Antilles of the New Republic. Repeat: This is Wedge Antilles of the New Republic. I am trapped on the Star Destroyer *Vigilance* in the space above Akiva, and I am in—"

A bright light. The bark of a blaster.

He cries out in pain as a laser bolt burns a hole through his shoulder. His hand reflexively opens—the microphone clatters away. He paws at his hip for his own blaster, but another shot and the weapon that hung there is quickly spun to slag and knocked off his belt.

Wedge, breathing deep, gritting his teeth against the pain, wheels on his attacker. He expects to meet some stormtrooper, or ironically a comm officer who is just returning from a meal.

But no.

The woman standing there is in a crisp admiral's

uniform. She's dark-skinned, with cold brown eyes to match. In her hand, a long-barreled pistol—a unique blaster of elegant, mirrored chrome.

"Please," he says, clutching his shoulder, favoring his leg.

She takes three steps into the room. "I cannot have you complicating what's about to happen. The future of the Empire—of the whole galaxy—is at stake." And then, a flash of surprising empathy. "I'm sorry."

"Wait. Let's talk this out." He swallows hard, wincing. "It's over. You know it's over. We can negotiate a surrender, a *meaningful* surrender. Right here, right now, you and I can—"

Behind her, a small squadron of stormtroopers catch up, their armored boots clattering in the hall behind her. They raise their blasters as she lowers hers. "I'm sorry, Captain," she says. Then, to her backup: "Arrest him. Take him to detention level— No. Wait." She snaps her fingers. "Have him shackled and taken to my shuttle. Have a medical droid in attendance." With a stiff smile she says (as if for his approval): "We are not animals."

CHAPTER SIX

FOR YEARS, Norra did not weep. *Could* not weep. She joined the Rebel Alliance as a pilot and when the decision was made—a decision made less in her head and more in her gut—she cinched everything up. Put extra steel in her spine. All the fears and worries and emotions became extraneous things: anchors, she thought, mooring her to an old life, to an old way of thinking. If she was going to make it through this, then she had to cut those fetters with a cold, merciless knife. Leave them behind her.

The Alliance deserved that much from her. This fight afforded them no time for weeping. They did not possess the luxury of looking back.

Since she joined the fight, she has had two moments when she wept. The first was only months earlier, after the battle over Endor had concluded; after she and her Y-wing (and her laser-crisped astromech) emerged from the labyrinth of half-constructed passages inside the second Death Star—just escaping in a plume of flame as the whole thing began to implode and then explode behind her, the shock waves causing her little fighter to tumble end-over-end until she almost passed out. That night, she sat alone in a changing room on the star cruiser *Home One*, and sitting there half in and half out of her jumpsuit, she wept.

Like a baby without its mother. Hard, racking sobs hit her like crashing waves until she was curled up on the floor, feeling gutted. A day later, she got her medal. She smiled, turned toward the applause of the crowd. She didn't show them how stripped-down and scraped-clean she really felt.

The second time is right here, right now. Holding her son and feeling his arms around her in turn. The tears that spill now are not the throttling sobs of that night months ago, but tears of happiness (and though she is hesitant to admit it, even in her own mind, of shame). It feels like a completed circuit: What she lost that night in the battle is returned right here, right now. Then she felt gutted. Now she feels filled up once more.

And then, everything snaps forward. Time unfixes its feet from this slow, perfect moment (she has not seen her son in years, after all), and suddenly Temmin reveals himself less a child and more a man: He's young, but starting to grow into himself. Lean, ropy, a muss of dark hair sprouting up off the top of his head. He's snapping to the strange battle droid on the floor, clapping his hands: "Bones. Pull the speeder around back. We need to load these slime-guzzling Hutt-mothers up and you need to fly them out *far as you can* along the Trabzon Road, I'm talking all the way to the Kora Biedies—" Here he turns to her and says: "These eddies of water where the river meets the road. Rapids." Then back to the droid: "You hear me, Bones?"

The B1 battle droid stands up, all the bones dangling from its body rattling as it does. The mechanical man gives an awkward salute and in a garbled, distorted voice says: "ROGER-ROGER. BODIES BE-GONE, MASTER."

Then the robot hums a discordant tune as it begins

to drag the thugs out toward a back portal door. Temmin calls after: "Cover them up before you go. Use that blanket!" From outside, the mechanized voice: "ROGER-ROGER, MASTER!"

Norra says: "Temmin, I don't know what's happening—"

"Mom, not now," he snaps. "Here, come on." He hurries across the room, hopping over a pile of spilled junk. He reaches up for the dented skull of an old translator droid and with his fingers forked, presses in on the eyes.

They depress with loud *click*s.

And a few meters away, a shelf slides away, and after it, a section of wall. Revealed behind the opening is a set of steps. Temmin waves her on. "Come on, come on." Then he ducks down the passage.

This is all a bit dizzying, but what choice does she have? Norra skirts the edge of the junk shop and follows her son down the staircase. Her boots clank on the metal steps—it gets darker and darker until she can't see anything. And then—

Click. Lights. Garish, bright, coming on one bulb at a time.

A room like the one upstairs—except the shelves are clean, shining, and home not to junk, not to trash, but to bona fide treasures. Treasures ranging from top-shelf technology to strange artifacts.

"Welcome to the *real* Temmin's mercantile," he says.

She sees parts for droids that haven't existed since she was a little girl. A rack of high-end blaster rifles. A crate of thermal detonators. A shelf of old books and mysterious patina-darkened vases depicting images of men in dark robes with red faces. "I don't understand," she says.

"Upstairs, I sell junk. Down here? Different story."

"No," she says. "I mean, *we used to live here.* This . . . this was our home. What happened?"

He stops and stares at her. Regarding her almost like she's a stranger. "What happened is . . . you left." The sudden silence between them rises like an invisible wall. And then, as soon as it arrives, it breaks again, and Temmin is once more wheeling around the room, chattering as he does: "So. Surat knows all of this is down here. That's not good. And he knows I stole *this,* too—" Here Temmin points to a matte-black crate bound up with carbon-banded locks. "I stole it from Surat. Some kind of . . . weapon, I guess. No idea what it does. He knows it's down here, but what he doesn't know, what he *can't* know, is—"

Her son hurries over to the opposite corner and whips a blue tarp off something: an old valachord.

Their old valachord. The instrument wasn't an artifact from ancient history but rather, from Temmin's own. (And here the memory hits her like a gale-force wind: Temmin and his father, Brentin, sitting at that very valachord, playing one of the old jaunty miner songs together and laughing.)

Temmin says, "Watch. Or rather, *listen.*"

He taps out five notes on the keys—

The first five notes of one of those old miner songs: "The Shanty of Cart and Cobble." And with that, *another* door opens up—this one with a pop and a hiss. Even as it opens, a faint breeze keens through the old stone walls beyond. She smells mold, decay, something metallic.

"No way Surat knows about *this,*" he says. It hits her then—the glint in his eyes, the smirk on his face. At first she thought he reminded her of his father. But maybe, just maybe, he reminds her of *her.*

"Temmin—"

"So, if we go into the old passages underneath the city and—"

"*Temmin.*" She uses her *motherly* voice. The one she uses to get people's attention. Norra softens it: "Son. Can we . . . take a moment?"

"Time matters. Those thugs who were here? Eventually they're going to wake up and crawl back to their boss on the other side of town. Surat won't let that stand, what I did. He'll send someone bigger, meaner, or most likely? He'll just come here himself."

She walks closer to him. "Temmin, I don't know what's going on here. All of this is . . . alien to me . . ."

"Because you've been gone. For *three years.*"

"I know—"

"Three years you haven't been back here."

"The Rebellion needed people—"

The volume of his voice ticks upward as he grows more agitated, more angry. "No, I needed my father back and *you* thought joining the Rebellion might help find him. But did it?" He peers around her side, as if she's hiding something behind her back. "I don't see him anywhere. Is Dad here? Are you hiding him? Is he a surprise? A birthday gift to make up for the three you missed? No? I didn't think so."

"There was a larger fight taking place. It wasn't just about your father, it was about . . . all the fathers, all the sons and mothers and families lost to or trapped by the Empire. We fought. I was at the Battle of Endor—"

"Who cares? Spare me the heroics. I don't need a hero."

"You will respect your mother," she barks at him.

"Oh?" He laughs: a mirthless sound. "Will I? Here's the holonews, lady: I don't need to respect you. I'm not a little kid anymore. I'm grown."

"You're still a boy. Fourteen—"

"Fifteen."

She winces.

He continues: "I'm my own man. Other kids had parents, but I didn't. I had a mom who flew the coop. Months without hearing from you each time. I had to make do, so I did. Now? I'm a businessman, and I need to keep my business safe. You made your choice. Between me and the galaxy, you chose the galaxy, so don't pretend like I matter now."

"You matter. Temmin, by all the stars, you matter to me. I'm here to take you with me. I have a smuggler ready to take us offworld and—"

At her belt, the comm relay crackles to life, vibrating as it does.

Which means: an emergency call. A New Republic signal.

A voice all too familiar to her fills the air:

"This is Captain Wedge Antilles of the New Republic. Repeat: This is Wedge Antilles of the New Republic. I am trapped on the Star Destroyer Vigilance *in the space above Akiva, and I am in—"*

Then the sound of a blaster. Wedge cries out in pain and—

The call ends.

Her blood goes cold.

Her mind wanders—Norra tries to figure out what that even means. Captain Antilles is here? On one of those Imperial Destroyers? Something really *is* going on. And suddenly she's at the heart of it. *Again.*

"There's that look," Temmin says.

"What?" she asks, suddenly distracted.

"It's the face you make when you're about to disappoint me again."

"Temmin. Please. This is important."

"Oh, trust me, I know. I can always tell when something is important because you go chasing after it, leaving us *unimportant* losers behind."

And with that, he ducks down the side passage. She hurries after him, but he pulls a lever on the other side—

The door slams shut between them.

INTERLUDE:

SALEUCAMI

FAMILY DINNER at the Taffral house: The patriarch of the family, Glen, sits at the head of the table. To his left sits Webb, the older of the two brothers. To his right: Dav, the younger. Webb is broad-shouldered, full-chested, a rounder belly. His hair sits trimmed close to the scalp, like his father's. Dav is leaner, smaller, a little scruffier, too.

None of them speaks. But it's far from quiet. The loud scrape of knives on plates. The rattle of a serving spoon against a wooden bowl. The groaning judder of chair legs on the wooden floor of the old farmhouse. Outside, wind whistles through the popperstalks and it carries the chatter-sounds of the starklebird flocks migrating east.

Dav speaks. "Pass the beans." Webb gives him a look. "Please."

Webb grabs the dish, starts to pass it over, then pauses, the dish held fast in his hand. He sets it back down. His jaw is set and his teeth work on pulverizing some seed in the back of his mouth.

"I can't believe you came back here," Webb says.

The way he says it is like he doesn't want to say it, like he's trying to bite back the words. But they come out anyway. "You gualama-loving, tail-kissing scum-shepherd."

Dav sniffs. "Zowie, Webb, why don't you tell me how you really feel?"

Glen just stares out over the table, silent as a judge.

"Oh, I'll tell you. I'll let you have it. You betrayed this family the moment you went out there and you became a rebel-lover. Joining the star-damned terrorists like they're some sort of freedom fighters instead of . . . instead of the criminals that they are!"

Dav lets his fork and knife clatter against the plate and table. "They're not terrorists. They started out as an alliance of resistance, but now they're a legitimate government, Webb. They're the real deal." He dabs at his mouth with a napkin. "The Empire's days are done."

Suddenly Webb stands up. His chair is knocked backward. "You watch your mouth. That's treachery, what you just said."

"The word is *treason*," Dav says, staying in his seat. "And why's your nose so far up the Empire's can, anyway? You failed out of the Academy. They beat your hide senseless day in and day out."

Webb puffs out his chest. "Made me a better man."

"Made you a belligerent jerk."

"Why, you slime-slick no-good-brother—" And with that, Webb launches himself across the table. But he's half drunk on koja-rum and Dav is sober as the noontime sky and so he steps handily out of the way as Webb crashes into the empty chair and smashes against the wall.

But drunk is still dangerous, and his arms flail out against Dav and the two go down, punching and kicking and calling each other all sorts of names.

That is, until Glen clears his throat, picks up a bowl of greens, and wings it against the wall hard as he can. It bangs and clatters. Salad leaves splatter against the wall and ceiling.

The two brothers poke their heads up like whistle-pigs.

"Both of you, siddown," Glen says, leaning back in his chair. "Sit."

The two brothers do as their father commands.

"Pop, he started it," Dav says.

Webb interjects: "Pop, don't listen to this *treason* monkey—"

"Shut up. Both of you! You two are in dire need of a lesson. I'm an old man. Had the two of you later than I would've liked. Figured myself a single man, a simple farmer, until your mother came along—may all the stars welcome her soul." He holds his hand to his heart and closes his eyes. "So I've seen a thing or two."

Under his breath, Webb mutters in a mocking tone: "*I had to crawl to the academy house on my hands and knees through mud and briar and fell-bears ate off both my legs—*"

With his knife, Glen gestures: "Boy, you best clip that line of blabber unless you want me to tan your hide with a dry popper-stalk."

"Sorry, Pop," Webb mopes.

"Now, listen. What's come before will come back around again. Republic was the way of the world before, and it'll be the way again. And for a time everyone will cheer them on, and everything will be cozy-dosie, but there will come a time when things go sour and someone decides they got a better way of doing things. And the New Republic or the New-New Republic or the Republic We Got This Week will clamp down hard and then those people with the so-called better way will become the brave rebel alliance and the Republic will become the enemy and the wheel will turn once more." He rubs his eyes. "I'm old enough to remember when the Republic shot itself right in the knee. It wasn't taken over by the Empire. It *became* the Empire slowly, surely, not overnight but over years and decades. Fruit always tastes nice when it's ripe. But it can't stay like that. Every nice piece of fruit will rot on the branch if it hangs there long enough. You remember that."

"Pop," Dav says. "It won't be like that this time."

"He's chosen his side," Webb says. "And I've chosen mine."

"And that's the damn problem!" Glen says, pounding the table. "Both of you, picking sides. Side you *should* pick is your family. No matter what. Above all else. But here you sit, bickering like a bunch of starkles over which one gets the first and last worm. You know the Lawquanes? Old man Cut, he fought in the Clone Wars. He saw the truth of things: No side in war is the right side. He did the right thing. Settled down. Had a family. Never got drawn back into the muck. But you two. Not good enough for—"

A sound. A pair of screamers. TIE fighters.

The Empire doesn't come out this way. The realization settles in fast.

"You gave me up," Dav says, horrified.

Webb looks shameful. "The Empire pays to give up rebel scum." But his words don't sound as sure now. Regret and guilt mingle in there.

Suddenly, a stun blast. The air flashes with blue and Webb cries out, dropping face-first into a bowl of mashed chokeroot. Dav goggles. "Pop . . ."

"You believe in what you're doing, Dav?"

"I . . . do."

"Fine. Good enough for me. I hope you're right."

He sighs. "Best run now. Go out the back window. Take the speeder bike in the barn."

"Pop . . . thanks."

"Now go."

"What will you do?"

Pop shrugs. "I'll tell them the truth. That you overpowered me, shot me, and ran." He turns the gun toward himself and fires. The stun blast knocks the old man back into his chair. His heels kick up and he moans.

Dav blinks back tears. Then he rushes over, grabs the gun, and heads out the back window just as the front door breaks down.

CHAPTER SEVEN

ABOVE THE CITY OF MYRRA, a haze. Even the sun, bright and bold and punitive, seems to have to push its light through the thick and gauzy air. Heat vapors rise, distorting everything. The humidity of this place is seen as much as it is felt.

So it takes a moment for Jas Emari to confirm what it is that she's seeing—there, descending from the heavens as if a divine chariot, a ship glinting in the sun. A yacht, in fact: ornate and opulent, gleaming brass and carmine piping, a ship built as much for its looks as its function.

It is the yacht of Arsin Crassus.

The Galactic Empire is a leviathan of force—a carbon-armored fist crushing those systems that would dare to deny its authority. But such force and such authority could not be conjured out of nothing. Even the Sith could not manage such magic. It was one thing that made the difference:

Credits.

Money.

Crassus is one of the Empire's main moneylenders. Has been for decades. The story goes that he was once a young man in the Trade Federation, and helped the as-yet-unformed but burgeoning Empire lead the Federation heads to slaughter on Mustafar while then plundering all their accounts to help fund the new government. And that's where he's been, since: helping the corporate side of Imperial government.

He's also a slaver.

And today, he is her target.

Jas clings to the rusted old tower rising high above Myrra's defunct capitol building. Cables cinch around her waist and her right thigh, belting her to the structure so that she can lean out with some freedom of movement and, more important, freedom to both of her hands. All without falling.

The bounty hunter has been here for some time. Waiting. Barely sleeping. She's tired. Her muscles ache. But this is the job. (The life of a bounty hunter offers a great deal of watching and waiting—those long stretches accompanied by very short, sharp bursts of action.)

She unbuckles the rifle from her back: a long-range rifle the Zabrak constructed herself. Based on an old Czerka slugthrower, she modified it to fire different rounds according to her needs depending on which barrel and which chamber she brings to the weapon. Jas once heard the story that the Jedi constructed their own lightsabers and she figured, well, why can't she do the same with her rifle? So she did. Because she can do whatever she wants.

Jas lifts the rifle to her shoulder, then with her left hand pulls down the telescoping unipod that clicks into the D-ring at her waist. (It gives the rifle that little extra stability, especially in such an unstable position as this, hanging a hundred or so meters up in the air, staring out over the sprawling city.) She presses her eye to the scope.

There, the yacht. The scope gives her critical data— the heat coming off the back of it, the ship's speed and trajectory, any biological signatures (those are presently nil given the yacht's shielding).

She points the weapon toward the raised landing platform atop the satrap's palace—the home of Satrap Isstra Dirus, a venal governor known for caring very little about the people of his city and very much about how fat his pockets have become with other people's credits.

In a perfect galaxy, he would be a target, too.

But Jas Emari is a professional. No collateral damage. Whether it's justified or not.

Through the scope she sees it:

The yacht, easing in for a landing. Steam burns off in ghostly plumes. It lands, rocking softly as it does. A gangplank descends. The satrap emerges: a tall man, handsome once, though even through the scope she can see the lines etching into his stony face like water carving channels into a mountain. He's all smiles and gentle applause. Bowing and scraping because he knows which side of his muftari bread is spiced and salted; Jas has seen his records, seen how the flow of credits stems from various Imperial corporations and trickles into his limitless coffers. The planets of the Outer Rim are a very good place to hide money and procure illicit goods (slaves included), and Akiva is just such a world. Behind the satrap: two of his guards. Tall helmets with red plumage. Each with vibro-pikes taller than those helmets, their blade tips pointed skyward.

Crassus steps down off the plank, attended to by his own guard: women in hardened-lacquer animal masks. Slaves, too, most likely.

The man himself makes no small target—he's big and round, with a beard dyed the color of deepest space, a glittering robe trailing behind him like a peacock with its tail in the dirt. He claps his hands and then takes both of them and clutches the wrists of the satrap.

They laugh.

Ha, ha, ha.

Time to end your mirth, Arsin Crassus.

But then her scope flashes—

Incoming ships.

Jas pivots the rifle, following the arrows inside the scope's display—and there she sees an Imperial shuttle, *Lambda*-class, descending through the spiraling cloud cover. A second and third arrow blip.

Two more shuttles.

And with them, TIE fighters.

She swings the rifle back to the platform. Crassus is still there (she hisses panicked breath through her teeth, glad to have not missed her opportunity thanks to a distraction), now standing elbow-to-elbow with the satrap. His own guards have lined up, waiting. Crassus has taken off his robe and one of his guards is now cooling him off with an unfolded fan.

Then, walking in from the rooftop door: three stormtroopers.

Curious.

Take the shot, she thinks. *Earn the credits.*

But—

But.

Something's happening. Her intel didn't detail any of this, and now she curses herself for falling into a familiar trap. She operates too often with blinders on. She sees the target and makes a beeline for it—and sometimes, when she does that, she misses things. A bigger picture. Unseen enemies. *Complications.* The view of the scope is all the view she needs, or so she believes until reality proves otherwise. She's been hunting Arsin Crassus now for a month, following his self-important vapor trail as he flits about the galaxy like a scared thatch-sparrow, and when she heard of the meeting between him and Satrap Dirus, she looked no farther.

Turns out, she should have.

Her finger hesitates, and one by one, the shuttles begin to land.

The shuttles, alighting in a half circle, begin to open up.

Their guests begin to spill out.

And with it, her breath catches in her chest. She feels like someone who has dug a hole in their back-yard only to find a trunk full of Old Republic dataries—a box of unexpected treasure.

Arsin Crassus, yes.

Then: someone she doesn't know, someone in an absurd piece of headwear (if Jas had to describe the hat, she would suggest it looked like someone had killed an emerald kofta-grouse and stuck it on his head) with the lush, plush, purple robes of an old Imperial adviser.

Out of the next shuttle comes someone she recognizes instantly: Jylia Shale. An old woman, shrunken up like a gallstone and with all the hardness of an uncracked koja nut. Shoulders forward, hands clasped behind her back, Shale wears the crisp Imperial-gray uniform, her hair done up in an austere bun atop her head. She comes with a pair of red-helmeted, red-cloaked Imperial Guards. Part of Palpatine's own royal protection.

And then, from the final shuttle.

Moff Valco Pandion.

Stiff, hatchet-chinned, a scar running across his brow, the kind of scar that looks like it has a story behind it.

And there, on his chest, a curious emblem: a rectangular one, with six blue squares in the top row, and three red and three yellow below it.

That, the emblem not of moff, but rather: grand moff.

A title assigned, or a title claimed and taken?

There, on that platform, stand three significant targets. Crassus is the intended target, but Shale? Pandion? Better payouts. Pandion in particular is the highest number in the pazaak card deck handed out by her contact within the New Republic: The higher the number of the card, the more valuable the target. And there are three of those targets.

Butterflies turn inside her stomach.

Kill Pandion.

The New Republic will want them alive but will still pay quite a bit for their corpses. As long as they aren't disintegrated, of course—handing in a jar of greasy ash isn't a good way to get paid. She always intended to kill Crassus. Better a man like that be put in the ground than be thrown in a cell. Penance for his crimes.

On the landing deck, Pandion joins the others, though he remains a step or two back: distant, haughty, purposefully separate. The others are having a conversation. Introductions, perhaps, or reintroductions.

Jas plays this out in her head. She takes off the blinders, tries to think beyond the moment, beyond the pulling of a trigger.

Killing Pandion, or any of them, is an option.

A single shot, and one is down. With it: a significant payday.

The others will scatter. Back to the shuttles or in through the palace door. If they go back to the palace, then maybe, *maybe* she will have a shot at taking out or capturing the others. But if they return to the skies? Then that chance will be gone.

A wind blows. A warm wind, even up here. Like the breath of a beast. Hissing past the thorny spikes rising off the top of her head.

That could work.

Let them go. Get one target.

But there exists a larger play. All of them together. A coup, for her. Jas had a name with the Empire. A name, too, among many of the crime syndicates here at the Outer Rim—with the Hutts, Black Sun, the Crymorah, the Perlemian Cartel. But with the destruction of the Death Star (*again*), and with the switching of her own allegiance, her name and her reputation are in flux—as is so much of the galaxy. If she's going to earn her keep, that means taking bigger risks. Playing it safe—slow and steady—is not an option. She reaches the decision and puts away the rifle.

One target is not enough.

She has to take them all.

And I have to do it right now.

Turbulence as the shuttle enters Akiva's atmosphere. Sloane sits in the navigator's chair—a non-essential role given the short distance they're flying, though she could fill it capably if needed—and watches the darkness of space give way to the washed-out light of the planet below. Clouds brush past the glass, and the heads-up display designates the horizon line, their trajectory, their plotted course.

Next to her, her pilot—Morna Kee. Been her pilot for some time now. A capable pilot. A loyal Imperial. A *faithful* Imperial. It's nice to have people around whose names she knows. But their defeat over Endor, plus the New Republic making deals with governors and sector heads left and right in order to scoop up Imperial naval ships? Not to mention the threat of internal schism. It's left her reeling. Grasping for details she once found vital. Details that can no longer be important.

Behind her: the archivist, the little man who will take notes on the meeting, inscribing the results of the summit so that the history of the Imperial resurgence is neatly writ and officially recorded. Next to him, her assistant on this mission, a bright-eyed young Corellian woman named Adea Rite. Then a half squadron of stormtroopers. Those with the best test scores, taken from the rosters of the *Vigilance*. They stand guard over her new prisoner: Captain Wedge Antilles. The rebel lies on a floating medical table, unconscious from the drugs pumping into his arm. The medical droid hovers over him, checking vitals, securing the tubing.

A fly in the ointment, that one.

A dangerous one. The rebels will come looking.

And then what?

Pressure lives in the hinge of her jaw. This has to work. All of it. The meeting must yield results. The future of the Empire—and the stability of the galaxy—is counting on that.

The meeting wasn't her idea alone, though those gathered think it is. All the more reason for this to play out according to her design and without any further hitches. *If this falls apart, they'll blame me.*

Below, the city of Myrra. A sprawling, choked mess. Strange-angled buildings pushing up out of the jungle, though not without the jungle trying to fight back: vines like cruel fingers draped over the walls and clay-tile rooftops as if they're trying to pull apart the city in slow motion. Between the buildings are pathways too narrow to be called roads—just alleyways, really, and one of the things that makes Imperial occupation here tricky. Those "streets" are too narrow for any of their transports with the exception of speeder bikes, and even then the corners are too sharp for those speeders to turn.

It won't matter, she tells herself. *This is temporary.* The meeting cannot last forever (though she's sure it will feel like it, at times).

The shuttle pivots hard, swooping low over the city. Dead ahead, the palace of their ally, the Satrap Isstra Dirus, an execrable sycophant, though she reminds herself that his particular brand is a necessary one sometimes—the machine only works when all the parts agree. The palace itself is a pompous affair: an old city temple repurposed to fit the satrapy's opulence. Quartzine walls shot through with bright vermilion—walls tipped with useless golden pikes, windows so multifaceted and crystalline that while they look beautiful, they fail to maintain the characteristic that windows are meant to demonstrate: transparency. She far prefers the stern, uncompromising design of the—

Ahead, movement.

Someone is zip-lining across from a nearby comm tower—a tower that looks to long have been out of use, once part of a capitol building that has failed to maintain proper government since the satrapy seized total power out here (not coincidentally when the Empire seized the Galactic Senate). Rae taps a button, spins a dial—

A portion of the HUD captures the image of the zip-lining interloper, zooming in. Zabrak, by the looks of the horns on the head. Female. Rifle on her back. A long rifle, too—a sniper.

Bounty hunter.

Rae Sloane growls, springs up out of her chair and

to the chair and console behind her—the gunnery station. Whoever that Zabrak is, Rae has neither the time nor the patience to figure it out—and while it's likely gauche for an admiral to man the guns, it is what it is.

Let them worry.

She pulls up the controls and begins to fire.

Jas prays the cable she fired from this tower to the roof far across the way will hold her. It's long and the tower it's moored to is weak. Even now she hears it groaning behind her.

Turns out, it doesn't much matter.

The shuttle appears to her left out of nowhere. Another *Lambda*-class Imperial transport. Black window glass above the nose cone.

Implacable and uncaring.

The cannons begin to fire. Jas sucks in a breath and tightens her body up. She pulls herself close to the cable. Her muscles burn. She brings her legs up tight to her body, knees tucked into her stomach. All in an effort to make herself as small as possible as the blaster cannons spit lasers—

They sear the air in front of her. Behind her. Below and above. She knows she's making a sound—a long, steady scream of rage and fear—but she can't hear it. All she hears is the wind and the cannons.

Good news is, the blasters under each wing of that shuttle aren't meant to hit relatively tiny targets like herself. Unless the person piloting that thing has Force sensibilities—a Jedi or some Dathomirian Nightsister—hitting her would be an act of pure cosmic providence.

Bad news is, whoever is operating those things just figured that out.

The shuttle turns just slightly—

And fires at the tower behind her.

A bright glow of flame behind her. The shriek of metal. And then it's falling—she knows it's falling because suddenly, the cable on which she's traveling goes slack in her hands. From a rigid line to a loose noodle. She thinks: *Hold on to it, hold tight, it'll swing you down—*

But the tumult is too much. The cable slips through her grip.

Wind whipping past. The city rushing up to greet her.

Jas Emari falls.

CHAPTER EIGHT

NORRA COMES BACK DOWN into the basement. The secret door is still closed, the valachord still sitting there. She growls, more at herself than at anything. Now she has to do something she's never been good at.

She has to remember how to play the valachord.

Well—she has to remember how to play a few notes on the valachord, because it's not like she ever had 1 percent of the musical talent of her husband and child. She sits down, taps a few keys, each note a melodious tone tinged with a faint mechanical susurrus behind it. Tap, tap, tap. She's not making music. She's just making a mess.

But then—*ahh*. There. That's the one. That's the start of the "Cart and Cobble" shanty, isn't it? The old miner song. Norra closes her eyes. Remembers her husband's hands on the keys. The way the thumb and last finger splay out. The progression of notes, one-two-three-four-five—

She takes a deep breath and plays them.

The door pops open with the sound of air rushing.

Relief floods in and Norra steps up and through the doorway. Again that smell hits her—the smell of age, of dust, of mold. The smell of a dirt clod broken in your hand, or the smell of dry and crumbling moss.

The walls ahead look to be old stone. Myrra used to be Norra's home, and she knows that underneath the city are the old catacombs—a city beneath a city, a maze from a much earlier time. Rumors about the maze abounded: a Jedi training temple, a Sith trap, the first dwelling of the primitive Uugteen, some slimy Hutt breeding ground. Stories about people getting lost down here, never found. Eaten by rancors. Falling forever down into the depths of bottomless pits. Stolen by the Uugteen and made into one of them, whatever they even are. Even ghost stories, as if the place is somehow haunted.

She knows the stories.

Norra hadn't known the old catacombs connected right up to her damn house. Isn't that something?

She takes one step and nearly screams.

Temmin is sitting right there, in a small alcove, his face highlit by the blue glow of a small holotab computer. On it, a map. He quickly turns it over and the screen goes dark. He sniffs. Wipes his eyes with the back of his hand then thrusts his chin up as if to cover up the fact he's been crying.

Norra says, "I'm sorry."

"Yeah. Me too."

She holds out her hand and he takes it. Norra gives a little squeeze.

"I didn't know this . . . was here."

He looks up and around. "The catacombs? Yeah. I got hold of a map a couple of years back. The underground connects to a lot of the houses, especially here on Chenza Hill."

"I spoke to your aunts."

"Yeah?"

"They said you don't even stay with them anymore."

He clears his throat. "No. I stay here now. I'm independent." He sighs. "You gonna see them while you're here?"

"No," she says.

"Figures."

A spike of anger stabs her insides. Anger not at Temmin, but at the two aunts—her sister, Esmelle, and Esmelle's wife, Shirene. It's not their fault, she knows that, but she can't help what she feels. They couldn't handle Temmin and now here he is. Running this shop. Leading this life. Almost getting killed by . . . who? Local criminals. Thugs. Brutes.

"I spoke to them. They don't want to leave Akiva. They're settled here and I suppose I don't blame them."

Temmin stands up. An incredulous, sarcastic grin on his face. "Leave? What do you mean, leave?"

"Temmin." Norra holds his hand tighter. "That's why I'm here. I'm here to get you. We have to go."

"Go? No way. This is my life. This is my shop. This is my *home*. You're crazy if you think I'm gonna leave."

"Listen to me. Something's happening here. The Empire is down but they're not out. The city is crawling now with stormtroopers. The Empire is here. They've instituted a blockade and a communications blackout."

He narrows his eyes. He didn't know about that, did he? Most of Myrra probably didn't—though they'll figure it out sooner than later. "Whatever. I've got an in with some Imperials. I sell them stuff. I'm not worried. You should go and save your . . . friend. Wedgie or whatever."

"Wedge."

"Sure."

She says, "I'm not. I heard what you said, Temmin.

I'm making a choice and you're it. You're the priority. I'm taking you away."

"Nope. You're not. I'm staying here. You can leave if you want, though. I'll keep doing what I've done: survive fine without you."

She bites her lip, trying not to say all the things that are threatening to come out. He was always head-strong and willful, but this is taking it to a whole other level. Temmin pushes past her, heading back toward the shop's basement, back through the secret door.

"Temmin, wait—"

"I have to start loading this stuff into the cata-combs. Hide it from Surat. It was nice to see you, Mom. You can go."

She grabs his arm as he steps through the door. When he turns around, he sees what's in her hand and his mouth forms an O of protest—

Norra sticks the needle, the half-broken one she stole from the interrogator droid, into his neck. She only needs to press the plunger part of the way—Temmin's eyelids flutter like butterflies in a jar.

He passes out, and she catches him.

"I'm so sorry," she says.

Then she starts dragging him back upstairs.

CHAPTER NINE

AS ADMIRAL RAE SLOANE ENTERS the room, they swarm her. This room is tall and broad and arched—in the center sits a massive table made from some old tree, the wood inlaid with tile of mirrored glass—but the way they come up on her makes her feel suddenly claustrophobic, as if this very big room is all an illusion, as if it's far smaller than its dimensions would suggest. Rae lets it come. She doesn't waver. Doesn't show the pressure.

They're all demanding to know what that was, but it's Moff Pandion who speaks with the clearest demand. And when he speaks, the others quiet.

She makes a note of that. Unsurprising, perhaps, but still.

"What, pray tell, was that sound?" he asks, stepping forward. Meeting her almost nose-to-nose as he enters uncomfortably into her personal space.

"The blaster cannons, you mean."

"No," he says with a blistering eye roll, "I mean the squawking of birds, the barking of dogs, the tune you were whistling as you walked in." He somehow smiles and scowls at the same time: "*Yes,* I mean the sound of the blaster cannons. What was that?"

"An insurgent," she says.

"A rebel?" says the onetime adviser to Palpatine,

Yupe Tashu, horror struck on his face like the gong of a bell. "Here?"

"No," she lies. Likely not the last lie she'll tell during this summit, either. "Not even that. Some local. As you well know—" She stops suddenly and says: "May we push back? Sit down? Enjoy the food Satrap Dirus has provided for us?" That suggestion met with reluctant nods and grumbles. Rae moves with the crowd, giving small nods of greeting to the others: Jylia Shale, Arsin Crassus, the satrap, the satrap's own cabal of bowing and scraping advisers.

Servers move around the room with shallow wooden bowls. They offer the bowls to those gathered so that the guests of the summit may pluck various foods—foods that Rae does not recognize. Little squirming things with black, inky tentacles. Small dumplings that smell of fragrant plum. Little seed-speckled balls that smell like the inside of her boots after she takes them off following a long day on her feet. Yupe Tashu picks at the food. Crassus eats greedily. Jylia has put a small plate of the food in front of her but seems hesitant to touch it. Pandion, predictably, has waved off food.

"As you know," she continues, settling in at the head of the table—and standing, not sitting. "The rebels have begun to disseminate propaganda in the form of various holovids. In some cases they have literally stolen and subverted some of our probe droids and are using them to spread their lies."

"Are they really lies?" Shale says. Just loud enough to be heard. "Or are we the ones lying to ourselves?"

A chill, after that. Pandion stares daggers at the old woman.

Rae ignores it and moves on: "We have been betrayed by various sector heads and governors across the galaxy. The so-called New Republic has led at-

tacks on a number of our freighters and transports—
successful attacks, I will add. Thus diminishing our
numbers. We are, to be frank, on the defensive. An
inopportune time to be scattered and leaderless.
Hence the purpose of this meeting. I'd like to thank
you all for—"

Pandion interrupts: "So, just now. We were attacked by a local insurgent? Not a . . . proper rebel?"

"No." Rae bristles at the interruption, but it's to be
expected from him. "As noted, just a local. Likely one
inspired by the aforementioned propaganda. Now,
the summit begins tonight—"

"First, you're late. Then you open fire outside the
satrap's palace. What of the rebel you took prisoner?
Or of the smuggler's ship that ran the blockade and
escaped? Are we truly safe here, Admiral?"

A sinking, sour feeling pulls at Rae's gut. Her stomach acid churns. If Pandion knows that, it means she
has a leaky ship. *A spy.* Betrayal. Already the feeling
that she's lost control and they're not even an hour
into the meeting.

Yupe Tashu looks delighted. "We have a prisoner?"

"And you didn't tell us?" Crassus says.

"This is quite concerning," Shale says. "*Quite* concerning."

Rae turns, looks toward her own squadron of
stormtroopers, all of whom guard the door. To them
and the pilot, she gives a small nod.

They disappear.

"The rebel was not part of any concerted attack,"
she explains. "Just a lone rebel. Likely scouting for
Imperial presence."

"Well, he found it," Pandion says, smirking.

With that, the door opens again and the stormtroopers usher in the hovering gurney. The medical

droid accompanies the prisoner. Captain Antilles remains sedated. For now.

"That," Sloane says, "is a danger to us, but also a fortune. For we have captured no small rebel here today. That is Captain Wedge Antilles, one of the heroes of the misguided Rebellion, present and instrumental in both of the Death Star attacks. Not only will Antilles be suitable to plumb for information, but should the rebels suss out this meeting, we can use him as a bargaining chip."

Tashu raises a hand. "May I be involved in the . . . interrogation?"

She ignores him.

Pandion says: "Is this who we are now? Reduced to common hostage-takers? Perhaps the Galactic Empire truly is fading, like a star gone bright and then soon to dust. At least with the likes of you at the helm." That last sentence a barb delivered right to Sloane.

"The summit begins tonight," Sloane says. "So rest up if need be. Time is of the essence. The future of the Empire will be decided by us." She looks to the archivist, a small, brittle man named Temmt. Februs Temmt. "Note in the official record that we will be referred to in history as the Imperial Future Council, or the IFC." A sharp nod to those attending. "Thank you, and see the lot of you tonight."

She moves quickly toward the door. Sloane fishhooks Adea, her new assistant, with the crook of her arm and pulls her close. She hisses: "Any sign of the bounty hunter?"

Panicked, Adea gives a small shake of her head. "No, Admiral."

"Problems?" Pandion says, suddenly appearing by her side. That reptilian grin on his too-pale face.

"None," Sloane says.

"Admiral, I admire what you're doing here. I do. You are not wrong that now is the time to act. The Empire I love will not easily come back from the blow of losing not only the Death Star but also our leadership. But I want you to realize that the future of the Empire has never been decided by something so *spineless* and *spiritless* as a council. An Empire needs a leader. An Empire demands an *emperor.*"

"Then perhaps that is what the council will discover," she says. Her eyes flit down to the rectangular bands across his breast. "I see you are elevated to grand moff. A self-proclaimed title, I'm guessing."

That wicked grin. "If one wants power, one must take it."

"True, perhaps."

"Not perhaps. And you know it in your bones. I know that you have wrested control of not only the *Vigilance,* but of the *Ravager,* too. And likely the fleet that goes with it. Imagine that. Little Rae Sloane, manning an entire Super Star Destroyer all by herself. Our last, isn't it?"

She says nothing. All she does is stare, stone-faced.

He goes on: "That was the fleet admiral's ship, wasn't it?"

"It was."

"Was. So he's truly gone?"

"Truly. And sadly. He was one of the best of us."

"He was." A trickster twinkle in Pandion's eye. He's got secrets. They all do. She just hasn't figured his out yet. "I'll see you at the meeting, Admiral. I am eager to get started."

INTERLUDE:

NAALOL

A SMALL TOWN in the mountains, reduced to rubble. A wind whips up, and dry leaves scrape the road between bodies. The corpses are everywhere. Two stormtroopers across the street. Two soldiers from the New Republic slumped up against a burning house, the roof still smoldering.

More down the lane, and more behind them.

Mon Mothma walks among the wreckage, attendants on each side of her: Hostis Ij to her left, and Auxi Kray Korbin on her right. Each serving the role of angel and demon on her shoulder (though the role is never fixed and one becomes the other depending on the situation). Behind them, four New Republic soldiers walking with blaster rifles at the ready.

This is the reality of war, Mon Mothma thinks. It has to be over soon. It *must* be. Ending this conflict was priority one. Naalol was strategically insignificant. Here, a series of little mountain towns with their little crooked mountain houses, and people who were valdeer shepherds or artisans or miners. But not far away was a small Imperial garrison, and when the

Empire began to lose ground elsewhere, it tried to gain it on planets like Naalol—fallback positions. What was a small garrison became a large one, and then war came to these people. And now those people—or the people in this town, at least—are either dead or have found their lives in ruins.

It's as if Hostis hears her thoughts. As she walks, he strokes his long beard and makes lots of *hmm*s and *ahhh* sounds. Finally he speaks, unprovoked (as he often does): "This is the price of war. It is not the New Republic's fault, Chancellor."

"I've seen war," Mon Mothma says. "I know its shape. I know its margins. But I'll never be comfortable with it." *As some most certainly are,* she thinks. She walks among some villagers who have gathered along the length of a low rock wall. Two Republic soldiers ladle hot broth out of a pot and into cups for them. As she walks, Mon Mothma takes hands and shakes them, pressing a few credits into palms as she does and saying a few small words of apology and gratitude. As they pass she says: "It is our fault and we must act that way to uphold our responsibilities. And it's why the war must stop soon. We cannot keep fighting it. We are not equipped to."

Hostis blusters and says: "That's hardly true. We're more equipped than ever, Chancellor. The Empire is waning and the whole galaxy can sense it. We can barely contain the lineup of recruits willing to fight for us now that the conflict is more out in the open. We have more ships. More equipment. More weapons. The tide has turned and—"

"I don't mean equipped in the literal sense, Hostis. I mean that this is not our heart. War is not a state of being. It is meant to be a temporary chaos between periods of peace. Some want it to be the course of things: a default fact of existence. But I will not let that be so."

Here, Auxi leans in and the Togruta woman whispers: "Chancellor, just to be mindful: We will have to leave soon if we are to be home on Chandrila in time for the Senate's first official day back."

"Yes. Of course."

She stands in the middle of it all. The rubble. The bodies. In the distance: a wrecked Imperial AT-AT walker, slumped forward like an animal with its neck broken. Not far from it: the cross-foils from an X-wing fighter broken and burning on a mountain ledge. One street over, a lineup of Imperials bound in a cascading series of shackles, each connected to the other by a buzzing thread of electricity. The prisoners are marched forward toward a transport by New Republic troops.

The chaos here flared up and is now dying down. The Imperial garrison is diminished. They fled into the mountains, pursued now by the New Republic soldiers. Naalol's time steeped in the boiling waters of war will be short, she thinks. Which is how it should be. Though war leaves its scars no matter its duration: Naalol will not forget this day.

To Hostis, Auxi says: "You do realize we are still going ahead with the relinquishment, yes?"

"What? You can't be serious." To Mon Mothma he says: "Chancellor. I beg of you. Now is *not* that time."

"It is and must be that time," she says, her voice quiet but firm. "Right now, I put my finger down anywhere on the star map, and our troops will go. They will fight. Some will die. That is my responsibility, but I do not want it. I never wanted it. The charter of Chancellor maintains the emergency powers granted by Palpatine, and they can persist no longer. They are a poison to democracy. They undercut my role."

As Hostis starts to stammer, she turns to him and takes his hands in hers. Mon Mothma says: "I am not a military leader, Hostis. I am the leader of the Senate, and if we're really going to attract more worlds and convince them to return to this process, it must not seem to be under threat."

"But the army and navy of the Republic—"

"Will continue for a time, but not under my leadership. Rather, it will exist under the arrangement that already exists in practice, just not in law: I will be part of a council of wise voices who will determine the best course of action in terms of our military presence in this civil war." She pauses to consider her next words. "It is vital we demilitarize our government so that a galactic war cannot happen like this again."

The wind whips up and lifts his wispy hair from his liver-spotted head. "We are not yet at that day. We must show military strength. If we project weakness, the Empire will capitalize on it. Giving the war over to the fickle vagaries of politics will slow our response time, weaken our resolve, and make us appear vulnerable—in part because we *will* be vulnerable."

Auxi offers a wry, knowing smile—she's enjoying this, isn't she? "Oh, it gets worse, Hostis. Tell him, Chancellor."

Mon Mothma sighs and says, "I will today put up a vote that resolves to cut our military presence by ninety percent once we are able to officially confirm an end to this war."

His face falls. Eyes wide, mouth open as if the old man is hoping to catch a winged meal of one of the orange-eyed deer-flies that buzz around here. "You cannot be serious."

"I am quite serious. Look around you. The dead on

our side are not proper soldiers, no matter how much we pretend they are. They're farmers and miners, pilots and smugglers, all drawn into this conflict against the greater evil of the Empire. Once our conflict is over, what do we say to them? Keep fighting for us? Against what? To what end? For what ideal?"

"For democracy, of course—"

"Democracy is not in need of defense. People are. And it's why we'll keep that ten percent. A peace-keeping force. The rest of our efforts will go toward training the militaries of other worlds. We will be a true Galactic alliance, and not a false one with an authoritarian sun at its center."

Hostis scowls. Gravely he says: "Then we shall see only endless war, Chancellor. Smaller armies just means smaller civil wars all across the galaxy. It means oppression will grow like weeds and we won't have the eyes or the control to stop it. In this time of upheaval, the galaxy will need law and order and you will grant it only chaos. It is that vulnerability that caused the rise of the Empire in the first place. The people of the galaxy reaching out, looking for a central authority, desperate for protection . . ."

It's Auxi who speaks up next. The woman is always wry, spunky, even a little venomous at times. "It sounds like you are on the wrong side of this conflict. I'm sure the Empire would be glad to have you, Hostis."

"Why . . . how *dare* you . . ."

Mon Mothma holds out both hands. "Stop. Please. No bickering. Not like this. We must respect disagreement. That being said, Auxi has a point. We are not fighting the Empire just to become the Empire. This is not a power grab, and that's what I want to show the galaxy. I want them to know that we trust them, as the Republic has always trusted them. If we're going to ask anybody to fight for us, they need to know what they're fighting for. And they will fight for a unified, democratic galaxy. Not one that merely pretends to be as it's squeezed tighter in an unyielding fist. We must yield. And to your comment about earlier history . . . we will put safeguards in place. We will move forward, smarter this time. More aware."

"Chancellor . . . ," Hostis says, but his plea dies in his mouth.

"My mind is made up. It's why I brought you both here. I need you to see the bodies. The waste. The tragedy of war. I need you to see why we need to end it. I cannot ask our people to fight for this again and again. Not once the Empire is truly diminished."

Auxi nods and says: "It's time to go, Chancellor. History awaits."

Hostis says nothing further. He just screws up his face into an uncomfortable smile and offers a grim, placating nod. "Of course."

"Thank you both," Mon Mothma says.

Together, they walk back through the debris of war. For it is time to return home. It is time to return democracy to the galaxy.

CHAPTER TEN

"I NEED TO PROCURE a way off this rock," Sinjir mutters, pushing on through the narrow streets of Myrra. He passes by a food vendor—the big-headed Bith, like most of the vendors, have their tables and shops pressed into the nooks and alcoves of the city's buildings. As he passes by, he grabs a crispy something-or-other from a dangling rack. He quick-pops it to his other hand so nobody sees, then looks down: some manner of little bird. Batter-dipped, deep-fried. He bites into it. Warm, juicy. Too warm, too juicy. It'll do, though, since suddenly he's starving.

Behind him, the Twi'lek man from Pok's bar hurries after. "But why would you want to leave?"

To get away from you. The alien has been following him for the last hour. Sinjir left the bar to clear his mind and, better yet, to get far away from that foolish scuffle—which he would have been wise to avoid—and this gawping blurrg who's trailing Sinjir like a lost nek.

Instead, Sinjir says: "I don't want to be here when it all goes to pieces. All the running around and the yelling and the . . ." He gesticulates with his hands to indicate a frenzied mess. "Chaos is most unpleasant."

As if to emphasize his point, a pair of TIE fighters roar over their heads, not far above the city buildings.

This may not be an occupation, but something's up.

"But—you're a rebel. You're here to fight the Empire."

Sinjir stops. *You're a rebel.* He almost wants to laugh, but the idea is absurd, too absurd, so absurd he can only stand there, his breath caught in his chest. Might as well take the lie—a lie that really began on the forest moon of Endor many months ago—and run with it.

"Yes," he says, wheeling on the Twi'lek. Firmness in his voice. "I *am* an agent for the New Republic. That is correct. And I must take what I have learned here and bring it back to my loyal allies at the Alliance."

From over the Twi'lek's shoulder, he spies a trio of stormtroopers pushing up through this crooked alley—shoulder-to-shoulder, blasters out. They're looking for someone, something. Maybe him.

Sinjir grabs the Twi'lek, pulls him into a small alcove. Finger to his lips. The stormtroopers pass.

"See? We are in danger."

The Twi'lek man nods.

"My name is Orgadomo Dokura," the Twi'lek says, his head-tails twitching like serpents as he speaks his name with some pride. "Please. Let me help you. Make me an agent of the Rebellion."

"You mean, the New Republic."

"Yes! Yes."

"My name is Markoos . . . Cozen." A name he just makes up right there on the spot. Cozen is a family name—distant, on his mother's side. Markoos is . . . well, he really did just make that one up. "You want to help me? Help me find transport off this planet. If there's a blockade up there—" He points heavenward, and even as the swirling clouds part he can see the distant shapes of triangles floating up there in the sky. Imperial Star Destroyers. "Then I need a sub rosa way of escape. Who can grant me that? Who do I go to, Oga-doki Domura—"

"Orgadomo Dokura."

"Yes, excellent, whatever. Just answer the question."

"You're going to need to see Surat Nuat."

The gangster. "Him? Really? No other competing syndicates? No smuggler's guild here? No fellow-who-knows-a-fellow-who-knows-a-very-nice-lady-pilot? None of that?"

The Twi'lek offers a wan smile with those little sharp teeth. "Sorry."

"Fine, let's go. You can show me the way."

They step out of the alcove—

And there stand two stormtroopers. Centimeters away—so close, in fact, they almost run into each other.

"Out of the way," one of the troopers barks, then reaches with a sweeping arm to push them aside.

The other stormtrooper, though—his helmeted head turns for a quick second look. "Hey. *Hey.* Grab them!"

So much for that.

Sinjir ducks a grabbing arm, and knees the other's blaster up so that the barrel points toward the sky as it fires. He snatches the rifle and cracks one across the helmet, knocking him back.

To the Twi'lek, Sinjir mouths the word: *"Run."*

She literally cannot see the forest for the trees.

In her sights: Princess Leia Organa. Dressed not as a princess, not as a dignitary or diplomat or envoy from one world to another, but garbed instead in the raiments of a soldier. It's no costume. Jas has read the files. And even without the files, the stories are known: Leia is a powerful woman. As capable with a blaster as ten stormtroopers. Twenty, even.

And right now, she's injured.

A bird with its wing broken. An easy target.

Jas sits up in one of the Endorian trees—massive-trunked things. Impossibly large. They make her feel very small. It has taken her quite some time just to get to this spot—navigating the battle, skirting laser-fire, avoiding those little black-eyed rat cubs that are native to this place. Now she's in place. All around, the fighting has died down. The fuzzy natives are all around, wrenching helmets off stormtrooper heads. Bashing them once more before dragging them back through the jungle.

Then an Imperial scout walker comes tromping through the woods. Brush crackling beneath its feet. Guns pointed at the shield bunker. Han Solo emerges, while Leia remains crumpled against the door. Hands up. The golden droid frittering about, an astromech down for the count.

If the walker blasts them into oblivion, then what? Could she still recover the body? Cash it in for cred-its? Claim success?

A deception. One she does not prefer. Jas Emari is a professional. And though she despises the Galac-tic Empire, they are the client and if they ever found out . . . though, suddenly she wonders if that even matters.

That is not for her to worry.

Her worry is this moment.

An opportunity to finish the job.

She again returns to Leia in her scopes. Her fin-ger coils around the trigger like a starving vine snake and—

* * *

The scuff of a boot. Jas opens her eyes, stands up. Moving quickly reminds her of the hit she took falling down from that zip-line—then she fired a secondary grapple line late, *too late,* and its anchor claw moored onto a balcony just three stories above the road. The line jerked her arm damn near out of its socket, and then she swung down and slammed into the side of the palace wall. A wall brushed with rough, jagged stucco. Her arm now scraped up, the skin in tatters. Already crusting over with scabs.

That doesn't matter now. What matters is—

"Who might you be?"

A Sullustan stands there. One of his eyes is dead—an opalescent cataract over it, and around it a starburst of scar tissue. A small nose of two pinholes and pursed lips sit underneath the double flaps of jowl tissue. Atop his head: a skullcap, black. Like a spider clutching his scalp.

"Surat," she says.

He is, of course, not alone. Six others stand behind him. Various thugs of various races: two Narquois with blasters pulled, an Ithorian with a long rifle and one eye bruised shut, a pair of gray-faced Duros, and at the back, a heaving, seething Herglic, the blowhole atop its slick black skin puffing out and hissing gouts of breath and spit. The Herglic has an ax. A very big ax.

Jas Emari curses herself.

She fell asleep. Here in the boy's junk shop. She came in, didn't find Temmin Wexley anywhere, then curled up on a back bench next to a table holding the board to some . . . child's strategy game.

"I know you," the Sullustan says. His face is wet and thick with flaps, and one would expect his voice to be some slurry gargle of sounds—or, as with some of those from Sullust, a gabbling jabber. But his voice is smooth, almost velvety. A deep bass. "You are that bounty hunter. Jas Emari."

"Glad my name gets around in the proper circles." She offers a stiff smile. Utterly fake. "Whatever this is, it doesn't involve me. Excuse me."

She moves to skirt past him.

But he sidesteps back into her path. He offers a raised finger, then tick-tocks it side-to-side. "Ah, ah, ah. May we talk?"

"I'm on the job. So unless you have credits to spare—?"

"Please. You have enough time for a *nap*. Surely you have the luxury of speaking with a friend." That, a jab at her for sleeping. A deserved one.

"A friend. Are we friends?"

"We could be. If you're honest."

She pauses. Then sighs, and takes a step back. "Let's talk."

"Why are you here? Seems a strange place to find a hunter of your caliber. This boy . . . his shop . . ." The Sullustan makes a face like he's just licked the hind end of a bantha. "It's really beneath your level."

She shrugs. "I need a part for my gun. He has parts."

"I have parts."

One of the Narquois chuckles.

"It's no slight against you. It's a small component and, really, beneath your level. So I came here."

Surat claps his hands together. A moist sound. Clap, clap, clap. "Very good. Very good." But then the little smile drops off his puckered lips. He steps forward. "But may I offer a countermanding theory?"

Jas is good at reading body language. A talent that has been practiced—one of her many senses she endeavors to keep sharp, like a knife. All of the gangster's body has tensed up just now. His eyes narrowing, then going wide again. Paranoia bleeds off him in waves. A not-uncommon characteristic of individuals in his position—certainly *head of a crime syndicate* is a life replete with nigh-constant threat. Her life is similar. But she knows not to give in to it. Paranoia is a deadly emotion.

Deadly for you. But deadly for those around you, too.

"Whatever you're thinking—"

"I am thinking that insolent grub, Temmin Wexley, has decided to make a play. He orchestrated the theft of . . . something important to me. And now he intends to dispatch me." Another step forward. "He is a crafty little trilobite, that one. Smart, if not smart enough. He comes at you from the side, as he has done to me for the last year. *Nibbling* away at my business like the *hiss-wyrmgrubs* of Sullust, chewing up our subterranean gardens, eating the roots of our underground trees." The gangster's moist face-flaps tremble. "You. He hired you. To kill me."

There it is.

"You're being paranoid," she says.

"Paranoia has kept me alive. Even when it has turned out misguided, I remain happily paranoid and have no regrets about it. Better safe than sorry."

"I'm not here to kill you."

"So you say. I let you go, I'll likely get a slug in the back of my skull before I lay my head to rest tonight."

Jas thinks: *If I wanted to end your existence, I could do it right here, right now.* At her back is a small utility knife. The blade would spring out with the tap of a button. She's fast. Faster than him. But not faster, she suspects, than the cadre of his cohorts. Certainly not faster than their weapons. Another option is to run—duck, dodge, feint, move. Attack them, not him. Distract. Fling junk. But they're all blocking the door out. And she's both tired and injured. Not an ideal situation.

She does calculations.

Only one option presents itself. An excruciating solution, in fact, but she has no other reasonable choice. "I'm not here for you. I'm here for someone else. The pay is good. I'll cut you in, seventy-five–twenty-five."

"Oh, my." He fans himself. "Twenty-five percent?" His mouth twists into a sour curve. "You think that's what your life is worth?"

Just kill him.

No.

"Sixty–forty split," she offers. "And you facilitate. You help get me close. At that level, I expect my partners to earn their pay." A true statement, that. Or would be, if she ever worked with partners.

"Let me guess. The target is Imperial? I see what's happening out there. Stormtroopers in the streets. Officers clucking along like little gray birds. The TIE fighters. The shuttle." He smirks. "Rumor has it one such shuttle—of a Lambda designation—fired on the old capitol building."

"So you'll help."

"By the stars, *no*. The Empire is an ally. You think I haven't heard? You're no longer offering contracts to the likes of them. Or the likes of me. You're a kept dog now. On the Alliance's leash. Really quite sad."

Her muscles tighten. This isn't working. She makes one last plea: "You need to watch the stars, Surat. The galaxy is wheeling on its axis. It's turning against the Empire. Don't tie your fortunes to that ship, because it's about to come crashing down. The New Republic—"

"Is a bastion of fools!" he suddenly screams, foul-smelling saliva flecking her cheeks. She pivots on the ball of her foot—

A blast from one of the Narquois hits her in the side. Her foot skids out—she crashes down on a table full of spacer parts. Metal clatters against the floor as she slides off. Her body, slack. Her mind, suddenly disconnected from her muscles. A stunning shot, not a killing one.

Surat stands over her, hands clasped in front of him. He seethes: "The New Republic will make no room for the likes of me. I will not face extinction at the hands of a choir of overly moralistic do-gooders. The Empire allows me to work, and so the Empire remains my friend. And now, as it turns out, I have a new gift for my friend."

He claps his hands again, and suddenly his cohorts are picking her up. The Herglic tosses her over his slick, cartilaginous shoulder. She wills her hands to move. Her legs. Her *teeth*. Anything at all. But it's all for naught. Her efforts are futile.

As they carry her out, she thinks: *You should have killed me.*

Sinjir steps out of the fading light of day and into the dank underground—well, what to call it? It's a cantina, probably, at least in part. The name hanging on the door outside says: THE ALCAZAR. But it's more than just a cantina. By the look of it, it's also a gambling house. And a house of ill repute. Probably also a slaver market, and black market, and—it's a whole damn compound, frankly. In this room sits an elevated stage on which plays some warbling gang of so-called *musicians*. Along the far wall is a long black bar carved out of some dead hunk of lacquered driftwood—and everywhere else, tables of gamblers sit, all praying to catch a little of that magic, whether at pazaak or rolling sheg-knuckles or yanking the lever on the One-Armed Smuggler.

Gambling. Sinjir never understood it. He had to take punitive measures against any Imperial soldier or officer attempting to gamble in the bunks, the mess, on a long and lonely shift. He decided that gambling was never about the credits. It was always about the risk.

The risk, and the thrill it brings.

Sinjir has no love of that thrill.

He wants to get off this planet as soon as possible.

"Come on, Ogly," he says, waving his new friend farther.

"Orgadomo."

"Uh-huh. Let's get a drink." His own sogginess is starting to dry up and wear off—now's a good time to replenish that pleasant feeling. And of course find out a little information. He grabs a length of the Twi'lek's head-tail and pulls him up to the bar. Sinjir gives the bar top a good, wet slap.

The bartender—a human man, as scruffy as a Wookiee yet somehow slimy like a worrt—turns, popping some kind of thin green leaf in his mouth. He chews it. Green fluid runs down his chin and he licks the one good tooth in his mouth. "Wuzzat?"

"Two drinks. I'll have a . . ." He turns to the Twi'lek. "You first, friend. What are you having?"

"An . . . ale?"

The Twi'lek looks nervous.

Sinjir makes a face. "He'll have an ale. I need something stronger. You got ahh, let's see. Jogan fruit brandy?"

"Kind of a fancy place you think this is?" the bartender rumbles. "I got ale. More ale. Other ale. Different ale. Grog. And starfire 'skee."

"I'll take that last decoction, then. A jorum of 'skee for me."

The bartender grumbles. Begins pouring a glass of something brown and muddy before sliding a bottle of foaming ale to the Twi'lek. "That'll be ten credits."

Sinjir catches the man's wrist—a gentle hold, and the man's skin is, as its appearance suggests, sweat-slick and slimy. The man gives Sinjir's hand a poisonous look as another squirt of green fluid runs down his chin. Sinjir laughs, withdraws his hand, and says, "One more thing."

"Go on."

"I need to see the man in charge of this establishment. Surat Nuat."

"Oh, do you?"

"I do. And I will pay."

The bartender's eyes flit about. "Then let's call it a hundred."

Sinjir winces. *That's valuable drinking money.* He reminds himself that now, it's also valuable *escaping* money. He unpockets the credits and slides the small cairn of filthy lucre across the table.

"Now," he says. "Where can I find him?"

The bartender gets a big, nasty grin across his face. Like a smear of mud across the wall, that grin. "He's coming in the door right now."

Sinjir sighs. He turns and looks.

A Sullustan is coming in the door. Milky eye. Smug, self-satisfied look. He's trailed by a pack of punks and thugs. The way all eyes turn toward him—a mix of genuine awe and utter fear—tells Sinjir that this alien is the real deal. That this is, indeed, Surat Nuat.

He's about to turn and demand his credits back.

But then he sees someone else.

A woman. Zabrak—or is it Dathomirian? Or Iridonian? He's not sure of the distinction or if one even exists. Those pale eyes. The dark tattoos forming spirals and knots on her cheeks and brow and chin.

His breath catches in his chest—

Sinjir stands there. Ferns up to his hips. A fallen tree across the soft, spongy moss of Endor. Beneath him, a rebel. Dead. The man's outer clothes—vest, poncho, camouflage pants—now hanging on Sinjir's frame. He puts the helmet on, too. Blinks. Swallows. Tries to focus.

A bead of blood drips down Sinjir's head. To the end of his nose. It hangs there before he sneezes it away.

His ears still ring from the sound of the shield generators going up.

His hands are filthy with dirt and blood. His own blood.

Superficial cuts, he tells himself. Nothing deep. He's not dying.

Not today, anyway.

Then: the snap of a stick.

He turns—and there she is. An alien. Sharp thorny spurs forming a crown on her moonlight-blue skin. She turns and sees him. The tattoos on her face— whorls and corkscrews of black ink—almost seem to turn and drift, like snakes entwining with other snakes. But when he blinks again, that stops. Just an illusion. He's still shaken up. Maybe she's not even real.

She nods at him.

He nods at her.

And then she yanks on what looks like a vine—and a whole swath of netting, netting woven through with sticks and blankets for purposes of hiding something in plain sight—pulls away. Underneath is a speeder bike.

The woman cinches a rifle up on her back.

She gives Sinjir one last look. Then the engine of the speeder bike revs and she's gone, whistling through the underbrush and between the trees.

—he knows her.

"I know her," he says. Low enough so that only his new friend hears.

The Twi'lek grunts in confusion.

"*Her,*" Sinjir clarifies. "The one with Surat's thugs." *I saw her on the moon of Endor.* "I don't *know* her know her. Never mind. Come on."

He hops off the stool—

Then quick-darts back to the bar, and slams back the 'skee. It tastes like he's drinking pure laserfire, and it carves a hot, burning channel deep through his core. Sinjir shakes it off, then pursues Surat and his entourage.

CHAPTER ELEVEN

OUT THE WINDOW, past the endless black, a repair droid totters past, carrying bits of scrap, its welding torch dangling by a long, black tube. Even after these many months, *Home One* still requires a last few repairs from the battle over Endor. Ackbar thinks: *It is a good thing we won that battle.* It was their last true shot. They gambled everything. And they almost lost it all. By the grace of the stars and the seas and all the gods and all the heroes, somehow, *somehow,* they managed.

He clears his throat. His time is up. With a webbed hand he grabs the plastic bottle and squeezes moisturizer into his palm and then rubs it on his neck, his bare shoulders, down the length of each red arm.

A deep breath.

Then, he is again under attack. He moves fast, picking up the kar-shak—the net-pole, a traditional Mon Calamari weapon—and whirls about in the padded room. A stormtrooper rushes up, the blaster rifle raised.

Ackbar grunts in rage, spinning the kar-shak and cracking the stormtrooper in the helmet. The end of the stick: barbed like a gaff hook. It whishes clean through the air, and clean through the white Imperial helmet.

As it passes, the stick interrupts the hologram for just a moment—

Then the stormtrooper is back, and Ackbar's enemy topples.

A second one comes up, and a third, and Ackbar captures the one's head in a net, and flings him into the other—again their holograms disrupt, then flicker back to life before dropping.

One, two, and now three stormtroopers enter from the corner projectors and—

Someone clears his throat.

Ackbar stops.

"Pause," he barks. The trio of incoming troopers freeze. Shimmering.

There, at the door, a young man. A cadet. "Sir," he says. A small fear shines in his eyes. But he stands tall, just the same. Chin up and out. Hands holding a screen pressed to his chest. "If this is a bad time—"

"Deltura, isn't it?"

"Ensign Deltura, yes, sir."

"No, now is a fine time," Ackbar growls, and sets his stick down. "I am to assume this is important?"

"You assume correctly."

"And why isn't Commander Agate bringing this to me?"

"She is occupied with repairs, sir."

Ackbar harrumphs, then steps forward. His sharp fingers click together. "Very well. Let's see it."

Deltura hands over the screen.

The admiral looks over it. His big yellow eyes turn back toward Ensign Deltura. "And you're sure about this?"

"Yes, sir. Captain Antilles hasn't checked in, and his comm won't answer. We can't even ping it."

"His last known location?"

"Raydonia."

"And he found nothing there."

"No, sir."

"And I will hazard a guess that says we are not certain of his next jump?" The ensign shakes his head because that's not how Wedge wanted to play this, was it? Captain Antilles saw no harm in doing some light scouting. He said it would feel like a "vacation"— just him and the Starhopper. Alone with his thoughts.

Ackbar thinks: *I warned him of this.*

I'm sure I won't find anything, Wedge said at the time.

You don't know that. One does not want to casually stumble upon a pit of eels, Ackbar cautioned. *But it can happen.*

Just doing my due diligence. It'll be nice.

"Nice."

Harrumph.

The ensign says, "The five closest worlds to Raydonia offer a glimpse of where Captain Antilles could have been heading next." On the screen: a list of five planets. Mustafar. Geonosis. Dermos. Akiva. Tatooine. Any of them could make sense—they know the Empire has gone to ground. "Mustafar makes some sense, as does Geonosis—"

Deltura is looking at him. Wanting to say something.

Ackbar pauses. "What is it?"

"There's more."

"And?"

"Something more than what's on that screen."

"Spit it out, Ensign. I don't care for this waffling."

"We have intel. From the Operator."

Ackbar steps closer to Deltura. "And how do *you* know about the Operator? That is classified information, Ensign."

"Commander Agate cleared me."

"Commander Agate seems to trust you."

A curt nod. "I hope so."

"Then I do, too. What is this intel?"

When Deltura tells him, Ackbar feels all the moisture go out of him. They keep the air in this ship as humid as possible—it is a Mon Calamari ship, after all—but he suddenly feels bone dry. Desiccated. He feels again on the precipice of something bigger, something *dangerous*. Some shadow unseen in the margins. "Are you certain?"

"No. We have no spies in the region that we know of."

"I'm older," Ackbar says, suddenly. Staring off at nothing. "The reason I do this—stand here and take my kar-shak and continue to practice my kotas—is because I wish to stay sharp. And flexible. And ahead of my enemies. I know one day that I will fail at this, and we almost failed above Endor. We rushed in. Careless. It almost cost us everything."

A moment of silence between them. His nostrils flaring.

"Sir—"

"Yes, yes, send scouts to each of those planets. But send *two* scouts to Akiva. We must be sure before we commit to anything."

Deltura salutes. "Sir, yes, sir."

As the ensign leaves, Ackbar is left alone once more. And he truly feels it, for a moment: the weight of the galaxy on his shoulders. An illusion, of course. He is not the standard-bearer for the New Republic, and nothing hinges on him. But the pressure remains, just the same.

And with it, a worrying thought persists: As an informant within the Empire, the self-titled Operator has not steered them wrong yet. His pinpointing of vulnerable Imperial routes and convoys, as well as supplying them with a list of likely governors and other galactic leaders who would gladly betray the Empire, was all of immeasurable help.

So why, then, can't Ackbar shake the feeling that once again they are about to fall into a trap?

PART TWO

CHAPTER TWELVE

"We have a problem."

Someone shakes Temmin awake. He gasps and sits up in the bed in the nook upstairs in their house. Thunder booms like cannon fire outside, like ships in the sky tearing one another apart—flashes of lightning like fire. It's a mausim—*an old Akivan word for one of the annual storms that rise up and signal the start of the wet season. The clouds turn black and tighten over the city like a noose. A mausim-storm can last for days, even weeks. Flooding the city with heavy rains. Heavy winds stopping traffic.*

Temmin sniffs, rubs his eyes. It's his father. He stoops down and kisses Temmin on the brow.

"Dad . . . whh . . . what's going on."

A voice from the door. Mom. "Brentin. What is it?"

Dad answers: "I'm sorry. I'm so—"

Downstairs, a pounding at the door.

Then another boom of thunder.

Brentin stoops, holds his son tight. "Temmin. I need you to be good to your mother. Promise me."

Temmin blinks, still sleepy. "Dad, what are you talking about—"

Mom is there, now, standing by the bed, a concerned face revealed with every pulse of lightning. Downstairs—more pounding, and then their visitor seizes upon impatience as they break in. Mom cries out.

Brentin says to his son: "Promise. Me."

"I . . . promise."

His father gives him one last hug. "Norra. Help me with this—" He hurries to the window, a window covered with a slatted metal shutter. Meant to keep the storm out—should the wind break the glass, the shutter will react, the slats will slam shut, and the whole thing will vacuum-seal. The two of them go over, one on each side, pulling the levers that hold the shutters to the frame. Mom says:

"Brentin, what is going on?"

"They're coming for me. Not for you. For me."

Voices. The crackle of a comm. Footsteps. Suddenly others are in the room. The white armor of a pair of stormtroopers. The black outfit of some Imperial officer. Everyone is yelling. Blasters up. Dad is saying he'll go peacefully. Temmin cries out. Mom gets in between the troopers and Dad, her hands up—one of them hits her in the head with the back of his rifle.

She cries out, goes down. Dad leaps, calling them all monsters, banging his fists against the one's helmet—

A pulse from a blaster. Dad cries out and drops. They start dragging him out. Mom starts crawling after them on her hands and knees and the officer in black stays behind, stoops low, and shoves a datapad in front of her face. "The arrest warrant for Brentin Lore Wexley. Rebel scum."

She claws at his boot and he shakes her free.

Temmin checks on his mother. She's collapsed in a heap, crying. Grief and fear are tamped down underneath a sudden surge of anger. Temmin gets up, runs downstairs. Already they've got his father out the front door. Dragged out into the rain, into the street where water runs over their boots as they splash forth.

Temmin bolts outside into the hard slashes of rain—everything feels like a nightmare, like this couldn't be real, like the sky has cracked open and all the evils have come tumbling out. But it is real.

He calls out for them to stop. The officer turns and laughs as the two stormtroopers toss his father into the back of a bala-bala, one of the small speeders used to navigate the tight channels and streets of Myrra.

The officer pulls his pistol.

"Stop," Temmin says, his voice more like an animal in pain than his own voice. "Please."

The officer points the blaster.

"Do not meddle, boy. Your father is a criminal. Let justice be."

"This isn't justice."

"Take a step and you'll see what justice is."

Temmin starts to take a step—

But a pair of hands catches him around the middle, yanking him up off his feet. Temmin kicks. Screams. His mother in his ear: "Temmin, no, shhh, not like this. Back inside. Back inside!"

"I'll kill you!" he screams, though at who, he doesn't even know. "I promise, I'll kill you for this!"

"We have a problem."

His mother, in his ear.

Whispering.

"Wuzza," he blurts, his mouth tacky and dry.

"Shh," she cautions him. "We're in danger."

He draws a deep breath. Temmin tries to get his bearings. Cargo bay. Small ship. Freighter, maybe. Corellian design. They're behind a stack of carbon-shell crates on a pallet. A hoverpallet, by the look of it, though right now it's powered down and set against the metal of the ship's floor.

Then he spies it:

A body.

A dead man. Turned on his side. Half of his face a moon-skin of scars, cratered with old burns. His eyes are empty, have lost their luster.

To his left, the bay door. Large enough for a trio of these crates, side by side. To his right, the sealed door—should go to the rest of the ship. The bunk, the gunner station, the cockpit, the head.

From beyond that door—the sound of comm chatter. And voices through helmet speakers. "Stormtroopers," he says, his voice low.

He tries to remember what happened, how he even got here. It's like trying to catch clouds with pinching fingers. But then the memory starts to resolve. He was down in the catacombs. Not far in. Just sitting. He'd just argued with his mother. He turned to go back and . . .

She stuck something in his neck.

His mother starts to say something but he whispers: "You brought me here!"

Alarm in her eyes. "I had to."

"Oh. You just *had* to?"

"We *need* to leave this planet, Tem."

"Where's Mister Bones? Where even are we?"

"Your droid?" she asks, sounding almost irritated. "I don't know. *We* are on a ship. On the outskirts— near the Akar Road." Gods, how far did she bring him? All the way out here? Near the canyons and old temple complexes? Panic seizes him. *My shop. My goods. My droids.* "That's the pilot." She gestures to the dead man. "He was going to take us out of here. The place was crawling with stormtroopers, so I snuck us on board and found him here, already dead. The stormtroopers came back in—I don't know why. A second sweep. Looking for contraband, maybe."

They're looking for us, he thinks.

"We need to take the ship and escape," Mom says. "We can do this. Together. I'll need you to be my navigator—we don't have an astromech." She must see the look in his eyes because she says: "I'll guide you."

She gives his hand a squeeze.

He seethes: "I *can't* leave here. This is my home."

"We have a new home now."

"You don't get to just kidnap me and—"

"I can because I am your *mother.*"

A thousand angry rebuttals run through his head like ring-dogs chasing their own banded tails. But now isn't the time.

"I . . . have a plan," he says. It's not a lie. Not really.

"I'm listening."

"Stay here. Follow my signal."

She starts to protest, but he darts out from behind the crates. Temmin hurries up to the cabin door. Next to it on the wall: a panel. He casts a look to his mother, who gives him a quizzical stare.

I'm sorry are the two words he mouths to her, silently.

Her eyes go wide as she figures it out.

I have a plan, it's just not one you're gonna like.

He quickly punches a few buttons on the wall panel. He overrides the cargo bay's pneumatic hinges—the ones that would open the bay door and ramp slowly, settling it against the ground as gently as a mother resting her baby in the cradle. Temmin doesn't have time for that. He pops the pistons with a screaming hiss and the bay ramp drops with a resounding *gong.*

Outside—a cracked, shattered landing pad. Roots and shoots pushing up through the plastocrete. Jungle and city beyond.

And stormtroopers.

A whole squad of stormtroopers.

They seem taken by surprise. They aren't lined up, ready for battle. They're out there milling around, standing about, poking through the underbrush and cracking open crates.

That gives Temmin one shot.

He yells, running forward, slamming his shoulder into the pallet full of crates. With a quick shove of his knee, he jams the button on the pallet handle and the thing suddenly pops up off the ground, hovering a few centimeters above the bay floor. His mother rushes for him.

But she's too slow.

Temmin hurries forward, pushing the hovering crate stack out the bay door with his shoulder. He hides behind it, shielding himself from the sudden fusillade of blaster fire. His mother calls after him, but all he can think is: *This was a stupid, stupid idea.*

"Do we have a problem?" Surat Nuat asks.

Sinjir crossed the gambling floor, shoving past dice throwers and card holders until he was standing in front of the Sullustan gangster. And now that gangster stands there, regarding him with one good eye. Sinjir feels suddenly dissected, like a winged insect pulled apart by a cruel child's plucking fingers. The feeling is only made more intense by the clatter of blasters raised in his direction and ready to fire.

Gasps all around. The music stops. Eyes watch.

He feels his new Twi'lek "friend" trembling behind him.

Sinjir clears his throat and smiles.

"Not at all," Sinjir says. "No problems here. A polite entreaty, if you will. May I appeal to your . . ."

What word will satisfy this self-important thug? What will tickle the Sullustan's ego, an ego sure to be as plump and bloated as a sun-cooked shaak carcass. "To your limitless grace, your many-faced wisdom, your eternal might?"

Surat smacks his lips together. "You have an eloquence. Manners. I like that. Even if your crooked human nose is dark with excrement. So. Make your plea. But make it quickly."

The thought runs laps in Sinjir's mind: *Just walk away. This does not involve you. She is no one. She does not matter. You don't know each other! You had a moment, one singular moment. Moments do not tally to anything meaningful. Run away, like you are so good at doing.*

But that woman? The Zabrak is watching him. And he might be imagining it, but—is that recognition in her eyes? A familiar scrutiny?

As if to confirm it, she gives him a small nod of her head.

To Surat, Sinjir says: "The woman. Is she yours to sell?"

"She is," Surat confirms, pursing his lips in amusement.

"Then I would buy her. I would pay well for a first chance—"

"The process," Surat interrupts, "for a prime candidate such as this, would be an auction. To maximize the effort and to ensure that all interested buyers have a chance."

"I will then offer to pay extra to undercut them."

Surat holds up a hand. "It does not matter. Because there shall be no auction for this one. We already have a buyer lined up. Unless you think you can equal the endless coffers of the Galactic Empire?"

Sinjir's heart sinks in his chest like a stone in swamp

mud. But he refuses to show the fear and disappointment on his face. Instead, he claps his hands and
smiles big. "Then there must be some confusion—
a muddled communication. You see, I am *from* the
Galactic Empire. An emissary. I am loyalty officer
Sinjir Rath Velus, last stationed at the Imperial shield
base on Endor, and now here on Akiva as part of
a . . . diplomatic mission. Did they not tell you I was
coming? We used to have it *so together* before those
rebel pigs blew up our favorite toy. I apologize, but
I'm here now—"

"I have not yet informed the Empire of this prize,"
Surat says.

"What? I don't follow."

"They do not know I have this one." The gangster
gestures toward the woman. "Perhaps you have a
Jedi around somewhere who predicted my call? Or
maybe you, loyalty officer Sinjir Rath Velus, are some
kind of wizard in possession of great precognition?"

"Well, I am quite gifted."

"Or maybe you are a rebel. Or just a con artist.
Does it even matter?"

Sinjir swallows hard. He forces a smile and says: "I
assure you—"

Surat scowls.

"Kill him!" the gangster barks.

Surat's men start firing.

"We have a problem, Admiral," Adea Rite says.

Sloane marches down the palace hall, the walls
lined with gold-framed portraits of satraps past: the
sluggy, jowly face of Satrap Mongo Hingo; the jaundiced, sickly countenance of Satrap Tin Withrafisp;
the handsome, smoldering portrait of young Satrap
Kade Hingo, a young lad governor who died too early

(written history says *by assassin* but whispered history says *by venereal disease*). Sloane skids to a halt and says: "What kind of a problem? I'll remind you that I am heading to a meeting that will make or break the back of the Empire *and* the galaxy it endeavors to rule."

Oh, the look of fear that rises on the poor girl's face . . . like a sun darkened by clouds. Sloane feels a small pinprick of shame over that—whatever the problem is, it's not likely to be the girl's fault. Still, to her credit, she summons her courage after drawing a breath.

"Two rebel scout ships," Adea says. Again to her credit, she says this quietly. Who knows if anyone could be listening?

"Where? Here? Above this planet?"

A small nod. "Yes. Tothwin claims both were rebel-designated A-wings."

This is happening too soon.

"And what became of them?"

Not that it much matters.

Adea says: "Both were destroyed before they could return to hyperspace."

Rae winces.

"Did the other Star Destroyers see?"

"I don't think so. At least, they haven't indicated such. The ships came in on the starboard side, away from the other two Destroyers. The distance between the Destroyers suggests they couldn't have."

That may buy them a bit more time—if the A-wings were able to return successfully and make a report, the swiftness of a rebel attack on their burgeoning blockade could be profound. But since the A-wings can't return, the rebels won't have any useful intel. It will give them pause. The A-wings could be dead from an Imperial attack, yes. Or a volatile Oort cloud.

Or an unexpected debris field. The rebel fleet will exercise caution.

Regardless, that leaves her with a new problem:

Does she tell the others? She could attempt to supersede their authority. Neither Shale nor Pandion is an admiral. Neither *technically* possess the authority to command fleet movements like Sloane does. But each is still in command of a Star Destroyer, and the rules these days are not so clear on who truly has *proper authority* to do anything at all.

If she tries to run an endgame around them . . .

They will try to run one around her, as well. A coup, perhaps.

Then the meeting will become a different game altogether.

She bites back a curse.

"Right," she says, then thanks the assistant.

Sloane marches toward the first fateful meeting of the summit.

"What's the problem in—*hey!*"

Norra wheels toward the voice and sees that it belongs to a stormtrooper—one of three standing there at the door between the bay and the bulk of the ship. The three step in, blaster rifles up and ready.

Temmin, why did you have to run?

A smaller voice inside her answers: *Because you gave him no choice.*

Outside the ship, past the bay door where she can't see, Norra hears the sounds of battle: Blaster rifles. Men yelling in alarm.

"There!" one of the stormtroopers says, spotting her.

The three turn toward her, pointing and gesturing with their weapons.

"Freeze."

The third says, "Stand up."

Slowly, Norra stands. The blaster at her hip feels heavy, as if burdened with great purpose and great risk. Her hand itches to reach down, pull it out, take her chances—her blood roars in her ears, a river of fear and anger. It rushes back to her, them kicking down her family's door, the Imperials dragging her husband out of her son's bedroom, the stormtrooper slamming her in the head with the end of his rifle.

She thinks: *You're fast. The bucketheads are slow. Take the shot.*

One of the troopers turns back toward the bay. He startles, taken by surprise, and for a moment she doesn't know why. "Look out—!" he starts to say, and then blaster fire pins him to the wall. The other two pivot, blasters up and firing, but it's too late for them, too—

A speeder bike bolts in through the bay doors and drifts as it enters, its back end sliding hard and clipping the two stormtroopers in the knees. They cry out as the speeder wipes them out, knocking them to the floor.

Temmin lifts the brim of his new helmet with his thumb.

"Let's go!" he says. "*Go go go go.*"

Norra takes a deep breath and hops on the back of the speeder as Temmin twists his grip forward. The vehicle takes off like a proton rocket.

"We have a—" Rae starts to say.

Pandion answers: "A problem, yes, I should say so. I have heard that Captain Antilles is not yet responding to any of our . . . efforts."

Tashu, having arrived late wearing a strange red

metal mask, one that appeared quite demonic, spins the mask (now facedown on the table) with his hand. "Do not worry, Moff Pandion. My technique takes time, but I have been trained by the best. The ancient Sith art of—"

"It's *grand moff,*" Pandion says, "and I may remind you here that the Sith are all dead and you carry none of their magic with you."

"*The problem,*" Rae says, putting some fire in her voice, "is that the *Vigilance* encountered two rebel A-wing scouts. We dispatched both—"

Arsin Crassus stands up. The man, already white as ground-down bone powder, goes almost translucent. Panic coils around his voice, tightening as he stammers: "The rebels will come for us. We must end this meeting immediately, as I am no warrior, but merely a merchant—"

"Sit down," Rae says.

Crassus hesitates, rubbing thumbs against fingers. A nervous habit.

Pandion says: "Don't be a coward, Crassus. *Sit.*"

Crassus sits, then. Though, Sloane notes, only when Pandion says to.

"I have a plan," she says. "Though it may seem unconventional."

Jylia Shale leans forward. "We're listening."

"I want to move the Star Destroyers to hyperspace. Not far. But out of both optic and far-sweep sensor range."

"That will leave us exposed!" Crassus says.

"If the rebels find nothing here, they'll move along. They don't have the time or the resources to monitor some backwater fringe territory such as this. But if they see a trio of Imperial Star Destroyers . . ."

Pandion leans back in his chair. Sneering. "Apparently, I'm at a *table* full of cowards. Let me posit an alternative solution, Admiral. You are in control of the *Ravager* fleet. Our last Super Star Destroyer, and you have it and—well, how many ships? We don't even know. An unknown quantity, hidden away the way a greedy child hides his best toys." Here he leans forward, pointing an accusing finger. "Perhaps it's time to *share,* Admiral. Bring your fleet forward. Let's not run with our tail tucked betwixt our legs. Let's go the *other* way. Build up our presence. The rebels come poking around, they'll find they have stirred a nest of vipers."

"No," General Shale says, giving the table a pound with her small, wrinkled fist. The old woman gives a firm shake to her head. "None of us is ready for that. This is a game of chatta-ragul. All the tokens are on the board, whether we like it or not. Minions, Scouts, Knights, all the way to the Pontiffs, the Alcazar, the Empress. You never move the Empress out unless you have no other choice. That was our failing with Palpatine's grand battle station: The Death Star was our Empress. We moved it forward too quickly: a chatta-ragul gambit that failed spectacularly."

"Speak plainly," Pandion says. "This isn't a game."

"It *is* a game," Jylia says, her jaw set. "It is a game with very high stakes where we must second-guess our opponent. The head of the New Republic fleet is Grand Admiral Ackbar. He is a genius tactician. A warrior of the mind. But he will not be quick to jump into this. One rebel missing, then two more on top: He will fear something is going on, that this could be yet another trap for him to blunder into. But without any information at all, he will be hesitant to send one more rebel to the grave. His next play will most likely be to send a drone ship."

"Or a droid," Rae says.

"Yes. Yes! A long-range probe. That is likely. Sent

from a ship kept at a distance—close enough for scanner range, which means, if we have ships here? That droid will be wholly unnecessary. And that ship will be out of range of our weapons. It will jump to hyperspace, and Ackbar will mobilize his fleet. And then it is open war once more. A battle that we cannot afford to lose, because, as I will remind you, we are expending resources at a greater rate than we produce them. We've lost ships, weapons factories, droid factories, spice mines, fuel depots. You want to risk more of it? We cannot afford to pay that debt."

"*Cowards,*" Pandion rages, standing up so fast his chair almost knocks over behind him. "The *Ravager* is a powerful weapon, and Sloane is sitting on it like a fat nuna hen upon a nest of already hatched eggs." He points to Crassus and Tashu. "This is a meeting where every voice counts, does it not? Then let me ask you two. How do you vote? Are we an Empire of curs and cuckoo hens? Clucking and whimpering in the dark? What say you?"

Crassus gives a nod. "I say we bring that Super Star Destroyer forward. I say we attack." He awkwardly thrusts a fist into the meat of his open hand.

Rae says, "Crassus has already admitted that he is no warrior. Just a merchant, wasn't it, Arsin? You're going to take his advice?"

Tashu speaks, jumping ahead of Pandion's next outburst. "I will say this: The Sith are masters of deception. It is no cowardice to hide in the shadows and strike when your enemy passes. I agree with the admiral."

Sloane nods. "That's three to two. We move the Destroyers."

"No," Pandion says. "One of those ships is under my command. And I won't move it. It stays."

The defiance in his eyes flashes like starfire. This is

happening earlier than Sloane expected—she always knew one of them, probably Valco Pandion, would test her. Fine. She marches around the side of the table and meets him nose-to-nose.

"I am the admiral of this naval fleet. You do not have the authority, self-proclaimed or not, to command one ship against the movement of its fellows. You do not have the authority to deny me in this."

Pandion grins. "And what if I do, anyway?"

"Then the *Vigilance* will shoot your ship out of the sky. Its pieces will rain down upon us, and that is how the Empire will end. With us destroying one another, like rats driven mad by hunger, rats who eat one another instead of hunting down a proper meal."

"I could take my ship. Flee to some distant system—"

"Flee?" she asks. "You want to run. So *you're* the coward."

From Pandion: a small intake of breath. A tiny little gasp.

I have you.

For now.

"Admiral," he says, his tone suddenly changing. He even offers a wan smile and bows his head. "I am of course just playing the Imperial advocate. One must attempt to fully dissect the animal to understand it, and so I appreciate you letting me challenge you in this way. Do as you see fit."

She nods. A temporary victory, she thinks. But Pandion is doing exactly what she wants to do with the fleet above Akiva: He's retreating temporarily in the hope of fighting again another day. What was it Tashu said? *Hide in the shadows and strike when your enemy passes.*

* * *

Seems we do have a problem, after all, Sinjir thinks, ducking blaster fire and leaping up, running across gambling tables. He kicks a set of chits up into the air—the gambler, some degenerate nerf herder with a sweat-slick face, chases after his lost chits and gets blaster fire in the back for his trouble. Sinjir knocks a set of dice off another table, then nearly trips on a gambling wheel before taking a running leap—

. He catches the bar top across his middle. The air goes out of his lungs. Blaster fire peppers the wood and sends bottles and glasses spinning to the ground, shattering. Sinjir *oofs* but still clambers up and over, holding his arms above his head to protect his skull from the falling barware.

Then everything goes quiet.

He thinks: *Is it over?*

A shadow descends over him.

The bartender looks down. Greasy grin on his face. His chin still green and slimy with leaf-spit.

"You got a problem," the bartender says.

Then the bartender drops a fist like a falling meteor. It hits Sinjir like a malfunctioning bay-door piston, and his eyes roll back in his head as everything goes slippery and he tumbles toward unconsciousness.

INTERLUDE:

UYTER

"WE HAVE A PROBLEM," the driver says.

Young Pade sees the smoke over the hills long before he sees what's making it. Though the boy can certainly take a guess.

He looks around at the other recruits—or potential recruits, anyway. They're all whispering about it now. Murmuring and opening the windows on the transport and looking out.

The hoverbus driver—a bewhiskered, round-muzzled Nimbanel—looks back with eyes that look beady under its huge brow. The Nimbanel says to Pade and the other boys: "You . . . you tell them. You tell them I don't work for the Empire. I'm just a driver! You all know that, right?"

"Go on, mister," Pade says. "Just turn around and get us there."

The Nimbanel mutters something mean under his breath.

One of the other boys—a pudge-bellied kid with dark, coarse hair and a speckling of moles on his cheeks—turns around and stares over the seat at Pade. "You think we're done for?"

"I dunno," Pade says with a shrug. "Wait and see, I figure."

He puts on a tough face. It's a lie, though. Because he's scared, too.

The bus continues on, riding over the broken roads of Uyter. Hills rising up on either side—the grass once green, now bleached pale. And soon, tucked between those hills: the Imperial stormtrooper academy here.

It's burning. Or, rather, it has burned. Half of it is torn open by the tearing hands of old fire, and now black smoke drifts from inside it.

On the ground, a dozen dead stormtroopers.

Among them: other men and women. Not Imperials. Simple vests and utility belts. They have rifles and blasters. All the boys on the bus lean out and stare. They, like Pade, have never seen weapons up close. Pitchforks and spanners and a few blunt instruments here and there. Mostly, they're farm boys. Locals from the fringes. Some of them recruited by officers.

Some of them, like Pade, were simply . . . sent away.

Sent here.

To a place that is no longer a place.

The bus stops as one of the men—*one of the rebels*, Pade thinks—steps in front of the vehicle. The door opens and the Nimbanel steps out. The boys stay seated, not sure what they should do.

Pade thinks to look tough. He gets off the bus.

The Nimbanel and the rebel, a man with a scruffy beard and a scar running across the side of his neck, are arguing. The Nimbanel is waving his hands saying, "No, no, these kids are not my responsibility. No! I won't drive them back. I'm not paid for that—"

"Sir," the rebel says, "as you can see, the Imperial

academy is closed. This isn't a place for kids anymore—"

And then he sees Pade standing there. The man
turns away from the driver and looks down.

"Mister," Pade says.

"Son," the man says. "We'll get you back on the
bus and on your way home in two twitches of a nerf
tail—"

"I don't want to go home."

"Just the same, home isn't here."

"Home isn't anywhere, then. My parents kicked
my can down the road and moved on when I wasn't
looking. Went off to be nomads somewhere. It's the
Imperial academy for me, or it's nowhere."

The rebel chews on that. He looks off at the hills.
Then to the Nimbanel and the bus and back to Pade.
"What'll you do if you can't go here?"

"I told you, go nowhere." Pade leans, lowers his
voice. "You kill the kids in that academy? Ones who
were gonna be baby stormtroopers?"

"What? Stars, no."

"What'd you do with them?"

"You sure stick your nose in it, don't you, kid?"

"Maybe that's why my parents fixed to get rid of
me."

The man sighs. He kneels down. "Some of those
kids will go home. Some of them are heading out to
the New Academy on Chandrila. If they're of an age,
we'll take them and teach them how to be soldiers, if
they care to join the cause. Otherwise, it's back to
their parents. Or to orphanages."

Pade thrusts out his chin. "Then that's where I
wanna go, too. The New Academy."

"Hm." The man narrows his eyes. "All right.
Here." He dives in his pockets, pulls out a handful of
credits, then turns and slaps them into the Nimbanel's

palm. To Pade he says: "Central City's still in the Empire's back pocket, so make sure he drives you to Riverbreaker. Shuttle's leaving there tomorrow morning for Hanna City. Be on it."

Pade nods. "Thanks, mister."

"Other boys are welcome to catch that ride, too. You tell them."

"I will." Pade turns, then calls over his shoulder. "Thanks. May the Force be with you, mister."

"You too, kid. You too."

CHAPTER THIRTEEN

A STRANGE THING, being a parent. A parent raises
a child with the expectation that it's her job to teach
the child how to . . . well, how to do everything. How
to eat, live, breathe, work, play, *exist*. A mother ad-
vises her child on how to deal with bullies at the academy, or what streets are safe and what ones aren't, or
how to drive a bala-bala cart without crashing it into
a wall. The parent teaches these things because the
child needs to know. Because the child isn't capable.
Not the child's fault, of course. They're born a clean
slate. It's the parent's job to put the first writing on
the wall, to make sure that writing serves as an instruction manual. To ensure, well, the kid doesn't *die*
trying to figure out how to *live*.

It's hard to get out of that mode. Hard to see when
one's child has cast off the mantle of ignorance and
figured out how to do things.

Or just how to *be*.

And right now, Norra isn't seeing it.

Because her son is about to kill them both.

She leaps on the speeder bike and Temmin launches
back out of the *Moth*'s bay doors like a jogan-bat
with its wings on fire. She tugs on his arm, points
toward the jungle—the rain forest is thick, and it's
easy to get lost out there. These stormtroopers aren't

wilderness-ready. They're not proper speeder pilots. Out among the trees and vines, Temmin and Norra will be able to disappear. Maybe even down into the canyon.

But Temmin doesn't listen.

Listening, it seems, is no longer his strong suit. He used to be a good listener. A good *kid*. Always headstrong, sure, but he listened to his mother. Took her advice, did what she told him to do.

That has changed. Plainly. She tells him to go toward the jungle, and he goes the other way. Temmin points the speeder back toward the *city*.

The streets are too narrow! They can take some of the main thoroughfares, yes—whip the speeder down the CBD or across Main 66—but the former will be choked with people, and the latter choked with vehicles and herd animals. She tries to yell at him again, trying to get him to turn back around and head toward the rain forest, but he brushes her off—

Just as laserfire kicks up mud and stone around them.

A glance over her shoulder reveals: two speeder bikes, coming up fast.

The stormtroopers are hunched forward, throttling the speeders to their maximum. Red blaster fire sears the air from underneath the bladed steering vanes at the fore of each vehicle. She yells in Temmin's ear: "Incoming!" And he gives her a quick nod and then cuts the speeder sharply to the right. He takes it over a small berm, and then beneath them is the shattered plastocrete that takes them right down a winding alley.

Walls whip past on each side. Norra finds her breath trapped in her lungs. Just a few centimeters one way or another, and they're toast. If she moves *even a little bit,* the wall will wear down her kneecap or elbow like a macrosander, and that'll be the end of them. Suddenly the speeder jerks up and over a bundle of wire fencing crossing the alley.

Behind them, both the pursuing speeders manage the same jump. One after the other—now in a line, not next to each other. Which means that only one can fire its cannon. A shrewd move by her son. *Maybe.*

As long as they don't die from taking a too-sharp turn.

Temmin does indeed take a sharp turn—around the bend of an octagonal building. An old bank, she thinks, which means they're headed toward the markets, toward the CBD avenue. There, a wider place to drive, but more dangerous, too. All those people will complicate the equation. Like asteroids floating in wide-open space—and the last thing she wants to see is what happens when they clip some poor ship merchant or quilka-leaf vendor and turn him into a red spray.

Ahead, between a stack of boxes, the way toward the CBD.

Blaster fire pocks the boxes. They jump and judder.

The turn comes—

And Temmin doesn't take it.

He keeps going straight.

Ahead, a low wall. A *dead end.* Just a pile of junk: more bundles of wire, more crates, a piece of corrugated aluminum.

She begins yelling Temmin's name—"Temmin! *Temmin!*"—but he just gives her a thumbs-up. He yells back:

"Trust me!"

Trust in her son.

Trust him to make the right decisions.

Trust him not to kill him, her, and those two storm-troopers hot on their tail.

The wall approaches fast—boxes, wire, sheet metal. It's then she realizes:

He's not going to go straight forward.

He's going to take them straight *up*.

One quick shot from the blaster at the fore of his speeder and the aluminum does a quick hop—it slides a bit to the left, creating a shallow ramp. He turns the speeder *just so,* and next thing Norra knows, her stomach is left somewhere about three meters behind them, down on the ground.

Norra feels her son tense up. And then turbothrusters push them forward, fast and hard.

The speeder zips up the ramp, over the boxes, and along the top of the short wall. A wall that's scalloped, the concrete shaped with wavy contours—and the speeder follows them like a boat skipping across rollicking tides. They zip fast with sickening dips and Norra holds on for dear life.

Behind them, one of the stormtroopers tries the same move.

The front foil catches at the lip of the wall, and the back end of the vehicle flips up and over. The storm-trooper shrieks as he pitches forward, the whole speeder crashing down on him. It bursts into a plume of flame.

The other speeder makes the jump. Through the belching fire of the first speeder it roars, cannon on full-auto. Peppering the air around them with screaming laser blasts.

Temmin cuts to the right. He takes the speeder over a plank sitting catty-corner from the short wall to a taller one: a house with a decrepit rooftop garden long gone unused. They whip past a saggy-bellied, shaggy-chinned Lutrillian sitting in a half-collapsed lawn chair, a half-eaten amphibian in his grip. He barely startles as they zoom past.

Temmin, she realizes, isn't planning on dropping them down to the street level *at all*. The rooftops—of course. You want to travel Myrra, most people stick to the streets. But Temmin and his friends always used the rooftops. Making jumps from building to building that would cause Norra to snap her ankle like a piece of brittle driftwood. Temmin and the others set up planks and sheets of tin. Ropes and balance poles, too.

He knows the rooftops of this city well.

And it occurs to her: This probably isn't the first time he's taken a speeder bike up here, either.

Her son, she realizes, is a damn good pilot.

And a smaller voice chides her: *Just as reckless as you, too.*

Suddenly—a shower of sparks behind them. Her tailbone vibrates as a blaster hit clips the back end of their own speeder. The vehicle starts to wobble and drift just as they cross over another set of planks to an even higher rooftop. But Temmin manages to keep it steady.

He reaches back, grabs his mother's hands, and pulls her forward, placing both her hands on the handlebar controls.

"Your turn!" he yells. Then starts to squirm under her arm.

"What?" she yells back, in panic.

Ahead, a metal pole thrust up out of a greenhouse at a forty-five-degree angle. As Temmin snakes his way to the back of the speeder—leaving her in control of it—he yells: "Meet me at Aunt Esmelle's!"

Temmin, no!

He jumps off the speeder.

She continues to rocket forward—ahead, a cobbled-together crossing of hull metal between one roof and another. Norra thinks to jam on the brakes, but doing that now? She'd lose too much momentum. Probably drop the front end of the speeder over the edge of the wall and go over with it.

And so she does what she can. She accelerates.

Behind her, she sees her son spin around the metal bar like a circus performer—*when did he learn to do that?* she wonders—and then he swings back down, landing right behind the stormtrooper on the Imperial's speeder.

Norra takes her own jump, crests another roof, and then: *brakes.*

The speeder protests the fast deceleration. She cocks the maneuvering controls so that she skids to a halt, parallel to the roof's edge—

Her heart sinks when she sees:

There, on the roof, a stormtrooper. Supine and still.

And going the other direction:

Temmin's new ride, disappearing back down the way they came.

Norra grits her teeth, pivots the vehicle back around—but she hasn't ridden a speeder in years. Everything feels clumsy, and even as she throttles it forward again, the realization hits her like a fist to the chin:

I've lost him.

CHAPTER FOURTEEN

THUNDER THROTTLES THE SKIES over Myrra, lightning flicking between bands of dark clouds like a dewback's tongue. Darkness has settled in, and with it the rains have come. Norra stares out the window. Rain streaks the circular glass. Every boom and flash makes Norra flinch.

"I'm sure he's fine," says her sister, Esmelle. Esmelle is older than she is by a good number of years—when Norra was born, Esmelle was already running around the city with a gang of hooligans all her own. She's lost a lot of that rebellious edge since then—now a woman content to sit in her home on Orchard Hill, as if waiting to die and join the rest of the graves that wait just up the road. Graves underneath fruiting trees. SO THAT WE MAY EAT OF THOSE WE LOST AND REMEMBER THEM, a plaque says on the gate into the orchard. That idea always turned Norra's stomach.

Norra turns to meet Esmelle. She's been trying to keep the anger inside the bottle, all stoppered up. But she's nervous, on edge, and she feels the bottle shaking, the glass cracking. "Really? Why would you say that?"

Esmelle, a wispy thing, just smiles. "He's always been fine."

"Yes. Fine. Perfectly, utterly *fine*. Like how he

doesn't live here with you, but how you let him live in our old house. And how you let him turn it into his own personal little black market, where he gets threatened by . . . by *criminals,* where he steals and sells *the-stars-know-what,* where—"

Esmelle, always the smiler, pats Norra on the shoulder. "Norra, honey, you should be proud of him. You raised him to be smart. *Independent.* You can't be mad at him for being what you taught him to be."

Norra laughs—a hollow, bitter sound. "I'm not mad at him, Esme. I'm ticked at *you.* I left him in your care. You were supposed to be a parent to my son. And now I find you've given that up. Did you ever even try?"

"Did I?" The smile falls away from Esmelle's face like the last leaf on a storm-shook tree. Her eyes narrow. *Good,* Norra thinks. *Let's do this. Let's scrap this out.* "Might I remind you that you, dear Norra, took off. I thought better than to chase some fool's crusade halfway across the galaxy like you, choosing to make other people your responsibility and not your own blood-born son. And—" Here Esmelle makes an exasperated sound, *pfah!* "—and if you wonder why the boy enjoys hanging around criminals, might I remind you that your own husband was—"

Norra raises the back of her hand. "Don't."

Esmelle blinks. Swallows. As if she realizes she danced right up to the edge of the cliff and now it's breaking apart underneath her feet. "I'm simply saying: The boy's last memory of his father is of them coming and dragging him out into the streets like a common thief-runner."

"Brentin was a *good man.* He carried messages for the Rebellion even before there *was* a Rebellion. And now there's more than that. There's a new dawn, a new day, a New Republic. In part because of people like *him*."

Esmelle sniffs. "Yes. And I suppose you think you're just such a hero, as well. You saved the galaxy, but lost your son. Worth it, dear sister?"

Why . . . you venomous canyon adder . . .

Esmelle's wife, Shirene, steps in. She secures Esmelle's elbow with her own, giving the woman a kiss on the cheek. "Esme, how about a hot tea? I've left the thermajug on the stovetop in the kitchen."

"Yes. Yes, that sounds good. I'll . . . I'll get tea." Esmelle offers a stiff smile, then fritters off as she is wont to do.

Shirene sighs. Shirene is the opposite of Esmelle in many ways—Esmelle is thin, reedy, pale as a ghost. Shirene is rounded, pillowy, skin as dark as a handful of overturned soil. Her hair is short and curly and close to the scalp; Esmelle's is long, a silver cascade down her back.

"Shirene, you don't need to step into the middle of this—"

Shirene clucks her tongue. "Please, Norra. I'm in this. I have skin in this game. I love Temmin like my own son. But what I need you to realize is that he *isn't* our son." Norra starts to protest, but Shirene shushes her—and somehow, Shirene has the magical ability to make that shushing feel gentle and welcome, soft and necessary. "Don't misunderstand me. I just mean that we were never ready for this. For *him*. He's got your spark in him. Yours and Brentin's. He's challenging *because* he's smart as a whip-snake, savvy as a sailbird. Forgive Esmelle. Forgive me. We just weren't ready. And you were gone, so what choice did we have?"

"I had to go. I had to fight."

"I know. And I'm sorry you never found Brentin."

Norra winces at that. It's like being slapped. Shirene doesn't mean it that way—the look on her face tells Norra that the thought is a sincere one, and not a barbed lash. But it stings just the same. "He wasn't a criminal."

"I know. And Esmelle knows it, too."

Outside, the sky splits with a close clap of thunder. Rain batters the side of the house. Normal for this time of year—the mausim-storms have already come and gone and ushered in the wet season.

"Here's the stars' own truth," Shirene says. "Temmin takes care of us more than we take care of him. He helps pay for things. Shows up at the start of the week with a basket of fruits and bread, sometimes some wyrg-jerky or some of that spicy arguez sausage. If our evaporator or our flood-pump breaks, he shows up with the parts and the tools and he fixes it. We're a couple of old cluckers, and he takes care of us good. We'll miss him."

"You can come with us. That offer is still on the table—"

"Pssh. Norra, better or worse, we put down roots. We're as grown into this hill as the orchard up the road, as settled as the bones in the dirt. You take your boy, though, and get him somewhere better."

Norra sighs. "It's not like he wants to go."

"Well, he's built up a life here. That shop of his—"

That shop of his.

It hits Norra like a beam of light.

"That's where he went," she says, scowling. "Temmin was never planning to come here. He went back to his shop." *I never should've taken him away from there in the first place.*

"Well, that's probably all right—"

"It's not all right. Those criminals I mentioned? They'll be looking for him. Damnit! I'm too caught up in everything—I didn't even see it. The storm-troopers didn't get him. He just bailed." She sighs, presses the heels of her hands into her eyes. Hard enough that she sees stars streaking and melting across the black behind her lids. "I need to borrow your bala-bala."

Shirene offers a sad smile. "Of course, Norra. Anything you need."

Damn this rain! Temmin thinks. He lies on his belly on the rooftop of Master Hyor-ka's dao-ben steamed bun shop that sits across the alley from his own—and though he sits under a tarp, he's still soaked through like a red-eyed silt-rat that drowned in a cistern. The rain pins him there like a divine hand.

He again lifts the macrobinoculars to his eyes. Flicks them over to night vision.

Two of Surat Nuat's lackeys—a potbellied Rodian and that oil-skinned Herglic—continue to do what they've been doing for the last hour. They pitch junk from Temmin's shop into the street with a clang, clatter, and splash. And then the same pair of Kowakian monkey-lizards descend from the nearby rooftop and canopy to pick through the shiniest bits before fleeing once more, cackling like tiny wizened lunatics.

Inside, he hears more banging. Drilling. Yelling.

They're trying to find out how to get into the sub-layer. They want what he stole from Surat.

Not that he knows what exactly it *is* that he stole from Surat.

A weapon, he figures. Has to be.

And whatever it is, it's *his* now. Not that Sullustan frag-head's.

When they have the door open, he can see just inside—and there, he sees the familiar pointed feet of his own personal B1 battle droid bodyguard: Mister Bones. The feet are still. They look collapsed against the legs, which means the rickety droid is collapsed and in storage mode. Worse, Temmin can see a slight blue glow around the metal.

That, he suspects, is the glow from an ion lock. It explains why Mister Bones hasn't been responding to his comlink. They've got the droid locked up and shut down in an ion field.

Smart move.

And it leaves Temmin with one less option than before. In fact, Bones was his best chance to reclaim the shop quickly (if temporarily): Send the refurbed, modded B1 droid in to whip everybody's tail so that Temmin could sneak in and get back into the sublayer to secure his stuff.

With that option off the table, it means the longer, more arduous path awaits: He has to go find one of the bolt-holes into the old catacombs beneath the city, then wend his way back to his own shop. He knows the way, but it won't be fast. Better to get to it, then. And hope he gets there before Surat's entourage of space-brains figure out how to gain entry.

Temmin starts to put his binocs away—

But then, off to his right? A shrill cackle.

He knows that sound.

Suddenly a flash of movement—a darting shape moves toward him, and one of the monkey-lizards has seized his binocs. The little demon hisses and spits at him, then pecks at his hands when he starts playing tug-of-war with it.

"Get! Off!" he growls.

But then something cannonballs into the small of his back.

The second monkey-lizard.

That one begins clawing at his ears and biting tufts

of hair off his scalp. Laughing all the while. It's enough of a distraction. The binocs slip from his grip and the monkey-lizard gambols about, delighting in its prize.

Temmin lurches to his feet, lunging for it—

And the second one drops to the ground and darts in front of him.

His ankle catches on the creature's body—its tail around his thigh, giving a hard tug. Next thing he knows, Temmin is going tail-over-teakettle as he tumbles over the edge of the roof. He hits the awning over the dao-ben shop and rolls off it, landing in a deep puddle. *Splash.*

He splutters and spits, lifting himself up. Water streaming down in a small dirty waterfall, his hair now in his eyes. Temmin wipes locks away—

And the curled tip of a giant ax blade hooks just inside his nostril and tugs his head up. *Ow, ow, ow!* The Herglic stands there, its mouth twisted into a sinister grin—rows and rows of serrated teeth sliding together with the sound of a rasp running across wood.

The Herglic cries: "It's the kid! We got the kid!"

Above, the monkey-lizards chant and cackle.

He staggers through the forest. The burning forest. Bits of brush smoldering. A stormtrooper helmet nearby, charred and half melted. A small fire burns nearby. In the distance, the skeleton of an AT-AT walker. Its top blown open in the blast, peeled open like a metal flower. That burns, too.

Bodies all around.

Some of them are faceless, nameless. To him, at least. But others, he knows. Or knew. There—the fresh-faced officer, Cerk Lormin. Good kid. Eager to please. Joined the Empire because it's what you did. Not a true believer, not by a long stretch. Not far from him: Captain Blevins. Definitely a true believer. A froth-mouthed braggart and bully, too. His face is a mask of blood. Sinjir is glad that one is dead. Nearby, a young woman: He knows her face from the mess, but not her name, and the insignia rank on her chest has been covered in blood. Whoever she was, she's nobody now. Mulch for the forest. Food for the native Ewoks. Just stardust and nothing.

We're all stardust and nothing, *he thinks.*

An absurd thought. But no less absurd than the one that follows:

We did this to ourselves.

He should blame them. The rebels. Even now he can hear them applauding. Firing blasters into the air. Hicks and yokels. Farm boy warriors and pipe-fitter pilots.

Good for them.

They deserve their celebration.

Just as we deserve our graves.

A pebble wakes him up. *Pock!* It beans off his head—a head that feels like it's been stepped on by the crushing leg of a passing Imperial walker—and lands next to his face. Clattering into a small pile of other pebbles.

Sinjir groans and tries to stand.

The ground beneath him shifts and swings—and he feels suddenly like he's falling, even though he's not. Vertigo assails him.

He blinks. Tries to get his bearings.

He's in a cage. Iron. Rusted. Shaped like a birdcage, except *person*-sized, though only barely. It dangles from a thick, heavy-gauge chain. A chain that ascends through the jagged, dripping rock above into a long, dark well. Below him—

Is nothing.

A massive rift, a black chasm between craggy, wet walls. Walls barely lit by braziers of light along a far wall—a wall that sports a narrow metal walkway bolted into the glistening rock.

A figure walks along that path. A Sakiyan, by his hairless scalp and ink-black skin. The guard has in his hand the end of a leash, the leash wound up around his wrist all the way to the elbow. At the other end of the rope? A long, red-eyed beast. Skin as rough and ragged as the wall it passes. A narrow maw with many teeth. A sallow belly dragging along the ground.

"You're awake" comes a voice from behind him.

Sinjir startles. It causes his own cage to swing, which in turn makes his head pound harder. He idly considers throwing up.

There, behind him: another half dozen cages like his.

Only two of them are occupied.

In one: a skeleton. Not human, though humanoid. Something with a horn on its head. What little skin is left on those bones looks like tattered rags and strips of rotten leather.

In the other: It's her. The Zabrak bounty hunter.

Thankfully, it's she who spoke. Not the skeleton. Because . . . gross.

"You," he groans. "You were throwing pebbles at me."

"Yes. Me. The one you tried to buy."

"Not like that. Not like you think."

"Then like how?"

He leans his forehead against the cool iron. Water drips down on his head, runs down to the end of his nose (*a bead of blood hangs there until he sneezes it away:* a returning memory that hits him like a seismic wave). "You really don't remember me, do you?"

"I do not."

Disappointment pulls him down like quicksand. "I thought we shared a special moment."

"Clearly, we did not."

"Endor," he says. "After everything. After the rebels secured their victory, I . . . we saw each other."

She hesitates. "Oh. Right."

"So, you remember."

"I suppose."

"Well, come now. Don't you think that's something? A moment of cosmic significance? The galaxy trying to tell us something? I mean, what are the chances?"

She sniffs. "I don't have a droid around to tell me."

"Let's just assume *astronomical,* then."

"And that means what?"

"I . . . I don't know, I just expect it means something." Suddenly, a pebble appears out of the half darkness and *thwack*s him in the head again. "Ow! Do you have to keep doing that? I'm awake."

"Everything means something, but not every something *matters.* I don't believe in cosmic significance. I don't care for magic or the Force or kissing a chit and throwing it into a fountain for good luck. I care about what I can see, taste, smell, and—most important— what I can do. You mean nothing to me until you do. You're a rebel?"

He chews on his lip. "Yes?"

"Why are you here?"

"I came to see Surat to find a way off this damp, jungly rock. Incidentally, did you see what happened to my friend? The tail-head?"

"They carried his body out after they dragged yours away."

"Is he . . . ?"

"Dead, yes."

Sinjir shuts his eyes. Says a small, meaningless prayer for the eager-eyed fool. What was his name? *Orgadomie, Orlagummo, Orgie-Borgie, whoever you are, you didn't deserve that.*

"Why are *you* here?" he asks.

But the Zabrak ignores the question. She cranes her neck, staring out.

He follows her gaze. On the walkway, the guard and the leashed creature disappear into a tunnel and are gone.

"I'm planning on getting out of here," she says.

"Ah, well. Good for you. Can I come?"

She reaches up, fidgets with her scalp. He watches as her fingers drift along the barbed horns that form a thorny crown on her head—she grimaces as she breaks one of them off with a loud *snap*.

He says, "That looks like it hurt."

"It didn't. It's fake." She teases something out of the horn—something metal. Like a key. She begins to use it on the lock at the door.

A lock pick.

Clever.

"You can come with me if you're useful," she says.

"I'm very useful. A very useful rebel, indeed."

The lock pops, and her door clangs open.

"I'm not hearing much in evidence of that."

She jumps out of the cage backward, catching the lip of it with her hands. The whole thing swings back and forth. The Zabrak swings a few good times, then bends her back in a way that Sinjir is fairly certain would shatter his spine like a falling icicle. Her legs swing all the way up, her feet closing around the top of the cage. Her hands let go.

Her legs swing her upper torso back up.

"You're . . . limber," he says.

"And you appear useless. Condolences."

She quickly climbs the chain above her cage, disappearing into the hollow space. *No, no, no!* She's his one chance! He's in this cage because he tried to save her!

"Wait!" he calls. "I'm not a rebel! I'm an Imperial!" He shouts louder: "An ex-Imperial loyalty officer! I stole a rebel's clothes on Endor! And his . . ." But she's gone. Her cage has already stopped swinging. "Identity." *And his life and his ship and apparently his moral center.*

Well then.

He groans. Again considers puking.

But then: His cage shudders.

And the Zabrak's upside-down face appears level with his own.

She scowls. "A loyalty officer. You just became interesting. And useful." The bounty hunter holds up her lock pick. "You're going to help me catch my quarry. That's the deal. Take it and I open this door. Leave it, and Surat will likely sell you to the Empire. They don't care much for deserters, I hear. Once, there might have been a tribunal, but these days they will shoot you in the street like a lowly cur."

"I'll take the deal, as long as you help me get off this planet after."

She considers it. "Done."

As the Zabrak goes to work on the lock, she says: "I'm Jas Emari."

"Sinjir Rath Velus."

"A pleasure. If you try to frag me over, I'll gut you where you stand."

"Noted."

The door pops open and she offers a hand. "Let's go."

* * *

Toomata Wree—aka Tooms—pokes around the boy's junk shop. The others have gone. Once the boy himself showed up, all the digging and messing around in here stopped. Surat said they'll get the information from the kid *proper-like,* because while the kid's a punk, he's just that. He'll fold like a bad gambler and tell them how to get into the down-below of this joint, so they can steal back Surat's prize and any other goodies they find.

Tooms fishes in his pocket, pulls out some numb-spray. He gives his bruised face a couple of good mistings—*psst psst psst*—and instantly the pain subsides underneath a carpet of sweet anesthesia.

That battle droid did a number on him.

A *battle droid,* of all things.

Kid might be a punk, but kid's also got talent.

Whatever. Right now, Tooms looks around the shop. Maybe he'll find something here for his girl, Looda. He's on the outs with her (the same rigmarole: *You work too much, Toomata, you do not care about me, if you like Surat Nuat so much why do you not make him your lover*), so a little prize might go a long way. But all this stuff? Droid parts and conduits and pieces blown off spaceships. Over there are evaporator parts. Below them: vaporator parts. Then circuit boards in a half-rotten box. Then a box full of wonky thermal detonators—paperweight duds.

Then he sees something:

The head of a translator droid. Tarnished up, but still shiny. Looda, she likes shiny things. Maybe he could do something with it. Put a couple blood orchids in it, or hammer open the head and use it as a . . . a dish.

He reaches up for it, his fingers grabbing for the eyes—

The head doesn't budge off the shelf. It's bolted down.

He pulls harder—

And the eyes suddenly sink into the droid's skull with a *whir-click*.

A door opens up. A small wind kicks up through the open space and the Abednedo sees a set of steps down. This is it. *This is it*. This is the way into the basement! Into Temmin Wexley's *special stash*. Tooms grabs for the comlink at his belt but then pauses. Maybe he should go down there, take a quick look for himself. You know. For Looda.

He chuckles, then steps toward the door.

Behind him, a voice: "Where is my son?" A woman's voice.

The Abednedo purses his cracked, split lips—then he moves fast, spinning around, reaching to draw the blaster at his side—

The woman shoots first.

The shot takes him in the stomach. He cries out, staggering backward as he tries to raise his own blaster—but the woman shoots again, and his weapon spins out of his hand. He clutches at his seared, smoldering middle.

She steps closer to him, revealing her face under the hood. A dark-eyed, steely glare awaits. He recognizes her from the shop that day. The scowl on her face is deep. The boy's mother thrusts the pistol under his chin.

"I'll ask one more time: Where is my son, Temmin?"

* * *

The boot presses down on the back of Temmin's neck.

His hands are pulled taut behind his back, swaddled in chains and held fast with a pair of magnetic manacles. He tastes blood and dust.

"You stole from me," Surat says, pressing down with his boot. Temmin tries not to cry out, but it hurts, and a sound escapes his throat without him meaning—a wounded-animal sound.

He's here in Surat's office. It's a spare, severe room—red walls lined with manacles. In the middle, a desk whose surface is made from some Sullustan frozen in carbonite. On that desk is a blaster, a collection of quills in a cup, a bottle of ink. The room features only one other piece of furniture: a tall black cabinet, sealed tight with a maglock.

"I . . . didn't . . . ," Temmin says. "It was an accident. I didn't know—"

He's yanked up off his feet. The Herglic does the lifting. Surat stands there in front of him, pursing his lips almost as if he wants to kiss the air. The Sullustan gangster runs an index finger under his own cheek flaps, flicking dirt away with thumb and fingertip. "You are lying to me, boy. And even if you were not lying, what does it matter? You have slighted me and that slight must be repaid in kind. Otherwise, how will that look?"

"It will look merciful—"

The Sullustan grabs Temmin by the throat. He squeezes. The blood starts to pound in Temmin's temples as he wheezes and gurgles, trying desperately to catch a breath—his whole face starts to throb. Blackness drifts in at the edges of his vision like pools of spilled oil.

"The only Mercy I have ever had was a Corellian slave girl. She was nice to me. I was nice to her. Mostly."

Then the criminal overlord lets go. Oxygen rushes back in through Temmin's burning throat. He gasps and coughs, spit dangling from his lip.

The Herglic kicks him in the back of the knee and Temmin falls once more. And with his arms behind his back, the best he can do is take the hit on his shoulder so his head doesn't snap against the hard metal floor.

"Let me tell you who I am," Surat says. "So you know what I can do. I killed my own mother for daring to speak back to me. We lived in a wind-harvest tunnel on Sullust, and I threw her into the blades. When my father found out, he of course wanted to hurt me like I hurt her, but my father? He was a soft, pliable man. He tried to hit me and I cut his throat with a piece of kitchen cutlery. It was my brother that proved the greatest challenge. We fought for years. Back and forth, from the shadows. He was ruthless. A worthy challenger, Rutar was." The Sullustan nods sagely, as if lost in memory. Suddenly he perks his head up and nods. "That's him there." He points to the desk. "He's the one frozen in carbonite. Some say I learned that trick from the Empire, but I assure you—they learned it from me."

"Please," Temmin says, bubbles of saliva forming and popping on his lips. "Give me a chance to make it right. I can repay you. I can be in debt—"

"The question is, what can I take right now? An ear? A hand? My brother took my eye in our final battle—" Surat cocks his head so that the Sullustan's one milky, ruined eye is pointed right at Temmin. "And that has become my way. My foes must leave having given something vital. Not just money. Credits are so *crass*. But something necessary. A piece of themselves offered and taken. What do you offer?"

"Not that, not that—you can take my shop, you

can have my droids, I'll give you back the weapon, anything. Let's just . . . let's talk it out. We can talk this out. Can't we?"

Surat sighs. "I think the time for talk has passed." And then he thrusts his finger up in the air and a big smile parts his strange face. "Ah! Yes. You do love to talk, don't you? I shall take your tongue."

Temmin gets his legs underneath him, tries to stand as he cries out in anger and fear. The Herglic knees him in the side and knocks him down.

The slick-skinned brute laughs.

Surat says, "Gor-kooda, take him to the cistern. I will get my things." Then Surat saunters over to his cabinet. He pulls back a sleeve and reveals a bracelet, then waves the bracelet over the maglock. It pops.

As Gor-kooda the Herglic drags Temmin out of the room kicking and screaming, Surat removes a long surgical gown and begins to put it on. Humming as he does.

"This *doesn't* seem essential."

"It is."

"He's not our problem."

"They're going to cut out his tongue."

"Oh, *now* you have a soft spot? I thought you only helped those who were—how did you put it? 'Useful.'"

"The boy is useful. I believe he can furnish the repairs on my gun. Otherwise, I would leave him to his fate. Would you?"

Sinjir flinches at that. Again the questions hit him: *What kind of man am I? Am I capable of walking on past? Am I different now, or the same?* He changed that day on Endor. Something turned inside him. The short, sharp shock of losing everything made him a new person.

But to what end? Who is he now?

A coward, or someone bigger, someone better?

The two of them crouch down in the tunnels below the Alcazar, Surat's cantina and criminal compound. After the bounty hunter hauled him up out of the dungeon he found himself in, they crept through this space looking for a way out—and there they happened upon voices in the other room. Surat, as he abused and threatened some young kid.

The shuffling of the Herglic's feet approaches. With it come the boy's grunts and bleats—plus the echoing sound of his feet kicking the floor and the walls as he struggles to escape.

"You first," Jas hisses in Sinjir's ear.

Then she shoves him out in front of the Herglic.

The Herglic: a huge, shiny creature. Tiny eyes in a massive head. No neck. Tiny teeth in a massive maw. No chin.

"Unnh?" the Herglic says.

Sinjir winces, then stabs out a foot to catch the beast in the knee: a common weak point among most humanoid beings. But it's like kicking a tree. *Thud.* The Herglic just looks down, then snorts. The alien lets go of the boy's bound wrists and grabs Sinjir with both hands—hands big enough to tie a speeder bike into a pretzel twist. But slippery hands, too, and Sinjir slides out of the grip and quickly goes for another weak point—the monster's throat. He flips around, trying like hell to get his arms around the creature's neck, but oops, no such neck exists. The Herglic chuckles, then jams his massive frame right, then left, each time smashing Sinjir into the wall—*Wham! Wham!*

Sinjir sees stars, his brain shook up like a cocktail.

A voice. Her voice. The Zabrak's.

"The nose," she says.

Then thrusts the heel of her hand forward.

Smashing it right into the Herglic's nose.

The alien howls, his eyes squeezing shut. Some kind of saline slime-snot begins pouring out of his nasal perforations, and the poor lug slaps at his snout like it's on fire.

"Get the boy," she says.

Sinjir slides around the hulking bulk of the Herglic's frame, and helps the boy stand. The kid looks like some ratty street punk. Tan skin, hair up in a messy knot. Someone here has worked him over pretty good. Blooms of bruising on his cheek. A split lip.

"Rescue party," Sinjir says, offering a stiff smile.

Then he shoves the boy forward. Out of the range of the Herglic's meaty, blind pawing.

The kid looks at the bounty hunter. "I know you," he says.

"We'll get into that," she says. "We need to go. *Now.*"

This is her life. This is the life of a bounty hunter. It never comes easy. Many try. They pretend at doing the work, but aren't ready for what awaits. Because the job? The job never comes easy. You think the job to extract some Quarren bookie who's been stealing from the Empire is gonna be a cakewalk, and it turns out he's got six squid-head egg-brood brothers and sisters who look just like him. Another job comes and *that* one seems easy, too—all you have to do is kill some soft-handed Black Sun accountant, but then it turns out there's a bounty on *you,* and next thing you know you're trussed up in the cargo bay of a ship belonging to that slovenly leper-head, Dengar, all while your prey has hightailed it to the far corners of the Outer Rim. You think, *yes,* I'll kill this spunky rebel princess-warrior like the Empire wants, but then you watch the rebels turn the tide and you realize the winning side isn't the winning side anymore and if you wanna survive, you'd damn well better change your skin or just plain disappear.

You think: *I'll just take out Arsin Crassus.* One shot, boom.

And then you realize: He's sitting there in a whole nest of Imperials. High-ranking players with big bounties. And next thing you know, you're falling, your gun breaks, and a local gangster with delusions of grandeur forces you to bust out of his prison and out of his cantina, but when you go upstairs and plan to head right for the door—

You see an Imperial officer standing there with a quartet of stormtroopers. And another cadre of Surat's thugs—not to mention the ones that will probably be coming up behind you *any second.*

Because you just escaped their prison.

And because you just released another couple of prisoners, too.

The job is always complicated.

It's never as easy as it seems. Even the hard ones always end up harder. But this is the life Jas took for herself.

And she's learned to handle it without panic. (Or, at least, without letting that panic out of its cage. Fear can be a strong motivator, provided you control it rather than letting *it* control *you.*)

The cantina and gambling house is full, even at this hour. Fuller now than it was earlier. A haze of smoke hovers in the air, so thick you could grab a handful and form it into a ball. The sound of the room is a low roar: a din of voices yelling, cards shuffling, knuckle-dice clattering against tables.

There—off to the side. A small doorway out. Probably into an alley. The *shame door,* they call it. You get too drunk on 'skee, you lose your pants in a game of Kessel Wheel, you meet a new friend and don't want anybody to see you leave . . . you head out the shame door. Or maybe you're ushered out quietly by Surat's men—no good to just throw those people out on the street. That tends to have a chilling effect on anybody wanting to come in through the door and spend their credits.

Thing is, the shame door is always guarded.

Tonight, by an Ithorian with one side of his hammerhead swaddled in a bandage. The wrapping covering one eye.

Jas doesn't tell the others the plan.

She just points and moves. They follow after.

The Ithorian grunts as he sees them come up. The alien gurgles at them in the Ithorian tongue, waving them off—

But then his one good eye widens. He recognizes them.

In Basic he says, "Hey!"

Jas hooks the inside of her leg around his tree-trunk limb, spins around him like he's a pole, and uses the momentum to smash the side of his head into the wall. His other eye shuts and he topples like a felled ashsap tree.

Sinjir goes to open the door, then curses under his breath. "Bug-hugging piece of star-burned flog-waste." He kicks the door.

At first she doesn't see what he's going on about but then—

The door is locked. The Ithorian was standing in front of the *wheel-lock:* three colored metal plates inside a circle, like wide, flat spokes. Hit the three plates in the right combination, then spin the wheel? The door will open. Problem is: They don't have the right combination.

Her planet for an astromech droid.

She senses movement—

Across the room, at the fore of the cantina, a storm-trooper is tapping the Imperial officer on the shoulder with one hand. And with the other?

He's pointing right at them.

"We're spotted," she hisses.

She gives a quick kick to the Ithorian's hip, catching his blaster holster with the tip of her boot. The gun juggles out and she punts it up into the air, where she catches it.

Behind them, from the door they just fled, come another trio of Surat's men. "There!" a thin-necked Rodian cries. "Kill them!"

He raises his pistol—a little BlasTech bolt-thrower—and fires.

Jas grabs Temmin, pirouettes, and moves him out of the way.

Just as the blaster bolt sizzles past, and hits the wheel-lock panel. The panel pops in a rain of sparks, and hops off the wall like a framed painting during a groundquake. Jas grits her teeth—*can't get out that way.*

But then the door shudders and whips open, sparking. The whole system malfunctioning in their favor.

"Out!" she says, moving the boy and the ex-Imperial out through the door and into the hammering rain. She sidesteps more incoming fire, then pivots and hops out the door—

A storm rages overhead. Water runs down the crooked alley: neon light trapped in it, moving like hot pink and glowslime snakes. The rain is coming down so hard and so fast it's hard to see. Then the sky flashes—blue pulses of lightning followed swiftly by ground-shaking thunder—and it forces the eyes to re-adjust.

Just pick a direction, she thinks.

She takes a step one way—

"There!" comes a shout. White shapes that direction. Stormtroopers. Coming around from the front side of the Alcazar. Jas takes a few shots, then pushes Sinjir and the boy in the other direction.

They bolt down the alley. Feet splashing. Rain threatening to push them to the cracked plastocrete and drown them like unwanted cats. The three of them turn a sharp corner—

Lightning flashes again, revealing a dead end.

Voices behind them. More splashing.

The alley was supposed to be their way out. Now it's just a murder chute. "We're trapped," Sinjir says.

Temmin shoulders into her. "My cuffs. Shoot 'em off!"

He turns his back toward her and cranes his arms. Jas holds one of his wrists, then puts the end of the stolen blaster against the cuffs—

A red glow and rain of embers as she pulls the trig-ger. The bolt shrieks through the middle of the shack-les, and Temmin yelps, staggering forward, shaking both hands as if they're bee-stung.

"C'mon," he says. "Look—a storm ladder." He points and she follows his finger. At the end of the alley, sure enough, there's a ladder—a jointed ladder made of chains bundled up at the top of a narrow roof. *Storm ladders.* Right. During bad storms, they get you off the ground quickly in case a flash flood comes churning through. A lot of rooftops have them here.

The three of them hurry to the end. Temmin slams

up against the wall, feeling around until he finds the button.

He slams it with the heel of his hand. Above his head, a clicking as the ladder is released from its mooring—a rattle-clatter as it drops and smacks down against the wall.

Footsteps. Shouts. Coming around the corner, now—not even fifteen meters away. A blaster bolt hisses through the rain, hits the wall. Temmin begins to clamber up the ladder—

But up above, a metal squeak. Then a reverberating groan.

The ladder above becomes suddenly unmoored, the brackets holding the chains in place popping free. Temmin falls a meter, lands on his back, gasping. Jas yells at him to move, and he does—rolling out of the way just in time, as the ladder mechanism comes crashing down where his head was only a second before.

Jas helps him stand.

Their one way up and out of this dead end is gone.

They await no more incoming fire. Because their enemies have them. What approaches is a curious mix of the *Imperial* and the *criminal*. Surat's thugs at the edges, and the Imperials—one officer, four stormtroopers—coming down the middle. The officer is a beak-nosed prig, grinning like he gets first bite of the bird on Founder's Day.

"Drop that blaster," he calls over the roar of the rain.

Jas sucks in a breath, ponders on the way out. Shove the boy and the ex-Imperial forward. Leap on their heads, use the stormtrooper helmets as stepping-stones—hoping she can use the cover of night and the bad weather to escape. Hoping they'll be content with their prize of Sinjir and the boy.

It won't work. Too risky.

She growls, and lets the blaster drop into the water streaming around their feet. Lightning flashes again.

And that's when she sees it.

That thing almost just crushed my head, Temmin thinks as the water gurgles past his ears. Above, storm clouds glow pregnant with lightning before discharging forked bolts across the sky. The woman—a bounty hunter, if he remembers her right—reaches down, helps him up.

He's still dazed when he realizes, the gig is up. Show's over. They're like droids on the sundering table: about to be ripped up for scrap.

They tell Jas to drop the blaster.

She hesitates, but then does it.

Temmin's heart sinks. So close. Surat will take more than his tongue for this. But then, another pulse of lightning.

And a smile spreads across his face.

The light illuminates a figure. The figure stands on a rooftop above and behind the pack of Imperials and thugs. When the lightning flash is gone again, once more the figure merges with the darkness. But to Temmin's eyes, the shape of the thing remains emblazoned upon his vision like an X-ray—he knows that skeletal shape. That beaked head. The knobby joints.

Mister Bones is here.

The next lightning flash—

There he is. In midair. Claw arms around his knees. Spiraling through open space, captured in the strobe-light pulse of the storm, gone again once darkness resumes—

But not really gone at all.

The droid lands on the ground with a hard *clack* and a splash.

It begins.

What happens next is like something out of a nightmare, Sinjir thinks. (Though it seems to be a nightmare dreamed up in their favor.) They're standing there, about to surrender. Then he sees something—movement in the air, something spinning. Then he hears something land.

The Imperials and Surat's men are slow to respond.

Too slow, as it turns out.

Two strangled cries rise up, swiftly silenced—and two stormtrooper helmets vault up into the air, turning like pinwheels. It occurs to him moments later: *Not the helmets. But the heads.*

The two other troopers turn—and so does Surat's collection of thugs. The officer, slow to realize, is knocked to the ground as *something* moves into the middle of them, wading in like a threshing machine. Some *shape,* some *bony configuration of limbs,* begins wheeling about—a vibroblade buzzing through the air. Men scream. They discharge their weapons, but this thing is fast, *too* fast, improbably fast, and they end up shooting one another as the thing ducks under, its whole body bent and suddenly scuttling like a stirred-up spider. It gets underneath the officer just as he stands up. Then he's dragged down to the ground once more, thrashing about—bones crack and shatter as the Imperial's screams are cut short.

Sinjir gapes.

What mad hell is this?

But the boy is at his elbow, urging him on. "We have to *go!*"

Sinjir nods, gamely. Yes, yes they do.

* * *

They run. Past the chaos. Past the throng of bodies battling a singularly insane battle droid in the rain—the droid now crowing a discordant song as he spins about, blade out, knocking stormtroopers to the ground and dispatching Surat's thugs with a mad, dancing whirl.

Temmin charges hard—almost losing his balance from the water rushing around his feet. Doesn't help that he's dizzy, hungry, and shot through with so much adrenaline he's pretty sure he might vibrate into a cloud of disconnected molecules at any given second.

Ahead, a three-eyed Gran steps out. One of Surat's many enforcers. The alien's caprine muzzle bleats out in alarm—the Gran raises a netgun, and Temmin winces, waiting for the incoming blast. But there's a flash in the rain from behind the enforcer, and suddenly the alien's three eyes roll back in their fleshy stalks before he plunges face-first to the ground.

Mom!

Norra stands there, straddling a bala-bala speeder—a narrow, stumpy vehicle meant to take the tight channels and sharp-angled turns of the streets of Myrra. Everyone uses them to go to work or move crates. On any given morning or evening, the CBD ends up choked with those speeders: every one in a different color, each one modded at least a little bit by its owners. This one is blue, with a braced box-rack in the back, where a chain and ball-hitch are hooked as well.

Temmin instantly recognizes it as belonging to his aunts.

Norra waves them on. "Come on! *Come on.*"

Temmin hops on the back of his speeder behind his

mother. Norra starts to hit the throttle—Temmin yells at her. Tells her to wait for his friends. She turns, emotions warring on her face.

"We have to go," she pleads.

"They saved me. They're coming, or I'm not."

She gives him a nod.

The other man, the tall one who came in with the bounty hunter, runs forward ducking an incoming bolt of fire. He nearly falls over—but catches himself against the side of the speeder. Temmin points him to the box-rack in the back. The tall man makes a disgruntled face, but climbs into it and wads himself up like he's a too-big animal for a too-small crate.

The man yells: "What about her?"

Jas comes up—she's got the blaster back in her hand, apparently having scooped it up. She's laying down covering fire.

The Zabrak bounty hunter turns, sees the stumpy speeder.

They all look to one another in panic.

The doors of the cantina burst open. More thugs and brutes. The Herglic leads the charge. Surat is in the midst, still in his surgical robe—he points and shrieks.

The bounty hunter moves fast.

As she runs, she tucks the blaster in her pants.

She claps her hands, yelling to the man: "Throw me the chain!"

The tall man wings the end of the chain at her—she snatches it out of the air like it's nothing, then winds it around the dead Gran laying there.

Temmin's eyes boggle. Is she doing what he thinks she's doing?

She is. Because as soon as she has the chain around, she flinches away from incoming blaster fire and yells: "Go, go, go!"

Norra hits the throttle. The bala-bala lurches forward like a tauntaun with its tail stepped on—the three-eyed alien's body goes with it, at first splashing through the street water but then skimming above it.

The bounty hunter rides the body. Like it's no big thing at all. Just another day in the life of Jas Emari.

CHAPTER FIFTEEN

IN THE DEEP WELL of Outer Rim space, a *Carrack*-class light cruiser—the *Oculus*—sits quiet and still amid a field of debris. The debris: the pulverized leftovers from the comet Kinro, a celestial object once predicted to carve a path clean through the Core Worlds many eons ago, sure to destroy one or several planets and the people on them. The history books suggest that it was the Jedi who banded together, and several gave their lives (some, just their minds) willing the comet to break apart before it ever even punched a hole through the Mid Rim.

Ensign Deltura cares little for that history. Not because it doesn't interest him—it does. His father was a history buff. Their home had little furniture, but stacks of books and heaps of maps.

Right now, though, the only thing Deltura cares about regarding this comet field is that it provides him and the cruiser perfect cover.

He looks over to the young Togruta woman next to him: Science Officer Niriian. She cocks her head toward him. Niriian is cold, efficient. All business. The woman keeps her head-tails pulled back behind her, bound with a small black cord. She studies him and everyone around her like they're winged insects pinned to a board. He likes that about her. Deltura suspects it's why she's good at her job. Speaking of that—

He gives her the nod. "Launch the probe droid."

She returns the nod. "Launching viper probe droid, designation BALK1." A tap of the button, and—out there, in the void of space, a plume of gas, and the droid launches. It's an Imperial droid, stolen and subverted for Alliance—he has to correct his thinking, *New Republic*—purposes.

"We good?" he asks her.

She turns a dial on the console and flips a switch—the screen starts to fill up with data and the speaker plays the strange encrypted droid-song.

"Already reporting in with atmospheric data."

"Thank you, Officer Niriian."

He takes her hand and kisses it.

She offers him a small smile. One of his greatest, most cherished things, that smile. The fact that he alone seems able to crack the ice wall façade she's thrown up gives him faith in himself, herself, them as a pair, the New Republic. Heck, the *whole galaxy*. Optimism blooms.

He comms in. Ackbar's face appears on the screen. The admiral looks tired. Unsurprisingly. Holding together the pieces of a broken galaxy is a strain. Deltura can only imagine the toll it has taken on the Mon Calamari.

"Probe launched," Deltura says.

"Excellent," Ackbar answers. "See you again in six hours, Ensign." Six hours: the time it will take for the probe droid to enter the space around Akiva. Though even now he can see the planet: just a small marble floating out there beyond the debris field.

She smiles. "We have time. Dinner, then rest?"

"Dinner, then something else, then rest?"

She chuckles. A musical sound.

＊　＊　＊

The argument, raging long into the night. As turbulent as the storm outside the satrap's palace. (Though the satrap seems to be the only one utterly disinterested in the storm outside and the storm raging in this very room—he sits in the corner, slumped against the wall, snoring.)

"—we mustn't forget that we have the *credits,*" Arsin Crassus says, rapping his knuckles on the table as he speaks. He does this whenever he feels he's making an important point, and it would seem that he always feels he's making an important point as he makes this *knock-knock-knock* gesture with irritating frequency. "The credits to spend how we see fit."

Jylia Shale sits stone-faced. Barely having moved in the last many hours—as if this isn't taking the toll on her that it is on the rest of them. Shale says, "Credits will not buy back our galaxy. They will not buy the hearts and minds of the people. And the Imperial coffers are far less formidable than they once were, Arsin."

"We still have the reserve accounts. The Banking Clan has wealth, tangible wealth we can plunder yet—"

"And plunge the galaxy into a recession?" Shale barks in a huff. "Oh, yes, that will surely win us the confidence of the people."

"It's not about winning over all the people," Crassus says. *Knock, knock, knock.* "I told you already, the best way forward is to establish a formal splinter Empire. Set up a truce with these New Republic slime-dogs, allow them to go their way, and we go ours. We're already locked in something of a cold war with those *ninnymanderers,* so we make it official."

Shale rolls her eyes. "Yes. Let's build a wall down the middle of the galaxy. They can have their half and we'll keep ours. It doesn't work like that. Let me make this abundantly clear to all who dare listen: We lost this war. We played with a foolish, overconfident, *reckless* hand, and we paid the price for it. There is no truce to be had. The New Republic will not abide us taking our toys to the Outer Rim. They will hunt us down. They will try us as war criminals. They will jail some of us, and execute others."

Sloane watches as the archivist struggles to keep up, hurriedly taking notes. He and the satrap are the only others without a formal stake in the meeting allowed in the room. Even Adea must be elsewhere. (Though stormtroopers guard the door, of course.)

Once again, Arsin leans forward and starts to speak, rapping his knuckles on the table to punctuate his words: "Shale, you were a vital strategist for the Empire and yet you lament the Empire's strategy—"

"*Arsin*," Rae blurts out. "If you bang those knuckles on this table one more time, I will break them with a stick."

"I . . . that is no way to speak to me," he blusters.

Pandion smirks. "She's right, Crassus. It's deeply irritating. Do it again and I'll break the other hand to make sure it's really truly done."

The banker sits back, arms crossed over his barrel chest. He mopes like a scorned child.

"The strategy of the Galactic Empire," Shale begins, "was not under my supreme control. I'll make it clear *yet again* that I disagreed with *both* implementations of the Death Star. I opposed its creation from the very beginning—and in fact, that opposition marginalized my input going forward. Except, perhaps, at Hoth. But the Death Star was our undoing. That old phrase, *Don't work your children in the same mine,* applies here. Putting so much time, and money, and effort, *and people* into the ecosystem of that massive battle station was a fool's crusade. Palpatine was arrogant."

Tashu, who has been mostly quiet this entire time—frittering with his fingers and the tassels at the ends of his sleeves as if this is all very boring to him, or as if his mind is simply elsewhere—finally speaks up:

"Palpatine's arrogance is undeniable. One also cannot deny that without it, the Empire would never have existed in the first place."

Moff Pandion—*Grand* Moff Pandion, apparently—stands up, begins to pace a semicircle around his end of the table. "I for once agree with Jylia Shale. Not just that the Death Star was our greatest mistake, but also that no truce will suffice. That will not slake the so-called New Republic's thirst for our blood. They've got it in their heads that we're monsters. It is decided. But that also means we cannot merely surrender. They'll want their taste of blood—don't be surprised if the best of us get dragged out into the streets so we can be shot by some savage with a slugthrower."

"Yes, Valco," Shale says. "We know that you want to attack, attack, attack. No matter how much it will cost us to do so."

He sniffs. "So you'd rather lay down arms and bow your head for the executioner's ax? You wouldn't want to go out fighting?"

"This isn't some kind of *inspirational story.* Some scrappy, ragtag underdog tale, some pugilistic match where we're the goodhearted gladiator who brings down the oppressive regime that put him in the arena. *They* get to have that narrative. *We* are the ones who enslaved whole worlds full of alien inhabitants. *We* are the ones who built something called a *Death* Star under the leadership of a decrepit old goblin who believed in the 'dark side' of some ancient, insane religion."

Yupe Tashu raises a quizzical, academic eye toward her.

Pandion just sneers. "Were this a better day, you'd be executed for treason, General Shale."

"See?" Shale says. "*We* are the ones who do the executing, *Grand* Moff Pandion. If we surrender, the aberrant kindness of the New Republic may translate to us. We may get to keep our heads still." She huffs. "Besides. We don't have a meaningful strategy of attack."

"Of course we do," Pandion says with a laugh. "Are you mad? The *rebels*—because that's what they are, rebels, criminals, deviants—did what they did with almost no war machine in place. Insurgents, all of them. They managed a few lucky shots with their slingshots but we still have the ships, the men, the training." He points to Arsin. "The *money*."

"Then why do governors turn away from us every day? Why do we lose more ships every week? Why do we see holovids of freed worlds throwing parades and tearing down statues? They did so much with so little, Pandion. You misunderstand our place in history."

"Then *we* do much with little. Besides—" He waves his hand dismissively. "Those holovids are propaganda, and you damn well know it. The reality is, the Rebel Alliance doesn't have the resources to keep control of this galaxy. But we still do. And—" Here he turns toward Rae Sloane. "Let's not forget we still possess a Super Star Destroyer. Isn't that right, Admiral Sloane? Or—do we possess it? Perhaps only you possess it. Perhaps you're being a greedy little child who doesn't want to share your fleet with the rest of the academy."

An expected commentary. One he's been making

again and again since they began this thing. Rae says the same thing she says every time he brings it up: "The *Ravager* and its fleet are at the disposal of the Galactic Empire, Valco. The question remains—"

He echoes her response even as she speaks it (though with a considerably more mocking tone): "—*the question remains, what even is the Empire at this juncture and who controls it?* Yes, I'm aware of your stance. I just want the room to be aware that you're the one with your finger curled around the trigger of our greatest weapon, and yet you keep it hidden . . . well, we don't even know where, do we?"

"Your spies haven't served you that slice of pie, yet, hmm?" she says, putting a small curl at the corners of her lips. Pandion starts to protest, but she wants to control this meeting, so control it, she does: "This meeting is to decide the fate of the Empire with the input of several advisers, not just one. If I wanted to take the *Ravager* and seize control, I could make that attempt and I might even manage it. But I'd rather not make the same mistakes as in the past. Now, Grand Moff, we have heard from you. We know your position." *Again and again.* "One person we have not heard from is you, Adviser Tashu. Would you enlighten us?"

Tashu looks up once more as if all this is a distraction. "Hm? Oh. Yes, yes. Of course." Tashu was a close adviser—and a friend, as much as one could be, apparently—to the former Emperor Palpatine. The man who was once senator, and then chancellor. And the man whom rumors said was also a dark Sith Lord. Amid the Empire, the presence of the Sith was less a fact and more a myth: A few spoke of it as being possible, but most believed it to be concoction. Palpatine would not be the first ruler to invent stories of himself as if he were of cosmic import: The history 'crons say that a regent of the Old Republic, Hylemane Light-bringer, claimed he was "born in the dust of the Typhonic Nebula" and "could not be killed by mortal weapons." (A fact proven untrue when he was indeed killed by a mortal weapon—bludgeoned by a chair, apparently.) Palpatine's legend extended, too, to his enforcer, the brutish Darth Vader. Sloane believes their powers to be real, though perhaps not as omnipotent as Palpatine would have preferred everyone believe.

It is then no surprise that Tashu cleaves to those ways when he speaks.

He says, "You chastise the dark side as if it is an evil path, laughable for its malevolence. But do not confuse it with evil. And do not confuse the light as being the product of benevolence. The Jedi of old were cheats and liars. Power-hungry maniacs operating under the guise of a holy monastic order. Moral crusaders whose diplomacy was that of the lightsaber. The dark side is honest. The dark side is direct. It is the knife in the front rather than one stuck in your back. The dark side is self-interested, yes, but it is about extending that interest outward. To yourself, but then beyond yourself. Palpatine cared about the galaxy. He did not wrest control simply to have power for himself—he already had power, as chancellor. He wanted to take power from those who abused it. He wanted to extend control and safety to the people of all worlds. That came with costs. He knew them and lamented them. But paid them just the same because the dark side understands that everything has a cost, and the cost must always be paid."

A moment of silence.

Then Pandion snort-laughs. Rae thinks, *If the Emperor were still around, that single utterance would earn Pandion the loss of his head. That's the cost that would be paid for such treasonous disdain.*

The moff holds up a hand and operates it like a babbling puppet. "You say all these words, Adviser Tashu, and yet, none of them sound like they have any bearing on . . ." Another snort-laugh. "Anything at all."

Tashu offers a beatific, self-assured smile. "What I mean to say is that Palpatine was a smart man. Smarter than the combination of all of us here. We must emulate his path. The Emperor knew the dark side was his savior, and so we too must make the dark side ours."

"Hnnh," Shale grumps. "And how do we do that? I don't think any of us are trained in the ways of the Force."

"No Sith remain," Tashu says. "And the lone Jedi that exists—the son of Anakin Skywalker—possesses an untouchable soul. At least for now. We must instead move toward the dark side. Palpatine felt that the universe beyond the edges of our maps was where his power came from. Over the many years he, with our aid, sent men and women beyond known space. They built labs and communication stations on distant moons, asteroids, out there in the wilds. We must follow them. Retreat from the galaxy. Go out beyond the veil of stars. We must seek the source of the dark side like a man looking for a wellspring of water."

Crassus twists up his pudgy, jowly face so much it looks like a wrung rag. "You're saying we . . . leave? We pack up our ships and run away? Like fearful little children afraid of Daddy's belt?"

"Not fearful," Tashu says. "Hopeful."

And from there, a brand-new fusillade of arguments rise up—this time from each corner, all at the same time. A cacophony of the same arguments. Truce. Money. Surrender. Cold war. Hot war.

All of it, nonsense. None of them agree. Sloane wonders if ever they will. Which means this summit was a foolish endeavor.

But we still have to try.

The Galactic Empire is a broken mirror. Many reflections of itself, shattered and separate. Sloane tells herself: *It's up to me to repair the glass. To fix the reflection.* She believes in the Empire. And she believes that she is the one who can and must fix it. An ascendant Empire will again rule the galaxy. And her place in it will be cemented—no longer kept to the margins, no longer left off the ledger. Sloane will matter.

She stands up. "Please continue. I'll be back."

They don't even notice that she leaves. She's not sure if that's a good thing or a bad thing.

In the space above Akiva, a viper probe droid decelerates with cautious bursts from its retrothrusters. When finally it stabilizes, its five spiderlike limbs extend outward. Its eye glows. A series of small antennas emerge from the top of its domed head, all meant to take measurements.

It begins its scans.

A hard hand cups under his chin. Moves his head up, back, left, right. The flat of this intrusive hand slaps his cheek. Not hard. Just: *pat, pat, pat.*

Wedge inhales sharply. His eyes open.

It's her. The one who caught him at the communications station. The one who put a blaster round in his back.

"What now?" he says. "Come to torture me your-self?"

The other one, the one with the pale face and the dark wrinkles—skin marked with bold striations, as if he were half dead—isn't here, but he appears now and again. Maybe once an hour, though it's hard to say because time is slippery. It's always just as Wedge starts to sleep again. And this strange man, he hurts Wedge whenever he shows. He cut into Wedge's side with a knife—no deep slashes, always shallow cuts. He thrust a spark-prod against the inside of Wedge's thigh, and when he did, everything inside Wedge lit up like a malfunctioning console. One time he just came in and noisily ate fruit. At no time has he said anything. Then he just licked his fingers. The other times he just chuckled quietly as he delivered pain.

But this one. This woman. An admiral, isn't she?

"No," she says. "I'm not a torturer."

"No," he wheezes. "Of course not. You're the questioner."

"I thought so. But I'm not sure." Nearby, the medical droid checks the tube that winds around his arm and plunges into the skin. "You wouldn't answer me anyway, would you?"

"No," Wedge says. He tries to put some carbon steel in his voice. He tries not to let his fear creep into that word. If she senses fear, she'll pounce. Tear into him like a wampa scenting blood on the snow. But he *is* scared. He came all this way, through countless battles in space, over snow, across desert and swamp and open sky, and now at the end of it he's here. Wounded and strapped upright to a table. Tortured to death.

"It wouldn't matter anyway. I ask you about vital New Republic details—ship movements, base locations, attack plans—what could I do with it? Not much, I'm afraid."

"Ready to surrender yet?" he says, giving her a smile. It's not a kind smile. It's cruel. He means for it to hurt. *I'm laughing at you,* he thinks.

"Let me ask you this. Why?"

"Why . . . what?"

"Why be a rebel? Why join?"

"To destroy the Empire."

She shakes her head. "No. Too easy. That's just the paint. Scratch off the color, there's something personal underneath it."

He again shows her his teeth—bared in a terrible smile. "Of course there is, Admiral. The Empire hurt people close to me. Family. Friends. A girl I loved, once. And I'm not alone. All of us in the New Republic, we all have stories like that." He coughs. His eyes water. "We're the harvest of all the horrible seeds you planted."

"But we kept order in a lawless galaxy."

"And you did it with a closed fist instead of an open hand."

"You have a way with words for just a pilot."

He tries to shrug but even that hurts. A grunt comes from the back of his throat and he bites back any further cry.

The woman nods, and then turns and leaves without another word.

Ensign Deltura's head hovers above the table. A blue glow surrounding the hologram. Ackbar leans forward at the table. "You're quite certain, Ensign?"

"No sign of Imperial ships, Admiral."

"But you did find signs of our own."

"Just debris. Nothing you'd find with the human

eye, but the viper is a surprisingly effective probe droid. It found molecular remnants indicative of our own ships, yes, sir."

"The A-wings." Ackbar hmms. "Something shot them down."

"Something from the surface, sir?"

"Unlikely. Couldn't hit an A-wing from that distance." Ackbar's long, webbed fingers mesh together. They rub against one another. He turns his chair to the other person in the room—

This person, also a hologram.

And this hologram is only barely a person.

The image stands there, off to the side. Like a ghost. The body and face shifting and distorting. Shadowy and unclear. This is their inside man: an informant known only as the Operator. So far, his intel has been trustworthy. Impeccably so. Which makes Ackbar all the more dubious.

"What say you, Operator?"

The voice that emerges is as distorted as the visual: a mechanized, warped sound. "Does the droid detect any traffic in and out of the capital city? Or around the planet at all?"

To Deltura, Ackbar says: "You heard the question."

"No, sir. No ships at all."

The Operator says: "Have the droid ping all the comm relays planetside. See what happens."

Deltura nods, says something to someone outside holorange. Likely his science officer: a young Togruta woman. Moments of uncomfortable silence spread out like something noxious spilling across the floor. Ackbar likes none of this. A septic feeling sits inside him, sucking up all the optimism he had possessed.

The ensign's glowing holographic head returns.

"Nothing," he says, almost shocked. "Ah, nothing,

sir. The probe droid cannot ping any of the relays. It's like they're dead."

"Communications blackout," the Operator says. "An Imperial trick. They are there, Admiral Ackbar. Their ships must be in hiding. But if no traffic is coming in and out, they have instituted a blockade. No ships. No communications. Something is happening. I do not know what."

"Thank you," Ackbar says.

"You will act on this?" the Operator asks. Eager. Too eager?

Ackbar doesn't answer. He turns off the hologram. Deltura asks: "Is there anything you want me to do, sir?"

"Hold position," Ackbar says. "I need time to think and confer with the others. Thank you, Ensign."

"Admiral, sir."

The man's face disappears.

Worry gnaws at Ackbar like a school of brine-maggots. He needs time to think, but too much time and they could miss a vital opportunity. *Or,* he thinks, *escape the jaws of yet another Imperial trap.* Is this a ruse, or is this the real thing? Could be a secret meeting. There, an irony too bold to ignore: Once it was the rebels who had to sneak around and hide their presence. Now it's the Empire. The roles are reversing. A sign of their nascent victory over Imperial oppression, perhaps. But he worries, too, about their overconfidence. The Empire isn't gone. Not yet.

It's waiting to strike again. Of that, he's quite sure.

INTERLUDE:

CHANDRILA

A PURPLE FRUIT COMES from off camera and crashes into the side of Olia Choko's face. The fruit pops. Juice runs down her cheek and drips from her jawline. She looks stunned.

From off screen, an angry voice:

"Boo! Boo to the Galactic Senate! Boo to the New Republic!"

Another fruit flies—this one misses its mark, sailing over Olia's head.

Tracene starts to say: "Okay, Lug, time to cut—"

"No," Olia says, interrupting. She swallows hard and wipes some of the goopy fruit innards from her cheek. "You. The protester. Come closer."

Tracene gives Lug a barely perceptible nod.

A pair of scaly Trandoshan hands appear at the edges of the screen and pivot the hovering camera toward a small Xan man in a dirty gray jumpsuit. He has a small basket of fruits and vegetables, mostly rotten.

He is alone.

He sees the camera is pointed at him and he waves

his hands. "No, no, I do not want to be on camera. Please."

Olia approaches. Gingerly. Hands out, beseeching. "If you have concerns, then I'd like to hear them."

"I . . . ," the Xan stammers, looking around. As if this is some kind of joke. Or as if he wasn't prepared to have this effect. "I am sorry, I should go." He starts to pull away, but Tracene steps in front of him.

"You can have your say."

Suspicious, he says: "Really?"

Olia answers: "Really. Tell me your troubles."

To the camera Tracene mouths: *Are we still on?*

A reptilian thumbs-up appears for a moment on screen.

"I . . . ," the alien begins. "I am Geeska Dotalo. I'm from Gan Moradir. Colony in the Mid Rim. The New Republic came. They . . . they destroyed an Imperial base. Now the Imperials are gone. The Empire was cruel. But at least there was order! We had food and water. Things *worked*. Now the rebels have gone. And the gangs have come. The *pirates*. We don't have enough food. The destruction affected our wells and . . ." He begins to sob. "We saved up enough credits to bring me here. I am all we have."

For a moment, Olia seems struck dumb.

Tracene looks like she's about to intervene, but then Olia speaks:

"It's good you came, Mister Dotalo. I don't believe Gan Moradir has a representative yet in the Senate. Today, you'll be that representative."

His eyes go wider than seems possible.

"Wh . . . what?"

"War is terrible. And an army isn't enough to fix problems. We need a solution for what happens after they do their job, and that's why the Senate is beginning again—and why we're doing it here, on the chancellor's homeworld. Some think of this place as a small, inconsequential world—but Chandrila has always been an origin point for big ideas and the citizens to carry them to the larger galaxy beyond. The galaxy needs help. It needs those big ideas but like you say, it needs the smaller things, too: food, water, shelter. Basic things. And after war is over, there has to be something else to fix what's broken. I invite you today to speak to the Senate about your people and your colony. Let them listen. Let us help you."

She summons someone from off camera. Another Pantoran—a man in blue administrative robes. Olia whispers to him. She makes a small introduction between him and Geeska Dotalo. Then the Pantoran man gently urges him away.

Tracene smiles and calls "cut." But her eyes flit to the distance.

Because there's a commotion now. People are looking up and away. Tracene motions with her hand and Lug spins the camera.

Over in the distance, a line of Imperial prisoners. Cuffed together, shepherded along by a New Republic officer.

"This is *unacceptable,*" Olia hisses, then darts off to intervene.

CHAPTER SIXTEEN

BAD DREAMS.

It's one of the classics, one of the dreams that re-plays inside Norra's head now and again—it's her and her Y-wing and her astromech, R5-G4, and they're in the twisting bowels of the Death Star again. She breaks off from the main conduit, drawing a handful of TIEs after her like flies on a gorth's tail. She can't swat them, can't bat them away, can't outfly them. And suddenly there are more ahead of her, and the inside of the battle station is a maze looping back on itself, and from somewhere she feels the concussive shock of the power source going up, and then everything starts to fall apart around her, and the fire fills the space behind her, and then it's there at the front, too, rushing up to greet her—

She wakes up bathed in sweat. Like she always does, no matter how warm or cold the air. Norra checks her watch. She has, of course, been asleep for less than an hour. After rescuing her son from the clutches of that vile gangster, she's still got the feeling—like they're being chased. Heart pounding, muscles tight, jaw set, adrenaline cooking through her like liquid blaster fire. Sleep was a bad idea.

Norra heads downstairs to get some tea. She ex-pects that everyone is still asleep—and here she reminds herself to thank her sister, Esmelle, for letting this crew of curious strangers stay the night—but as she descends, she hears voices coming from the kitchen.

There, gathered around a small table, are the two curious strangers: Jas Emari and Sinjir Rath Velus. They've set aside Esmelle's hydrodome (where she grows small herbs, like heartweed and sinthan seed) and have set out across the small table a series of odd objects: a saltcellar, a series of herb vials, a napkin dispenser, a bunch of quicksticks and fruit knives.

She enters, and the two of them straighten up.

Like children who have done wrong.

Hm.

"What's all this?" Norra asks.

"Nothing," Jas says.

"Just . . . playing a game," the other one, Sinjir, says with a smile. A strange couple, these two. She, a cold-faced, curt-tongued Zabrak. He's a tall drink of milk: a bit rangy, scruffy, the smell of wine or brandy leaving his pores. He's got a big, duplicitous grin. She's got eyes like cut stones.

Norra mumbles something and then taps the button on the side of the kettle. From the upper cabinet she selects a gesha tea, measures some into a cup. The other two are staring holes in her back.

The kettle whistles, and she pours. Ghosts of steam rise around her.

Then she turns and says, "That looks like a map."

"It's not," Sinjir says, still smiling.

"It is," the Zabrak says at almost the same time.

"Will you tell me what it is?" Norra asks.

"No," the other two both answer in unison. Jas and Sinjir give each other a look. A bit quizzical, a bit amused, that shared look.

Norra leans over. Scrutinizes their arrangement.

"This, the napkin dispenser. It's bigger than everything else. So it's meant to represent something big. The satrap's palace, I'm guessing. Which lines up with the rest—here's the old capitol building, here's the Avenue of the Satrapy, here's the narrow Withrafisp Road—this was once a secret road, I'm told, to sneak satraps in and out of the palace, but it's been public since I was a girl."

"Nope," Sinjir says, feigning total sincerity. "Sorry. Thank you, though, for playing. Now, if you'll excuse us—"

"Shut up," Jas says to him. Then to Norra: "Yes. You're right. Did you grow up here?"

Norra nods. "I did."

"You're . . ." Jas gives her a look-over. "A rebel?"

"Am I that obvious?"

The Zabrak shrugs. "No. But I'm no fool. You had no problem shooting at stormtroopers last night. And yet you don't look like another criminal. *Or* just another local. You . . . dress like a rebel. The utilitarian vest. The utility belt. Those boots." She squints. "Pilot?"

Norra laughs. "Yes, that's correct."

"I'm a bounty hunter," Jas says. "I'm here collecting a bounty for the New Republic. I think I could use your help."

"Wait one star-burned second," Sinjir protests, waving both hands. "You're cutting me in for a meager twenty-five percent, and now you're going to water down the bounty even more by bringing her in?"

The bounty hunter says, "I'm hoping she'll do it because it's the right thing and because it is an attack on the Empire. Not because of credits."

Norra feels the call of duty crawling over her like

ants. She wants to find out more, wants to throw in and spit in the eye of the Empire, *but*—

"I can't," she says, speaking through clenched jaw. "I really can't. My son and I have to leave this planet. My first priority is taking him away—"

"Go save your friend," Temmin says. "Antilles. Because I told you, I'm not going." Temmin shuffles into the kitchen. "And by the way, I know you people think you're not being loud, but you're totally being loud."

Norra catches his arm. "I'll let someone else . . . save Captain Antilles. My job isn't fighting this war anymore. My job is you."

But he pulls away from her. He grabs a glass of blue milk from the cold-chest. "Did my droid come home yet? He should be here by now."

Norra wants to keep fighting him, but she bites her tongue. He's as stubborn as she is. Pushing him is like punching a wall. She'll only break her hand trying.

Sinjir says to the boy, "That was your droid, huh?"

"Yeah."

"That was a *battle droid*."

"I *know*."

"They're the most inept fighting unit in . . . perhaps the history of the galaxy. And trust me, stormtroopers are basically just overturned mop buckets with guns, especially these days."

"Do not sell the stormtroopers short," Jas snaps. "In number, they are dangerous."

"So are swamp buffalo," Sinjir says. "It doesn't mean they're particularly effective. Battle droids, even less so. Kudos to you, young man. Turning one of them into a . . . bona fide war machine?" Sinjir softly applauds. "Though I think it's wise to prepare for the eventuality that they overwhelmed him. He's a battle droid, not a technological miracle."

"Yeah, well." Temmin stands there, looking surly, sipping his drink. "You don't know borcat scat from dewback dung, pal. Mister Bones is programmed with . . . well, just trust me. Mister Bones will be *just fine*." Norra watches her son—the way he stands with his fists balled up. His brow furrowed. He's angry. Like she was . . . and maybe still is, she admits to herself. But then his eyes narrow and he looks down at the table. "What's this?"

"Nothing," Sinjir says.

"It's a map," Temmin says. And Norra swells with small pride. A pride that grows as Temmin adds: "What's this? The satrap's palace?"

"By all the damned stars," Sinjir says. "Like mother, like son."

The boy frowns at that. Norra feels stung.

Jas Emari then jumps in with both feet: "Right now, at that palace—provided we have not missed our opportunity—a secret meeting is taking place. At this meeting are a small number of very important individuals within the Imperial ranks. Movers and shakers. High bounty values." She lists those individuals: Moff Valco Pandion, Admiral Rae Sloane, Adviser Yupe Tashu, General Jylia Shale, and the bounty hunter's original target, the banker and slaver: Arsin Crassus.

"That's it," Norra says, snapping her fingers. Part of her feels like she should've figured this out already, but then another part of her—a realistic side or maybe just the cynical side—says she's just some pilot, how would she have known? Still. "It all adds up. The Star Destroyers. The blockade. The comm blackout. They're protecting this meeting. And Wedge . . ."

The Zabrak raises an eyebrow. "What is a 'Wedge'?"

"Wedge Antilles," Sinjir says. "Right? Pilot for the Rebel Alliance?"

Norra nods. "Yes. How did you know?"

The man hesitates. "I'm . . . a rebel, too."

That strikes her as odd. He *is* dressed a bit like one. But something about him feels off, somehow. Still— the rebellion is home to all kinds.

Norra continues: "They must have him. Wedge. He was probably scouting the Outer Rim and ran afoul of . . . whatever this is."

"He's probably still alive," Jas says. "Which means you have an opportunity. Help me. We will strike a blow for your New Republic. We will undo the efforts of the Empire, cutting their hamstrings just as they're relearning how to stand. You will rescue your friend."

Again, duty swarms Norra. The chance to do right. But the opposing feeling rises true, too—for once, she just wants to keep her head down, her chin to her chest, and duck all incoming fire. She doesn't want to fly into the belly of the beast. Not this time.

"No," she says, staring down below her darkening brow. "The best way forward is to get *off* this planet. Soon as we get into comm range, we alert the Republic, they send in ships and troops and—"

The bounty hunter interrupts: "Wrong. By then the meeting will have concluded—if it hasn't already. And your friend will either be gone or dead. The way forward is now. The work is ours to do."

"I'm in," Temmin says. "But I want a cut."

"Young man," Sinjir says, chuckling. "Let's not *overreach*. We dutifully saved your little can from getting kicked—"

"Fine," Jas Emari says to the boy. "You can have half of his cut." She tilts her thorny head, gesturing toward Sinjir.

Sinjir objects: "Hey!"

"You'll still get passage off this planet," the Zabrak

woman says. She gives a haughty little flip—the ax-blade slice of hair between her thorns suddenly falls to the side of her scalp. "And the bounty is significant enough that even a fraction will buy you enough otherworldly liquors to keep you pickled until the New Republic once more becomes the Old Republic. Take the deal or leave it."

He rolls his eyes. "Fine."

"I don't know about this," Norra says.

"I could use your help. I bet your friend could, as well."

Norra hesitates. It's like being a kid again and jumping off one of the waterfalls in Akar Canyon. She literally has to hold her breath before she says: "I'm in. But I want passage off this planet, too."

"Done," Jas says. "Now I think we should—"

Wham wham wham.

The whole house shakes. Someone's at the door. As Jas pulls her blaster, the memory once more comes rushing back to meet Norra, coming at her as fast as the silver water after jumping off one of those waterfalls—that sound, fists pounding on the door. The sound of Imperials coming to take her husband away.

CHAPTER SEVENTEEN

AROUND THE TABLE sit three figures of flesh and blood and two holograms. Those present: Admiral Ackbar, Commander Kyrsta Agate, and Captain Saff Melor. The two holograms: General Crix Madine, and the newly appointed chancellor of the New Republic, Mon Mothma. All of them look tired and worried. Ackbar suspects he appears much the same. Everything feels to him on a pivot—balanced on the blade of a knife. Like it could go one way. Or with the barest breeze, it could fall back to the other side. A razor's edge of possibility, good and bad.

"Are we sure we can trust this informant?" Madine says. He scratches at his prodigious white beard. The lines in his face, seen even here in hologram, appear deeper than ever.

"So far," Agate answers, "all signs point to yes."

Ackbar interjects: "But we also must recognize the Empire's ability to play the long game. Our victory over Endor was fortunate, but the Empire orchestrated that trap with great patience."

"Send in a fleet," Melor says. The Cerean captain carries a certain haughtiness with him. His head—tall and ridged, a frustrated and dubious brow that extends upward to demonstrate excess incredulity. "Two light cruisers, a contingent of fighters from

Gold Squadron, and see what's there. If there's a fight, the fleet will be ready for it."

Mon Mothma speaks: "We must be cautious. Inroads to the Outer Rim are slow. Further, this is a time of relative peace, but that peace rests uncomfortably on very unstable ground. An incursion of that magnitude could be seen as overly aggressive. We must be seen as friends, not intruders. Occupying the airspace over Akiva could be trouble."

Melor shakes his head. "Chancellor—and congratulations, by the way—Akiva is, with all due respect, no feather in anyone's cap. It is a marginal planet at best, and the satrapy is in the Empire's pocket. They produce resources we do not require and the old droid factory beneath the city has been out of use for decades. As such, Akiva offers us very little strategic advantage *or* concern—"

"But the *people* there *are* our concern," Mon Mothma says. Ackbar detects that her hackles have been raised. Melor does that, sometimes. He's from a military family and though he carries some of that Cerean intellectual arrogance, his aggression is well known. Mon continues: "And we have intelligence that suggests our messaging has gotten through there. The people are ready for a change. The New Republic is that change."

Melor starts to speak, but once more, Ackbar interjects: "I am in accord with the chancellor here. This is a fragile peace. And we must be wary of any ruse set before us. General Madine, do you think you could put together a strike team? Small. Five to seven Republic soldiers."

"I think that's doable. You want them on the ground?"

"Mm-hmm," Ackbar says. "A suborbital landing squad. Special forces. Drop from high atmosphere.

We need reports from on the ground. This seems the most opportune way to do it. Small but effective. Can we all agree on that?" Nods all around except from Melor—the captain frowns, puckering his lips as if he's about to object. But then he sighs and nods, as well. "Good. Let's get this in motion. I want boots on the ground in six hours. Sooner if we can manage it. Thank you, all."

CHAPTER EIGHTEEN

JAS WINGS THE DOOR OPEN. Blaster up.

A droid stands there in the early-morning rain.

It's a B1 battle droid. *The* B1 battle droid—the bodyguard Temmin calls Mister Bones. Rain hits the servomotor in its exposed skull, sparking and turning to steam as it does. Temmin rushes past Jas.

The droid, painted red and black, laughs maniacally: a warped, mechanized sound. It raises its one arm (the other is now missing), and all the little animal bones that dangle from it rattle and clack.

The droid gives a robot thumbs-up.

"Bones!" Temmin says, throwing his arms around the droid.

"I PERFORMED VIOLENCE," the droid warbles. Jas wonders if that's pride she hears in the thing's discordant voice. "ROGER-ROGER."

Then a shower of sparks erupts from its head. Its eyes go dark.

It falls to the side like a felled tree.

Temmin makes a sad sound in the back of his throat. Sinjir peeks past and says: "I think that thing has seen better days, boy."

"Quiet," the kid snaps. "You'll hurt his feelings. He just needs work. Help me get him inside."

*   *   *

"It's night, you know," comes a voice.

Wedge, magnetically shackled to the table, startles awake. The dream he was in—a dream of being out in space in a broken fighter, the oxygen failing, his astromech blown to slag, the ship drifting through the void—falls apart in his hands like wet sand gone suddenly dry.

The voice. It's coming from the strange man—the man whose age is hard to tell, the one with the dark striations that aren't quite wrinkles. With the beady eyes and serpent's smile.

The one who cuts Wedge with the knife.

Right now, though, he sees no knife. Just the man clasping his hands within the bundled, puffy sleeves of his robe.

"You here for more torture? I won't break."

The man's spooky smile never wavers. "I know. I can see that. I can see your vitality will never waver." He thrusts up a finger, as if having an epiphany. But the epiphany is not his own—rather, he seems to wish to deliver one. "Did you know that Sith Lords could sometimes drain the Force energy from their captives? Siphoning life from them and using it to strengthen their connection to the dark side? Extending their own lives, as well, so that they could live for centuries beyond their intended expiration?"

"You fancy yourself some kind of wizard?"

The man tut-tut-tuts. "Hardly. I am Tashu. Merely a historian. An eager student of the old ways. And, until recently, an adviser to Palpatine."

"My friend Luke told me some things about him."

Tashu's grin broadens. Showing off his too-white teeth.

"Yes, I imagine he did. Seen through the lens of a

confused, naïve boy, most assuredly." His fingers pluck at the air like a spider testing its webs. "I know I won't break you physically."

"So why come here at all?"

"To keep you from sleeping well. And to help break you mentally. It may not yield us any information. But I like to practice."

"I'm a pilot. I'm used to not sleeping."

"Yes, but you're not used to hopelessness. Look around. You're locked away. Tortured without function. The Empire even now is resurging here in this very palace. Your New Republic has a moment to breathe and gain its footing—but we have a war machine. We have the blessings of the dark side. And even if your people continue to march forward, reclaiming system after system—we will be waiting. In some form or another. The Empire is just a skin we wear, you see. A *shell*. It's not just about law and order. It's about total control. We will always come back for it. No matter how hard you work to beat us back, we are an infection inside the galaxy's bones. And we will always surge forth when you least expect it."

"You're wrong," Wedge says, gritting his teeth. "The galaxy is home to good people. There's more of us than there are of you."

"It's not about numbers or percentages. It's about faith. The few of us have infinitely more faith than the many of you."

"I have faith in the New Republic."

Tashu chuckles. "And that faith will be tested."

"Your face will be tested when I kick in your teeth."

"There it is," Tashu says, snapping his fingers so hard it sounds like a bird's neck breaking. "A vital spike of anger and hate. Born of the hopelessness I've planted in you. A terrible little seed. I can't wait for it to grow its wretched tree and bear its ugly fruit."

INTERLUDE:

CORONET CITY, CORELLIA

LIGHTNING FLASHES, and the fight continues. On the roof of the old holoplex, against the backdrop of a bright, gaudy, ever-shifting billboard of advertisements, two men battle. They've been here for so long now, all sense of time has escaped them. They're tired. Bedraggled. Soaked by the rains that came through and have gone again.

But they keep going at it.

The older one—thick, slovenly, his body encased in loose rust-red armor, his head swaddled in rain-sodden wraps—circles. Both of his hands up in club-like fists. A line of blood snakes from his nose, and he licks it away, then grins like a drunk.

"We can quit this charade anytime, mate," Dengar growls. "We can sit down, have a proper pint somewhere, talk over the agreement."

"No agreement," says the other man—the one who calls himself Mercurial Swift. He's young. Agile. No armor at all. Dark hair now plastered to his pale brow. In his hands, a pair of batons. He gives them a twirl. "You gotta give this up, Dengar. You're reaching past the stars on this one. A fool's crusade—"

At that, Dengar rushes in again. Swinging fists like hammers. Like he doesn't just want to punch the younger, faster man, but wants to pulp him like a fruit for his morning juice. Mercurial catches a fist to his collarbone, and pain shoots up his neck and down his arm. One of his batons clatters against the rooftop, splashing into a puddle.

Mercurial cartwheels the other way. When Dengar moves to follow, the younger bounty hunter ducks, and pistons the end of his baton in the gap between Dengar's armor plates—right into his ribs.

The older thug howls and staggers back, clutching his side.

His smile is somehow a scowl at the same time. "Join me. You're good. You're *fast*. But dumb. Real dumb. Just look at you. Green as fresh doaki spice. You need a . . . guiding hand."

"From you?" Mercurial asks with a coughing scoff. "I can't see that happening, old man." Another flash of lightning. No thunder. "Don't you get it? I got into this gig because I like being alone. I *like* the rogue thing." He laughs: a curiously melodic sound. "I didn't become a bounty hunter so I could join a club, eh?"

Dengar begins to circle again.

Mercurial circles the other way. Toward his lost baton.

"We've always been a club!" Dengar shouts.

"Maybe that's what's been holding you back. Other hunters always scooping up the bounties before you. Beating you to the punch." There. At Mercurial's feet—the baton. He kicks it up into his hand.

"Oh ho ho, you think I've lost a step, huh?"

"Can't lose a step you never had!"

Dengar guffaws. "You little scrap-muncher. I was putting away bounties while you were still in your space diapers."

"What's it say about you that you're still *in* your space diapers?"

"You don't much like me, do you?"

"You want it point-blank? You're a strange, gross old man. Heart to the moon, truth on my sleeve? Nobody's ever liked you."

There. That got him. Dengar's like a crazy beast— you just have to wave the right bait in front of his nose to get him to charge. And charge he does, thundering forward like a starving pack animal.

But then, at the last moment, he jukes left. The older bounty hunter dives across the roof and tucks into a roll. When he springs back up on the other side, he spins around—and his particle array gun is in his hand. Ready to scatter Mercurial's atoms across the flashing billboard.

Again, the fight pauses. Mercurial with his hands up. Dengar on one knee with the wide mouth of the array gun pointed.

This time, they're silent. Tension drawn out like strangling cord. Lightning flashes again. Dengar's finger hovers near the trigger. The gun hums. Mercurial's hands tighten around the batons.

Something is about to break.

Something *has* to break. Or Dengar's going to shoot him.

Mercurial's eyes flash to a nearby rooftop. His eyes go wide. His jaw, slack. He summons the image in his mind and says:

"Boba Fett?"

Dengar wheels toward the rooftop, the gun barrel turning.

And that is Mercurial's opportunity. He flings one of the batons—it cracks Dengar on the top of his forehead as soon as he whips his head back around. As his skull snaps back, Mercurial is already leaping forward and driving a knee into the side of the old bounty hunter's face. Then an elbow against his collarbone. A baton against his wrist. The gun drops.

Mercurial picks it up and jams the barrel under Dengar's chin.

Just as fresh rain begins to fall. A spitting, flecking rain.

Dengar winces. "You're good."

"I've been told."

"That trick back there? Maybe I have lost a bloody step, mate."

Mercurial shrugs. "I used to be an actor and a dancer."

"No fooling?" Dengar croaks. "What turned you to this life?"

"The Empire doesn't much care for the performance arts."

"True that, true that." Dengar sniffs a bubble of blood back up his nose and sneers. "But all that's more to the point, innit? Things are changing now. Our profession is about to get *marginalized,* too. Those rebels won't put up with our special brand of sauce for too long, will they? It's why we gotta band together. Form a proper union. We'll be a force to reckon with. We'll look all official-like!"

"I'll take my chances alone."

Dengar nods. "Okay. Okay. You, ahh. You going to kill me?"

"No bounty on you. Why bother?"

"You watch. That day will come. Bounties on the

bounty hunters. We'll see it soon enough. Even in my lifetime. Just you watch."

Mercurial nods, takes the gun away. "Take care, Dengar."

"Not likely, kid. Not bloody likely."

CHAPTER NINETEEN

IT'S MORNING, and Adea waits for Admiral Sloane.

Adea realizes that in the grand scheme of things, she is of little import. An attaché. An assistant. She hands papers. Fetches cups of caf. Asks for signatures. Delivers communications.

But one day, maybe she'll be something more.

This is a glorious time to be alive.

The Empire is reeling. That is, itself, not a good thing. But in those cracks and fractures waits opportunity. Every crack is a place where Adea can ease the tip of her foot. She can widen those gaps and find a place for herself in there. It's why she admires Sloane so much.

The admiral understands. The admiral is making the best of this situation. And right now, Adea has bad news to deliver.

That thrills her, honestly. It shouldn't, probably. Bad news is, by its designation, declaratively and objectively bad. But it's the reaction that matters. People are made under duress. They are formed by crisis. Adea grew up on Coruscant. But her parents were not important people. Her father was a welder. Not so low that they had to work in the bowels of the city-world—he worked prime jobs for the Empire. But he still got his hands dirty. And burned, and cut, until one day they were arthritic claws of scar tissue and callus.

She always marveled how the laser-welders could make or break things. How they could join pieces together—or cut them apart.

This is like that.

Crisis will bring them all together or destroy them. But she believes that Sloane will be made by this crisis. Not just this small one she's about to hand-deliver, but the larger crisis.

She admires Sloane greatly.

She would hate to disappoint the admiral.

Rae stands under the spray of an ice-cold shower. *Piped in straight from the canyon,* the satrap said. *The purest water you will find on Akiva. The old Ahia-Ko people believed the water was so pure, it could take from you your sins and leave you a better person.*

If only that were true.

She keeps the water cold because that's how the showers were on her first assignment so many years ago. When she was just a cadet aboard the Imperial Star Destroyer *Defiance.* She grew to like it. The cold water toughened her. Woke her up. Just like it is now.

Plus, it's a necessary contrast with the heat here. Soon as she steps out of the shower, that heat assaults her—yes, the hot, humid air is invisible, but no less tangible. It feels like she's walking through boiling swamp water. Drowning while standing.

Out in the luxurious room that the satrap has furnished for Rae, Adea awaits. Morning light illuminates her as she stands there, dutiful as a coatrack, the holoscreen in her hand.

"You got some sleep?" Rae asks, toweling off her head.

"Yes, Admiral," Adea says, averting her eyes and blushing as Rae dries and dresses herself. Adea isn't true military. Rae sometimes forgets that those outside the navy or the army don't share the same experience. Sloane's nudity isn't meant to be anything other than a transitional state. Nothing romantic, nothing shameful. It is a practical fact of existence.

"Good," Sloane says. "Sleep will be necessary for the day ahead."

"I thought the meeting went well."

"The meeting went well the same way a crash landing goes well. It was an ineffective, inconsequential first step." Rae steps into her uniform, smoothing out the wrinkles—at least that's one good thing the humidity gives her. (And her hair looks actually sort of amazing for the first time in how many years. Appearance figures very little into how she sees herself, but once in a while it's nice to remember what she really looks like.) "We will try again today. That said, I don't expect much. This is just the first summit. We may need more. Bring in more voices. Tell Morna that she should have the shuttle ready just after dinner."

"Of course, Admiral. Do you expect that we will summon the *Vigilance* back to orbit, or should Morna plot hyperspace calculations into the shuttle compu—" Adea's screen flashes. Once, twice, then goes red.

Rae furrows her brow. "What is it now?"

"We have a situation. An . . . incursion."

CHAPTER TWENTY

THE TRANSPORT BUCKLES and bounces along the cloud tops of Akiva. The sun forms a hot line over the swirling curls of white, looking like melting steel. Down below, the barely seen city of Myrra. Hidden behind the clouds, and when sight of it emerges, it remains garbed in a gauzy pink haze.

Sergeant Major Jom Barell of New Republic Special Forces (SpecForces) looks to the five men and women standing to the right of him at the open door. On their torsos sit carbon-lace armor, the shoulders marked with the sigil of the New Republic: the Alliance starbird, now inside a sunburst. The symbol of a changed day, a new dawn. The phoenix, truly reborn.

The soldiers standing here with him: Corporals Kason, Stromm, Gahee'abee, Polnichk, and Durs. He knows which is which, even though their faces are concealed behind the orbital drop masks.

He gives the nod. "Drop!"

One by one, they unclip and leap into the clouds. Slugthrowers on their backs. Arms stretched out, as if trying to reach for the sun.

His turn.

Barell hates jumping. Give him anything else. *Anything*. Creeping through some Naboo swamp. Freezing his tail off in some ice-walled snow base. One time, they had to fly a gunship through an electrical superstorm over Geonosis to root out some Imperials that had gotten it in their heads to start up the old Geonosian droid factories again—the storm was all lightning and heavy winds and hail peppering the side of the craft so hard it left little *dents* in the metal. He was pretty sure they were dead before they even landed. And that was *still* better than jumping out of a ship.

Especially a suborbital drop.

Well, it is what it is.

Barell jumps after Durs, the last in the line. It feels like it always does—his guts sucking out through his hind end, his heart left somewhere behind in the sky above him, the panic, the terror. And then—

The air rocks. A concussive wave hits him. His body spins like a spun top and above him he sees it— the side of the transport, blown open, black smoke bellowing as flames flash and sparks shower. The ship lists and starts to tilt as it goes down—

He tries to comm, but it's no good, he knows that. There's a comm blackout. Nothing he says is going to go anywhere.

Best he can do now is drop and try not to die.

But that's a far trickier task than he expected— because below him, he sees Corporal Kason at the front of the line disappear in a flash. Something comes up from the ground: the blinding streak from a turbolaser. One minute, there's Kason, and the next he's just a red spray and a torn-up tatter of carbon-lace armor spiraling through the clouds.

We're dead, Barell thinks.

Another blast and Stromm is next—a flash and he's gone. Barell dives down through the space where Stromm was just two seconds before.

Barell signals the others: "We're pigeons to hunt up

here. We need to be falcons—engage para-wings." It's too soon, they're too high up. The winds up here could kill them. But what choice do they have? Below him, the other three snap out their arms and legs— and their wing-suits engage.

It's too late for Gahee'abee—the moment the Kupo-han's para-wings extend from wrist to ankle, he's gone. Another searing blast from the surface of the planet and he's just ragged wing strips caught on the wind.

CHAPTER TWENTY-ONE

A QUIET MORNING IN MYRRA. The rains have stopped. Heat rises off the rooftops and streets, leaving everything smeary behind the vapor blur. A pair of cerulean skycatchers duck and dive in the air above Norra's head, chasing one another in what might be a territorial dogfight or a mating dance. Or both, perhaps, given the nature of those plucky blue birds.

It feels calm up here on Esmelle and Shirene's rooftop as she sips her tea. But the serenity outside does nothing to quell the chaos inside.

Norra knows this feeling. Suiting up for her Y-wing. Sitting there in the hangar on *Home One,* waiting for the signal, waiting for the jump to lightspeed. It was quiet, then, too. A few murmured voices here and there. A droid burbling past. The sounds of the old frigate—a *tink-tink-tink* in the pipes behind the walls, a faint groan of metal on metal, the rumble of the air scrubbers kicking on.

She tries not to feel sick, but today is like that day.

She just wants to go home.

But duty calls once more.

Downstairs in the basement, Temmin works on his droid. The other two managed some sleep. Norra did, as well—though just a few hours, and even those were not without trouble.

But the boy kept working. She admires him. He's like his father, single-minded and driven. But he's got her stubborn streak. Her anger, her cocky sure-footedness—the same sure-footedness that made her leave this planet and join the Rebel Alliance under the foolish assumption she *alone* would be able to find out where they were keeping her husband and . . . what? Rescue him? Like he was a princess trapped in a tower like the old fairy tales? What a blubber-headed notion that was.

Across the way, up toward the orchard, she sees another rooftop—an older couple sits up there. She recognizes them. They've been here for years, those two. The pair: a couple of old shriveled Bith. She forgets their names, though Esmelle probably knows them. The two Bith sit there under an umbrella, watching the sunrise over the distant jungle, sipping from a single cylinder—probably a cup of oratay slurry. Bith seem to love the stuff.

Peaceful people, the Bith.

Norra wishes she could be like them—

Just then, a sound in the distance. A sound Norra knows deep in her bones before her ears even receive it—the roar of a TIE fighter.

It streaks past, flying low. Toward the city center.

The Bith—the peace-loving, oratay-sipping Bith—stand up. The old man has a blaster rifle he yanks out from under his chair, and next thing Norra knows he screams a babble of profanity in his native tongue before firing futile laser bolts at the screaming Imperial fighter.

The Bith woman, she shakes her fist and joins in the tirade.

It hits Norra, then. Of course. *Of course.*

She's about to turn around and head back inside when out over the city center, an explosion rocks the sky. Norra spins, and sees up there in the clouds something burning—a small black shape. A ship. Suddenly listing hard and plunging through the whirling clouds.

Another flash—a cannon blast from a turbolaser punches up through the sky. It hits . . . something up there. Something small.

A soldier, maybe.

Her middle tightens. A rebel soldier?

It makes sense.

But that means their timetable just changed.

Whong! Whong! Whonnng!

With the last hit from the spanner, the battle droid's eyes pulse and flicker back to life. The speaker underneath the thing's pointed metal beak utters a grinding, stuttering sound: "RRRRRRRRRggggRRRRR."

Temmin hits it again.

Whong!

"RRRRRROGER-ROGER."

The droid stands up. Servomotors whir as it regards its repaired arm—an arm that's not so much an arm as it is an astromech leg. It spins the leg around, slow at first, then faster and faster until it's just a blur. "THIS IS NOT MY ARM."

"I know, Bones. Sorry."

"THIS IS AN ASTROMECH LEG."

"No, no, I know."

"ASTROMECHS ARE INFERIOR. THEY ARE BEEPING BOOPING TRASH CANS. I AM MADE INFERIOR BY THE INCLUSION OF THIS NON-ARM."

Temmin shrugs. "I promise, I'll get you fixed up when we get back to the shop. Right now, this is what my aunts had around." Down here in the basement

workshop is where he first built Bones—cobbled together from scrapped droids he found in the catacombs beneath the cities. Debris and ruination from
the Clone Wars. When the factory down there—now
a gutted, flame-charred crater—still pumped out
droids for the Separatists.

He reaches for the spanner, and collapses it—it's a
little multitool he always keeps at his belt. Can become nearly any tool he needs just by telescoping out
different prongs. He twirls it, pops it back on his utility belt.

"PERHAPS I CAN STILL BE FUNCTIONAL."
The droid thrusts the astromech leg forward. "I CAN
BLUDGEON THOSE WHO WOULD HURT YOU.
I WILL BEAT THEM TO A GREASY TREACLE-
PASTE. DO NOT WORRY, MASTER TEMMIN.
YOU ARE SAFE."

"Thanks, Bones." Temmin throws his arms around
the droid. The droid returns the hug—admittedly,
with one arm. The astromech leg just kind of . . . pats
him on the side of his arm, *pat pat pat.* "I thought I
lost you."

He's had Bones for a while now. The thought of losing this droid . . .

"I DID GOOD. I CAME BACK."

"You did. Thanks, Bones."

"ROGER-ROGER."

A creak of a board—someone shifting weight on
the plankwood steps. It's his mother. They stare at
each other for a few moments. Like they don't know
how to deal with each other. Because they don't, do
they? They're strangers to each other. He realizes that
now. He lifts his head. He's embarrassed. Did she see
him hug his droid? Ugh. "Mom. You could . . . knock
or something next time."

"Temmin, something has happened. And . . . I think I have a plan."

"I'll be right up."

She waits there for a moment. "I'm . . ."

"What? Spit it out."

"I'm glad we're back together. And I'm glad your droid is fine. He seems to mean a lot to you."

"No! He doesn't. He's just a droid, okay? I said I'll be right up."

His mother offers a small smile and nod, then returns upstairs.

When she's gone, Temmin whispers to the droid: "I didn't mean that."

"I KNOW."

"You're the best."

"I KNOW THAT, TOO."

Esmelle meets her at the top of the steps. Her sister gently closes the door. Worry crosses the woman's face. Her features bunch up like a drawstring cinched tight. "Is the droid okay?"

"I think so." Norra neglects to mention the astromech arm that has now replaced his missing one. "Sort of?"

"That droid means a lot to him."

"So I gathered."

"No, you don't get it. He built Mister Bones the year you left. Temmin doesn't have many friends. That droid might be it."

"You can't be friends with a droid."

"Well, he is. Temmin was getting taunted and beaten by a gang of . . . young tyrants. Bones protected him. He's not just a bodyguard. When you took off on your . . . *trip* . . ."

"I get it," Norra snaps. "You think I should feel

bad about leaving. I do feel bad. I felt bad then. I feel worse now. I'm trying to fix things."

"And yet here you are. Doing more work for the rebels. It's your son that needs you, Norra, not this . . . crusade of yours."

Crusade. That's how Esmelle sees it. Norra snarls, "War is coming to Akiva, Esme. Not later. Soon. Now, maybe. You can pretend that it won't land on your doorstep, but trust me, you *soft-handed, weak-backed* sister of mine, no amount of wishing will hold back the tide. Now step aside. I don't have time for this conversation."

Her sister protests, but Norra pushes past her.

"Can't I just sit back and watch?" Sinjir says. It's just him and Jas. In front of them, another display of kitchen implements and foodstuffs. The map of Myrra has grown since last night. "All this business is really quite distasteful. I could sit back, hold up score-cards. Do a little proper cheerleading?"

He takes a nip from the unlabeled bottle. The liquor is sweet. Honey on the front, and lavender at the finish. The taste lingering on his tongue is coppery, almost electric, like he's licking the top of a thorium battery.

"I told you, I need actual help, not the illusion of help." Jas stares at him, sees him drinking. She snatches the bottle out of his hands, sniffs it.

"Hey! That's no way to be."

"You're a drunk."

"I'm no such thing. I'm no drunker than a pickle. I brine myself in order to maintain a low level of . . ." He waggles his fingers in the air. "*Fuzziness.* I find life is so much more pleasant that way."

"I need you clear."

"Oh," he mopes, "we're perfectly clear."

The bounty hunter stares holes through him. "What happened to you? On Endor. I do remember you. Standing there, covered in blood. Yours?"

He sneers. "I do not want to talk about this."

"And yet, here we are, talking about it." She sits down. Sighs. "I became a bounty hunter because I did not like the life my mother had chosen for me. It felt . . . overly arranged. It *choked* me. So I took after my mother's sister: Aunt Sugi was a bounty hunter, too. Thing is, Sugi always worked with a crew. She was no lone bird, no rogue operator. One thing I learned from her was, if I was going to work with a crew, I had to trust them. I had to know them. So I didn't work with a crew. Because I trusted myself above anyone else. Now, here I am. Working with you."

"Which, let's be honest, makes you very fortunate. I'm really very cool. It's almost as if you've won the Empire Day lottery." He smirks. "Hey, if you have a ship, where is it? Can't we use it to just . . . flit off this rock? Go find something better to do?"

"It's a few days' walk out into the jungle," she says, but the way she says it indicates that the Zabrak isn't buying any of it. "Had to make sure my trek into the city was unseen."

"Convenient. By way of grave inconvenience."

She stares holes through him. "What happened that day? On Endor?"

"You know what happened. You were there."

"To you. What happened to *you*."

"I . . ." Sinjir puts forth a grim smile, trying not to speak aloud the memories that are tearing him apart. "*Fine*. You really want to know? You won't stop poking? Let's have it, then." He swirls the honeyed liquid around the bell of the bottle. "So, like I said, I was an

Imperial loyalty officer on the base of Endor and—*oh look it's Norra!*" He nearly drops the bottle when he sees her step into the kitchen.

Her. Norra. Standing right there. Fuming. Chest rising and falling like that of a beast who smells blood on the wind. He should've heard her come up. But with the drinking and the talking . . .

"An Imperial," she says.

"I'm sure you misheard me," he says. "I said . . . mImperial?" He frowns and *hmmph*s. "That's not a word, is it."

"An *Imperial*," she says again. Louder this time.

"Norra, listen—"

She charges at him. Tackles him into the counter. Bowls clatter. The saltcellar spins off the edge of the table and shatters. Her hands wrap around his throat and her face hovers over his.

"I should've *known*," she says. "You didn't carry yourself like one of us. Too *superior*, too *nose-at-the-sky*. That accent, too. Crisp like a bitten cracker. You sonofagundark—"

The click of a blaster.

Jas presses it to the side of Norra's head.

The bounty hunter speaks in a calm voice. "Norra. You are going to have to make peace with this. If you can't make peace, everything falls apart. He was an Imperial. And we can use him."

It's like watching the mist clear out over lake water. The fight goes out of Norra and she falls into this thousand-meter stare. Sinjir eases out of her slackening grip and rubs his throat.

"We can use him," Norra says. "You're right." Her focus snaps back and it's as if she's made a decision. "Something has happened. The timeline has changed. We need to move now."

From behind them, Temmin says: "Am I interrupting something?"

Nobody says anything.

"What's going on? Hello? Anybody?"

Norra smiles and says:

"I have a plan."

INTERLUDE:

SEVARCOS

THREE SLAVES HUDDLE in the shadows of Imperial turrets, hiding behind a jagged rock as the battle rages: Hatchet, the Weequay, whose craggy face is marked by a central scar running down between his eyes, down the length of his nose, over his lips, and even to his chin; Palabar the Quarren, whose tentacled face is chapped and chafed and peeling (for the air here is so dry and full of particulate it will slowly abrade you sure as water erodes rock); and Greybok, the one-armed Wookiee, a beast who hovers over the both of them and protects them even as an A-wing slams into the red-rock mountainside above, raining debris upon them.

"We must run," Hatchet hisses. "The Imperials are winning this battle. And when they do, the mines will again be theirs. *We* will again be theirs!"

The Quarren nods. Palabar has been so traumatized over the years that he goes wherever the wind takes him, cowering and nodding and whimpering in the dark.

But Greybok roars: a guttural growl of dissent. He

shakes his one fist in rage, baring his teeth as he ululates.

The Imperial turrets spit fire across the open plain
leading up to the mouth of the spice mine. Other
slaves huddle about. Some wounded. Others dead.
Most just trying to survive however they can.

Greybok growls again, his head lifting, his filthy,
matted fur shaking.

Hatchet shakes his head. "You're mad! We cannot
help the rebels win. This is not our war, you walking
pelt! Our only hope is not to die."

But in a rare fit of dissent, Palabar says: "What . . .
what if the Wookiee is right? What if this is our only
chance? If we run, they will find us . . ."

Greybok barks in agreement. He shakes his arm
again. The Sevarcos slavemasters took his other one
many years ago when he tried to escape. Their masters were not themselves Imperials, but this mine has
long been in the grip of the Empire. Officers coming
to inspect the proceedings, to take a tithing of credits
and spice. The Empire does not frown on slaves, but
rather was built on their backs. The credits in the Imperial coffers are earned by those who are kept against
their will. Whole species! Greybok knows all of
this—he is no common worker, though that is his
purpose here, to swing a pneumo-hammer and pul-
verize rock. Once, he was a tribal diplomat. He knows
the rough shape of things. He is no fool.

And though he is no warrior, today he has cause to
try.

"Don't go out there," Hatchet spits. "Don't be a
fool, Wookiee."

But the Wookiee doesn't care.

Greybok just wants to be free.

He stands up. Roars the battle cry of his people.
Then he runs into battle, ducking laserfire. An Impe-

rial in mechanized battle armor wheels on him, turning a heavy handheld cannon toward him. But Greybok has speed and surprise, and gets under his attacker and flings the heavy trooper into a crevasse.

Greybok never stops moving.

He has a plan.

There, ahead: a corral. High fence with electrified gate. Inside are three more slaves—these easily ten times the size of Greybok. *Rancors.* Creatures made vicious by the slavers. Forced to march in the outer canyons to keep the slaves from attempting escape— everyone knows that if you did make it to those canyons, the rancors there would hunt you and eat you.

But when the Imperials come, the rancors are drawn back to their high-fence corral and kept—they don't like anybody. Slave *or* Imperial. The rancors are trained only to like the slavers who train them.

These rancors are here now. On the side of the Imperials. They gnash their teeth and scream. One of them is smaller than the others: bright yellow eyes and gray-green face. The others are rust red like the mountains in this part of Sevarcos: bigger, too.

Greybok bolts toward the corral, scooping up a heavy rock as he goes. The rancors turn toward him, shrieking. Greybok roars back and begins to bang the rock against the massive lock holding the electrified gate closed.

Wham. Wham. Wham. The rancors stop screaming and watch what he's doing with intense fascination. Imperials start to yell. Laser bolts pepper the ground near his feet, and sizzle against the fence.

He keeps going. *Wham. Wham. Wham.* Until—

The lock cracks in half and drops.

The crackling serpents of electricity that once crawled all over the corral fence suddenly flicker and die. The charge is gone.

And the gate starts to swing open.

The smaller rancor roars and bats the gate open with the back of its hand. The gate catches Greybok and flings him to the ground. His head cracks against a rock and everything goes blurry.

Above him, dizzy shapes as the three rancors escape. Screams ensue. Something explodes. Men, yelling in panic. Then, suddenly, someone appears over Greybok—a slaver. A Zygerrian. Mouth twisted up in feral rage. The master seethes: "What have you done, slave?"

Greybok tries to stand, but the Zygerrian points one of their terrible weapons—a blaster called a needler. The slaver spins a dial on the side and pulls the trigger. Ropes of red lightning flicker from the tip of the weapon and surround the one-armed Wookiee.

Everything is light and pain and fire.

He can't even roar. He can only choke and gurgle.

Blackness bleeds in at the edges. The Zygerrian means to kill him. That is one of the powers of the needler: It can cause a little pain, or a whole lot of it. Enough, over a short period, to seize your heart and kill you.

But then it stops—the fire recedes, the pain fades (though the memory will long remain). The Zygerrian drops.

There stands Hatchet, holding a bludgeoning rock of his own.

Greybok roars a thank-you.

And then darkness takes him. Though only for a moment. Or so he thinks: He opens his eyes and it feels like no time has passed at all.

Except, it has.

Hatchet sits there, picking his teeth with a broken stick. All around is the waste of war: the turrets on fire, rebels rounding up slavers, canisters of spice thrown into a crackling fire. One of the rancors lies dead: one of the big ones. The gray-green one and the other rust-red monster are nowhere to be found and no sounds of them can be heard.

Greybok roars a question.

The Weequay answers: "What happened is, we won. Or the rebels won. Well, *somebody* won, and it wasn't the Empire or the slavers."

Nearby, Palabar holds his knees close with his long arms. His tentacles search the air anxiously. He asks: "What happens now?"

Greybok echoes the question in a low, thrumming grumble. As a rebel soldier passes by, Hatchet calls out to her: "Hey. Honey. What happens now? For us, I mean. The slaves."

She smiles a little. But Greybok sees that she looks lost, too. All she can do is shrug. "I don't know. Nobody knows. You're free, though."

The woman keeps on moving. She kicks a storm-trooper helmet out of the way and then she's gone. In the distance, the sound of another battle. Greybok wonders if all of Sevarcos will fall. Or if it will be re-claimed by the Empire. The future is suddenly unpinned—evolving, spinning, leaping about like a panicked tree-loormor.

Hatchet laughs: a mirthless sound. "Nobody knows. You hear that, fellas? Nobody knows what happens next." He sniffs and stands up. "Whatever it is, I guess we're the ones who gotta do it. Let's walk. We're free now. Might as well act like it, see what the galaxy has to offer a trio of no-good, no-class ex-slaves, yeah?"

PART THREE

CHAPTER TWENTY-TWO

BLEARY-EYED, Admiral Ackbar stands, studying the data. It's a short packet of information, shown in a three-dimensional display—before him, the surface of the planet Akiva grows bigger, blowing up like a balloon until it seems like he could reach out and move the whorls of clouds with the flat of his hand. Like a god. But it's just a projection. A hologram. Data pulled from the probe droid still there in space. He sees what the droid saw: the small dot (illuminated by a red circle) representing the transport flying in, the SpecForce soldiers exiting the ship one by one (each a yellow circle). Then the flash of cannon fire. A turbolaser from the planet's surface. That, from somewhere down below the clouds.

The red circle flickers and goes dark, exploding in midair before it ever reaches the ground.

One by one, the yellow circles flicker and go dark, too.

Except for one.

They lose his signal when he reaches the planet, but it would appear as if Sergeant Jom Barell of the Spec-Forces survived the attack. To what end, Ackbar does not know. Information at this point is and will be sketchy. The communications blackout is doing them no favors—the probe droid only has the information it has because of a visual survey. And *they* only have the droid's information because it daisy-chained the communiqué back to the *Oculus,* which is far enough out of range that it can send it back to Ackbar here on the *Home One.* Short-range communication made long.

"And we think Barell survived," Ackbar says.

The hologram of Deltura's face nods. "We do."

He moves aside, and the science officer's face appears. Officer Niriian says: "Though his survival is not guaranteed. You'll note the erratic pattern he suddenly follows—a pattern that continues to the ground." She replays that last bit, where Barell's glowing circle suddenly darts right, then left, then zigzags down. "It suggests he deployed the para-wing too early. The wind at that level is intense. We cannot be certain that the man who landed on the surface is a man who is alive and well."

Ackbar nods. "Thank you, Officer Niriian. Commendable work, as always." He cranes his neck and massages it.

Deltura returns. "Sir? Our orders, Admiral?"

"Remain in place until further order. But remain wary. Something is going on there. It seems we will have to reveal the face of this thing with a far more active hand than initially anticipated."

If this is the Empire, as their shadowy informant suggests, then the war for the galaxy has preemptively come to this sector of the Outer Rim.

They already know by the time she gets to the room. The volume level of those present is already a clamorous din, and when Rae enters through the door, that vexed and fretful outcry turns toward her like a laser. The satrap, acting like a servant, hurries toward her and he's saying—not to her but to those gathered—"I told you, it's safe, it's safe, the walls here are stone as thick as you are tall." He gets to Rae and offers her a tray full of fragrant pastries: delicate little pinwheels with sweet, floral fruit pressed into the centers. She hand-waves them away, despite the hungry protestations of her stomach—she cannot seem like an effective leader if she has a funny little confection in her hand and crumbs at the corners of her lips.

No. Better yet—how best to downplay the severity?

She catches the satrap by the arm and plucks a pastry from the tray and begins to eat it.

Let them see she doesn't take this threat seriously.

A lie. It's serious. Or will be dire enough, soon enough.

The fact they already know something's going on is again a credit to Pandion. He has *someone* on the inside of her team. Tothwin? Could be. The prat. Adea or Morna? That, a more troubling concern.

Nothing to be done now. No time for a rat hunt.

She waves her hand, catching a few falling crumbs in the palm of her hand. "As you know," she starts to say, then has to say it louder again to quiet those gathered. "*As you know,* there has been an incursion into Akivan space. We discovered a rebel transport in the atmosphere above Myrra. We eradicated that transport with one of the suborbital ground-to-orbit cannons. That is the end of our present concerns."

"The end?" Crassus barks. "That feels hardly accurate. How dismissive! This is a threat, Admiral Sloane, the Rebel Alliance—"

Pandion interrupts: "The rebels will send a fleet. Not immediately, but soon. And when they do, we should meet them here. They are blind to the situation. Yet we see with clear eyes. That gives us a powerful advantage. They send a fleet and we have our own—led

by the Super Star Destroyer *Ravager,* of *course*—
waiting. A victory for the Empire. One that will serve
as a tolling bell ringing throughout the galaxy, herald-
ing the return of order."

Tashu and Crassus nod. Shale says, elbowing past
the obsequious satrap and his tray of pastries: "They
still have the military advantage. Particularly if they
send in a large fleet as a response. How likely that is,
I cannot say, but just the same, putting *any* of our
command ships into play right now is foolhardy. This
battle has no stakes except that of our survival. That
is a battle you only fight if you must. If we *lose* this,
then we lose our command ships, and likely our lives
or our freedoms. *That* will be a tolling bell, Moff Pandion. Do you want to lose here as you did on
Malastare? The loss of that communications station
lost us our meager hold on that world."

She, too, heard of his loss there—only he escaped.
Fleeing in an escape shuttle as the rebels took the base
behind him. In the navy, the admiral goes down with
the ship. Moffs do not hold such a code, it seems.

Bringing it up has stung Pandion. His anger at that
comment hangs on his face like an ugly mask. "You
coward."

Shale shrugs. "Not so much of a coward that I fled
as my men fell to capture or death."

It's time to step in before these two kill each other.
(Though that, she thinks, might solve a problem,
wouldn't it? If only she were so ruthless.)

"The plan as I see it," she again says quite loudly,
"is that we continue breakfast and continue discuss-
ing our greater purpose—the future of the Galactic
Empire and the galaxy it ostensibly controls. In the
meantime, our people will prepare our shuttles, pack
our things, and my assistant Adea will plot for us a
revised location for this meeting. By lunchtime, we

will adjourn to that secondary location and continue this there."

That statement is her trying to put her boot down on the neck of a wriggling serpent to pin it to the ground before it bites her. This whole thing threatens to be a rope sliding all the way through her grip. Right now her declarative statement seems to give them pause, but she knows at any moment someone like Pandion will step forward, call a vote. That, a precedent from the night before—and a mistake she made letting them all have a voice. (And here she wonders at the larger mistake: Is this meeting a foolhardy endeavor? Perhaps Pandion has a point. The Empire needs an emperor. Not some squabbling council. Councils are how you slow the wheels of progress to an imperceptible crawl. The Galactic Senate was known for its inability to accomplish *anything*.)

It is what it is.

"Let our meeting commence," she says.

Jom Barell coughs. His eyes refocus. Where is he? What happened?

It doesn't take long for it to come careening back— fast as the ground lunging up to meet him. The memory of falling. The transport in flames. His team erased from the sky, one by one, as if by the flicking finger of a callow and callous god. And him: his wings out. The wind taking him. Durs below him. Polnichk above him. A laser erasing Durs. The wind breaking Polnichk before the cannon claims him, too.

Jom fell into it, then—a jet stream of air pushing hard, a cold wind that swept him aside like a brutish hand. He dropped about thirty meters in a few seconds, then tumbled forward, the air gone from under his wings. He blacked out only to awaken again closer to the ground now—the city visible beneath him. He extended his arms once more, felt the air seize him—

His descent was ill controlled. He crashed into the side of a small wagon. And then crawled underneath a small wooden overhang strewn with hay and fruit rinds—the leavings of some domesticated animal— before passing out into what he feared might be death.

But alive, he remains.

It's hot as a rancor's mouth here. Jom pries off his mask, flings it to the ground. He tries to move—but his one arm gives out, and pain fires from the wrist to the shoulder like an arc-whip of electricity. He can't even close his fist. The limb feels useless inside the casing of carbon lace.

It's broken.

Frag.

He reaches around for the rifle strapped to his back with plans to use it as a cane—

But it's gone.

Double frag.

Must've broken off in the fall (or the landing). He rolls over, starts to push himself up onto his knees with his unbroken arm and—

When he lifts his head, sweat pouring off his brow, he sees the white boots of stormtroopers standing there. Three of them. Blasters pointed.

And that's a triple frag for the frag trifecta.

"Well, hey, boys," Jom says, words ushered out through gritted teeth. "Hot enough for you?"

"Freeze," one stormtrooper says.

"Stand up," the other says.

Idiots.

"I can't likely do both," Barell says. "I'm just one

man, not three like you fine soldiers—" And on that last word he pivots and kicks a leg out hard, stabbing his heel at the post holding up the wooden overhang. It's enough—the post cracks like a snapped bone, and the whole roof comes down. Clay tile clatters off and rains down upon the stormtroopers as the wooden platform separates him from them.

No time to waste. He springs up with both legs, urging himself past the pain and slamming his shoulder into the roof, shoving it forward. The stormtroopers give way, toppling to the ground with the rattle of armor. They're trapped underneath it. He crawls on top and slams his weight down a few times—but he sees movement at the edge. One of them is trying to crawl out from under. Blaster rifle in one hand.

Jom rolls over, pries the blaster from the stormtrooper's hand.

"Hey!" the trooper shouts.

"Hey," Barell seethes, standing up—using the blaster for support.

Then he fires the rifle down through the wood, peppering it with searing bolts. Splinters spray. Smoke drifts through the holes. The stormtroopers stop struggling and lie still.

He winces, spits, and then steps off the platform.

Time to move.

CHAPTER TWENTY-THREE

THEY WALK. Hard to keep your face hidden here on the streets of Myrra, especially in hot weather—a cloak is out of the question and a face mask will drown you in your own sweat. Veils are the way they go: Norra with a white veil over her nose and mouth, Jas with a full head veil, black as midnight. (Though the veil does little to conceal her head-spikes.)

Ahead, a pair of stormtroopers walk toward them.

From somewhere behind, a flung jogan fruit. It hits the one trooper and splatters—purple juice and pale seeds running down the white helmet in gooey rivulets. The two troopers wheel, blaster rifles up.

"Who did that? Who?"

"Show yourself!"

But nobody does. The pair of Imperials curse and keep walking.

Jas and Norra cinch their veils closer to their faces and skirt past the two stormtroopers on the far side of the crowded street. They make it.

Norra feels so tense she's afraid her teeth might break against one another. She tries to relax, tries to unclench. But everything feels like it hinges on everything else—one wrong move and the entire thing comes tumbling down around them.

"Your plan really might work," Jas says.

"You think?" Norra asks. "I'm suddenly not so sure."

Jas shrugs. "After seeing what we just saw? I feel considerably better about it. Here. Ahead. Your son's shop."

Temmin's shop. Norra thinks but does not say: *Once, my home.*

From inside, the sounds of banging. Metal striking against stone. A power drill revs up somewhere past the door. Norra can feel the vibrations of the drill in the heels of her feet up through her calves.

"You sure you don't want me to come in with you?" Norra asks.

Jas pops the knuckles on each hand with a pressing thumb. "Too crowded in there. You'll only get in my way."

"Thanks for the vote of confidence."

"You be the pilot. I'll be the bounty hunter."

"Fair enough. I'll get my gun fixed, then I'll meet you at the evil-eye."

Jas nods, then steps forward, blaster drawn. Norra waits around—just in case. As the bounty hunter steps forward, the door to Temmin's shop hisses open. The Zabrak steps in. The door slides shut behind her.

The drilling sound stops.

It's replaced by yelling. *They've seen her.*

Then the yelling cuts short.

Banging. A thud. Blaster fire. Another bang. Three more blaster shots in quick succession. Someone mewling in pain. One more shot. The mewling ends, cut off as fast as it began.

Moments tick by.

The door hisses open.

Jas stands there, a line of dark blood trickling from her nose. Her lip is split. Blood smears her teeth. She gives a wink. "We're clear. Now go."

* * *

"Stand down," Sinjir growls past the pair of blaster rifles shoved in his face. He lifts his chin and sneers. "Don't you know who you're talking to? Didn't anyone inform you of my presence?"

The two stormtroopers give each other a bewildered look. As if to say, *Is this some kind of Jedi mind trick?*

Behind Sinjir, in the narrow alley, a few Myrran citizens hurriedly pass—a scurrying Dug, a pair of washerwomen, an Ugnaught riding on the swooped and bent neck of an Ithorian.

And behind the stormtroopers is a door.

A door that leads to a local communications station. A three-floor dome-shaped building with a tall—if crooked—antenna at the top of it. An antenna that isn't much to look at. It's not big enough to climb or hang off of. Were the wind to kick up in a storm, said antenna would probably waggle back and forth like a judgmental finger.

It won't get a signal out into space.

But it will send one locally.

"Step back," one of the troopers says.

Sinjir feigns incredulity. "You really . . . hah, you really don't know who I am. Your faces will be *quite red* under those austere helmets when you find out. You have an officer present, I take it? *Get him.*"

Another shared look. One of the stormtroopers comms: "Sir? We have a . . . problem at the side entrance. Uh-huh. He's claiming to be an Imperial? Yes, sir. Yes, sir." Then to Sinjir: "Officer Rapace will be right down." He thrusts his rifle up and forward again as if to assert his dominance and to say: *Don't get any funny ideas.*

Sinjir is nothing but funny ideas, so, oops, sorry, too late.

Moments later, the door behind the troopers slides open and an Imperial officer—little hat and everything—steps out. A prig-nosed man with a soft, downy beard. "What is this? Who is this?"

"Are you Officer Rapace?" Sinjir says.

"I am. Who are you?"

"I am Loyalty Officer Sinjir Rath Velus."

There it is. That delicious flinch. A tightening of the eyes. A tremor in the hands. Fear and uncertainty doing a wild and whirling dance. Though Rapace tries not to show it, Sinjir sees it. Because it is his job to see it.

And because everyone is afraid of a loyalty officer.

"We don't have any, ahh, loyalty officers stationed here," Rapace says, a bit of a stammer in his voice. He pulls a scanner off his belt and holds it up to Sinjir's face while the stormtroopers keep their blasters trained on him—though now the barrels are pointed *just slightly* downward because they know the fear, too. Probably quaking inside that armor.

The scanner beeps.

Rapace seems taken aback. "Sinjir Rath Velus. You . . . you died on Endor. You are listed as a casualty."

"Ugh," Sinjir says, making a distasteful face. "This *clerical error* has been following me like a bad smell." He rolls his eyes. "*No,* I did not die on Endor, and *yes,* I am really here, right now, standing in front of you."

"I . . . ," Rapace says, bewildered. "You're not in uniform."

"I was on leave. But I'm reporting for duty and this local comm station was the closest place for me. An old comm station, wasn't it? Good for you. Lock down any points of information transmission. Nicely done, Officer." Before Rapace can blunder through a thank-you, Sinjir says, "May we go inside? I would like to evaluate the situation."

"Sir," Rapace says with a stiff nod. "Of course, Loyalty Officer Velus. Right away." He turns heel-to-toe, trying to put a ceremonial spin on it as if to indicate *what a good Imperial* he is, and marches inside.

Sinjir passes the two stormtroopers. "You two. Inside, as well."

"But sir, we're guarding the door—"

"Are you questioning a loyalty officer? Perhaps you should remain out here. I could search your quarters. Dig through your files. Speak to Rapace about any instances of . . . insubordination that may have occurred."

"Lead the way, sir," the other stormtrooper says.

(When Sinjir turns his back, the one elbows the other.)

They step in through the door.

The door closes behind them.

Officer Rapace walks ahead toward a set of dimly lit steps curving upward to the second floor.

At the door outside: a *knock-knock-knock*. Metal rapping on metal.

Which means: *Now is the time.*

The stormtroopers turn, grunting in confusion. Soon as they start to pivot, Sinjir reaches behind Rapace to snatch his pistol—while, with his other hand, he shoves the officer forward.

He shoots Rapace in the back. The officer pitches face-first.

The stormtroopers cry out in alarm and wheel back toward him. But for them, it's too late. The door opens. Framed there in the doorway is the battle droid—Temmin's droid. Bones. His astromech leg spins up like a turbine rotor and hits one of the troopers so hard in the helmet the white armor splits down the middle like a cracked kukuia nut. The other cries out in panic, and is silenced by a vibroblade punched through his chest plate.

The stormtroopers drop.

"HELLO MAY I COME IN," Mister Bones intones.

Sinjir sighs. "I think you said that part a little late."

"ROGER-ROGER."

From the staircase: the dull clack-and-thud of footsteps. Sinjir positions himself next to and just behind a small footlocker—and as soon as the other two stormtroopers appear, he squeezes off two shots in quick succession. The one tumbles forward. The other topples backward and slides down on his smooth armor. They lie still.

Sinjir nods to the droid. "Tell Temmin it's time."

"MASTER TEMMIN. HIS NAME IS MASTER TEMMIN."

"Yes, great, fine, tell *Master Temmin* it's time."

"ROGER-ROGER!"

Norra sits on the rooftop of the old outfitter's store. Used to belong to that old Tuskface—the Aqualish, Torvo Bolo—before it burned down. Bolo played at being a hard-ass, but he'd always sneak her and Esmelle little candy-swirl sticks while he sold provisions to their parents. Story goes that it was someone from the black market who burned it down. Simple enough to increase black-market profits if the black market suddenly includes items that were once easy to come by.

But that's Akiva. The corruption once held fast to the satrapy and its backstabbing aristocracy leaked out like a punctured slabin barrel, got all over everything. Became toxic in that dose. A changed world.

But that's a thought for another time. Now: There's a task at hand.

Across the narrow street sits another rooftop: the old Karyvinhouse Plantation. Home then and now to one of those duplicitous aristocrat families, the Karyvin clan. Old money. They own islands down in the Southern Archipelago, they own crystal mines in the Northern Jungles. All their children always seem to skip the Academy and head right to officers' school, not climbing the Imperial ranks so much as pole-vaulting over them.

On the rooftop: two TIE fighters. This quiet, sub-rosa occupation of Myrra has left a number of the Imperial short-range fighters parked on Empire-friendly rooftops all around the city.

Norra needs one of them.

She glances behind her, watching the rooftop of the Saltwheel Playhouse. The rooftop where a branch of a gnarled old-growth jarwal tree broke off and fell years ago, and still sits.

Norra waits and waits.

How long is this going to take? Jas should've been—

There.

A flash. A little mirror catching sunlight.

It's time.

Norra scoops up a bit of broken mortar from the rooftop, and then pitches it hard. It hits the vertical wing of the TIE—*pock!* And then, sure enough, from around the far side: Here comes the TIE pilot. Helmet off, tucked under his arm. Hand drifting to his pistol.

He bends down, picks up the thrown hunk of mortar.

Norra stands, whistles.

He perks his head up like a whistle-pig at its hole. It takes him a moment to even register that there's someone there. He starts to yell at her—"You there!"—and his hand moves toward his blaster.

From far behind Norra, toward the playhouse roof: a small sound.

Piff.

The pilot shudders just slightly. His words die in his mouth and he dips his chin to his chest and stares, bewildered, at the hole there.

He doesn't collapse so much as he just . . . crumples.

Norra psyches herself up. She's older now. Not as spry as she once was. Her bones don't ache all the time—just in the mornings—but it's enough to remind her she's not a young mother jetting around the galaxy anymore. Time has ground her down. She's a good pilot, but all this running and jumping? It's not really her bag.

It's a short jump. You can do it.

Deep breath and then—Norra runs. She crosses the general store rooftop, and ahead the narrow street gap looms and she tries not to think about falling, tries not to think about dropping three stories and breaking her body on the plastocrete below, and she plants her heel at the edge of the rooftop to make the jump . . .

. . . just as a second TIE pilot emerges and sees her.

The blaster is already in his hand and he starts firing.

Norra's foot skids out from under her and she falls off the rooftop.

* * *

Temmin kneels. Holds up both hands in front of his face. He stares through his fingers at the blaster barrel pointed toward him.

"Please," he pleads. "*Please.* I didn't do anything."

The Imperial officer chuckles and then says: "I know."

Temmin springs to his feet, feigns trying to run the other way—

The blaster goes off. The bolt hits him in the back.

He drops. The air gone from his lungs. He wants to cry out, gasp, roll around, try to suck in a fresh breath. But he has to hold it. This has to look convincing. *Stay still. Don't move. Don't even breathe.*

Play dead.

Moments pass. Temmin feels like he's going blue in the face.

Then, finally—

"Did we get it?" the Imperial officer—Sinjir, actually—says.

Mister Bones stands there, still as a coatrack. "WHAT."

Temmin lets out a breath as he stands up and pulls the comm-relay panel out from under his shirt. A deep dent sits in the middle of the steel grid. These plates line the outside of the receiver tower on the roof, and are meant to survive the mausim-storms, so they're pretty damn indestructible. "This dent looks awful close to being a hole," he says, chiding Sinjir.

"Well, *sorry,*" Sinjir snips. "It was your idea to use the relay panel. Besides, this was all necessary for the ruse. Now will you *please* ask your psychotic automaton if he captured the footage?"

"Bones, did you get that footage?"

"ROGER-ROGER, MASTER TEMMIN."

Then the droid starts humming to himself. Shuffling from foot to foot almost as if trying not to dance, but dancing anyway.

Sinjir asks the droid: "And you have Norra's recording?"

"ROGER-ROGER."

He turns to Temmin: "And you have the—"

"Yeah, yeah, I have the holodisk. This thing has gone everywhere. Everybody seems to have it. Or seen it." He reluctantly admits: *Mom had a pretty good plan.* This part, at least. The rest? He's not so sure. He definitely doesn't want to leave this planet. This is his home. This is where he has his business. His *life.* And she just wants to rip him away? Take him offworld to—where? Chandrila? Naboo? Gross. He tries to shake off the feeling. "You know, this place. It used to transmit the news. My mom and dad used to listen to it. But the satrapy shut it down on Imperial orders." He thinks but does not say: *And then it turns out my dad was using this very console to transmit rebel propaganda all across Akiva.*

The irony is not lost on him.

Sinjir pulls a chair away from the console and pushes it toward him. "And you really think you can hack the signal?"

"I built him, didn't I?" Temmin thumbs in the direction of the droid. He sits in the chair, blows dust off the console.

Mister Bones is slicing his vibroblade through the air, trying to attack a moth. Finally, he succeeds— then comes a tiny little *bzzt* as the moth is sliced in twain, two little white wings fluttering to the ground, smoldering.

"Yes," Sinjir says, voice as dry as an old biscuit. "*That* is what I'm worried about."

* * *

Norra's lungs and shoulders burn as she clings to the plantation rooftop, her hands scrabbling on the wet ledge. Her boot toes scrape futilely against the wall as she tries to pull herself up.

A shadow looms over her.

The TIE pilot. Standing there, pistol pointed.

"You killed NK-409. He was a friend. You rebel sssssss—"

He staggers back. His finger reaching to probe the hole in the dead center of his black chest plate.

"Scum," he finishes.

Then pitches forward—right toward her. Norra cries out and hugs the wall as close as she can. She can feel the air disturbed behind her as the pilot plunges through and plummets to the street below.

Her fingers start to slip. She thinks of the dead man below.

I'm about to join him.

Get it together, Norra.

Everything relies on this.

Make Temmin proud.

The tip of one boot anchors her against the wall. She presses up with her leg—the calf and thigh straining, burning. Then, groaning, she hauls herself up and over the ledge and onto the plantation roof.

Norra lies there for a moment. The massive black bat-wing of the TIE fighter—an *evil-eye* as she and some other rebels have called them, because that's damn sure what they look like screaming at you through the endless void of space—and thinks: *I'm about to fly one of those things.*

One last exhalation. Whew. *Better get to it, then.*

"We're in," Temmin says.

Just then: banging at the door here at the comm

transmission booth. From the other side: "Open up!"

Sinjir takes the blaster and fires a shot into the door mechanism. A flash of flame and a rain of sparks. The door judders, then locks.

"Do it," Sinjir says.

Temmin hits the button.

The transmission begins.

All across the city of Myrra, HoloNet receivers flick on. Above cantina bar tops, in little galley kitchens, appearing above the wristwatch projectors sported by those stuck in a long bala-bala commute down the Main 66 highway. It appears on the big, cracked screen hanging just outside the Hydorrabad Arena in the middle octagon of the CBD.

On all the projections appears the face of Norra Wexley.

A pleading face.

The projected Norra says:

Akivans, your planet has been occupied. Myrra is now under the control of the Galactic Empire. Long have we resisted total occupation, but now the war is at our door. And with war comes crimes such as this:

A scene plays out. A boy holding up his hands. An Imperial officer with a pistol. *Please. Please! I didn't do anything.* And the officer laughs and says, *I know.* Then the Imperial shoots the boy in the back as he tries to escape. The boy falls to the ground, dead.

The Imperial is not really an Imperial, and the dead boy is not really a dead boy. But few would even get the chance to recognize the artifice.

When they see it, all across Myrra the Akivans gasp. They shake their heads. They cluck their tongues. And all that soon turns to quaking in rage.

Norra appears again, her voice booming out:

Right now, at this very moment, a meeting takes place inside the walls of the satrap's palace. Already a hotbed of corruption, this Imperial meeting means to negotiate the total occupation of your city and your planet. Will you stand for this? Or will you fight?

I say: fight.

And know that the New Republic stands with you.

Then Norra disappears.

A new projection plays, this one on a loop. Princess Leia appears and speaks in the same video many of the Myrrans have already seen, a holovid going around and around. It begins:

The New Republic wants you. The grip of the Galactic Empire on our galaxy and its citizens is relinquished. The Death Star outside the forest moon of Endor is gone, and with it the Imperial leadership . . .

CHAPTER TWENTY-FOUR

RAE QUAKES.

Adea shows her the holovid outside the dining area—the others are still in there, once more arguing their respective positions. Now they've moved on to *who* exactly should become emperor in the wake of Palpatine's death. When Adea pulled her out of the room, Adviser Tashu was floating an idea where they used a proxy to show that the Emperor was "still alive"—after all, he had many body doubles. Easy enough to use one. To her surprise, they all seemed to *like* that idea. And that's when Adea got her.

And showed her the vid.

. . . at this very moment, a meeting takes place inside the walls of the satrap's palace . . .

"Someone has sabotaged us," Rae hisses. She sets her jaw and growls: "This is not known information."

"I know."

"Was it you?"

Fear travels across Adea's face like a crack in a wall. "No," she stammers. "I . . . Admiral, please, I would never—"

She thinks to press it. Reach out. Take the girl's throat. Make her confess through a collapsed windpipe. But such cruelty is beyond her right now. Adea didn't do this. No motive lines up. It makes little sense.

Who, then? Pandion? The satrap?

Someone else, someone unseen?

"Get me Isstra," Rae says. Adea nods, and ducks back in through the large red double doors leading into the dining room. Doors opulent with scrollwork and carvings of some satrap fighting off strange creatures—a nexu in one carving, a pack of feral humanoids in another. Rae stares at it and suddenly sympathizes: *I, too, am besieged.*

The doors open as she watches them. The satrap emerges, all sycophantic smiles and deferential bowing and scraping. "Yes, Admiral Sloane, please, please tell me what I can do—"

She shows him the holovid.

His eyes go wide, wide, wider as he watches it. "Oh, my."

"Show me a window that faces the front. Toward the Avenue of the Satrapy. *Now.*"

He nods, claps his hands, and with a lasso-whirl of a finger two of his attendants—young women garbed in soft, diaphanous golden scarves—follow after, feeding him small dried fruits as he walks worriedly and hurriedly forward. They go up a set of blue-tile steps, past a wall that is itself a burbling fountain, up another set of steps—these curving, and so tight that two cannot walk up them side by side. They reach a longer hallway, one lined with narrow, arrow-slit windows. "Here," he says, chewing on one of the small dark fruits nervously.

Rae walks over to one of the slit windows.

Even now, she can see Akivans gathering out front. Not a mob. Not yet. But they regard the palace as an unpleasant curiosity. Like they're trying to decide what they're seeing. Or what to do. Or maybe they're looking for a sign of what's really going on in here—already they've surely seen the Imperial ships parked along the landing ring that forms the top of the palace. And they've seen the increased stormtrooper presence, the TIE fighters swooping, the occupation of several key locations across Myrra.

The situation is a canister of fuel, stuffed with a rag, the rag lit on fire.

The rag will burn. It will burn faster than anybody likes or expects.

And when it does: *boom*.

To Adea, Rae says: "Begin to prepare the ships."

"It will take some time to calculate hyperspace jumps—"

"We can do that after we exit the atmosphere. Time is of the essence."

This meeting is over.

Time to tell the others.

INTERLUDE:

TARIS

IN THE DARKNESS, a red lightsaber rises from its hilt.

The blade gently sways—*vwomm, vwomm.* Leaving streaks of red in the black. Nearby, a fat assassin-spider dangles, its thorax glowing with a phosphorescent skull pattern. The arachnid spits venom at the red blade as the red glow moves closer. Then: The sword moves quickly.

The spider is bisected in twain with a little shriek and hiss.

Both halves plop to the floor.

The light returns to the room as a young rat-faced girl pulls back a black curtain over the window.

The wielder of the lightsaber: a long-snouted Kubaz, his eyes concealed behind gold-lensed goggles, the rest of his head swaddled in red leather scarves. He retracts the crimson blade into its hilt.

Three individuals stand before him. Two in black robes, their faces concealed. The third stands at the fore of them: a young woman. Pale. Hunched over, as if her spine refuses to keep her straight. Her hands play at the air—fingers like the legs of that spider, plucking invisible threads that perhaps only she can see.

They stand in a tenement on Taris—now, with the black sheet back from the window, this room is revealed as nothing short of a wreck. A tick-infested pile of pillows on the floor. Walls tagged with graffiti (one such piece of tagging: a stencil of a familiar Sith Lord's helmet with the phrase beneath it reading VADER LIVES). Rubble and ruin everywhere. Not much different outside: tenements stacked atop one another. Some are just shipping containers. Others are hulls from ruined spacecraft teetering precariously on top of or against each other. Rank pollution floats about: yellow like the scum on dirty water.

The Kubaz squeaks in his native tongue: "You have the credits?" The rat-faced girl translates for him, repeating his words in Basic.

"Is it really his lightsaber?" the young woman asks. Her voice is a raspy whisper, as if something is wrong in the well of her throat.

"It's the Sith Lord's laser sword, sure enough."

"May I?" she asks.

The Kubaz shakes his snout and says: "No. Not until I see the money. Money talks or Ooblamon walks."

Ooblamon's little friend, the rat-faced girl, giggles when she translates.

The pale woman looks to the other two in their dark robes. They whisper to each other. Almost as if arguing.

She turns back. "How do we know it is Vader's blade?"

"You don't. But it's a lightsaber, isn't it? And it's red. Isn't that the color you seek?"

More whispering, more arguing. A mad susurrus.

Finally, some sort of concession. The robed figures each give her a small box marked with strange sigils. She shakes them: Ooblamon the Kubaz knows the sound of credits rattling. It warms his unkind heart.

They hand over the boxes. He refuses to take them, and instead the rat-girl scurries over. "This is my co-hort and apprentice, Vermia." She takes one box in a clicking claw, and then the other. She hurries back to the corner to begin her count. Credit chattering against credit as she makes her tally.

The young woman offers her pale hand. "The . . . lightsaber, please."

"When the count is complete," Ooblamon says. He cocks his head and stares at them through his goggles. "What are you? You're no Jedi."

"We are adherents," she hisses. "Acolytes of the Be-yond."

"Fanatics of the dark side?" he asks. "Or just chil-dren who want to play with toys?"

"Judge us not, thief."

The Kubaz sniffs with his snout, a dismissive ges-ture. Vermia hurries back over and says with a chuckle: "The credits are all there."

Ooblamon goes to hand over the weapon, but as the young woman reaches for it, he yanks it back. Then he pulls back a bit of his own brown, grungy robe and shows the blaster hanging there. "You get squirrelly and think to use that laser sword on me or my cohort, this will not end well."

"We are not violent. Not yet."

The Kubaz grunts, then hands over the lightsaber.

The three strangers suddenly turn to face one an-other, holding the lightsaber among them. Whisper-ing to one another. Or to it.

The woman mutters a half-heard expression of

gratitude, then they start to hurry out the door. As they go, Ooblamon calls after:

"What do you plan on doing with that thing?"

The woman says, simply: "We will destroy it."

He laughs. "Why would you do that?"

"So that it can be returned to its master in death."

They scurry away. Outside, the sounds of Taris: a bleating horn, someone yelling, a speeder bike back-firing, distant blaster fire.

Vermia says: "Was that really Vader's weapon?"

The Kubaz shrugs.

"Who knows. And really, who cares?"

CHAPTER TWENTY-FIVE

A LINE OF SPARKS, red as a demon's eyes, runs up along the outside of the door leading into the console room of the comm station. Mister Bones stands in front of it, waiting. Humming a discordant little song—a song some maniac might think is pretty, the kind of song that sounds like wind howling through a cavern might sing. Sinjir waits, too, pistol drawn.

They'll come for us.

And then he wonders, *What then?*

Already he's alerted the Imperials that he is, indeed, still alive. They won't realize it, yet. But when all of this shakes out, someone somewhere in *some* office of the Empire will see that Officer Rapace pinged their networks with *his* name and *his* facial scan. What if they capture him?

Oh, irony of ironies—

He will likely be taken before a loyalty officer.

One such as himself.

He almost wants to laugh at that.

The line of sparks, halfway up the door now.

"Wait," Temmin says. "Wait, wait, wait. Look."

Sinjir looks. An evaporator unit hangs from the ceiling like a pregnant droid. "So? It's an evaporator. They don't use ducts we can fit through—it's just piping, isn't it? Unless you have a *molecular miniaturiza-*

tion ray handy that will magically shrink us down to hamster size, I don't think—"

"No, *look*." Temmin points to a pair of hinges. He gets onto his tippy-toes, then raps on the thing with the back of his knuckles.

It results in a hollow *bong, bong, bong.*

"It's not real," Sinjir realizes out loud.

"Right. It's a way out. Probably to the roof. They used to do rebel transmissions from this booth. My *dad* might've put this here. Or used it." Temmin jumps up, catches the metal lip of the device—his weight pulls the thing down, and it hangs off its hinges.

The welder line around the door is almost to its end.

"No time like the present," Sinjir says, and hurries over.

Up there, through the space: a ladder.

The boy was right.

They climb.

Temmin sticks his head up through a hatch. The door swings open and everything is washed out in a wave of searing white: The comm console room was so dark, and out here it's almost too bright. He pulls himself up, his eyes still adjusting. As he belly-flops onto the roof of the comm station, he can't help feeling an odd surge of pride. Inside his mind, he repeats what he told Sinjir: *My dad might've put this here.*

But then the familiar anger stomps down its foot:

Dad being a rebel is why he got caught.

And why Mom left.

And why everything fell apart.

That good feeling he had is instantly poisoned. Like

a beautiful flower sprayed with acid—it withers and rots inside him.

He looks up, then, blinking.

He hears the sound before he sees it.

A TIE fighter. He blinks again, staring up at the sky, toward the sun.

No. Not one TIE fighter. *Two* of them.

He helps haul Sinjir up—"We have to move! Incoming!"

The first TIE bears down on them like a meteor ready to roll right over them. It's then that he gets it.

Temmin knows what that fighter is here to do.

Bones hops up out of the hole—

Temmin tackles Sinjir and the battle droid. He knocks them both behind a metal fixture meant to look like the exterior mechanism of the (not-actually-working) evaporator system. They all hit the deck.

Just as the TIE fires its front cannons.

The building shakes and from the other corner of the structure there're streaks of fire and a small blooming cloud of yellow smoke. Temmin peeks his head out and sees the antenna array tilting off the roof and falling away, leaving behind a rain of electrical embers.

They killed the transmission.

He has to hope it stayed out there long enough.

And now, here comes the second TIE fighter. It starts firing at the rooftop, likely intent on bringing the whole building down. It's not a bomber, so it won't happen with one run, but those weapons at the front are no small popguns, either. A couple of passes and the top half of the comm station will be turned to flaming chunks of rubble.

He grabs both sides of Bones's head. "You got this?"

Bones says in that voice that warbles from deep to

shrill, a mechanized distortion: "CONSIDER IT DONE, MASTER TEMMIN."

The TIE cannons begin shattering the other half of the roof. Debris sprays. Fire plumes. The sound of the fighter and its guns and the explosions roars in Temmin's ears. Not just his ears. He can feel it in the back of his *teeth*. Sinjir winces, clearly feeling it, too, popping up to fire off a few futile shots at the incoming fighter—and then turning to pop shots at the stormtroopers now coming up through the escape shaft.

Bones shrieks: "ROGER-ROGER." Then the battle droid jumps up in the air, tucking arms and legs together, forming a cannonball—

And crashing through the TIE fighter's front windshield.

The TIE wibbles and wobbles in the air, careening drunkenly across the Myrran rooftops—it zigzags herkily-jerkily out of sight.

Just as the first TIE, now looping back on its return trip, begins firing its cannons. The blasts pepper the top of the building, crossing the rooftop, and coming right for them. Temmin turns and looks—there's no time to think, only time to act, but there's no other roof to which they can jump—

Sinjir points.

A third TIE has joined the fray.

It swoops in, front blasters flashing—lasers unzipping the sky.

Lasers that strike the first TIE in the side. Its hexagonal wing panel breaks off, hitting the side of the comm station. The rest of it spins off to the side, streaking along the building like a meteor—it crashes into the side of an old office building, erupting in a ground-shaking *boom*.

The third TIE—their *savior*—shrieks overhead.

Sinjir, panting, says: "I think your mother found her ride."

Temmin nods, checking himself over to make sure he's all there. *Mom really is one starcracker pilot.* No time to think about that—or her—right now. Instead he says: "We better go. They're gonna swarm us in no time."

Norra finds herself thinking about wasps.

Here, in Akiva, there exists a wasp: the redjacket. The length and width of the tip of one's thumb, the redjacket wasp is a scourge. They are mean, vicious creatures. They sting. Their stingers suck up blood. They take the blood to feed their young and use it to build their signature rust-red nests. Mostly, you find them out in the jungles, though once in a while they stray from their comfort and you find a nest under an overhang or a rooftop (at which point the common solution is just to burn the whole thing with a can of engine solvent and a flick-tip lighter, making a home-made flamethrower).

Thing is, those wasps fly a certain way. Individually, they're hard as anything to catch or kill, because they fly up, down, left, right. They can zip forward, then stop in midair and hover before zipping back the other way. (And usually that's when they go in for the sting—and one stick from a redjacket's stinger can leave your whole arm numb for an hour.)

Flying a TIE fighter reminds Norra of those wasps.

It's incredible. Such maneuverability. She can do just as the wasps do: thrust forward, then retroboost to a stop, then streak to the left or the right. On a lark she gives the whole thing a spin—literally corkscrewing the ship as she flies it over the city that was once her home.

Of course, the trade-off is this: The TIE is a suicide ship, isn't it? To get the speed and maneuverability, the Empire sacrificed safety and sanity in the rest of the design. The whole thing is brittle like a bird skeleton. Doesn't even have an ejector seat. It's not just a fighter.

In dire situations, it doubles as the pilot's grave.

Still, Norra isn't thinking about that when she takes out the other TIE fighter menacing the rooftop of the comm station. Her twin laser cannons tear the wing panel off and as it crashes, disintegrating, she thinks:

That's what you get for messing with my boy.

Norra whoops, exhilarated.

Now for the task at hand.

Ahead, through the sun-glitter haze hanging over the city, she spies the massive citadel that is the satrap's palace. Gaudy and opulent. All its towers and parapets splayed out in the asymmetry of an insane being. (Every satrap builds something else onto the palace, it seems—regardless of how well it matches the design of the rest. The result is something altogether more chaotic than intended. Beautiful, too, in its strange, slapdash way.)

Around the center dome and tower sits a ring, and around that ring are parked the familiar fins of Imperial shuttles.

Those are her targets.

Below her, her screen blinks, then flashes green.

Two bogeys on her tail. Another pair of TIE fighters, joining the fray. She thinks: *It's flashing green because it doesn't know they're enemies, does it? It reads their signature as friendly.*

She hopes they read *her* as friendly, too.

But she learns quickly the reality of that situation as both of the evil-eyes behind her open fire—muscle memory precedes proper thought (for her hands are fast even when her brain is slow) and she again spins the fighter through the air, spiraling it forward and then up as laser bolts pepper the air around her. G-forces put pressure on her temples like a crushing vise and it feels like her legs and guts are somewhere still down about a thousand meters below, and everything feels like it's going to be torn apart—

The blood rushes back into her head (or is it out of it? she can't really tell) and when she again rights the TIE, her two pursuers are now the pursued—the pair flying dead ahead of her.

She feels a surge of excitement. Her panic is buried beneath it.

Then Norra pulls the triggers on her twin flight sticks.

Green lasers cut through open air and rend the first TIE into shrapnel. The bulk of the destroyed fighter lists into the other. A flash. A great shuddering concussion of air and fire as her enemies spiral downward and disappear into the city in one final detonation.

She flies through the fading fire.

And again sets her sights on the palace ahead.

There, on the screen held vertical in Adea's hand. An incoming TIE. An enemy combatant flying it. Heading right toward the palace. Rae understands its purpose. It can't do anything to the palace. The walls are too thick. But one part is exposed:

Their ships.

Those shuttles are their lifeline.

It's too late to get their own ships back in the air. And they have no defenses, no cannons, no—

Wait.

She snatches the holoscreen out of Adea's hand and

punches up the controls for one of the three ground-to-orbit turbolaser cannons they set up across Akiva's capital city. Her assistant's eyes go wide.

"Admiral, the turbolaser isn't meant for this—"

"It's our only chance."

"It's pointed right at the palace."

Rae looks at the calculated trajectory.

It's not ideal.

But it'll have to do.

She fires.

One minute Norra is flying along, her path safe, secure, assured. And then the air lights up with blinding light and something shears the right wing panel off her own TIE, and suddenly—she's lost all control.

No, not all of it.

She's spinning, once more winding through the air, this time in an uncontrolled spiral, but she *does* have some control.

Just a little. Just enough.

She holds the flight sticks firm, locking one against the other, fighting against the spin. Her head is dizzy. Everything's gone loopy. Her guts churn and she wants to puke. *Steady. Steady.*

The distant thought reaches her:

I'm going to die.

This is it. The culmination of all she's done and all she is.

Part of her feels proud. *I've accomplished so much,* she thinks.

But then another warring thought intrudes like a rude visitor: *But I haven't accomplished so much. I have failed my son. And I failed my husband. Brentin, Temmin, I love you.*

She aims the spinning TIE right at the palace. Dead

ahead is the landing ring. The shuttles. A yacht. They're lined up *just right.*

Maybe, maybe I can take them out with me . . .

A stray, idle thought as the palace rushes forward to greet her.

I sure wish these things had an ejector seat.

CHAPTER TWENTY-SIX

THE PALACE SHAKES with the impact. The lights flicker. Dust streams down from the ceilings, where cracks appear in the smooth stone. Rae moves fast through the building. Running now, not walking. Someone calls after her. Adea. But then another voice: Pandion, too. Ahead: the staircase and doorway to the landing ring. A staircase in lapis blue and copper, ancient and elegant, beautiful in its construction— but Rae is blind to all of that.

All she sees is her pilot, Morna Kee, staggering down the steps. A line across her brow blackened with soot and dribbling blood. Rae catches her as she comes down. "Are you—?"

"I'm fine," Morna says. "Don't go up there."

"I need to assess," Sloane hisses, then hurries past her.

Again, Pandion's voice behind her. *Stay back, you prig,* she thinks.

She throws open the door. Sunlight. Bleaching everything out. The smoke catches in her nose and clings there like an infection. A merciful wind rises then, pushing some of the billowing black away, and she sees the damage done:

Three shuttles, in various states of destruction. Crassus's yacht is not here—it took off again and went to orbit, an act for which she is suddenly thankful—but at the end of the row sits a charred lump of slag:

A TIE fighter. One of their own. A suicide attack.

Easy enough to see its path through the wreckage. It cut a diagonal line across the three Imperial shuttles: smashing the back end of the first, the middle of the second, the nose and cockpit of the third. Effectively destroying each, rendering them useless.

A sound reaches her ears:

A dull roar.

She thinks: *What could that be?*

Rae steps through the smoke, past the wreckage. The landing ring shifts beneath her feet and the metal of one of the shuttles groans and bangs, but then everything is still once more. She shouldn't go farther, and yet she does—her feet urging her forward without her explicit consent.

At the edge, an old copper railing dusted with emerald patina.

She presses up against it.

The roar is the crowd below. A thin, wan crowd—

But one that is strengthening even as she looks down.

From other streets, Akivans move toward the palace. And that other sound she heard? Rocks. They're throwing rocks against the palace. None of them can hit her here—she's a hundred meters above them. They look small to her as a crowd, but as a mass: They're growing. Like a spreading cancer.

She turns around to behold the wreckage once more and she realizes:

That did it.

The fires of their shuttles burning lit the fuse.

Now the bomb is counting down—the bomb of riot, rebellion, insurgency. It is at their doorsteps.

Soon it'll be climbing up the walls. It hits her all at once: *This was engineered. This was orchestrated by someone, maybe one of our own. Maybe someone inside the satrapy. Someone has kicked over the pile of dirt to watch all the little ants spill out.*

And then, another thought:

We are trapped here now.

The ring shifts again. She jukes forward, catches herself on the railing. Hands catch her elbow, pull her back. Morna. "Admiral. Please. Back inside. Look." Her pilot points. Across the way, on the rooftop of the old capitol building—the one with the rusted tower they took out with the shuttle's cannons upon arriving here—she sees a few people climbing up there. Citizens, probably. Trying to get a look. *Or a shot.*

"Yes," Rae says. "You're right. Back inside."

Outside the cantina doors and windows, a small crowd surges, moving down the street and toward the palace. Sinjir catches a flash of white armor—the crowd carries a struggling stormtrooper past.

It worked, didn't it?

It worked better than we even imagined. The TIE fighters destroyed the antenna at the comm station, and he feared that the message hadn't gone out long enough. But then—explosions at the palace. Norra must've succeeded. That and the doctored propaganda they sent out. It worked. The city is responding. *Reacting.* All that pent-up rage? The cork has popped. Everything's foaming over now. It's not just from this one moment. Not just from the occupation. The Imperials have long toyed with planets like this one. Though never formally occupying them, they imposed tariffs and taxes on law-abiding establishments while letting the black markets and criminal syndicates go about their business as long as they tithed back to the Empire. That was one of the striking things about seeing the Imperials fighting alongside Surat Nuat's thugs: It exposed that alliance bold-facedly, revealing what everyone always suspected but few ever really knew.

Across the oka-wood bar, the Mon Cal with the droid arm slides across a bottle of something that glows green like industrial slimewaste. Sinjir gives him an arched eyebrow and Pok just shoves it forward another few centimeters as if to say, *Don't ask, just drink.*

Well, that squid-faced fellow hasn't been wrong yet.

Sinjir takes the bottle and heads to the table, where Temmin sits next to his droid. Mister Bones was here when they arrived—Pok's Place being the go-to meeting spot for the lot of them after the operation's conclusion—and the droid looked even rougher. Scuffed up. His metal scored in places. Several of his little osseous accoutrements have gone (which also means his bony jangle is no longer present). Otherwise the droid looks pretty good for having cannon-balled through the front windshield of a roaring TIE fighter.

Still, Temmin sits, chin on his folded arms, stewing. Eyes narrowed. The tip of one thumb sits thrust in the kid's mouth as he chews the nail.

Sinjir plunks down the bottle. Takes a sip, and immediately makes a face. A taste fills his mouth that is somehow both bitter and sweet. *Too* bitter and *too* sweet. And the liquid is thick. Almost gummy.

It's awful stuff.

His mouth goes a little numb.

Huh. He takes another sip anyway. Looks around

idly: The cantina is mostly empty. Just a few old salts in the back, drinking their drinks. Together but alone at the same time, somehow. Most of the crowd is outside.

"You *drink* that stuff?" Temmin says, not lifting his chin.

"I suppose I do. Not that I know what 'this stuff' is."

"Plooey-sap. Comes from one of the trees in the jungle."

Sinjir scrunches up his nose. "Well, it tastes like I'm licking the underside of a leaky droid, but I seem compelled to keep drinking it."

"More power to you."

"You're worried."

"Worried? About what?"

Duh. "Your mother."

"Whatever, Mom's fine. And if she's not, y'know. Whatever."

"Yes, you said that already. 'Whatever.'"

Now Temmin lifts his chin. His lips lift in a sneer. "What? You don't believe me?"

"I believe every boy worries about his mother just as every mother worries about her boy. My mother used to whip my back with switches she pulled from the tree in our front yard. I hated her. But I loved her and worried after her just the same because that's how sons and mothers happen to be. It is just one of the many truths of the universe."

"Well," Temmin sniffs, "*my* mother abandoned me to go fight in some dumb war. So, trust me: I don't care. *I don't care.*"

Mister Bones echoes: "HE DOES NOT CARE."

"If you say so."

"I say so. I. Do. Not. Care—" Temmin's eyes flit to the door.

Sinjir cranes his neck and sees Jas walk in. Her gaze finds them and she comes over. But there's something in her approach. The slightest hesitation. Her body language screams: *I have bad news and I do not want to deliver it.* Then the way she looks at Temmin as she steps up . . .

Oh. Oh, my. Sinjir realizes what it is even before she says it.

"Temmin," she says. "Your mother succeeded in her mission. But she didn't make it. Norra is gone."

Panic at the summit. A cacophony of competing voices like a roost full of ill-kept birds. They all stand around the grand dining table, yelling at one another about what to do next. Holoscreens are cast about the table, projecting data at various stations. Data showing surging crowds. Revealing their own casualties. Offering predictions of what comes next.

"How many TIEs do we have left?" Pandion barks. "Answer me, Admiral. How many are left on Akiva?"

Adea eases the base of one of the holoprojector disks toward Rae, and on it, a casualty report. Sloane turns it toward Valco.

"We lost five in that attack. Two at the roof of the comm station that served as the origin point for the rebel propaganda, and two from whoever was in that stolen TIE. That last fighter is the fifth. We lost half."

"Half," Pandion says with a huff. "We only have *five* short-range fighters stationed across the city?"

"Correct."

"And how many troops?"

"A single company, besides what's here in the palace."

"A hundred, hundred fifty stormtroopers? That's it?"

"And their attendant officers. Another twenty or so."

"So, one hundred and twenty Imperials for a city of—how many?"

Here, Shale speaks: "About a million."

Pandion asks the inevitable question: "Why don't we have more, Admiral? Why are we not better protected?"

Truth is, he already knows the answer to this question. They all do. Negotiating this summit into existence was quick, but took a hero's effort—sleepless nights, countless communiqués, ceaseless bickering. They exacted out each little detail, down to the food they would be served and the types of fabrics they desired in their bedsheets. They *know* why the city isn't locked down with whole battalions of stormtroopers, and yet, Pandion asks the question because he wants to whittle her authority down to splinters— she the stick, he the knife. So, she answers him:

"We couldn't have this look like a total occupation. The risk was low—"

"The risk is now considerably higher, wouldn't you say? We need more ships. We need to bring the Star Destroyers back. Recall them from the neighboring system, Admiral. Return them to orbit. We will return to our ships and make our escape."

Shale stands and throws her hands in the air—an unusual gesture for her, this physical act of exasperation. "How do you intend to make that escape? We have no ships of our own here. We are boxed into this palace by a population that has been long abused by the satrapy—"

Now it's Satrap Isstra's turn to speak up. Gone is his strident, fawning obedience. Present now: a taste of venom on his tongue. His handsome, smiling face twists into a mask of desperation. "No!" he says.

"You cannot mound this weight upon my back. I am not your pack beast here to carry your sins. I imposed the taxes the Empire demanded. I have been a loyal ally, implementing any program you wanted, and what do I get for it?" His voice goes suddenly high-pitched. A plaintive whine. "You shot a hole in the side of my palace! That turret took off the eastern-most tower—a tower that has stood tall over this palace for two thousand years."

A lie. Sloane knows that the tower the turbolaser destroyed was relatively new—built by one of the Withrafisps in the last two centuries. The design of that tower—the speckling of red brick spiraling up the side, the onion-shaped dome—matches the architecture of *that* period. Not millennia before. Sloane pounds the table with her fist. The satrap's jaw shuts.

"I will not order the Star Destroyers to return."

Mouths gape. Crassus says: "We get to vote."

"As has been noted," Rae says, "decisions like these are best left to a singular authority, not a voting body. I am the acting fleet admiral and I decide what to do with those ships."

Pandion counters: "You *will* bring them in. You must. From there we can bring in a shuttle, and the TIE fighters will give us enough cover. We must show strength. We will not merely *sneak out* and *flee* like scared ryukyu hares—we do not run from the fire. We must face it. Then, we use the Star Destroyers to dispatch bombers and we teach this city what it means to rise up against the Galactic Empire."

"Right now," Shale says, "the New Republic—"

"The *Rebel Alliance,*" Pandion says, correcting her.

"The *New Republic,*" she reasserts, "does not know what to make of this situation. They have not sent a fleet because they do not know what awaits them. And they do not want to destabilize a world that could end up as their ally. As such, they wait. Cautious. Hesitant to play too strong a hand. They have made big gains, but they are cautious gains. They are not playing a reckless game, and so neither should we, Valco."

"You craven, sniveling, soft-bellied—"

"We will use Crassus's yacht to escape," Rae says, disrupting the tired argument between the moff and the general. "That is our way out."

"What?" Crassus says. His face goes red as anger rises to his cheeks. "What did you say? I will support no such thing. That is my precious ship—the *Golden Harp*. I do not consent to this."

"And I do not care. You are not a true Imperial. You are a moneylender. A banker. There are others like you. And it would take only an Imperial writ to drain your accounts of their gold the way a swarm of redjacket wasps would drain the blood from their prey. Stand in my way, Arsin, and I will execute you myself."

Pandion whistles. "Look who has found her teeth."

Crassus pales, the blood draining from his face. "I . . . you wouldn't."

"I would. I will." She draws her blaster, points it. "Do you consent?"

"I . . ." She fires the blaster. Just above his head. He flinches, hands up and gesticulating wildly as he babbles: "Yes! Yes. By the stars, yes."

"Good. Make the call. Summon your *Golden Harp*."

Crassus nods, swallowing hard. And with that, the rest of the room goes back to tearing into one another. Pandion, though, for his part, gives Sloane a small, curious smile. She cannot dissect it. What lies behind that little grin, Sloane cannot say. Is he proud? Proud of her for asserting her authority, or proud of himself for pushing her to this point? Is he simply amused at her efforts? That smile worries her more than a scowl.

Adea leans up, whispers in her ear:

"We have a new problem."

Rae thinks: *Not another one.* "What now?" she asks in a low voice.

"You should see for yourself."

INTERLUDE:

HYPERSPACE

STARS STRETCHED INTO SPEARS, spears flung through the open black past the *Millennium Falcon* as it punches a hole through hyperspace.

Han Solo scratches at the weeks-long beard growth that's come up over his cheeks. It itches even still, and he makes faces as he scratches.

Chewie growls at him and points.

"Yeah, yeah, now I really *am* some scruffy scoundrel. I grow this face pelt long enough, maybe they'll think I'm you." He gives the Wookiee a smirk, and Chewie rumbles a response. "Okay, relax, big guy, nobody's going to confuse me with you. You're like a walking tree covered in hair."

Chewie leans back in the copilot seat, and the streaking starlines reflect in his eyes. He's bored. And a bored Wookiee is a dangerous thing. Last system they were in—Ord Mantell out here in the Mid Rim— Chewie got to messing around with the *Falcon*'s navigation system, trying to chase down a glitch that had been screwing up the hyperspace drive. He fixed it, so great. But then the guns stopped working—which, of course, they only discovered when they were ambushed by a trio of Krish marauder-ships. They got some serious char on their vector plates and hoverpads—almost didn't get out of there.

Still. It's nice, in a way, being out here with just Chewie. He misses Leia and Luke—even Lando, though he'd never say that out loud—something fierce, but being out here with his old pal reminds him of his younger days. Him, the Wookiee, and the *Falcon*. No responsibilities besides protecting their own tails—and, of course, getting rich. (Which, a small voice reminds him, never happened.)

"All right, coming up out of hyperspace," he says, reaching for the throttle to disengage. And as he eases it back, the starlines shorten and there's that dizzying moment. The one that's never gone away no matter how many jumps they've made, the one that makes him feel like his brain has been hurled through space while his guts are a dozen parsecs behind. Then the planet swells into view ahead of them:

Dasoor.

Another on the list of lawless places: an unruly world thick with thieves, run by gangs (who are in turn run by a crime cartel), and powered by slaves.

Too vile even for Solo in his younger days. Thieves he can truck with. Slaves—well, that sets the coals in his stomach to a hot, volcanic burn.

Chewie warbles and growls, and Han answers him: "Plan's the same as it's been." Same as it was on Ord Mantell, Ando Prime, Kara-bin, and all the rest. He affixes the cybernetic implant over his eye—a telescoping heliodor lens that, in fact, doesn't work and is totally fake. That plus the scruff and the ugly aviator cap he dons seem like enough of a disguise to make sure the people down there don't know him at first glance. When Chewie roars in protest, he nods.

"I know, pal, I know. I'd rather have you there with me, too, but if there's one thing that's gonna give us away, it's a smuggler walking around with one of the few dozen liberated Wookiees. But we gotta find the Empire's supply lines, and that means me going down there all by my lonesome and kicking up some dust and seeing what it smells like. You just . . . stay close in the *Falcon* in case things go to garbage."

The most recent whispers are that the Empire—after losing some of its traditional supply lines and ships over the last couple of months—has been tightening ranks around some of the criminal organizations they quietly supported during the last decades. Han's been going down, asking questions, getting into the occasional (fine, *more* than occasional) bar fight, and seeing if anything shakes out.

So far, it hasn't.

Chewie barks a sharp yip and Han agrees: "Yeah, I hope Wedge is having a better time with his mission, too. Let's get planetside and—"

The comm crackles. Above it, a shimmering blue hologram appears.

Han laughs and Chewie waves.

"Well," he says. "Look what's come crawling up out of the space waves."

The woman projected by hologram puts a cocky tilt to her hips. "Hey there, you old scoundrel."

"Old?" He feigns distaste. "Imra, that hurts me. That hurts me right in my heart." He puts on that winning smile. "I'll never get old."

"Think Leia will feel the same way?"

"Now, that's a low blow."

"You could ditch the princess, you know. Shake off the costume of a law-abiding, upstanding citizen and come back to the rogue's life."

"Imra, did you call just to taunt me, or you got something for me?"

"We've got an opportunity with a very small window."

Chewie gurgles and Han agrees: "Imra, like you said: I'm out of that life, so whatever it is you're bringing to me—"

She disappears and a new holo-image pops up: a planet.

Chewie, agitated, stands and roars, shaking his fists and knocking loose the stabilizer bar above his head—the *Falcon* suddenly shakes and shudders, and Han has to quickly reach up and reset the stabilizers. He's about to tell his old friend to calm down, relax, whatever it is that has the big fella worked up is—

Then it hits him.

The planet.

It's Kashyyyk.

It's Chewie's *home*.

A planet whose Wookiees are still in thrall to the Empire. Chewbacca was once a slave like the others: shackled, half-starved and half-mad, his fur matted, he'd worked to cut down the beautiful wroshyr trees for lumber and farm food that was once theirs, in order to feed the Imperial army. Wookiees were used across the galaxy, too, shipped away to serve as slave labor in mines and in building structures like the Death Stars. Sometimes, they even used the poor furballs as science experiments: ripping them open to test out medicines and weapons.

"Chewie, it's all right, pal, it's all right." Han pats his friend on the shoulder, helps him back into the chair. The Wookiee's muscles ripple under his fur, and his lips curl back to reveal his teeth. His breath comes in ragged gasps. To Imra, Han says: "Whaddya mean, a window of opportunity?"

"The Wookiee planet's still on lockdown. The Empire doesn't want to give it up, but their ranks are cut. Normally, ships come in and come out and they trade stormtroopers and officers, but the actual weight of their presence never changes. Except now, for a time, it's gonna change."

"I don't follow."

"They're gonna do . . . who can say? A changing of the guards or something. Or they need ships for some other planet or some other—I really don't know, Solo. The details are fuzzy, but what we *do* know is, the ships that are leaving won't immediately be replaced. Which means we have a few days."

"When?"

"Now."

Chewie raises his head back and howls.

"Now?" Han leans forward in his chair, suddenly agitated. "Like, today?"

"Almost. Clock is about to start ticking in the next day-cycle."

"The Alliance—the New Republic, whatever they are—they got me on this thing. I've got a responsibility. I can't just change the plan and go off half-cocked . . ." And he knows what the New Republic will say. They have a strategy. They won't divert attention to Kashyyyk, not yet. He's asked. More than once.

Chewie is giving him this look. Not even making a sound. The Wookiee's chest is rising and falling.

And it hits Han: The words coming out of his mouth don't sound like him. Being out here, though, with Chewie, it's made him feel like he used to. They'd just go places. Do whatever they wanted. Follow their noses to drink and contraband and stacks of credits and whatever good or bad deeds came along.

A fire lights in Han's belly.

It's time to do this. He tells Imra: "You owe me big, you remember that?" From that time he pulled that Star Destroyer off her tail (and got himself raided in the process). "Don't say you don't remember—"

"I remember, I remember, it's why I'm here. You said if I ever heard anything about Wookiee-world to tell you. Here I am, telling you."

"That's not enough," he growls. "You gotta do more."

She hesitates. "How much more?"

"Get everybody. Every right-thinking scamp, scoundrel, slicer, smuggler—anybody who owes me a favor. Anybody who hates the Empire like we do."

"That's not as long a list as you'd like."

"Fine. Offer them immunity. If they want their records clear, let 'em know the New Republic is adding names to a list. Full pardons."

"Is that true?"

"Sure is," he lies. It's not true. He's never heard it. But he'll make it true. Somehow. He turns to Chewbacca: "Hey, pal. You still know how to contact the other refugees? Roshyk, Hrrgn, Kirratha, and them?" Group of a half-dozen Wookiees who escaped Kessel and got away from the Empire when nobody else could. Group of the meanest, hairiest brutes. They're mercenaries now, and they don't have much care in them when it comes to the politics of the New Republic, but they damn sure will care about liberating their home.

Chewie nods and growls in assent.

"Good. Get 'em together. And, Imra, you get the rest. Tell them to meet us outside Warrin Station. Like, now. Hell, *yesterday*. We don't need the Alliance or the Republic. We do this our way."

The Wookiee pumps his long arms in triumph.

Imra gives her word, and then she's gone.

"We don't have any plan, pal," he says.

The Wookiee growls.

"We're making this up as we go."

Chewie nods and ululates.

"Good. It's like the old days, buddy."

Chewie grabs him with those big arms and shakes him like a cup of dice.

Han grins and laughs and tries not to get crushed. "C'mon, Chewie. Set new coordinates. It's time to get you home."

CHAPTER TWENTY-SEVEN

WEDGE STAGGERS DOWN THE HALLWAY of the satrap's palace. Pain pulls at him like heavy chains. Fatigue is sucking at him, and no matter how fast his heart is beating, no matter how much adrenaline he feels coursing through him, his bones still tell him one thing: *Give up, lie down, give in.*

The power failed only minutes ago—and when it did, his shackles fell off like they were a child's toys. Now he's free.

Or close to it.

Voices nearby. Alarmed voices. Followed by the sound of marching, clattering feet. *Stormtroopers.* Wedge winces and tucks himself into the nearest alcove—a narrow space with a ceramic pot that serves as home to one of the planet's jungle orchids. He squeezes in next to the pot and tries to still his breathing.

Footsteps closer, closer.

The chatter of troopers: "The admiral thinks it was some kind of distraction."

The other: "Or maybe they just don't want us to leave."

"Who is *they*?"

"Does it even matter?"

Their voices, louder now. Until they're walking past.

Walking past, until they stop. And they stop right by the alcove. Only a handful of steps away from Wedge hiding in the shadows of this interstitial space. He tenses his muscles. Readies himself for the attack—

No. It won't work. He's too hurt. On any other day, if he were healthy, he could take out a pair of these bucketheads. Slam their helmets together, grab one of their blaster rifles, head for the door. But they'll overpower him in this state. They'll put the hurt on him.

Instead, he remains. Quiet as the stars.

The stormtroopers look around. They comm in: "Nothing on the third floor. Moving to the fourth."

They keep on walking.

Wedge lets out a gentle sigh of relief as their footsteps recede.

His muscles ache. His leg almost gives out—his knee buckling suddenly, and when it snaps back per reflex, he nudges the ceramic pot.

It rattles and wobbles. Echoing in the hall.

The footsteps stop.

No, no, no.

One of the troopers asks the other: "You hear something?"

"Back there."

They start to approach once more.

Looks like I have no choice. It's fight or get found. Survive at any cost or get thrown back into shackles. He tenses up, planting his feet in the best fighting stance he can manage—and his foot presses back on that pot again. The pot slides back, the grinding of stone against stone.

And when it does, the wall in the alcove behind him opens up.

A thin, narrow door. A secret passage.

It's now or never. Wedge slides past the pot into the darkness of the open space. The footsteps come closer and on the other side, Wedge sees a stone button jutting from the wall. He slams it with the heel of his hand and the door closes behind him—just as he catches a glimpse of white armor.

Temmin sits, shaking. He feels woozy. Clammy and gut-sick. He tries to keep it together when Jas tells him that his mother's TIE fighter—the one that saved his life only an hour before—crashed into the satrap's palace.

They try to console him. Even Bones puts a metal claw on his shoulder. But he brushes them all off. Tells them he'll be fine.

He blinks back tears and turns away so they can't see. He faces the wall, jaw locked tight, hands trembling underneath the table.

The thing is, he's always known this day was coming. His mother, out there in the galaxy somewhere. Fighting for the rebels. Making supply runs through Imperial territory. Every day he didn't speak to her (which was most days) was a day he knew she might be dead. Her ship, floating out there. Her body, still strapped into the seat of whatever hunkajunk scrapboat the rebels had sitting in some dingy hangar. That thought sometimes came to him as nightmares. Her chasing after him, her eyes dead, her mouth hanging open. Or Imperials coming to his door to tell him they'd killed her. Or a coffin showing up at his door one day with her in it.

And now that day is come. Just after they'd made contact once more.

As Jas goes on about how the mission isn't scrapped,

about how they still have to do the job, all Temmin can do is navigate the all-too-familiar feelings churning inside him like a storm-tossed sea.

Anger is the king of those seas. Anger at her for leaving him and giving herself to a cause that was always more important than him. And anger at himself for being so selfish, and for not making better use of the time he had with her when she was here. Anger for everybody, in fact: anger at Sinjir and Jas for dragging them both into this, anger at Surat for being Surat, anger for the New Republic and the Galactic Empire and—

The sound of chair legs skidding against the floor.

He turns as the others gasp.

A woman sits down in the chair at the end of the table, and pulls back the veil that obscures her face.

"Mom," he says, his voice small, so small.

Her side is scraped up—and her face is dirty and a little bloody, too.

"You . . . crashed," Jas says.

Norra shrugs. "Turns out, TIE fighters have an ejector seat after all."

Temmin scrambles up over the table, knocking Sinjir's plooey-sap bottle to the ground. He barely notices. All he cares about right now is throwing his arms around his mother. She returns the hug.

It lasts a long while, though he suddenly realizes not long enough.

The power outage, Rae thinks. When the TIE fighter slammed into the palace, taking out their shuttles, the power flickered on and off for a few seconds. And apparently, that's all it took.

Because now, their prisoner is gone. Wedge Antilles is loose in the palace. The magnacuffs securing him failed when the power did. And an old building like this doesn't have backup reserves. No off-site battery, no supplementary generator.

"This is not good," Rae says, stating the obvious.

"We'll find him," Adea says, though her voice does not convey confidence. "I'll put the troops on it."

"Good," Rae says. Adea leaves the room and the admiral picks up the head of the medical droid. Dispatched by Antilles, probably.

This adds up to one more problem. A big one. This entire *summit* has been problems coupling with other problems to beget *whole new* problems. A mating tangle of errors and cock-ups. Fragged from sundown to sunup.

She was told that this was a bad idea. But Rae insisted. She cleaved to that idea, the one oft spoken by Count Denetrius Vidian: *Forget the old way.* She embraced that idea time and time again, because the old way had earned the Empire nothing but its unintended obsolescence. A new way forward, she decided, was what would heal the Empire and save the galaxy. That's what would secure a proper peace before chaos grew, renewed, from the seeds cast about by the destruction of the second Death Star.

But now she's not so sure. Perhaps the old way is the only way. Assertive control. Authoritarian strength. The steel fist in a black glove.

Sloane focuses.

She has to find Antilles. Again.

The passage is wide enough for one person—a stark difference from the grand hallways of the palace, hallways large enough to accommodate a line of guards, maybe even a couple of speeders if you could fit them through the door. This is smaller. Intimate. A passage for the satrap—or the satrap's guests.

It's all new to him, even now. Wedge isn't exactly part of the upper crusties of the galaxy. He grew up getting his hands dirty at the fuel depot and working local farms in his spare time. But just the same, it makes a kind of sense, this passage: Certainly the satrap would want a way to move unseen throughout the palace. Unburdened by advisers or dignitaries wanting this, that, or the other thing. And Wedge always heard that the cities of Akiva were riddled with secret passages, both aboveground and beneath it.

The big question is: Now what?

He's stopped to catch his breath long enough. As he slides down the passage, blue crystalline lights rise to a slow glow as he approaches. And when he moves past, they dim once more. Lighting his way three meters at a time. A beautiful, if eerie, effect.

Sometimes he passes small slits through which proper light shines—the light of the hot day outside the palace's cool walls. Those glimpses of light feel like freedom. It gives him hope, but it's agonizing, too.

"So close," he mutters to himself.

But then—he turns a sharp corner and sees. A beam of light with great substance. Shining through an old window, the glass warped with time.

It's not a big window.

But it's big enough. He could fit through it. If he breaks it, he could clamber through to the other side and—

He looks through the distorted pane and sees the drop.

Three stories up. And not three stories like in some small Corellian schoolhouse, but three *palace* stories. It's fifteen, twenty meters to the ground.

Maybe climbing would be an option. Or, if there's one window here, there might be others farther down. If the passage continues on . . .

The realization settles into his bones.

He could leave. He might be able to make it work. But then what? He goes out into the city. Hurt. Maybe he makes it, maybe he doesn't. Maybe they recapture him in an hour, or ten, or after a few days. What will he change? The occupation has happened. Something big is going on here in this palace, *right now.* Running away might save his life.

But would it save the New Republic?

No. His only chance is to stay here. To remain in the palace and learn what's happening—or, at the very least, find a way to send out a communication to Ackbar and the others.

He looks out the window one last time.

So. Close.

Then he keeps on moving.

Norra takes a moment to appreciate the reunion. She's tired, after all, and frankly just wants to soak it all in. Her body aches all the way down to the marrow of her bones. Every time she blinks, she pictures the palace rushing up to meet her. She remembers her hands reaching out to brace herself against the console (a dumb idea, because did she somehow think that would soften the crash?). Her palm mashed buttons.

One of those buttons was the ejector.

Next thing she knew—she was up and out, the TIE smashing into and rolling across the three shuttles. Her chute deployed late, too late, and a hard wind whipped up and yanked her to the right. Then she was down on the ground, dragged across it—the sleeve of her arm torn to tatters, her skin roughed up and scraped raw.

So, for a moment, she takes the hug and the smiles from the two people who are relative strangers to her but who now feel at least a little bit like friends, if not family: the bounty hunter and the ex-Imperial.

Even her son's crazy-eyed droid says: "I AM GLAD YOUR EXISTENCE HAS NOT BEEN REDUCED TO SCATTERED ATOMS, MASTER TEMMIN'S MOM."

She laughs. They all do. She pulls Temmin to her side and puts her arm around his waist as he stands next to her.

"I'm glad I'm alive, too," she says. But she feels it: The moment is over. It has to be. She darkens her brow and says with grave seriousness: "But we still have work to do. We have to get into the palace and I think I know how."

INTERLUDE:

CORUSCANT

IT IS JAK'S THIRTEENTH BIRTHDAY.

The young boy—no, the young *man*—needs a birthday present. Not that he has anyone around to buy it for him. But he's sure his father would've wanted him to have the very best.

He walks through the shattered conduits of 1313: Coruscant's most infamous underworld level, a dungeon so deep that the world above has forgotten about it. He walks past a pair of pale, wan Er'Kit scraping fungus from the walls and greedily sucking the spongy mess. He passes by a spider-armed Xexto pulling wires out of a dented panel, feeding them into a charger full of plump, buzzing batteries—the alien chatters irritably as Jak walks past: a warning not to attempt to plunder the spoils of stolen electricity. And there, past that, around the bend—

A pair of guards. A rough-looking ale-bellied human with food stuck in his beard, and a bigger, even fatter Kerkoidan. The Kerk stares out past a pair of blood-pink tusks. As Jak approaches, the Kerk shows the blaster at his hip. In Basic, the alien mutters: "Keep moving, rat."

"I'm no rat," Jak says, summoning courage. "I'm a buyer."

The Kerk pulls the blaster—it's not a real threat yet. His movement is slow, languid, the motion of a confident bully. "I said—"

Jak fumbles with the card.

It's matte black.

The ink on it is red—and it glows.

"Here," Jak says.

The human's eyes go wide. "A kid with a card."

"I'm no kid. It's my birthday."

"Happy birthday, skidstain," the Kerk says. "All right, you can go in."

The bearded man raps on the door. It hisses open.

Inside, the one Jak seeks: the horned Iktotchi scumlord, Talvee Chawin, aka the Thorn. Named maybe because he's got one horn broken, and the second horn loops down around under his chin, and then barbs outward like the warning thorn of a poisonous plant.

But maybe because he's been a thorn in the side of the Empire.

"You," the Thorn says. "You're the kid."

"I'm not . . ." *Oh, never mind.* "Yeah, it's me."

"I didn't think you'd ever show."

"Your friend gave me the card."

"But what cause does a boy like you have to use it?" The Iktotchi crime lord steps up from around his half-circle couch and approaches the boy. He licks the air. "You don't belong down here. You belong up there."

"I do. You're . . . right. But right now *up there* doesn't belong to me."

A smile curls at the crime lord's lips. "It belongs to them."

The Empire.

Jak continues: "I saved your woman from police custody."

"She's not my woman. Nobody owns Lazula."

"She works for you."

"She works *with* me."

"Fine. Whatever. I saved her. She gave me the card. Now here I am."

"The card, the card." He puffs and pops his pale lips. "Yes. It's almost as if you knew what you were doing, saving her." He turns one of his dark eyes toward Jak. "One even wonders if you set her up in the first place."

On this, Jak stays silent. He tries not to quake in his boots.

But then the scumlord claps his big hands together and waggles his pointed fingers. "Either way, I admire your *take-charge* attitude. You give me the card, I'll give you a birthday present. But it's a present that comes with a price tag, as all presents do. This price is not just another year added onto your life—the usual price for another year on this world—but something bigger. Longer. A different life. A life with me."

"I . . ."

"You can go. Think about it. Talk to your family. Ask your house gods. But that is my condition. Lazula already told me what you want, and I know what I want as recompense."

"I have no family." He has only a jar of ash with his father's name on it. And as for house gods . . . they never had those. Dad never believed. "I saved Lazula. That should be enough."

"It's enough for me not to gut you like a pipe-weasel."

". . . oh."

"Yes. Oh. You want the weapon you seek, you join the team."

"I'm in."

Those two words, spoken without hesitation—a lack of hesitation that surprises even him.

The Iktotchi smiles. "Good. Then you shall have your weapon. Why do you need it? What is your plan?"

I'm going to knock out all the power to Coco-Town. But he doesn't say that. He doesn't explain how the Anklebiter Brigade—kids younger than him fighting for the rebels—know all the bolt-holes and tunnels in that part of the city. How they know one such access port hidden in the back of old, defunct Dex's Diner—and how if one were to sneak into and through that tunnel, one could theoretically plant an EMP device underneath the Imperial front lines, knocking out their power. Their eyes. Their ears. Their cannons.

All he says is, "It's my birthday, but really, it's a present for the Empire. A cake I'm baking them." *And when the power is all out and they're fumbling around in the dark, I'm going to pop up out of nowhere and put a blaster shot right in Commander Orkin Kaw's back.* Then he will finally have his vengeance against the man who took his father from him. Because the battle—this war—still rages. And Coruscant is not yet won.

CHAPTER TWENTY-EIGHT

ADEA HURRIES along the long hallway, her feet echoing on the tile floors. She stares down at the screen in her hand, pulling up maps of the satrap's palace, trying to figure out where the captive may have gone. Ahead, a quartet of stormtroopers intersects her, then keeps moving down a perpendicular hallway. To the side, a few serving girls hide in an alcove, watching, waiting, frightened.

In the quiet, if she listens, Adea can hear the sounds of the crowd outside. A dull rush, like blood in the ears. She wonders how long it'll be before someone breaches the walls. Maybe even clambering up through the broken tower, the one shattered by the laser turret.

No time to worry about that.

Focus on the present problem, she thinks.

The palace map hovers in the air before her, a small holograph. She splays her fingers out and the map grows larger, and she touches an area to zoom in. The captive pilot had to have left the room and then—? No ductwork to speak of. Everything is open and obvious. Big halls and staircases. The problem isn't that everything is open, the problem is that the palace is *so large*. It would take her a full day just to walk every centimeter of it—up, down, all around. He could be hiding anywhere.

And what's this? Here. A fragment of a passage behind the walls. Flickering. A secret passage. Or the start of one.

Adea realizes: They're dealing with an incomplete map. The satrap has furnished them with a map that fails to show the clandestine passages—

Movement from her right.

Someone runs fast, catches her shoulder, spins her around—

She cries out as the small blaster she keeps in the holster right at the base of her spine is snatched away.

The captive stands only a meter away, with her pistol in his hand. Captain Wedge Antilles. His hair a muss. Eyes unfocused. His pallor is the color of ash, greasy and slick with sweat.

"That holoscreen," he says. "I need it."

"No," she says. Lifting her chin. Trying to look tough.

"See this blaster? I need that screen. And I need you to open comm channels. You can do that, can't you?"

Her mouth forms a flat, resolute line. "No."

"You're lying."

"What if I am?"

He laughs. Exasperated. Tired. He's in pain. He says, "I want you to think about this really hard. All this? The Empire? It's over. This is the end. You help me and I won't forget that. Nobody here has to know. Say I overpowered you. You don't look like a soldier. Or an officer. Do the smart thing. Help me. Give me that screen."

Hesitantly, she nods.

Whimpering, she leans forward, starts to hand him the screen.

He reaches for it.

Adea sneers, and turns the screen toward him, sliding her thumb along the side to jack up the brightness all the way so that the projector lights shine right in his eyes. He shields them, crying out—

Adea doesn't run. She thinks: *This is my moment. I capture him. I earn favor with Sloane and the others. I fix her mistake. I'm a hero.*

She lunges in, knees him in the gut. Her hands lash out, catch his wrist, and she gives it a twist—she's practiced in self-defense, having trained in the Imperial martial arts: a combination of Zavat, *echani,* and good-old-fashioned ICE—Imperial Combat Exercises, the same training that every stormtrooper and officer gets. The blaster drops out of the pilot's hand.

But Wedge, he's fast. Even in his condition. His other hand stabs out, catches the dropped blaster. She drives her head forward, catching him right in the nose with the flat of her skull—

Crunch.

He cries out.

The blaster goes off.

And pain fires through her. Adea staggers back. In her left leg, a hole from the blaster smokes. Wisps of smoke coil upward from the wound. Her whole leg goes numb and she tumbles to the floor.

The rebel scum says: "I'm sorry. I am."

Then he scoops up the holoscreen and hobbles off.

Adea cries out, calling for help, screaming that the interloper is here. And then she just crumples up and cries because she failed. Her chance to do right by the Empire has gone so very wrong.

Jas stands at the doorway to Temmin's shop. The journey here was not an easy one, though it should've been. Akivans stream past. Some of them are carrying signs.

On the way here, she saw an effigy of the satrap. Out there, right now: a clumsy scarecrow that looks like the dark Imperial enforcer Darth Vader. Someone sets it on fire and it burns. Black smoke rising from underneath, fire consuming the Sith lord scarecrow.

This city is a keg of cordylleum about to go *boom*.

She didn't make this happen, but she and the others definitely measured out the fuse and handed out matches.

Part of her is proud: This is her operating at a much higher level. This is Jas wielding an entire city population as a weapon against her target. She's used to manipulating people, but this? This is magnified. This is something sublime. The other side of it is, she's so used to working alone. Auntie Sugi always had a crew, not to mention a soft spot for the downtrodden. Farmers and slaves and fools.

Jas always figured that for weakness. Maybe it wasn't.

She looks behind her. Inside the shop, Norra and Sinjir work together. The boy, Temmin, had to make a side trip: He said he didn't keep his maps in the shop, just in case. Had to go to his "hidey-hole nook-and-cubby" (his words, not hers) to get them. So he and his lunatic droid went off.

I'm using these people to accomplish my goals. That's what this is, isn't it? They're not her crew. They're tools, same as any hydrospanner or Harris wrench. That's what she tells herself to harden against their loss. Because smart credits say that someone won't survive this mission. They already almost lost Norra. Another will fall.

She tries to ignore how that makes her feel.

She tries to ignore that it makes her feel anything at all.

This is a job. You hold no allegiance to the New

Republic or to this particular pack of freaks and devi-ants. They are not your people. You are not their people. Get the work done, get paid, get out.

That's what her head tells her.

But why does her heart tell her something else?

"Here we go," Norra says, bringing up a box and plunking it down on the table.

Sinjir leans over, sees what she's bringing up, then backpedals away. "That is an *entire box* of thermal detonators."

"I didn't think they were snow globes."

"Can I trust you not to blow us up? You handle those things like a dockworker dropping off a case of potted bantha meat."

She laughs. He frowns as she sizes him up and says: "You weren't a soldier, were you?"

"All are soldiers in service to Empire," he says wryly.

"Uh-huh. I mean, front-line soldier. Gun up. Taking blaster fire. Look—thermal detonators don't go off until you activate them." She picks up the box and gives it a shake. He winces, waiting to be blown to his constituent molecules. "They don't go boom if you jostle them. I could kick one and it wouldn't go off. Until you prime them, these things are basically just shiny rocks."

He clears his throat. "You'll forgive me if I stay a few meters away from that box of 'shiny rocks' at all times, then."

"Just trust me: We're safe." But now she stops and folds her arms. He can see she's got something on her mind.

"Go on. Say it. Unburden your soul."

"I . . ."

"Spill it, Norra."

"You can trust me. Can I trust you?"

"With thermal detonators?"

"With my life."

"Oh. That." He arches his eyebrow so high, he expects it's hovering above his hairline. "You mean because I was an Imperial."

"The Empire doesn't do betrayal very well. Its people are loyal because they know what happens if they're not. I'm your enemy. And you're mine. That kind of thing isn't easy to shake."

He snaps his fingers. "See there? You're right, but you're also wrong. Those loyal to the Empire are loyal because they know what will happen to them if they betray it. That much is true. And do you know why that is, Norra Wexley? That's because of *me*. I was a loyalty officer. Are you aware of the responsibilities of an Imperial loyalty officer?"

"I confess that I'm not."

"Oh, it's a truly charming role. I was trained to sniff out weakness in my cohorts. I learned how to read body language, how to detect lies, how to use people against one another, all in order to discover where my own people had committed trespasses against the Empire. Anything from small breaches of conduct to outright treachery against the throne. I was the shadow they couldn't shake. You put me in a base or battle station or office and they knew they were on notice. I'd scare up what they'd done like a hunter flushing prey from the brush. And I'd hurt them to earn a confession and correct the errors. Oh, it wasn't just physical pain I caused, though that was certainly a part of it. It was emotional pain. Can I tell you a story?"

"Temmin's not yet returned, so—have at it."

He leans back against a table. As he tells the story,

his long nimble fingers gesture along with it. "Most of the people I hurt were people I didn't much care for. Some were brutes, others were cowards, and all of them were people I was happy to hobble on behalf of the Emperor. But that wasn't always the case. Take, for example, young Gunnery Officer Rilo Tang. Rilo: an eager officer. Eyes bright like polished credits. A beautiful man. Pretty like a sunrise. Sweet like a jif-cake. And *sneaky* like a *monkey-lizard*."

"I don't follow."

"He was a thief, you see."

"What did he steal?"

Sinjir laughs and cocks his head. "Well, that's the thing. Nothing particularly important. It was a compulsion of his, I suspect. Grabby hands picking up anything that wasn't nailed down. Mostly he stole the personal effects of others. Silly things. Holopics and ID tags and—by the stars, one time I remember he stole a private's pair of shoes. Why do that?"

Norra narrows her eyes. "I'd ask the same. Why?"

"Best guess given his psych profile? Parents often sent their troubled children to the Imperial academies. An act meant to be corrective, as they assumed we could shape their sloppy, insubordinate progeny into something resembling a proper galactic citizen. The reality was often that those types washed out. Forcibly so. The Empire wanted its own heroes, not its own freak show. I suspect Rilo was like that."

"What happened to him?"

"We warned him. *I* warned him. Again and again. And then one day he stole something from a moff—a ring. A ring the moff said was personal to him, meaningful, but I realized had encoded information in its scrollwork, though that's a story for another day. So I was forced to . . . deal with Rilo in order to solicit his confession."

There. That look on Norra's face. Up until now she'd been following along with curiosity, but suddenly: That look falls away like bark off a dead tree. What's left is a cold, empty stare. One of horror.

"You killed him," she says.

"No. Oh, no, no. You misread me. I wasn't the executioner. I was the confessor. The secret police. I found the evidence, and then someone else signed the warrant and someone else beyond that pushed you out of the air lock. Or hanged you or put you in front of a firing squad, or, or, or. But to elicit that confession, I had to break many bones on this beautiful boy's body. I don't know if they killed him. I heard rumors he ended up working the trash compactors. What matters is that his face would never look the same. His beauty, his vigor? Gone. And that was my fault."

"You were a bad man."

"Still am, maybe, though I'm trying to do better. But that's not why I'm telling you this story. The reason I'm telling you this is that you think you're my enemy, and that's not true, not at all. The Empire is my enemy. The Empire has always been my enemy. I hunted my own kind. I hurt them. I was made to doubt them, to see the weakness in them. And I saw *so much* weakness and ruination. In them." *And in myself.* "They were my enemy then and remain my enemy now. I've just scrapped the uniform."

"So, you're with us now? You're a rebel?"

That thought twists inside of him. He is, isn't he? A rebel. He's turned like milk past its time. Gone to the *other side.* And why? Because he almost died there on Endor? Because looking at all that wreckage jarred him? Changed him? What a curious reason to desert your post. It can't be that simple. It can't be that *com-*

plete. He tells himself that it's temporary. That this crisis of conscience will one day resolve itself.

He lifts his chin and stares down his nose at her. He says: "I'm not with them, but not with you, either. I'm with me."

"I don't trust people who are only in it for themselves."

He shrugs and offers a sad smile. "Then you shouldn't trust me."

Everything's gone supernova. Jom Barell can see that. TIE fighters blowing each other up overhead. The city surging all around him. He hides in the sliver-sized alleyway between two buildings—an old kaffa shop and a rotten-walled tenement—and watches it all unfold. The anger. The chanting. Rage at the Empire. Fury for the satrapy. An Akivan resurrection: rebirth blooming bright in the fires of revolution.

Up until now, he had a goal: Get to a comm station, find a way to report in. He could hack it, or force the Imperials to give it up.

But all these people around him? This small rebellion unfolding before his very eyes? Well, that puts him in the fighting spirit.

He thinks back to that turbolaser turret, blasting apart whoever was in that rogue TIE fighter. That thing's a danger.

So, Jom changes his orders. Time for a new target.

Forget the comm station.

He plans on taking the turret. Single-handedly. Or the likelier result: He'll die trying. But if he wasn't willing to die for what he believes in, he wouldn't have joined the Rebel Alliance in the first fragging place.

* * *

Temmin's back now. All of them gather downstairs in the shop's cellar, and he has the maps of the city's subterranean passages spread out across a couple of weapons crates.

"A flimsiplast map," Sinjir says. "How quaint."

Norra shushes him. She admits it sounds a bit sharp, a bit too . . . *motherly*. (And her feelings about him ricochet around the room of her mind like a stray blaster bolt. She wants to trust him. But something about him rubs her wrong. Could he betray them? Would he?) Still, it works. Sinjir quiets down and Norra leans in.

"Look, this is our way into the palace. The tunnels connect all parts of the city. The access points have long been walled off—"

Temmin interrupts: "Yeah, which also means they've walled off the way into the palace."

"Maybe not," she says. "Everybody here has heard the rumors of how the satraps sneak in and out of the palace. This might be how. And even if it is walled off—that's why we bring the detonators."

The bounty hunter nods. "I like it." Norra feels an odd surge of pride, there. Jas seems a hard one to please. "It gets us off the streets and out of the way of the rebellion. Plus away from the prying eyes of both the Empire and any of Surat's men. This works. And that's our doorway in?" Jas points to the secret door behind the valachord.

"Yeah," Temmin says. "But I gotta say, I *don't* like this plan. It sucks. It sucks the fumes from a broken speeder bike. It sucks the vapor from the hindquarters of a gassy eopie. It sucks—"

"Evocative," Sinjir interrupts. "You should've been a poet."

"I'm just saying, look. This map? It's not gonna be totally accurate. This is hundreds of years old."

Norra says, "But you've explored the area. You'll be our guide. I trust you, Temmin." She offers a warm smile. To her surprise, he gives one back.

"Okay, *yeah,* I have, and the map has been wrong a lot of the times. Plus, I didn't go that far. If we're going all the way to the palace, we have to pass by the old droid factory."

"Which is where you got a lot of your droid parts to sell. Right?"

". . . not exactly. I picked scrap from the garbage pits down there. Holes full of junk from the factory. I never went to the factory itself."

Jas asks: "Why not?"

He hesitates, but then says:

"Because it's haunted."

A moment where they all share looks.

Sinjir cannot contain himself and finally bursts out laughing. "Haunted? By what? Droid ghosts?"

Norra elbows him hard in the ribs. He *oof*s.

"I don't know," Temmin says. "I don't know! That's just the story. That's the story of why they sealed it all up. It was haunted, so they sealed it all up. You know how many people have gone missing down there?"

"They went missing because they didn't have a map," Norra says. "They probably got lost, Temmin. Or never went missing at all and are just part of the stories. Spooky stories from some jungle scout camping trip do not reality make. This is our best, fastest way there."

Jas turns to Temmin. "Do you have a better way?" she asks.

"I do."

"And?"

"We don't go at all! Listen. I get it. We all wanna do right by the galaxy. But this isn't our job. Well—" He points to Jas. "Fine, it's *your* job. But the rest of us? This is going to shake out with or without our help. And . . . maybe the New Republic are the good guys, maybe they're not. Maybe nothing changes here. Maybe it even gets worse. We *are* the Outer Rim. We're the part of the toilet bowl nobody wants to clean, okay?"

Sinjir whistles. "And I thought *I* was cynical."

Norra kneels before her son and takes his hands in hers. Her heart breaks to see him like this. He *is* cynical. She understands it. She knows it. And she's pretty sure it's her fault. Which means it's her job to fix it.

"Tem," she says. "This is the kind of thing your father and I have fought for. We want to make a better galaxy. For you. For your kids." He winces at that—and she remembers that no teenager wants to talk about getting married and having a litter of puppies. "Please. Trust me on this one. We're doing the right thing. And we can make a difference. Even a small group of people can change the galaxy. It only takes one man to spit in the eye of a giant and blind him. So let's do it. Let's spit in the giant's eye."

Jas speaks up and says, "Your mother is right. If we don't act now, it's likely that the Imperials at that palace will squirm out of our grip. If that happens, we don't get paid. You want to get paid, don't you?"

Temmin nods. "I do."

Norra almost regrets that. That what moved the needle with him wasn't her earnest plea but rather, the practical, greed-driven entreaty put forth by the bounty hunter. But it works.

He's in.

The call goes out, and they find Wedge Antilles in the servile quarters in the bottom floor of the palace. Already here they're bringing steel shutters down over any of the stained-glass windows and fortifying the doors. Down at this level, the roar of the crowd is a living thing—still muted, muffled, but with a rise and fall that Rae can feel in her breastbone.

She steps into the bunkroom, with a trio of stormtroopers behind her. Adea is not present—she's already under the care of the palace doctors.

Antilles is facedown at the back of the room, dead. His arm is splayed out, his hand curled into an arthritic claw. A few centimeters away, the holoscreen he stole from her assistant after he shot her.

Rae eases forward and then she sees—his back gently rising and falling. He's not dead, after all. Merely unconscious. The pain and injury, too great for him. Good. That means this particular breach began and ended before the others of the summit could find out.

She signals the stormtroopers to gather Antilles up.

"Take the captive back upstairs. Use *actual* chains this time. Surely the satrap can conjure up some in this archaic palace." Then she snaps her fingers. "Hand me that holoscreen. I should return it to Adea." Just because she's injured doesn't mean she can't work. Rae needs her.

The stormtrooper hands over the holoscreen.

And her blood goes cold.

On it, a communications screen. He hacked their channel and secured a line. And it's open to a rebel frequency.

Antilles sent out a summons to war.

INTERLUDE:

THEED, NABOO

THE RED-HEADED BOY with the cleft lip stands there with the other kids. Kids of all shapes and sizes, all ages and alien races. Most of them are younger than him, and the younger the kid, the more attention that kid gets from the wannabes who gather around, looking to adopt. All of them, shipped here from various parts of the galaxy.

The boy leans over to the tail-head girl next to him, and he says: "We're never gonna go home with any of these people."

"Shut up, Iggs," she says. "You're being a huge bummer."

He shrugs. "I know it and you know it, Streaks. They want the kidlings. The young ones. We're too old."

"We're not *that* old," she whispers. "And besides, we're heroes."

"Heroes?" He rolls his eyes. "C'mon. They don't know that and if they did they wouldn't see it that way."

"We were the Anklebiter Brigade from Coco-Town. That means something."

"It means two things: zip and squat. People don't even know what we did. You think people care about a buncha orphans who hid in the sewers and messed with the bucketheads and other Imperials? I dunno if you noticed, but we aren't on Coruscant anymore. And even if we were—so what?" They got scooped up and brought here. Taken out of harm's way, so they were told. But Iggs and Streaks—they *were* the harm's way. They and the other orphans were doing rebel work. Striking from the shadows. Hiding in alleyways and shipping containers. They brought down a whole Imperial frigate—one resupplying the Empire's front lines.

"They care. We did more than that. We passed messages. Told them about troop movements. We gave them intel, Iggs. How do you think the rebels retook Coco-Town? That was us."

He waves her off. "I know that. You know that. But these people will never know. Or never care."

Her face sinks. "You think?"

Suddenly he feels bad. He squeezes her arm. "We always got each other. And the others."

Now the lady with the green skin and the other older woman—the "maven," the one who has been talking to orphans and the wannabe parents about this or that—come closer. Iggs hears the green lady talking to a pair of well-to-do humans, pink-skins in fancy clothes. They're talking about how important it is to try to get the galaxy "back to normal," about how a lot of poor kids have been displaced because their parents went to war or were casualties in this conflict or that battle and it's time to put families front and center again. And mostly Iggs, he just stands there making faces, rolling his eyes. All while Streaks stands there, vibrating visibly.

"Maybe they'll come and interview us," she says. "Maybe we'll go home with someone today." He hears the hope in her voice. Like she wants to say: *Maybe we can have parents again.*

"They won't come to talk to us. We look like dirty urchins."

"They might!"

"They won't."

But sure enough, here they come. The green lady and the maven. The adults hunker down and green lady says to the both of them:

"What are your names?"

They tell her. He's Iggs, she's Streaks.

The woman can't quite contain her amusement. A little smirk on her face. *Laugh it up,* Iggs thinks. She makes small talk with the kids. Just dumb stuff. Their favorite flavor of milk shake, if they hope the Grav-Ball Pennant will start up again this year, stuff like that. A small crowd of wannabe parents gather now—wealthy Naboo types in their finery and fanciness. Iggs only feels more like a stain on a nice tablecloth.

"What happened to your parents?" the woman asks.

Iggs freezes. He doesn't want to think about it or even say it. He tries to block out the memories of seeing his two fathers lying there like that . . .

Streaks, though, she jumps right in: "My parents were rebels. Their transport was attacked just past Tanis and I'm a rebel, too, me and Iggs here were part of a crew of kids called the Anklebiter Brig . . ."

Ugh. No. He feels out of place. A piece of trash left on a nice shelf. So while they're talking to Streaks, he ducks away behind a tent—he starts looking for ways outta here. Already he starts forming a plan in his head. Find the sewers—they gotta go somewhere. Work their way back to the center of Theed. Find a spaceport. Catch a ride back to the action. Back to the hot war of Coruscant. Home to Coco-Town, where the Anklebiter Brigade can ride again and help the rebels.

There. A grate. That'll do. Doesn't look bolted down. It's all gilded and pretty—like everything in this city of museums.

Iggs ducks back around the side of the tent. He's about to yell to Streaks that it's time to go, time to bust out of here and forget all this *getting adopted* nonsense, but he turns around and she's gone. No. Not gone. There, a few meters away. Talking to a nice-looking couple, a clean pair of pink-skins with good hair and shiny teeth. She looks happy. They look happy.

Iggs thinks, good for her, good for her.

Then, because nobody's paying attention, he slinks off alone. He finds that drain grate, pops it, and ducks down into the darkness. It's time to go home. It's time to go back to the fight.

CHAPTER TWENTY-NINE

THE CASE IS LIGHT. Though he's moved it before, it surprises him again: The crate with the black carbon locks looks like it should weigh a ton. And one might expect a weapon like this (er, whatever "this" is) would be heavy. But it isn't. It's light as air. Hollow as a balloon.

As the others move into the passageway leading into the catacombs beneath the city, Temmin lifts his end and Bones lifts the other (the droid helps not because the crate is heavy, but rather because it's cumbersome).

They get it inside the door.

Temmin looks at his shop, says a small and silent good-bye, then shuts it. Ahead, Sinjir snaps on the illumi-droids: little floating lanterns, each with a trio of tentacle arms dangling beneath. Arms that dead-end in pincer grips.

The light from the droids is mottled, greasy. (They're dirty and dinged up.) But it's enough.

Norra and Sinjir forge ahead. Temmin starts to follow, but Jas catches his arm first. "This crate," she says.

"Surat's weapon," he says. He tries to say it with some authority, like, *Yeah, this is Surat's, and I stole it. What of it?*

"It's not a weapon."

"What? Yes it is."

"Maybe it can be. But it isn't literally a weapon."

"I don't understand, how did you—" He touches one of the carbon locks, and it springs open. His eyes widen. "What? *What.* I've been trying to open these for days. For days!"

"I picked them."

"You . . . you just picked them. Do you have magic fingers? Are you some kind of wizard?"

"I have talents. And I used them while I was down here repairing my gun before I helped your mother claim one of those TIE fighters for herself." She gestures toward it. "Go on. Pop it."

He does. Like a kid on his naming day, he rips into this present with greedy gusto. Soon as the lid lifts, a blue glow emerges. He has to squint against it, it's so bright. Then he sees. It's a box of data cubes.

"Data cubes?" he asks. "That's it? It's not a weapon at all!"

"It's not. It's something far better: *information.*"

"Surat was protecting information?"

"I don't know about what. But if we get through this, I'll help you figure out what that information is. And then together we can sell it."

Ah. There it is. There's her angle. He knew there had to be one. He clucks his tongue. "And I assume you get a cut. For your benevolence and wisdom and your connections to whatever market would buy this—"

"Sixty–forty."

"Oh, whoa, hey, that's not fair—"

"I'll give you the sixty."

Oh. He hesitates. Ahead, the light recedes as the others walk on, the illumi-droids bobbling after them. His mother calls: "Are you coming?"

"Deal," he tells Jas, then shakes her hand.

"Deal."

"We're coming!" he yells. Under his breath, he adds: "So impatient."

Sinjir is used to tight spaces. The Empire was not known for its *roomy* architecture. It was fond of austere pragmatism (that term, *austere pragmatism,* or sometimes *pragmatic austerity,* found its way atop many Imperial brochures and propaganda tracts), and so kept its hallways low and narrow. Stormtroopers were literally supposed to be within the same range of height and weight in part because of exactly that—he wasn't joking when he said he was too tall to be a stormtrooper.

The catacombs, as such, do not give him claustrophobia. Not strictly speaking. No, the anxiety in his chest is from something else: the way they wind around. It's not enough that the maze asks them to go right, left, or straight. Instead some passages go up, others down, and others yet wind around in a spiral. One pathway will be dry as dust, and the smell coming out of it will be of pulverized bone. Another pathway will be wet, heady, almost fungal. They walk through puddles and over crumbling stone and mortar. Sometimes the illumi-droids highlight a wall as they pass, and the wall shows off filthy handprints streaked across the rock, or instead shows something in a language far off from Basic. Some curse, perhaps, some profanity. Or perhaps some threat.

Occasionally, sounds wind their way through the labyrinth, too. Scraping. Scuffing. A hiss. Once: A pair of green eyes sat shining in the darkness like glowing crystals. When their light reached it, Sinjir saw it was just a fengla—a pale, hairless vermin. High haunches and crooked incisors. It spits and hisses before scurrying off, claws clicking.

They walk for a while. Stopping sometimes to check the map. Then they continue on. Walking underneath dripping water—lingering rainwater, Temmin assures them, not, like, the bodily excretions of some Ithorian doing his business up above. They cross a long, narrow bridge—only halfway across it does Sinjir realize that it matches the battle droid, because the thing is mostly bones. Larger bones. Not human. Bound up with rusted wire. It sways over a chasm, and Sinjir remembers the great rift below him as he dangled there in Surat Nuat's dungeon. A dungeon that must connect up to the city's underground space.

Soon, they start to see droid pieces. And blaster scoring on the walls. Sinjir even thinks he sees scarring from lightsaber blades: This was the site of an old battle during the Clone Wars. When the Jedi were populous and not on the edge of extinction.

Temmin says, "We're coming up on the junk pits."

The map says as much, Sinjir thinks.

And then he watches Temmin. He hadn't been, not really. The boy seemed fine, if a bit shook up from all of this. He can pretend he's hard against it, but between almost getting killed by a Sullustan gangster and losing his mother, it's to be expected that the boy is off his kilter.

Something else is going on, though.

It's in the way the boy looks around. And fidgets. He's nervous. Like he's hiding something. *Temmin has a secret.*

Sinjir hangs back, and urges Jas to hang back with him.

"What is it?" she asks in a low voice.

"We need to talk."

"Mm," she says, nodding like this was inevitable. "I knew this would come. And yes, I concede."

"You concede what, exactly?"

"You are satisfying."

"I . . . don't follow. Satisfying? I don't know what that means. I do know that it sounds awfully . . . milquetoast. Drinking a cup of protein slurry when you're truly hungry is *satisfying*. And yet, disgusting."

Jas gives him a frustrated look. "I mean that I find you capable. You interest me. And so, *yes,* when all this is over, we may couple."

"Couple. Like—" His face goes suspiciously and surprisingly red. "Like you and me? Together?"

"That is indeed what I mean."

He laughs. "Oh."

"If you're going to laugh about it," she says, suddenly stung. "Then you can take my invitation and stick it in your exhaust port."

"No, I just mean . . . I'm not into . . . this."

"This?" Her scowl deepens and her teeth bare. "Aliens?"

"*Women.*"

"Oh. *Oh.*"

"Yes, oh."

"Oh."

Moments pass. The awkwardness between them is a living thing—like a cloud of flies you can't ignore no matter how hard you try. Eventually she blurts out: "You wanted to speak to me about something else, apparently?"

"Ah. Yes. The boy. Temmin."

"He's clearly too young for you."

"Would you stop? That's not what I mean. Listen. He's lying to us."

"Everybody is lying all the time, Sinjir. I recognize

that your former role in the Empire makes you *excessively* paranoid, but—"

"The map," he says, finally. "It's about the map."

"What about it?"

"Temmin told us the map had changed. That it was wrong."

He sees the realization hit her. It lands on her the way a fly lands on someone's nose. "But it hasn't been wrong," she says. "It's been right."

"Exactly."

"He's hiding something." Her brow darkens. "Something down here he doesn't want us to see, perhaps."

"A stash, maybe. A trove."

"Could be. Keep your eyes peeled."

"You too."

The junk pits: massive craters dug out of the catacombs. The stone brick gives way to natural rock, opening into chambers wide and deep that house heaps and mounds of old scrap. Droid parts, mostly, and a great deal of it largely unrecognizable or unusable. The good stuff likely picked over and pulled out—*by my son,* Norra thinks.

She stands by it, looking around. She kicks a stone forward. It *pings* off what looks like a half-melted protocol droid arm. Other parts clang and clatter, sliding down—a momentary avalanche of scrapscree. All of it echoes. Temmin sidles up next to her. "There goes us being quiet," he says.

"We're alone down here."

"You hope."

She rolls her eyes. "Where are the other two?" Mister Bones stands about three meters back still cradling the crate of thermal detonators while humming. But the other two aren't here.

"They're back a way. Talking. I saw the light from their droid."

"Hm." She wrinkles her brow. "Temmin, do you trust Sinjir?"

"I dunno. Why?"

"He's an Imperial. He hurt people for a living."

"You trust the bounty hunter but not the Imperial?"

She shrugs. "A bounty hunter lives by a certain code. They want to get paid and this mission gets her paid. I trust her as far as all that."

"But Sinjir, not so much."

"I . . . don't know. I want to trust him."

"He got us this far."

"That's true."

"He hasn't fragged us over yet."

"Language," she chides.

"Sorry."

"And you're right. But we could be walking into a trap."

Temmin tenses up and looks away. She sees now she's given him cause to worry. "They aren't family," he says. "We're family."

"We are. But I'm sure we'll be fine. It'll all be okay."

"Yeah." He thrusts his tongue in the pocket of his cheek and idly nudges a stone with his shoe. "Mom, I'm sorry."

"For what?"

He dithers a bit. "For . . . being a real sleemo to you. It wasn't right. I just . . ." His nostrils flare as he draws a deep breath. "I missed you. And I miss Dad. And I was mad that you left and then even madder that maybe you died and I . . . I don't have what you have. I don't have the . . . courage, I don't have that

fire in my heart for the New Republic like you. I
just . . ."

She puts her arm around him. "It's okay. You're a
kid, Tem. You got enough to worry about. Don't
worry about this. I love you."

"I love you, too."

A flutter in her chest. She knows he loves her. But to
hear it? It makes all the difference.

From behind them, Jas calls: "Are we stopping?"

Norra answers: "No. Just waiting for the pair of
you to catch up."

They keep on.

It's time, Sinjir thinks, to pry.

They walk past the junk pits, toward the direction
of what the map says is the old droid factory. Or its
entrance, at least. Temmin says they'll have to go
right past the front of it—though thankfully not inside.

As they pass by a wall of glowing fungus—the stone
beneath their feet loose and slippery, slick with spongy
moss—Sinjir catches up with Temmin and his B1 battle droid, Bones.

"That droid of yours," Sinjir says. "He's something."

Temmin looks up. A dubious brow raised. "Yeah. I
know."

"You find him down here?"

"Uh-huh. In one of the pits."

The battle droid saunters alongside. Singing a quiet
(well, not that quiet) little song: "DOO DEE DOO
DOO BAH BAH BAH DOO DOO."

"He's obviously no longer standard-issue," Sinjir
says. "You've done some modifications."

"Thanks, Darth Obvious. Or is it Emperor Palpable? Next you'll tell me which end of a blaster is the shooty-shooty one, or why I wouldn't do so hot in a Wookiee arm-wrestling league."

"You can't out-snark me, boy, so don't even try. I'm just saying—how exactly did you program that droid to be so . . . *that*." He gestures to the droid, who stops singing long enough to do a high kick.

Temmin sighs. As if this line of questioning bores him and yet he must persevere. "Bones is primed with a high-octane cocktail of programs. Some heuristic combat droid programs, some martial arts vids, the moves of some Clone Wars cyborg general, and also, the body-mapped maneuvers of a troupe of la-ley dancers from Ryloth."

Dancers. That explains some things, actually. The occasionally graceful way the droid moves, but also: the humming and singing.

"Crafty," Sinjir says.

"That's me."

"What else is down here?"

"I dunno. Your guess is as good as mine."

That answer: It reads true. Temmin doesn't appear to be lying, but as Sinjir just noted: The boy *is* crafty. "Is there something down here you don't want us to see, Temmin?"

"What? Are you accusing me of something?"

"I just want you to know we're not going to . . . plunder your wares."

"I don't have any wares down here to *plunder*."

Sinjir sniffs. "I thought perhaps you didn't want us getting to the droid factory treasure before you did. But that means it's something else."

". . . *what's* something else?"

"You're hiding something, Temmin. I can sense it."

There! There it is. Temmin's whole expression shifts just slightly—there's a flicker on his face like a disruption in a hologram, a sign that Sinjir is right. The boy *is* hiding something. "I . . . I'm not—"

Ahead, Jas says: "The factory."

She points to the side.

To Temmin, Sinjir says: "To be continued." Then they jog to catch up, the little illumi-droid burbling a meter behind.

Here, the passageway opens up. The droid factory entrance is a wide mouth framed by metal arches, two booths, an old corroded sign that says: SUPPORT THE CONFEDERACY OF INDEPENDENT SYSTEMS! Another sign says: BUY A DROID FROM THE SEPARATIST ALLIANCE! A third hanging from above—at an angle, since one of the bolts has come free—says, RALLY AGAINST REPUBLIC OPPRESSION. On that one, some of the letters are so rusted they've essentially gone missing.

Norra says: "This, from the days when the Separatists brought the war to the Outer Rim in the later years of the Clone Wars."

"How'd they get the droids out?" Jas says. "They didn't march them through these . . . sewers."

Temmin shifts his weight nervously. Sinjir watches him. The boy says: "Used to be a telescoping platform. They'd raise the droids up for delivery and ships would pick them up. It's all destroyed, sealed over. I thought once you could get down here from there, but it's too wrecked." He scratches his head. "Can we go? This place gives me the hypers."

A small technique for *rooting out* truth is to make the subject—Sinjir actually thinks the word *victim* but he tries to shove that kind of thinking back in the dark hole from whence it came—uncomfortable. Put them off balance. Do that, they make mistakes. They say things they don't mean to say. And so, that is Sinjir's plan of the moment.

He picks up a hunk of stone. "It's not haunted," he says. "Look."

Sinjir wings the stone toward the gate. It *bongs* off one of the booths. Rust flakes rain and the stone drops.

"Don't!" Temmin cautions.

"There's nothing to worry about, the factory isn't—"

Inside, deep within the bowels of the factory, something howls. A mechanized sound. Not human. Maybe not altogether robotic, either.

"The gates," Jas says. "This place should be sealed up."

"But it's not," Norra adds. "Everything's open."

Another wail. And a third after that. Closer now.

"I HAVE A BAD FEELING ABOUT THIS," Mister Bones says.

"We need to go," Temmin says.

From inside the old factory, a sudden scramble of sound—metal on metal. Like footsteps. Coming toward them, and closing in fast.

"Run!" Sinjir yells.

CHAPTER THIRTY

HIS RED NOSTRILS FLARE. Air in and out. Ackbar longs for water. He has a small tank here—a bacta healing tank retrofitted with water possessing the salinity and pH balance of his homeworld, Mon Calamari. Sometimes he goes into it and just ... floats. But he has little time for such moments.

Maybe one day. But not today.

The message from Captain Antilles plays again and again in his mind. It came in on an Imperial channel, of all things. Ackbar wasn't the recipient, but saw it soon after. Wedge looked ragged, injured. His message before he collapsed and the communications ended was brief. Too brief. *High-level Imperial meeting. Blockade on ... Akiva. Palace at Myrra. Now is the—*

And then it was over.

He tells the others—Agate, Madine, Mon Mothma, Ensign Deltura—that Antilles was right. Ackbar presumes to finish the captain's statement:

"Now is the time. Prepare a small fleet, but have other ships in reserve, fueled up with full loadouts. Agate, I want you to lead the charge. Be ready for anything. If this is the Empire, you can be sure they will not go easily. And they are overly fond of tricking us into doing what they want."

* * *

It's like inverting a pyramid and carrying it, point down, on your back. All that weight. The sharp peak between your shoulder blades. Built of bricks of blame. A terrible and uncomfortable burden.

Sloane is feeling it now.

The others are driven now by panic, rage, opportunity. Pandion, trying to winnow her down to particulate matter. Shale, the doomsayer who thinks they must surrender now or die soon. Tashu, interjecting now and again with some parable or pabulum about the wisdom of the dark side and if only they followed its teachings and oh, Palpatine said this, the old Sith writings said that. Crassus wants to buy their way out. He's waving around his metaphorical credits-purse thinking that the Empire can bribe its way free of New Republic persecution. *Best of luck with that,* Rae thinks.

The satrap, at least, remains quiet. He sits in the corner, staring down at his hands. The writing is on the wall for that one. He knows the Empire will abandon him. He will be left with a city that seeks his head on a pitchfork so they can wave it around for all to see.

In the other corner of the dining room—as they have never yet made it to the meeting room near their quarters on this troubled and turbulent day—stands Adea, her leg already bound up in a foam-layer cast printed by the medical droid. The assistant hobbles over and Rae thinks: *I must keep her close. She has shown more steel than most of these so-called Imperials.*

"The yacht?" Rae asks her, ignoring the shouts of vitriol from the rest of the room.

"Had to stop for fuel one system over. But in hyperspace now. Will land soon after. Expected within the hour."

Rae tenses up. "That's longer than expected. I don't know if I can keep these animals at bay until then." *They might tear my head off, too.* "Any chance Crassus is delaying it behind our backs?"

"Possible, but can't see why. He's eager to leave. Truth is, those big ugly barges are—" Here Adea winces in a bit of pain and shifts her weight. "They guzzle fuel like it's free drinks at the Death Star Commissary." Sloane spent plenty of nights drinking at the commissary with her comrades. A pang of nostalgia plucks her strings.

Rae turns to the room. She makes her voice louder than everyone else's. "Shale. How long before we can expect a rebel fleet?"

The woman scrunches up her face and frowns. "Hard to say, Admiral. They'll send something, probably soon. One suspects it'll be a reasonably sized fleet. Expect them within the hour if they're feeling aggressive. Three if cautious."

That's cutting it awfully close. "Our own Star Destroyers. It's time to call them back. Our ruse is over."

Shale objects: "Admiral, if we bring them back, we have no guarantee that those three Destroyers will survive the ensuing battle—"

"Caution I admire. Cowardice I do not. Though our TIE regiment is reduced somewhat, our Destroyers are more than capable of cutting down a rebel fleet. Especially if we are ready for the fight. I don't want to make our escape into space just as the rebel scum come dropping out of hyperspace." To Adea, she says: "Call them back. Now."

"Yes, Admiral." Adea leans in. "Also, you have a call."

Sloane mouths the question: *Who?*

She tilts her screen toward the admiral so that the rest of the room won't be able to see it.

Rae sees a face she recognizes, though it belongs to someone to whom she has never been introduced.

The Sullustan gangster, Surat Nuat.

But why?

CHAPTER THIRTY-ONE

TIME, broken out into the moments between trigger pulls. Jas drops to her knee and faces the coming horde as the others flee. The long rifle in her hand. Eye against its scope. Down there, toward the entrance, they pour out.

A flash of corroded metal. Piston legs. Dented chest plates. Long, gangly, many-jointed limbs. *Droids,* she thinks. Mad, lunatic droids. Each different from the last. Glowing eyes. Mechanized wails.

They rush down the passageway. Some thirty meters off. Surging forward like feral things, like the bristle-backed boarwolves of Endor. Running on all fours. Up the walls. Skittering along the crumbling ceiling like spiders.

Boom. Boom. Boom.

The slugthrower launches round after round.

They drop, one by one. She takes the legs out from the first—it crashes down, neck breaking as it hits. A spark as a shot punches through the metal skull of one, and it tumbles into another of its swarm. They shriek and screech. She fires again, and one of their skulls pops off, clanging against the wall with a loud echo—

That's when she sees.

They're not droids. They're something *else.* Creatures. Black-eyed things, noseless. Mouths open, showcasing a pincushion of wild needle-teeth. The thing that loses its skull plate dashes to the side, grabs it, and reaffixes it before joining the rushing throng anew.

Twenty-five meters.

Boom.

Twenty. Eighteen.

Closer, closer.

There's too many, she thinks. A dozen here, and more pouring out of the factory. A whole tribe of these things. *A hive.* But she has the slugs. She can do this. But there, Aunt Sugi's voice whispering inside her ear:

You have to know when to run, girl.

That, a message to Jas only weeks before Jas took her advice. Maybe how Sugi meant it, maybe not. But she ran away from her home planet. A terrible place. A *strange* place, Iridonia. Brutal and unforgiving.

Fifteen meters.

Both her hearts beat fast in tandem, outracing the speed with which she can pull the trigger.

Twelve meters.

Boom.

They shriek and click and swarm.

A hand at her shoulder—a voice, numb and almost lost underneath the ringing of her ears. It's the boy.

"We have to go," he's saying. *"There's too many."*

"I can do this!" she roars.

But she can't. She knows she can't.

You have to know when to run, girl.

Now is the time to run.

The stories were true, Temmin realizes—from a certain point of view. What came spilling out of that old droid factory weren't ghosts. The place wasn't haunted by specters or Force wraiths.

And it isn't haunted by old, malfunctioning droids, either.

It's the Uugteen.

When he goes back to get Jas, he sees one—what they thought were droids were just the Uugteen wearing droid parts like armor. The pale, feral things—near-humans, but far enough to still be monsters—usually keep to the jungles and canyons. Sometimes, though, they find caves to live in. The catacombs beneath Myrra aren't just caves, he realizes.

They're a whole cave *system*. Maybe they connect out elsewhere—to the Canyon of Akar, or even all the way to the coastline far south. This pack has been living down here for a long time, hasn't it? It doesn't even matter now. Because he and his friends are besieged. Chased. And the monsters are gaining ground fast.

Jas turns suddenly—she fires a shot at a half-collapsed stone beam hanging above the passageway. One shot, it cracks. Starts to splinter. Two shots, those cracks spread. But the pack is almost upon them. Gibbering and screaming like men on fire. Again Temmin tries to pull her along—

But she takes one last shot. The beam crashes down. Water streams along with it. It crushes the front line of the monsters.

It slows them down.

For a moment.

They run once more, rounding a corner. Here it goes up—and he knows that they're nearing the ground underneath the Royal District. Another half-hour walk and they'll be at—or beneath—the satrap's palace.

Mister Bones skids to a halt. He sets down the box of detonators. His astromech arm spins up, blurring the air. His other arm snaps back, revealing the vibroblade. Bones makes sounds like the Uugteen—threatening howls, barks, gargled blasts of mechanical distortion.

Temmin yells at him, tells the droid now isn't the time.

But Bones is programmed to protect Temmin. That is the programming that overrides all else. Fierce, loyal, psychotic.

The Uugteen swarm up over the broken beam.

Temmin hears his mother calling for him. He tries to tell Bones to move—even pulling on the battle droid's arm. But he doesn't budge.

Then he looks down. Near the droid's feet. The box of detonators.

The box of detonators.

"I've got a plan!" he yells at Bones. "Come on, come on!"

He grabs one of the detonators out of the box. Just one. Then he pops it open, spins the top to its shortest fuse, and flings it back into the box from whence it came. Then he yells: "Run! Everybody run!"

Temmin bolts forward, his legs straining—all parts of him tensing up as he waves everyone away. Bones sprints alongside of him, the droid's feet smashing hard into the brick. The battle droid yells:

"ALL WILL GO BOOM."

Six seconds. The Uugteen swarm.

Five seconds. Norra waves her son and the others on.

Four seconds. The droid-clad monsters rush up to the box.

Three seconds. Jas pivots, fires her rifle over Temmin's shoulder.

Two seconds. Bones cackles.

One second. Temmin winces and dives to the ground as—

He lifts his face from the ground. His head pulses like the engine of an idling speeder bike. Temmin pushes himself up on his hands, dust and rocky bits raining down from his hair. He flinches just in time to see Jas leap forward and jam the butt of her gun into the faceplate of one of the Uugteen—a protocol droid face painted in what looks like blood, the mask rent in half with a jagged rip so it looks to be some nightmarish mouth—and the thing pinwheels and goes down. Bones stomps on it again and again.

Temmin thinks, *It didn't work. The plan didn't work.*

But then he braces himself against the wall and pulls himself up. Jas offers him a hand and he takes it. Two of the Uugteen lie on the broken floor—here the floor is crooked, sporadic tile. All of it shattered.

The tunnel is sealed.

"Stragglers," Jas says, gesturing toward the two monsters. Up close, he can see their pale flesh underneath the armor—revealed between the joints, like the flesh of a krillcrab when you turn it over to get at its meat. "You okay?"

He nods, numbly.

"That was a good idea," Jas says, and then she quick-steps out of the way as Norra launches herself at Temmin, wrapping her arms around him.

"It was a good idea," Norra says. She kisses his brow. Idly he thinks, *Even though I'm dirty.* That's what a mother does.

"Thanks," he says, that high-pitched tone still moving from ear to ear, his head still pounding like heavy rain on an old fuel drum.

Sinjir steps up, dusting off his officer's uniform. "Let's not all crack open a case of fizzy drinks *just yet*. I'll casually remind you all that the boy just detonated our key into the satrap's palace."

Yes, Temmin thinks. *Now we'll have to turn back around. And everything will be fine again.*

"We can't go back," Jas says.

"Guess it's over," Temmin says with a shrug. He tries not to play it too eagerly. "This'll all . . . it'll all shake out. We'll find a way back up to the surface, and—"

Sinjir lifts his head. "Way up to the surface? Can you find us a way out nearby?"

"Absofragginglutely," Temmin says.

"Language," his mother says.

"Sorry. But yeah, um, hold on . . ." He unrolls the map, his heart beating a kilometer a minute in his chest. *We're in the clear.* His second thoughts about everything no longer matter. "Here. Close by. Five minutes and we're there—should take us up right into the old Banking Clan building."

"Not *us*," Sinjir says. "Me."

That earns him some quizzical looks.

"I'm dressed for the occasion of duplicity," he says, demonstrating his officer's uniform with an open-handed gesture. "I'll find a way up and out. I'll contact the Imperials at the palace—I should be able to find the frequency, because, oh, that's right, I was an Imperial with high-level clearance. And then I'll get *them* to open the door for us."

Jas frowns. "And how do you plan to do that?"

"That is the brilliant part. I'll tell them the tunnels are their one safe way out of the palace."

INTERLUDE:

TATOOINE

JAWAS STINK.

That's something Adwin Charu didn't expect. Most of this planet has that *hot sand* scent to it—like the inside of his mother's clay oven before she put dough into it. Like everything's baking. But soon as he stepped inside this sandcrawler, the odor hit him like a fist. A musky, animal smell. And suddenly he's forced to wonder if each Jawa is just a fraternity of wet rats gathering together under brown robes and a black face veil.

They hiss and jabber at him. And he tells them again, like he's been telling them for the last half hour: "I don't *want* any of this. *This*—" He sweeps his arms in a broad gesture, indicating the dimly lit heaps of junk all around him. "—is all *worthless* to me and my company. I need to see the *real* goods." He enunciates words like he's speaking to someone hard of hearing. As if it's doing any good at all—these stubborn little stink monsters don't seem to hear him, or understand him, or maybe they just don't care. But he knows the stories: They sell the dross to the rubes, but every sandcrawler has a real collection, too. Valuable goods to those in the know.

Adwin has a job here. And it's not to come back to his boss with an armload of malfunctioning garbage.

The Jawas click and whisper.

"I *need* droids, weapons, mining tools. I *know* these sandcrawlers are old mining vehicles. You *stole* them. Least you could do is—"

From behind him, someone clears his throat.

Adwin glances back, sees a man standing there. Angular fellow. Leathery skin. Pinched eyes. Amused smile.

"Ahoy there," the man says.

"Uh-huh," Adwin answers. "Fine. If you'll excuse me?" Irritated, he adds: "I hope to be done here soon, provided these *things* comply."

"You're not from around here, are you?" the man says, still grinning like he knows something. He steps in out of the bright desert sun, brushes some dust off his long jacket. "Not a local."

"No. How did you know?"

The man chuckles: a rheumy, growly laugh. "You're too clean, for starters. Spend some time here, you get dust all up in your fingernails and nose hairs. Sand in your boots. But the other thing is, you gotta know how to handle the Jawas. These little scavengers, they work on rapport. You buy something now, something small, then you come back and then you buy bigger. And eventually, after a dozen or so visits, you start to see what they really have on offer. The real goods."

Adwin scowls. He doesn't have the patience for this. "I don't have the luxury of time. My boss won't allow it." He sighs. This is worthless, then. "I suppose I'll have to take my chances in . . . what's that town? Behind us?"

"Mos Pelgo," the man says.

"Yes. Well. There or Espa, I suppose." Adwin sighs. He begins to push past the man. The man extends the flat of his hand—he doesn't touch Adwin, but does block his way out.

"Now, hold on, friend. I happen to have the rapport you need with these little fellas. I'd be happy to vouch for you."

Adwin narrows his eyes. "You would?"

"Sure thing."

"And why would you do that?" He squints harder, suspicion twisting his face into an uncertain sneer. "What's the price?"

The man laughs again. "No price, no price. Just hospitality."

This planet: back-end water-farming bumpkins. Fine. Adwin can use that. He's comfortable exploiting the naïveté of others. "Yes. Yes. That would be excellent. Thank you—ahh? Your name?"

"Cobb Vanth."

"Mister Vanth—"

"Cobb, please."

"Ah. Cobb. Shall we, then?"

The man steps forward, scratching at his stubbled face. He starts talking to the Jawas. They gabble at him in their rat-tongue and he says, "Uh-huh, no, I know, but I come bearing credits and so does he." Cobb turns to Adwin and gives a wink. The Jawas whisper and babble. "Okay, then.

"Come on," Cobb says, and they follow a pair of the little hooded weirdos to another door in the back next to an upside-down gonk droid. The door hisses open, then shuts again behind them. Lights click on. Brighter here than in the other room. And sure enough: These are the goods.

A protocol droid. A pair of astromechs. A rack of weapons—Imperial-issue, by the looks of it. Against the far wall: a series of panels from what looks like a Hutt sail barge, plus a few other Huttese artifacts—some charred, others twisted. All of it, wreckage.

"Perfect, perfect, *perfect*," Adwin says, clapping his hands. He immediately heads over to a shelf and starts looking through bins, boxes, wire crates. Cobb pokes around, too, though Adwin mostly loses track of him until Cobb says:

"You're with that new mining company."

Adwin turns. "Hm? Oh. Yes."

"The Red Key Company, isn't it?"

"That's the one. How'd you know?"

"I have a way of sussing things out. I know that things are changing. Not just in the galaxy, but here at home, too. The Hutts still haven't shaken out who's next up to fill Jabba's throne—if you can call that flat slab of his a throne. Seems like this might be a new day for Tatooine."

"Yes, we certainly hope so," Adwin idly responds, mostly ignoring the man's small-talk prattle. He's happy Cobb got him in here but now wishes the man would just leave him alone.

Adwin spies a large, long box on the floor. He whips off the ratty cloth that's covering it and—

Oh, my.

From the box, he withdraws a helmet. Pitted and pocked, as if with some kind of acid. But still—he raps his knuckles on it. The Mandalorians knew how to make armor, didn't they? "Look at this," he says, holding it up. "Mandalorian battle armor. Whole box. Complete set, by the looks of it. Been through hell and back. I think my boss will appreciate this."

"I actually think I might take that home with me," Cobb says.

"I think *not*," Adwin says, turning around, the helmet tucked under his arm. The blaster at his hip suddenly feels heavy, pendulous. Eager to be drawn. A strange sensation, that. Adwin feels like he's really getting into the spirit of this planet. He's never had to shoot a man before.

Maybe that day is today. An exhilarating feeling, oddly.

Cobb grins, crosses his arms. "What are you thinking, company man? See, I could really use that armor. I figure being a newly appointed lawman—"

"Self-appointed, I think," Adwin says.

But Cobb doesn't take the bait. "Being a lawman, I could use some protection against those corrupt types who might think to seize the opportunity here on my planet. That armor is mine."

Adwin smirks. He takes his thumb and pulls back his tunic, revealing the blaster. "Cobb—"

"Sheriff Vance, to you."

"Oh." Adwin laughs. "*Sheriff,* I'd hate to have to draw this blaster—"

Cobb Vance's hand is up in a flash—there's the shriek from his own blaster, and it punches a cauterized hole clean through Adwin's shoulder on his right side. His hand goes limp, lifeless. The helmet clatters out of his other hand. He backs against the shelf, terror-struck.

"You, you monster . . ."

Cobb shrugs. "Oh, now. I'm no monster. No worse than your boss, that Weequay dung-muncher, Lorgan Movellan. I know his scam. I know all the scams. Afraid the Republic is back and gonna put their boot down on all the lowlifes and scum-lickers, the syndicates are trying to find new ways to appear legit. And with the Hutts fighting one another for control, bunch of these little quote-unquote *mining companies* are swooping in with brutes like your boss at the helm. A new age of mining barons. Won't fly. I'm here now.

Me and others *like* me. Bringing the law to this lawless place. And that starts with me shooting you and taking that armor out from under you."

Adwin whimpers. "Please don't kill me."

"Oh, I'm not. I'm leaving you alive so you can go tell your boss that he'd best pack up and hit the hyperspace lanes out of this sector, lest he wants me coming for him in my new—well, new to me—suit of armor."

"I will," Adwin says, sinking to the floor. He watches Cobb pick up the box of armor before heading to the door.

On his way out, Cobb says: "Next time you wanna pretend to be a gunfighter, best to shoot first, talk later. Bye now."

CHAPTER THIRTY-TWO

WHAP.

The rock crashes hard against the stormtrooper's helmet. The helmet spins and visibility is lost. Jom Barell dances around to the front of the armor-clad Imperial and gives a hard kick upward—the toe of his boot catches the stormtrooper's blaster hand. The hand snaps back. The blaster leaves the grip and spirals forward.

Jom catches it and fires three bolts into the stormtrooper's chest.

The body drops atop the other three troopers.

Jom's one broken arm still dangles at his side.

Not bad for a bird with a busted wing, he thinks.

He starts to climb up the ladder that leads up to the turbolaser ground-to-orbit turret, but as it turns out, climbing up the ladder is the hardest part. He has to lean into it. Take it slow. Haul himself up with one good arm, the stormtrooper's blaster rifle bolted onto his back.

It's a miserable endeavor.

Lots of grunts and growls.

It takes what seems like a galactic epoch, but somehow he manages to get to the top and pop the hatch. He starts to climb inside—

"Don't move," comes a voice.

A young Imperial gunnery officer in his little officer's hat stands there. A small Imperial blaster pointed. That hand shakes just so.

Jom sighs. He climbs all the way through—"Slowly!" as the Imperial warns him—and lifts his one hand up to placate.

"Both hands," the officer says. He's a fresh-faced nobody. Cheeks like marshmallows. Scared eyes like livestock about to meet its maker. The kid stands in front of the gunnery console—through the glass, Jom can see the twin turbolaser barrels aimed heavenward.

"One's broken," Jom says.

"I said . . . both hands."

Jom growls. Fragging kid. He winces as he lifts his broken arm. White-hot pain arcs across both shoulders. He bares his teeth and stares through watering, wincing eyes. *"There."*

"Now . . . on your knees."

"You're young."

"Wh . . . what?"

"Young. Like a baby whilk calf—don't know a whilk? I grew up on a farm. Long-legged critters. Meat tastes stringy, but the milk is good, and their hides make for fine leather. Their babies are clumsy, fumbling things. Knock-kneed and dumb as a box of retainer bolts. You're just a baby."

"I am not," the officer insists, gesturing again with the blaster.

"Uh-huh. Lemme guess how it's been. Your top officers are mostly gone now. A lot of them went up with the Death Star or the ensuing battles. Some got sold out by governors. So now the officer pool is either guys like you who are really young and untested, or really old and are being brought back in from the pasture because they got nobody else."

"I am not untested."

"Not anymore, you're not. Because I'm testing you. Here's my test: You can run or you can die. I'd not fault you for running. You wouldn't be the first Imperial to abandon his post. Some of you are finally figuring out you lost the war and you're just clinging to debris. It's okay. You can go, and they won't ever find you." Jom steps sideways, circling a bit closer to the officer and the gunnery console behind him. "Go ahead."

"I . . ."

"No judgment here, pal."

The officer lowers the gun, takes one ginger step forward. Like someone easing across the surface of a frozen lake, moving slowly lest the whole thing crack and shatter and dump them into the hoarfrost depths.

Jom thinks: *Well, that went better than expected.*

But then a look crosses the young officer's face— another flash of fear, but this time it's different. A greater fear. A fear of his own people and what they'll do to him if he runs.

The officer makes a decision in that moment. He raises the blaster anew—but by the time it's up, Jom is already charging forward like a bull. He slams into the Imperial, lifting both of them off the ground and slamming the young officer back onto the console. The young officer goes still, and rolls off onto the ground. He curls up, moaning.

Jom takes the blaster pistol, picks up the kid, and shoves him in a footlocker trunk toward the back. "Shoulda made a different choice, kid," Jom says, then slams the trunk down. Inside, the officer yells and weeps.

Jom winces and sits at the console.

He pulls up radar—one ship.

Incoming.

He taps on it, and data cascades across a trio of screens in front of him—it's a yacht. A Ryuni-Tantine Vita-Liner. Fancy ship, if a little old, for the richest in the galaxy—what Jom and his friends used to call the "upper-atmos," because on his world, Juntar, the richest of the rich used to live up in the sky in these floating mansions while the rest of the world toiled on the farms and in the dirt-cities below. The yacht is from an older day—Clone Wars era. A day of greater pomp and circumstance.

It's got a trajectory toward the palace.

He checks its signature, because somehow, it's made it through the blockade—and sure enough, the code that flashes checks out:

It's an Imperial code. Which makes that an Imperial ship.

Jom chuckles and spins up the cannons. He pulls out the manual controls and tilts the two barrels of the massive turret toward the yacht—the ship coming in low and slow out of the clouds, its side gleaming in the sun like a sheen of liquid light. Jom grins and winks. "Bye-bye, little ship."

He pulls the twin triggers.

Nothing happens.

Pull, pull, pull. *Click, click, click.*

Nothing.

"Fraggit!" he bellows. Slamming the officer into the console must have damaged . . . *something.*

He watches the yacht ease toward the palace. Safe as a star-whale in an empty ocean. *No, no, no.* He has to fix this thing. And he has to fix it now. Because he's taking out that ship, one way or another.

CHAPTER THIRTY-THREE

THE VERY SIMPLE PLAN IS THIS:

They find their way to the entrance into the satrap's palace. It's obvious enough: It's not sealed with some inelegant crumble of rock and stone, but rather with the finest brick. Blood-red bricks embedded with flecks of lucryte—a semiprecious stone that glitters and flashes when light touches it. Upon the brick is a sign in ornate script: SEALED BY THE AUTHORITY OF THE SATRAPY OF MYRRA, AKIVA.

Then, they move down the hall, just around the bend.

And there they wait.

The officers will come past. Likely with a handful of stormtroopers or palace guards in tow. And once past, they will have a surprise waiting.

Norra's not sure about this. She hunkers down behind a pile of mossy rubble and leans back toward Jas. "You're sure this will work?"

"No," Jas says. "I'm never sure. But this is our best bet."

"We won't be able to take them all."

"Among the four of us, I trust in our abilities. Particularly with my skills and the droid's programming, we will be just fine."

To Temmin, Norra says: "Are you okay?"

He nods. But he's not okay. She can see that. Something is bothering him. He tries wearing a confident, even cocky mask—giving her that wry smile of his. But it's false. She's his mother, so she knows. Something is eating at him—chewing him up from the inside out.

He's afraid, maybe.

But is that all? He's usually so fearless. This feels like something else.

No time to find out now.

She hears something. To her son and the bounty hunter, she raises a finger to her lips and then mouths the words: *They're coming.*

Moments pass. And as they do, confusion and then horror settle into her, because what she's hearing *isn't* from the direction of the sealed portal. It's from the other direction. It's coming from *behind* them.

A faint shudder to the ground. Footsteps. Coming closer and closer.

"The Uugteen," Jas says, and jacks a slug into her rifle.

"No," Norra says. "I know that sound." It's not the mad scramble of those wretched things—the Uugteen swarmed with scrape of metal and machine wails. This is a measured step. The clatter of armor, not of repurposed droid limbs. "Stormtroopers!" Norra says.

And down the long, cragged passage behind them, she sees the first flash of white armor. A red laser bolt punctures the air just above their heads—a spray of stone and debris. Norra fires back, and then suddenly the air is peppered with streaks of light. "Fall back!" Norra says.

They have only one fallback position.

Back toward the sealed gateway into the palace: a dead end.

But what choice do they have? They pull back around the corner, and as they do, she tries to get a quick count of what's coming—a dozen or more stormtroopers. A tough fight, but maybe doable. *Maybe.*

They round the corner—

Just as the gateway detonates. Crimson bricks clatter against the wall as the explosion eradicates the barrier.

Through the dark haze of smoke and dust, more flashes of white.

Stormtroopers pouring in from that end, too. Now they're trapped on both sides, caught like a rat between two cats—

It hits her, then. A sinking feeling as she realizes:

Sinjir sold them out.

They're caught at the corner, hunkering down next to one another, she and Temmin firing in one direction, Jas and the droid—Bones with a blaster in his clawlike grip, too—firing in the other.

A voice cuts through the hellstorm—

"Put your weapons down." A woman's voice.

The look on Jas's face is a lightning strike of sheer rage—a mask of fury and murderous determination. "Eat slugs!" she barks, and raises her long-barreled rifle again. But Norra puts a hand on her shoulder. Jas looks—a confusing stare. Pleading in its own way. *Let me kill them,* it says.

But Norra shakes her head and drops her weapon.

"Norra," Jas says.

"You can't claim that bounty if you're dead," she answers.

"I'm so sorry," Temmin says.

The woman's voice calls out again: "Weapons down. Stand up with your hands up. Move slowly."

Jas curses in a tongue Norra doesn't know, then

lays her rifle down. Temmin's blaster is already down and he tells Bones to do the same.

They stand, hands up.

Stormtroopers emerge through the haze. A dozen on each side of them. Too many to take, even *with* a skilled bounty hunter and psychopathic battle droid on their side. Norra's insides twist up.

Through the stormtroopers on the palace side, a woman—the one who commanded them to lay down their weapons, it seems—walks through her soldiers and toward the fore. Her hands are clasped behind her back. The woman has dark eyes and skin, and her face is pursed into a dissecting stare. Her back has an arch to it, and her posture is one of authority and confidence.

An admiral, by the bars across her chest.

"I'm Admiral Rae Sloane," the woman says. "You are under arrest for conspiring against the Galactic Empire, long may it reign."

Jas curses again in an unknown tongue: *"A-kee a' tolo, fah-roo kah."* Then she spits on the ground.

"You'll never get away with this," Norra says. "The end of the Empire is here. The comet is coming that will smash the rest of your rule to dust."

"Yes, well. The comet has not struck us yet, Norra Wexley. Come. For a short—very short—while, you get to be guests of the satrapy of Akiva."

Jom lies down underneath the console. Wires dangle in his face like the face-tentacles of a Quarren dentist. He ties off one wire, then pairs another two together. It sparks and he curses. He fights desperately to by-pass the trigger mechanism—which must be broken— and allow firing control to route right to the console itself. He ignores the pinprick burns on his face and tries a third wire—

Above him, he hears a hum. The console is back on.

That did it. Yes!

He bites the inside of his cheek to distract from the pain as he hauls himself back to standing, then he again aims the cannons—now the yacht has landed at the palace. Well, no, not exactly—it can't land, not now. The landing ring is a mess. Even from here he can see that the whole thing leans at a bad angle and looks as fragile as a house of pazaak cards. So the yacht hovers, burning fuel and staying aloft just nearby.

It gives him a clear shot.

He takes it. Jom finds the button to which he re-routed the firing mechanism—a button once used just to turn the lights on and off inside the turret—and smashes it with his thumb.

Nothing happens.

He roars in frustration and presses it again.

The console lights up bright, then too bright, and then sparks crackle out of the sides and seams and then the whole thing goes dark.

Norra is forced to her knees on the palace floor. A beautiful floor: a cerulean blue like she's never seen before shot through with veins of copper and bronze. It has the look of seawater catching sunlight, and part of her wants to stare down at it forever and ever, pretending that none of this is happening. But it is happening. Sinjir has sold them out. They are captives. Their mission has failed and they will be imprisoned or executed.

Despite her best desires, Norra isn't the type to turn away from what's coming, no matter how terrible.

She lifts her chin and meets it, scowling.

Next to her, Temmin and Jas kneel, too. The droid remains standing, warily pivoting his head around, looking at all those who surround them—every time his skull turns on its axis, she hears its little servo-motors whine.

She thinks: *The droid is scattered. Upset. Unpredictable.*

She whispers to her son: "Control your droid."

But Temmin just looks ashen. He says nothing.

The admiral paces alongside them. At the top of a set of grand steps stand others of import: Norra sees a tall, fox-faced man in a dark moff's uniform and a smaller, older woman. That must be the general: Jylia Shale. Behind them, a round-bellied, rubicund man with a wispy beard and another individual in a tall, pompous hat. That one has a strangely beatific smile.

Rae gives a nod to someone.

Through the crowd, they bring Sinjir.

His eye is swollen shut. His nose, plugged with blood, and the bridge of it looks scabbed over, maybe even broken. Sinjir's hands are bound behind his back. They shove him forward and he lands hard against his shoulder with an *oof.*

"Sinjir," Norra says. "I don't understand."

Stormtroopers approach with magnacuffs.

"LET ME FREE, MASTER TEMMIN," Bones says, his astromech arm starting a slow whir.

Temmin, in a small voice says: "No, Bones. No."

A trooper grabs roughly for Norra's arms, yanking them back. The cuffs snap around her wrist. They grab for Jas, too, and she fights a little—yanking her shoulders away and growling like a feral beast—but that small act of defiance isn't enough. The shackles hum and snap around her wrists.

Temmin, though: He stands up.

"Temmin," Norra says. "Son, this isn't the time."

But he ignores her and steps forward. Stranger still, nobody stops him.

"Let me go," he says. "Me, my mother, and the droid."

Jas says, "Oh, no. Temmin, no."

The sound in her voice: disappointment. Norra doesn't get it at first, but then Temmin says: "That's the deal. Honor the deal."

Rae holds up a small holoscreen. She taps a button and a projection emits. There stands a flickering blue hologram of a Sullustan with one eye. She knows who that is. That is Surat Nuat.

"Your deal was with *him*," Sloane says, and the Sullustan smiles.

The projection of Surat speaks: "Regrettably, boy, the Empire has negotiated their own deal. And they have changed their terms."

"No!" Temmin says. "You said we could go free."

"Temmin," Norra says, and she hears the terror in her voice. *This can't be true. He couldn't have. He wouldn't* . . . "Temmin, what is going on?"

He shoots her a look: sad and panicked. "I'm sorry."

From the floor, Sinjir groans. "He sold us out."

"I wanted to stay here," Temmin says. "I didn't want to leave. This is my home! I had to give Surat something or he'd kill us. Mom, please." Then to the admiral: "No! This wasn't what we said. The deal was for me, my mom, my droid—we all get to go."

"You may go," Rae says. "The others remain. Unless you'd like to stay behind, as well? I'm flexible on how tight we tie this noose."

Surat chuckles.

Jas looks at the boy and says, "You'd make a good bounty hunter, kid."

"He'd make an even better Imperial," Sinjir says.

Temmin, rattled now beyond measure, wheels on his droid. "Bones! Save us!" And the droid utters a mechanized war whoop and leaps up—

The battle droid never had a chance.

Laserfire cuts the metal man down in midair. The B1 droid screams and lands hard on the ground, so hard he shatters the blue-and-bronze tile. His legs go out from under him and he slams onto his side as Temmin races to him. Stormtroopers shove the boy out of the way and then hold him back. Norra tries to get to her feet but they hold her there.

She watches with inevitability as Sloane steps over to the droid. She draws her blaster and fires round after round into the machine's head.

After the sixth shot, it pops off and spins away, smoking.

The droid's limbs go still, clunking to the ground.

Temmin weeps.

"As was our deal, you may go," Sloane says to the boy. To the stormtroopers holding him, "Escort him out of the palace. By way of the roof, if you please."

No!

Norra launches herself up and starts to run toward Temmin.

A flash of white behind her as a stormtrooper steps in and clubs her in the back with the butt of his blaster rifle. She goes down amid broken droid parts. Sinjir lies nearby—she cries out as they carry Temmin away, the boy kicking and screaming and calling for his mother.

CHAPTER THIRTY-FOUR

WHAT HAVE I DONE?

That thought runs on an endless loop inside Temmin's head. Guilt cuts through him like the vibroblade at the end of Mister Bones's arm—the memory of the droid's destruction joins his guilty thought. That, his mother crying for him, the look on the faces of Jas and Sinjir . . .

At the time, it seemed like the right move. He knew he never wanted to leave Myrra, but that meant making peace with Surat or finding his own tongue cut out of his head. So he went and made a call to Surat—and the Sullustan gangster took the deal. Temmin excused it that the ex-Imperial and the bounty hunter would do the same. They'd sell his skin soon as someone offered enough credits—he said to himself, *They don't have any scruples. They don't have a code.*

But it turns out he was the one without scruples.

Temmin is the one without a code.

He hoped against hope that it would all fall apart and he wouldn't have to go through with it—that it would all work itself out and the snare he'd tied around his own stupid leg would just . . . *untie* itself, the knots going loose as the whole situation resolved itself without his plan coming to fruition, but now here he is—dragged up steps by a pair of stormtroopers. His heels kicking against the hard stairs, his hand trying to catch ahold of something, anything—a railing, a light fixture, a door handle.

Ahead, another staircase—

Temmin darts his hand out, catches the lip of a small fountain pressed into the wall. He curls his fingers around the stone and pulls himself free. Both stormtroopers cry out in alarm and come after him.

He stabs out a kick, catches one in the chest.

The stormtrooper *oofs*—but captures his foot. Then the Imperial pistons a fist into Temmin's stomach. The air goes out of him. An ache runs through him—down his legs, up his arms.

Again they pick him up. Carrying him up the second set of steps and through a set of red doors—out onto the roof. Temmin coughs, blinking back tears. He hears it now: the sound of chanting. Yelling. The crowd.

"No, no, please," he pleads with them as they haul him toward the roof's edge. The two stormtroopers lift Temmin over their heads. He can see the crowd now. Massive. They're streaming in from all directions. Signs. Effigies. Rocks, bricks, bottles thrown. Akivans. Protesting the satrapy. Protesting the *Empire*. Temmin missed it. He thought everyone just wanted to keep their heads down. Like him. *I'm on the wrong side of this thing.*

Mom, I'm so sorry.

"Time to join your friends," one of the stormtroopers says. He doesn't even know which one. All he knows is he screams as they pitch him over the edge of the roof. Temmin falls.

The yacht floats in the heat haze above the satrap's palace. Its front end hangs forward like a falcon's beak

dipped in bronze; black windows between bony pipes
of red and gold; two wings that angle down and lift
upward at the end, appearing like the hands of a plaintive, supplicant monk. The yacht drifts so that it faces
its side toward the palace, getting close to the corner of
the rooftop as its gangplank extends out horizontally,
dropping only at the last minute toward the roof to
form a ramp.

From the street, a few rocks fruitlessly pelt the underside of the ship.

Stormtroopers move to the edge and fire their blasters down indiscriminately into the crowd.

Norra thinks: *You only dig the Empire's grave with
actions like that.* Because everyone sees. The Empire
is a thug, a bully. It's no better than Surat Nuat, or
Black Sun, or the syndicate of Hutts. The Empire pretends it's about law and order, but at the end of the
day, it's about dressing up oppression in the costume
of justice.

The admiral must understand it, too. She catches
up to the stormtroopers and pulls them back, rebuk-
ing them loudly.

Ahead of Norra, the other esteemed guests of the
Empire—their targets, the ones they hoped and failed
to stop—board the ship. The fox-faced man, the one
she believes is Moff Pandion, gives them a dismissive
look. As if they're greasy swamp clay stuck to the
underside of his boot. A mess that must be scraped
off and flung away.

Then he, too, ascends the ramp.

Norra looks to Jas and Sinjir. Both of them standing there, hands bound behind their backs. Each
hedged in by stormtroopers so that there's no way to
run and nowhere to go if they did.

Then the door opens again, and Norra finally sees:
It's Captain Antilles. Her heart breaks. His injuries

have him in their grip. His hair is spackled to his fore-head with sweat. His pallor is the color of fireplace ash. He's strapped down to a hovering table ushered forward by a pair of stormtroopers and a 2-1B medical droid.

As he passes, his eyes flutter open and he sees her. "Pilot," he says.

"Captain," she responds.

He gives her a weak smile as they push him onto the yacht.

Norra looks to Sinjir. "What's going to happen to us?"

"Well." The ex-Imperial sighs. "I will probably stand trial. Jas will probably die. You, I cannot say. Prison. Execution. Perhaps you'll join your rebel friend and be part of a peace settlement."

"I'm sorry about all of this."

"Not your fault," Jas says.

"He was her son," Sinjir notes, staring at them with his one good eye. The other remains swollen shut. "Her blood in his veins. I can reserve a *little* bit of judgment for her. I think I've earned that luxury."

Jas starts to protest, but Norra interrupts: "He's right. You can lay the blame at my feet. I just hope, despite it all, my son is okay."

Sinjir smirks. "Norra, I don't think any of us is okay."

"Norra, Temmin is a survivor," Jas says. "He has what it takes. If anybody will make it out of this alive, it will be him."

Temmin is dead.

He's sure of it. He could not have survived. And now, this feeling, this *strange and impossible* feeling— he's floating. Drifting across what feels like the calm waters of Farsigo Bay in the south. He and his mother and father used to go there sometimes on vacation. There they'd fish or sail spray-boats or try to scare up some of those gleaming korlappii shells—the ones that caught the sun just right and gave off a rainbow of light.

He doesn't hear the water. Or smell its brine.

And Temmin doesn't much believe in an afterlife anyway.

The boy opens his eyes.

He *is* floating. Buoyed. Carried on the hands of the crowd.

They caught him. *By all the stars and all the satellites, they caught me.* He laughs: a mad cackle that sounds not unlike that of his crazy droid.

Then he remembers: his mother. And Jas. And Sinjir.

He doesn't have much time.

He lifts his head and rolls off the carpet of hands that's been carrying him, and he drops down into the crowd itself. For a moment, he's lost—it's hard to get his bearings in this sea of people. The throng overwhelms. But then he spins and sees the massive palace walls rising up.

I have to get back up there.

He starts to push his way through the crowd.

Rocks pelt the walls and rebound. He sees people trying to climb up—a Rodian scales the wall and dangles from a balcony. A pair of humans try to help each other up. And Temmin thinks: *That's my way.*

He hasn't played with his friends in a while. Hasn't been the street rat urchin for a few years now. But he still knows how to shimmy up a drainpipe, or clamber up a wire-mesh grate, or find handholds where none seem to exist. He doesn't have time to figure out the best way up.

Instead, all he can do is climb with the others.

* * *

As they load the final passengers—the prisoners taken from the catacombs beneath the palace—the satrap catches up and drops to his knees. "Please, please, please. You must take me with you. I am besieged! They are climbing the walls like monkey-lizards. *They will tear me asunder.*"

Sloane puts her hand on his shoulder. "You've done the Empire a great service, Satrap Isstra."

The smile on his face spreads like butter. He believes he is being saved. His chest rises and sinks with relief. "Thank you. Thank you, Admiral. You are too kind."

"But we no longer require your aid."

"Wh . . . what?" Bewilderment crosses his face. He doesn't know if he's being punished, rewarded, put out to pasture, or what. "I don't—"

She gives a nod. Two stormtroopers grab Isstra and drag him back toward the doorway. He kicks and yells like a petulant child.

"You cannot do this!" he cries, froth forming at the corners of his mouth like so much flotsam. "I have been good to you! Guards! *Guards!*"

Two of his palace guardsmen come rushing through the door.

They are cut down by the stormtroopers' blaster rifles. Dead before they even had the chance to protect their erstwhile leader.

The satrap bleats like a throat-cut stock animal. The troopers toss him to the ground and he crawls between the corpses of his guards, weeping.

Sloane steps aboard the yacht.

* * *

The crowd roars. Temmin's fingers barely hold on, crammed into a tight crack running up the palace wall. His muscles ache. He hasn't done this for a while. He lifts himself up—

Just as the crowd surges. They pull back from the walls. Someone lobs something against the palace doors.

What was that—

The building rocks. A thermal detonator blast buckles the doors. The fingers on Temmin's left hand slip out of their mooring—

He dangles, one arm straining, his feet scrambling to find any kind of ledge to bolster himself.

The crowd surges again. They swarm against the injured door. Pushing in. Some four-armed Besalisk comes bounding through the mob with a massive forge hammer, and charges the door.

No time to worry about that.

Temmin screams through clamped teeth as he reaches up and regains his handhold. The boy continues his ascent.

Morna sits in the captain's chair of the yacht. Rae enters, sits next to her. "Cushy," she tells the pilot.

Morna nods. "No kidding, Admiral. Everything gleams. And these chairs . . . I feel like I'm still sinking into them."

"Don't get used to them. Comfort is not an Imperial priority." At that, Rae offers a faint smile. "Any problems with Crassus's pilot?"

"He fought me, but I made him recognize the Empire's authority and I assured him he would still be paid for his time."

"He's locked up, isn't he?"

"In one of the bedrooms, yes."

Adea, too, is in one of the bedrooms. Rae exhorted her assistant to go lie down, for stars' sake: The woman has been impeccable in her aid, and brave in her defense of the Empire. Rae told her to rest up. She put her in one of the cabins next to Captain Antilles and his guard.

"Excellent. Are we ready to depart this execrable planet?"

"We are, Admiral. And I just got the report that the Star Destroyers have returned to orbit from hyperspace. We have coverage from the *Vigilance*, the *Vanquish*, and the *Ascent*."

"Then let's bid farewell to this sweat-slick steam bath."

Morna nods. She powers the engines up.

The yacht begins to move.

The yacht begins to move.

Temmin scrambles over the edge of the palace roof and sees the gangplank pulling back and the yacht easing away from the edge.

I'm too late.

He looks around, eyes darting quickly.

There.

The satrap. Blubbering between the bodies of two of his own guard retinue. Their vibro-pikes lie off to the side.

This is stupid, Temmin thinks, hurrying over and kicking one of the pikes up into his hands. *This is the worst idea,* he thinks as he turns and runs full-tilt toward the edge of the roof. *I am a laser-brained moon-calf who is going to die,* he decides as he plants the tip of the pike down hard and uses it to launch himself off the palace roof.

I'm dead.

I can't make this.

I have made a huge mistake.

The pike is out of his hands. Temmin's arms pinwheel through open air as the yacht drifts. The side of the ship comes up fast—

He slams into it. *Wham.*

His hands reach for a hold. But they don't find one. He hears the pathetic squeak as he paws at the metal and starts to fall.

But then—

He stops falling.

His hand catches one of the decorated pipes outlining one of the windows. Temmin clutches it tight, and brings his other hand up and pulls himself up. There's a moment of triumph—a flutter in his chest as he thinks, *I made it! I totally made it!*

And then the yacht starts to lift up and he realizes:

Why did I do this? I'm going to die!

The ground beneath starts to shrink as the yacht ascends.

So close, Rae thinks, easing back into the copilot's chair. *Almost there.*

This entire trip has been a failure. She realizes that now. But failure cannot be the end of it. Failure has to be illuminating: an instruction manual written in scar tissue. What, then, are the lessons of this? What has been learned and what can be built from the wreckage?

One: Consensus will not be easy. And it may in fact be difficult enough that it is not worth pursuing.

Two: The Empire is fractured. That is not new information, but it has been clarified here. And a new dimension is revealed to her, as a result: Many inside the Empire do not want to heal those fractures but rather, want to use the division for their own designs.

Three: If the Empire is to survive, then they must—

A red blip on Morna's screen. The pilot frowns.

"What is it?" Rae asks.

"Could be a bird," the pilot says. "Though, if it is, it's a very big bird." She shakes her head and clarifies: "Something's on the hull."

Rae nods. "I'll send some men to look into it."

Sinjir kneels next to the others. His face feels like pounded dough. There they wait in this opulent room toward the back of the yacht, kneeling like slaves in a plush room of couches and tables. The fat banker, Crassus, sits in the corner, smoking spice out of a long obsidian pipe. His slave women in their beastly masks buff and trim the nails of his plump, desiccated feet, cutting the calluses off his awful toes.

On the one side of Crassus sits Jylia Shale. A general. Sinjir knows her—or, rather, knows of her. Depending on who you talk to inside the Empire, she's either a legend or a traitor. A conqueror or a cur. She has a pair of red-cloaked Imperial Guardsmen with her.

On the other side of Crassus: the purple-robed adviser. Sinjir doesn't remember that one's name, though he's fairly sure Jas told him. One of Palpatine's inner circle, most likely. An acolyte of the Sith side of the Force, though certainly not a proper practitioner of it. Essentially, a cultist.

Across from Sinjir:

Pandion sits, stock-straight.

Staring at them.

No. Staring at *him*, at Sinjir.

"I know I'm handsome," Sinjir says—an unintentional growl in the back of his throat as he speaks. A rattle from injury, not rage.

Pandion only chuckles—it looks like he's about to say something, but then a small contingent of stormtroopers hurries past, toward the middle of the ship. They look alarmed. Pandion tries not to flinch, but it happens.

Sinjir says with a smirk: "Something's wrong, isn't it?"

"Still your lips, traitor, or I'll cut them off."

Gonna die, gonna die, gonna die. Temmin holds on with every ounce of willpower he can. Already wisps of clouds are passing by. The air grows cold. The ship starts to shudder with turbulence. He starts to think: *Maybe I can crawl down underneath the ship. Use my multitool to pop a maintenance hatch, climb into the belly of the ship and*—

The window above him pops open with a hiss.

A stormtrooper's head pokes out.

"Hey!"

That's as good an invitation as Temmin's going to get.

He reaches up, hooks his hand behind the stormtrooper's helmet, and yanks the Imperial soldier out through the open space.

The trooper's scream is loud at first, and then fades as he falls.

Temmin crawls up inside the open window.

He belly-flops to the floor, panting. He shakes the blood flow back into his arms. He's in a hallway full of doors. Cabins for the yacht. He stands up, dusts himself off. Then someone taps him on the shoulder.

Uh-oh.

He turns. There stand two more stormtroopers, rifles up.

And behind them come a pair of red-helmeted Imperial Guards. Their cloaks sweeping the floor behind them.

"Hey, guys," Temmin says, giving a fake laugh. "Is this not the twelve thirty space-bus to the Ordwallian Cluster Casino? No? Ooh. Awkward!"

He turns and runs.

"Fragging frag it!" Jom Barell snarls, his face red. Nothing he's done has made this thing work, and now his target is fleeing toward orbit.

He stands for a few moments. Chest rising and falling.

Calm down, he tells himself. *Think.*

But he doesn't think and he doesn't calm down.

He roars in rage and brings his good fist down on the console again and again, because whatever chance he had has been squandered, and the effort undertaken to capture this turret in the first place didn't do a damn thing to help the New Republic and—

With the last hit, the console suddenly glows bright.

"What the . . ."

Outside the window, the twin cannons adjust, tracking the target.

The whole turret shakes as it fires, filling the cockpit with the bright, demonic light of turbolaser blasts.

It's going well. Too well. Sloane feels the twist of dread in her gut, and that twist only tightens when Morna turns and says with a frown:

"We have a problem, Admiral."

Of course we do.

"What is it, pilot?"

"A rebel fleet. Coming into space above Akiva."

Perfectly atrocious timing.

"How big?"

"Big enough to be a problem."

"Let's just get us to the *Vigilance* safe, Morna. Then we can—"

Again, the pilot's screen starts flashing.

"What *now*?" Rae snaps.

Morna's eyes light up with panic and confusion. "One of our turrets. From the ground. It's tracking us. It's about to—"

The ship rocks and shudders. Rae's head snaps back and she tumbles out of her chair. Everything goes dark.

Lasers scorch the air above Temmin's head—he runs, ducks, and dives onto his belly to avoid getting cooked. He rolls over and puts his hands up to surrender—

He can see they're not going to let him.

The stormtroopers raise the rifles again.

And the wall next to them suddenly disappears.

The ship jolts hard to the right as a bright flash tears through it, ripping it open from underneath. Taking the wall, the floor, *and* the Imperials away—what's left of them spirals away out the open hole. Wind keens like a mournful beast. Temmin feels it start to pull at him as the whole hallway depressurizes: He grabs out with a hand as the yacht starts to dip, catching one of the cabin door handles. Fixtures start popping off the walls, vacuumed out into the swirling clouds. At both ends of the hall, pressure doors start to close, sealing off the middle portion of the yacht.

Temmin kicks open the cabin door, pulling away from the hungry winds trying to suck him out into the void. He throws himself inside.

Emergency klaxons blare. The panel dash on the shuttle is lit up in an array of panicked flashes. Rae hauls herself back into the chair. Morna never left hers. Her arms are extended outward, and the tendons in her neck stand taut like bridge cables. She fights to keep the yacht aloft—it starts to dip but she pulls back and she again lifts its nose.

"Status!" Sloane demands.

"Kinda busy, Admiral," Morna hisses through her teeth.

Rae wants to chastise her, but the pilot is right. She instead pulls up the screen, sees the damage was straight to the middle underside of the yacht. Near to where the first-floor cabins are. Both halves of the ship are sealing off with pressure doors, which means they're not dead yet and nobody has to abandon ship. But it *does* mean that the front half of the yacht—in which Rae sits right now—is separate and in fact *inaccessible* to the back half. And the middle of the ship is a no-being's-land.

The ship bounces and judders like it's about to come apart. Morna warns: "The atmosphere is rough up here. Could tear us apart. Almost to orbit. *Almost there.*"

"Keep it together," Rae demands.

If anybody can do this: Morna can.

The lights buzz and flicker. They go from darkness, to red emergency lighting, back to full lights—then back to darkness once more.

Jas doesn't know what happened, but best guess is that they took a hit. From where, she cannot say. She's surprised they're still aloft. Good thing this is a pretty big ship, but even still, they're all lucky that the whole thing didn't get sheared in half with both pieces plunging to planetside.

Panic has filled the Imperial ranks now. Murmuring and frittering about. Crassus whining about his yacht. The adviser, Yupe Tashu, praying in some heretical tongue to beseech whatever Dark Force he calls upon in times of crisis. Shale simply leans forward, head between her legs. Like she might be sick. She's a general—used to, in part, being on the ground. Or in a cloistered war room somewhere. She's not a soldier, or at least hasn't been for years.

Jas, for her part, just sits still.

Like Pandion, who seems to have a real hate for Sinjir. It's there in the way he stares at the other man. Black eyes like a pair of blaster barrels ready to fire.

A stormtrooper enters. "We're cut off from the front of the ship. Pressure doors have sealed us off."

Pandion, without turning his gaze from Sinjir, picks up his communicator and speaks into it: "Admiral Sloane, are you there?"

His comm crackles. Her voice emerges: broken, staticky, but there.

"Moff Pandion. We're presently occupied."

"Should we expect to die? This ship has escape pods, does it not?"

Sloane's voice returns: "We're safe. Almost in orbit. Patience."

Jas doesn't know what's going on.

But chaos has sunk its teeth into the situation.

And in chaos, there lurks opportunity.

INTERLUDE:

BESPIN CLOUD CITY

"THEY'RE COMING IN!" Borgin Kaa cries to his young girlfriend: the dancer Linara. She gives him a look of panic as he gestures toward the front door of his luxury domicile where a line of sparks is drawing its way up the outer edge of the magnalocked portal. The sparks burn bright and ease upward with the speed and perfection of a confident, practiced hand.

The older man fumbles around the foyer table and finds a ceramic vase from the Vinzor Legacy. It's an artifact many millennia old, dating back to the Old Republic. Or so he's told. All he cares—or cared—about is that it's worth something. The way it's shot through with blue lacite. Like gleaming cerulean spiderwebs. Blazing blue.

He hates to do it, but he palms the vase.

It's a weapon, he thinks. *Not an ancient, valuable artifact.*

His heart hammers in his chest.

Did he take his tincture this morning?

Did he forget?

Is he going to die?

No! I've lived this long. I'm on the list. Cloud City has become quite the destination to procure rare implants: new oculars, custom-tailored hands, whole new organ systems for whatever human or alien can pay. He needs a new heart. He was on the list—still is, he hopes. But then the rebel villains had to muck everything up and the Empire stepped in and took over this sector and now all those implants are on hold.

The Imperials will fix this. The Emperor has assured the galaxy of peace.

The embers dance around the final curve of the door, then down to the floor.

The portal hisses and slides open.

Through the smoke he sees the shapes of the trespassers—Linara cries out, and Borgin grunts and heaves the vase hard. It hits to the side of the door, missing. It doesn't even break. The thing just goes *thud* and lands on the floor.

Apparently the Vinzors knew how to make a vase.

Figures storm in, blasters up. Two of them he doesn't recognize: a Devaronian woman and a lanky, clanking PAD—a personal assistant droid—on whose tarnished silver faceplate someone has painted a black skull.

The other two he does recognize: the local miscreant, Kars Tal-Korla—aka, the Scourge of Cloud City. Hard not to recognize him. He's on every poster and cautionary holovid here in the city! The Empire wants him bad, and now here he is—live inside Borgin's own apartment. Wearing his trademark armor: a mismatched patchwork set of Mandalorian, Corellian, and even bits of Imperial trooper thrown in for good measure.

Next to him, though, is the real surprise:

Jintar Oarr—

Fellow Onderonian. Wealthy beyond measure. One

of the residents here in the luxury levels of Cloud City alongside Borgin.

A friend. Or was, once.

"You," Borgin says, pointing a thick finger at the man. Jintar, that handsome prig. Sharp-cut beard. Eyes like gray clouds. Even the lines in his face look distinguished.

But as Borgin thrusts his accusing finger up, the Devaronian steps in, grabs his finger, and bends it back. Pain arcs like a blaster bolt up to his elbow. He howls in a way that shames him—a piggy, high-pitched squeal, like the sound one of those Ugnaughts makes when it tumbles into the machines—and then he drops to his knees as she with her other hand jams the barrel of her blaster rifle against his forehead.

"Wait," Jintar says. He reaches for her wrist, and she hisses at him like a snake. He stays his hand, but then says to her: "Let me talk to him."

Kars gives a nod. "Let them speak. But we're on a timetable here—so make it snappy." To the assistant droid he barks: "Go find that access panel."

Access panel? Borgin's gaze follows the droid as it totters out of the foyer and down the hall—but before he can see where the metal man is going, the Devaronian grabs his chin with a rough pull and turns his face toward her.

"Your friend would like to speak with you."

Jintar kneels. "Bor," he says. "Listen to me. We've been lied to. Adelhard has sealed off the whole sector. Massive blockades with a ragtag Imperial remnant. But that's not how they keep control. They keep control by lying to us." He takes a deep breath. "The Emperor is dead, Bor. It's been confirmed."

"Lies," Borgin hisses. "Of course, that's what *his* type would have you believe!" He gestures with his chin toward the rebel, Kars. The scruffy pirate in the patchwork armor does nothing but scowl and shake his head. "I've seen the holovids. You have, too. Palpatine is alive and well on Coruscant and—"

"He's just a stand-in. A proxy. *An actor*."

"No. More rebel lies."

"We've done the comparison. The vids don't match. This . . . person in the dark robes isn't Palpatine. Different chin, different gestures. A poor facsimile."

"You're a traitor."

Jintar's face falls. Sadness flashes in his eyes. "No, Borgin. You're the traitor."

"The Empire's been good to us."

"It has. But it hasn't been good to everyone else. And the righteous folks of the galaxy will see that. Which means I'm calling on you to act." Jintar's voice softens. That man could coax a slakari-hound off a rotten carcass. "We could use your help."

Help. They want *his* help?

That's not happening. Borgin roars—he's been in a few fights back in the day, back when he was a young mining baron on the Sevarcos moon. Sure, he's older now, much older, and heavier, but he lurches upward, slamming his head into Jintar's—

Stars explode behind his eyes. He falls back on his tailbone. Someone reaches for him, but he cries out and swats the hand away.

Jintar is wincing, his forehead already showing the bloom of a future bruise. Borgin, though, tastes blood.

It's the rebel's turn. Kars steps into view. Blurry. Borgin blinks. The pirate scratches at his stubble and twirls the pistol at his hip. "Let's talk this through. You've got an access panel in the back. It's tied into the same conduit as Governor Adelhard's chamber up on the prime tower. We need that panel opened. You give us the code, we'll be happy. You don't give us the code, we'll have to do it ourselves." Kars's mouth sharpens into a wicked razor-angle grin. "And we won't be happy."

"Brutes! Bullies! *Criminals*."

Kars sighs. "Okay, then. Rorna?"

He gives a nod, and the Devaronian woman pistons a fist into Borgin's side. Borgin bleats and flails— Jintar catches his hands and wrenches them behind his back. He feels his hands being stuffed into something. A fabric bag. A sock, maybe. Then the rip of bonding tape coming off its roll as it winds around his wrists.

"Linara!" he cries. "Linara, save me!"

But his girlfriend merely looks down at him the way a disappointed mother looks down at her troublemaker child. She asks Kars: "Is there anything I can do?"

The pirate chuckles, then tosses her a roll of bonding tape. "Why not close up that gassy vent of his he calls a mouth?"

Borgin protests: "Linara, I've been good to you. We love each other. Don't you do this to me. I'll punish you! I'll punish your whole family! I'll end their loans and stack debtors against them and—"

She slaps the tape against his mouth. And she doesn't stop there. She winds it around his head once, twice, a third time. It looks like she's enjoying it.

"Mmph! *Mmph*." Translation: *The Emperor will have your heads for this.*

Kars nods. From the back of the domicile, the sound of a whirring drill. Kars lifts a wrist-comm to his mouth: "Tell Lobot we have to do it the hard way."

The Devaronian says in a lower voice, "We could torture the code out of the rich man. It would be no small pleasure." Said with a feral smirk.

The pirate waves her off, then away from his comm he says: "No. We have specific instructions. No such shenanigans. We're to keep this clean, aboveboard. Blah blah blah, the Alliance doesn't do it 'like that.'" Then, back to his wrist: "Yeah. Yeah, I'm listening. Tell Lobot to make sure he's standing by with the intrusion team. And get a message to Calrissian. Tell him we're almost in and that he can transfer the credits—" He pauses. "No, you know what? Tell him we're doing this one gratis. On the house. He and his New Republic pals can owe me a favor. Make sure to emphasize that. A big favor."

Scum. Scum!

Jintar once more kneels down. "You're on the wrong side of history, Bor. You never did understand that the galaxy was more than one man."

CHAPTER THIRTY-FIVE

AND LIKE THAT, the pale blue skies of atmosphere give way to the gradient darkness of space—and that gradient fades, too, becoming not part shadow, but all dark. The comforting void. Because that's what it is, to Rae: a comforting emptiness. It gives her pause. The vastness. The endlessness of it all. To feel small in it, but also powerful enough to matter in its midst.

At present, though, she can find no comfort.

Because, ahead of them: War rages in the black.

A brute-force battle. No elegance, no aplomb. On one side, a trio of Star Destroyers firing salvo after salvo of blasts. Those attacks met by the incoming rebel fleet: five ships, each smaller than the Destroyers, but no less potent. And between the two of them, a swarm of ships like flocks of night birds. Trading fire. Some of them burning bright as they spiral like the crackling, wheeling fireworks set off by laughing children.

She chews her lip.

"How are we doing?" she asks Morna.

The pilot answers: "Limping along."

"Sprinting or limping, just get us home."

* * *

Commander Agate is shaking.

It's normal. At least for her. The battle here has begun, and in the beginning of any battle, she shakes. It's a combination of jangled war nerves and the rush of adrenaline hitting her like lightning overloading a ship's systems. For years, she tried to hide it. She took meds to still her hands. Tried to remain hidden and alone during the first moments of a battle. Because she couldn't have those with her see. The shaking was a sign of weakness. But eventually she came to realize:

Showing it off—and not caring who cared—was a sign of strength.

So now she trembles. And she lets it happen. It's a natural part of who she is as a warrior and a leader of soldiers.

She calms herself by staring out at the black and then back again at the battle map holographically projected above the table. All the pieces moving along as they must. A chaotic dance, but one given over to a kind of precious, special order.

Now, though: a new blip.

She taps the air, zooms in on this uninvited guest.

A yacht? Uninvited *and* unexpected.

Imperial? Or some unlucky Akivan land baron who thought to make a hasty escape during . . . an unfolding space battle? That's either an idiot or a genius piloting that thing. Agate asks Ensign Targada— a gruff Klatooinian with a high brow and a frowning mouth, an ex-slave who is loudly loyal to the New Republic—to track that ship's course.

"It's headed for that Star Destroyer," he says.

An Imperial, then.

Shoot it down?

She hesitates. Things move more slowly than one would think—big capital ships firing fusillade after fusillade at one another while the fighters swoop and spin among the stars—and careful thinking can be a strength of its own. But hesitation can fast become a liability.

Targada echoes her question: "Concentrate fire on the yacht?"

"No," she says sharply. "It's damaged. It may play host to a target of high-value intelligence. Destroying it means destroying information we may need." She curses under her breath. In an ideal world, they'd swoop in and capture. But the battle won't allow for such a precision maneuver. "Let's remove their options for landing. Concentrate fire on that Star Destroyer. If they don't have a place to land, they become quicker pickings."

The strange man throttles Temmin. He's ruddy-cheeked, with a warty nose and pock-cratered cheeks. The man wears a pilot's leathers.

"What's happening?" he asks. The lights flick on and off. "What's happened to my ship, you little urchin?"

Temmin shoves him back. "Get! Off!"

The man snarls. "You'd better tell me what happened. Did you do something? Are you an insurgent? A rebel terrorist? Scum. Scum!"

Then he rushes Temmin.

Temmin cries out and throws a punch. The man's nose pops like a blister and he goes down, whimpering. "My ship. My ship!"

The boy has no time for this.

He looks around, his eyes having a hard time adjusting when the lights keep strobing like that. The pilot starts crawling for the door, and Temmin moves and kneels down in front of him. "Out that cabin door, it's death. You hear me? Death."

"You don't know that. I need to get to the cockpit! I can fly this ship. Me. Only me! I'm a good pilot. Or . . . was. Once."

"Then we need to get to the cabin. The pressure doors are sealed, you nerf-wit. You know this ship? Tell me how to get . . . somewhere, *anywhere*."

The man groans as he stands. His joints and bones creak and pop. "Move the . . . move that bed back. There should be a maintenance hatch under there. But I don't have a tool to open it."

Is nobody ever prepared? Temmin rolls his eyes and pops the multitool off his belt. He starts to move the bed. Sure enough: a flat hatch sealed with flanser-bolts. They'll take time. He gets to work.

Pandion stands. Norra watches him take slow steps toward Sinjir, on whom he seems singularly focused. "You were an Imperial, once," Pandion says. "A loyalty officer. Is that right?"

"That is accurate," Sinjir says.

"Ironic, then. That your own loyalty was in question."

"Not really. I was taught early on in my training to see the weakness in others. It was only a matter of time before I saw the weakness in the whole of the Empire." Sinjir grins past bloody teeth. "Look closely and you see the whole thing is shot through with cracks and fractures."

Pandion walks closer. A slow, measured step. A cruelty flashing in his eyes, pulsing and flaring like the lights overhead. "The only weakness in the Empire is men like you. Men who are not committed enough. Men who betray the cause because of a failing inside them. Bruised hearts and diminished minds. The Empire is made stronger when fools like you fall."

Even with his hands behind his back, Sinjir manages a shrug.

"Seems to me," he says, "that the weakness in the Empire is in men like you, Moff Pandion. Paltry, ineffectual idiots. Men who want to be leaders more than they want to actually *lead*. And besides, what is a *moff*, anyway? A meager sector head. Even the name sounds weak. *Moff. Moff.* It's the sound a dog makes as it regurgitates its dinner—"

Whap. Pandion backhands Sinjir.

A line of blood snakes down the ex-Imperial's chin from his lip.

Sinjir licks it away.

"*Moff, moff, moff,*" he says again, mocking.

Norra warns him: "Sinjir, don't—"

But it's too late. Pandion is on him again, this time hauling Sinjir up by the collar of his stolen officer's uniform. He hits him once, twice, a third time and Sinjir's head rocks back on his shoulders.

"Stop!" Norra cries. "Stop."

Pandion hisses at her. "Shut up, scum."

Sinjir seizes the opportunity. He spits a tooth—one of his own—at Moff Pandion's face. It bounds off the space between the Imperial's eyes, and as he blinks in surprise, Sinjir head-butts him.

Crack.

Pandion staggers back. Twin streams of blood trickle down his nose. His face twists up like a terrible knot. "You. Traitor." He wipes blood from his nose, then draws his blaster. "You won't make it to trial."

Jas speaks up: "Let me do it."

Pandion squints. "What?"

"I'll do it. For the right price."

"Price? After you've thrown in with *this* lot?"

"The bounty on your head was too good, Pandion. But I'm sure there's more than enough credits to compensate me. Looking at this yacht alone, I can see we're on a banking ship. Surely you're willing to pay me more than the New Republic was to capture you."

"Capture me?"

"It was all about you. You have a very high bounty."

He sneer-smirks. "Yes. I should have expected that. How high was the bounty?"

"Ten thousand credits."

"Should've been higher," he snits. "Still. I'll give you twenty thousand from Arsin Crassus's coin purse to execute this traitor. Right here, right now. What say you?"

Crassus stands, blustery and blithering: "What? You can't. I didn't make that offer!"

"And yet I take it on good faith you wouldn't want to deny the Empire," Moff Pandion says. He turns the blaster toward Crassus. "Right?"

"Ah . . . absolutely. What's mine is yours."

Pandion chuckles. "Good." He spins the blaster around and approaches Jas Emari, extending the weapon out. "Here you go, Zabrak. Take it. It's yours. Oh. What's that? Your hands are bound?" He clucks his tongue. "What a shame. Guess we don't have a deal. Because the Empire doesn't *do* deals with bounty hunters anymore."

He wheels back with the blaster and moves to strike her.

Norra cries out.

But Jas is fast. Her hands—they're free. Somehow. She catches his hand and twists his wrist. Pandion cries out and she snatches the blaster from him and wheels him around, pointing the gun to his head.

"Nobody shoot, or I take off the top of his head with his own blaster," Jas warns. Jylia maintains her seat, and Crassus keeps standing. Stormtroopers and Imperial Guards point weapons, but Pandion waves them off, saying:

"No. No. Wait. Put them down. Let her speak."

Norra thinks: *How did she get free?*

But then Sinjir steps up. The shackles fall off his wrists, too.

Suddenly a voice calls from beneath her. She turns and looks, sees a pair of eyes looking up through the room-length vent that runs along the seam between the wall and the floor. A little multitool reaches out through the vent. She hears a voice:

"Mom, move your wrists closer. I can pick the lock."

Out the front of the yacht, a TIE fighter spirals toward them, fire jetting from its one side into the unforgiving maw of space. Morna yanks back on the flight stick, moves the flying brick out of the way just in time. Their own ship shudders as the TIE explodes somewhere out of sight.

Ahead, a pair of TIEs chase a rebel X-wing. They swoop and dip. Beyond them: the Star Destroyer *Vigilance*. *Not far now,* Rae thinks.

She brings up Tothwin on the comm.

His nervous face appears on screen.

"We're coming in," Rae says. "Bay G2D1."

"Of course, Admiral. We're taking a lot of damage and the shields—"

Morna leans over. "We're coming in hot. I can't slow this thing down. Something is fritzed."

Rae adds: "Have extinguisher droids on hand, we're coming in—"

From one of the rebel frigates, a massive blast arcs through space, striking the *Vigilance*. A burst of fire and debris from the bridge. Tothwin's image dissolves and the link is gone.

"Admiral?" Morna asks. "We can't land there. The *Vigilance*—"

"Remains for the moment. The plan is the same."

"Admiral, I strongly advise—"

"I have a plan. Take us in.

"Same bay. The *Vigilance* remains, and I have a plan."

Tension in the room runs so high that, should a pin drop, everyone might start firing their blasters. Jas stands with Pandion's blaster held to his temple, her other hand clamped around his neck. Norra is up now, shaking off her shackles. Sinjir is helping Temmin crawl up through a maintenance hatch in the middle of the floor. Norra rushes over and picks him up and gives him a long, crushing hug.

Pandion jeers: "How touching. But what now, bounty hunter? You've got one weapon among you, and a dozen pointed in your direction."

"That one weapon is pointed at your head," she says.

"Ah, yes. But *then what*, exactly? We land and . . . you continue this threat? Eventually you'll meet someone who doesn't care if I live or die."

"I'd say we've already met several."

He scoffs. "This charade is temporary. What is your plan?"

She wears a feral grin and licks her lips. "I have no plan. What I do have is *your* blaster and *my* friends and luck on our side. Plus: We're very good at improvising, as you can well see."

"You'll pay for this."

"No," she says. "We'll *get* paid for this."

* * *

Rae straps in.

The Star Destroyer looms closer and closer. Bay G2D1 awaits covered with the faint blue shimmer of the shields. Shields that she believes are failing, which means soon, the *Vigilance* will be no more.

To Morna, she says: "I trust you not to kill us."

The pilot nods. "That's the plan."

She winces as she brings the yacht in through the front of the bay. Rae feels the speed now, sees everything zooming up to them fast, too fast, and the deck rushes up—

The yacht hits it hard. Pain goes through her—an ache through her wrists and neck as the g-forces threaten to rip her asunder. The yacht lands hard, and as the lights again go out all she hears is the grinding of metal on metal as the whole thing shifts sideways, skidding fast and loose across the Imperial Star Destroyer's bay.

CHAPTER THIRTY-SIX

FZZT. FZZT.

Sparks in the dark. Circuits pop and fizzle. Panels swing, hanging by loose wires. A haze of smoke fills the air. Smells duel for supremacy: the stink of hot metal, the odor of melting plastic. A third stench: electric ozone.

Light comes in from outside. Garish, bright, artificial light.

Norra groans and lifts her chest off the uneven ground. She tries to figure out what happened, but it doesn't take her long to realize, because she's been in this situation too many times before:

We crash-landed.

Underneath her, Temmin lies unmoving.

Oh, no.

"Temmin. Temmin!" She pulls him up and he suddenly draws a sharp breath, his eyes fluttering open. She laughs and pulls him close.

"Ow," he says.

"Sorry."

"No. I'm sorry."

"Not now," she says. "Later. Now we have to—"

Someone moves through the space. Norra's eyes adjust and she sees Jas stalking through the ruined room, emerging from a whorl of black smoke. She stands over a body, points the blaster down, and fires.

The blue pulse from a stun charge warbles in the air.

Whoever is lying there shudders and goes slack.

Jas looks over. Sees Norra—she reaches out a hand and helps her up, then Temmin. To the boy, the bounty hunter says: "You're late."

"Jas, I'm so sorry, I didn't mean—"

"Stop there. We're fine."

From behind them, a cough and sputter before Sinjir says: "Yes, please. I'm not dead but I may yet choke on your rank sentimentality. I cannot say for sure *exactly* what happened, but I'd put considerable credits down on a bet that says we should not dally."

"You talk a lot for not dallying," Jas says.

"And you certainly do love an unnecessary retort—"

Norra interrupts: "Focus up, crew. What's our status?"

"We crashed," Jas says. "Obviously." She gestures with her foot by way of a gentle kick. "That body belongs to Adviser Yupe Tashu. Now stunned. I also secured Jylia Shale, the general." She points, and Norra can make out a crumpled shape. "Beyond her is Crassus. He didn't make it. Along with most of these stormtroopers."

One starts to stir, and she fires a stun blast at him. He thumps back down to the ground with a gurgled groan.

"And Pandion?"

"Gone."

Norra nods. "Come on."

They step toward the back of the room, and together they push on a scrap of metal—that's where the light's coming in, and collectively they peel back part of the hull. Enough for them to slip through.

Out there, the bay entrance—a rectangle looking out into space. And onto a space battle: New Republic ships launch a fusillade from their cannons. The darkness is lit up with the vigor of war.

In here: an Imperial Star Destroyer bay. Alarms go off.

The entire ship rumbles and vibrates.

A TIE interceptor screams past the bay entrance, chased by a pair of arrowhead-shaped A-wings. Norra thinks: *I want to be out there.* An odd feeling. A scared feeling. But eager and hungry for it just the same.

"Look," Temmin says. She follows him pointing—

At the other end of the bay, a line of *Lambda*-class shuttles and a pair of TIE fighters. One of the shuttles lifts up off the ground.

"You." Norra points to Jas. "Take the others. Get your bounties and haul them on board one of those shuttles. You can fly it, right?"

Jas nods. "Not as well as you, I wager, but yes. I'm capable."

"Capable," Sinjir says. "There's that word again."

"You help her, Sinjir. Temmin, I need you to do something real important. Are you listening?"

"O . . . okay. Say the word."

"Go back inside that yacht. Find Captain Wedge Antilles. You hear me? Find him and get him out." *Please let him be okay. After all this . . .*

Temmin asks: "Mom, what are *you* doing?"

"I'm going to take one of those TIE fighters and I'm going after whoever *that* is." She points to the shuttle as it roars toward them, its cannons firing—she pulls the others down behind the wreckage of the yacht as the laser blasts stitch a line of craters along the docking bay floor before the shuttle races toward the exit and off into space.

Norra wastes no time because there is no time to waste.

She's up on her feet, hard-charging toward the TIE fighters. She hears her son calling for her—asking her not to leave, asking her not to die, telling her to let it go. But she knows she can't. She knows who she is and what she does. And this is it. It is time to fly once more.

CHAPTER THIRTY-SEVEN

ONCE AGAIN, the almost lunatic freedom of the TIE fighter. Norra plunges the small Imperial ship into the maelstrom of battle. Cannon fire is tearing past her in both directions, laser blasts crisscrossing the void in front of her. She hunts the stars for her prey, and just as she sees the *Lambda*-class signal out there in the dark, an X-wing comes diving from above her like a raptor bird and she realizes: *I'm in an Imperial ship.*

The Jedi are known for having the Force—she doesn't know what that is or if it's even a real thing (though Skywalker certainly makes it look like it's no myth), but she knows she doesn't have it. Just the same, she has what she has, which is an uncanny ability to just *turn her brain off*. Stop her mind from chattering. Stop thinking about details.

Stop thinking and just *feel*.

The X-wing comes down on her and she reacts without thinking, bringing the TIE fighter up where the X-wing goes in the opposite direction. Then a Y-wing is in her sights, and she has to juke the TIE back and forth, starboard to port and back again, in order to avoid the incoming blasts.

She quickly fumbles with the communicator and signals to rebel comms: "This is Norra Wexley, call sign Gold Nine. I have taken command of this TIE. Repeat: I have taken command of this TIE."

Inside her head she adds: *Please don't kill me.*

Commander Agate stands on the bridge of the old Alderaanian frigate, the *Sunspire*. Out there, she watches the battle unfold. It's easy to stare at it and be lost—not lost because you don't know what's happening, but sucked into it, drawn to it like a winged thing toward a plasma torch. Hypnotized, in a way. Idly, she realizes: *We're winning this battle.*

Which means they're winning this war.

There, though, a new question haunts Agate in the back of her mind:

What then?

Behind her, Ensign Uray stands. The blue-skinned Pantoran says: "We are winning this engagement, Commander."

"Winning does not mean won. Keep up the pressure."

"Yes, Commander. There's something else." A pause, then: "There's a pilot out there in a TIE fighter. Claiming to be . . . well, one of ours. From Gold Squadron."

"That seems unlikely."

"And yet it's what she claims."

She ponders. Could be a trap. But to what end? A single TIE fighter could do what? They are suicide machines, but why this ruse?

Her gut twinges, tells her which way to go.

"Give her support. Get her on the comm. Let's see what's going on."

* * *

Plugging in hyperspace coordinates is no easy feat during a space battle. Get it wrong and put the ship in the wrong space and the only place you'll end up with great speed is the grave. (Though here Rae admits: If ever she is to die, it should be out here, in space. Born from stardust, returned to stardust. She cares little for such poetry, but this appeals to her, somehow.)

"Almost there," Rae says. "Keep us flying, Morna."

Her pilot nods.

Inside her heart, Rae regrets the loss of those they left behind. Adea in particular. Whether the woman is alive or dead, she cannot say. Adea certainly deserves life, but if death is her end, then it was a noble one in service to the great Galactic Empire.

The door to the cockpit hisses open.

Which is curious, because she and Morna Kee are the only two on this shuttle—or so she had thought.

She wheels around, knowing already who she'll see.

Pandion.

He's got a blaster in his hand. A line of blood is drying upon a long cut crossing his brow. His nose appears broken. His mouth, bloody, and the rest of his uniform looks dirty, dusty, in tatters.

"You survived," she says.

"I did," he says with a curious smile. A smile that quickly dies on his face. "Let me tell you how this will go. You're going to the *Ravager*. You will take me to that Star Destroyer, and then I will take control of it in return. It is mine, now, Admiral. Not yours. The last great weapon of the Empire is in my control because you are incapable of wielding it."

The shuttle quickly ducks a hail of incoming blasts. Rae steadies herself on her chair. Pandion remains standing, leering, scowling.

"You fool," she says. "You eager, egotistical fool. Grand Moff. *Pfah*. You have so much, so wrong. The

Ravager is not the last weapon. Nor do I even control it. There is . . . another."

His face twitches. "You don't mean . . ."

"I do mean. He's not dead."

"But you said he *was*."

"I lied." She shrugs.

"This was . . . all his plan. Wasn't it? I should've seen it. I fell for a trap. We *all* fell for your trap. You betrayer. You foul, wretched betrayer."

Panic seizes her. She thinks: *No, it wasn't supposed to happen like this.* But then the more terrible realization hits her: *But what if it was?*

What if this was the plan all along?

Suddenly the ship shudders. Morna, without taking her eyes off the console, says: "We have company. It's a lone TIE fighter. It's firing at us! And rebel ships, too. Incoming."

Rae scowls. "New plan, then. You might want to buckle in, Valco. This is going to be a bumpy ride."

It feels good to be up here again. The TIE fighter makes Norra feel like she could thread a needle. And there, ahead: the shuttle. She takes a few shots, though the shuttle's deflector shields hold. But they won't for long. Especially with the squadron of Y-wings coming in behind her for support. But then, just as she's got the shuttle in her sights—

TIEs. Swarming like wasps. They're on to her. She no longer flags as Imperial to them and they're taking their shots. She pulls away, leads three of them off— they're on her like magnets, following her every swoop and turn, her every roll and lurch, so she draws them back toward the Y-wings.

The rebel fighters, dead ahead.

Into the comm she says: "Stay on target."

It looks like a suicide mission. A game of chicken with her own people, her own ships. But they know what she's doing. This is a practiced move. One the Imperials never expect.

At the last minute, she pulls up, and the Y-wings open fire.

The TIEs, dispatched in gassy plumes of quick-burn fire.

Now back to that shuttle.

It takes her a moment—the shuttle has deviated from its course.

There. *There.* Heading toward another of the Star Destroyers. The shuttle swerves toward the massive Imperial ship. Norra lines up her weapons. And she starts to fire.

Pandion has chosen to remain standing.

Which is as expected. He won't sit. He won't risk looking weak.

Rae thinks: *It will be his downfall.* "That's your Destroyer. The *Vanquish.* I'm going to take it."

He laughs. "I think you overestimate your—"

Rae moves fast, grabbing the flight stick out of Morna's grip. She pushes it hard to the right and the ship goes into a quick spin.

Pandion loses his footing. Morna quickly rights the ship, and when the moff reclaims his balance, Rae is up out of her seat. She pistons a fist into his middle, then wrestles the blaster out of his hand.

She fires a shot into his belly, then kicks him out of the cockpit.

The door seals behind, and her fingers dance on the keypad next to it to ensure the seal holds. He wails on the other side. Pounding.

The ship shudders with blasts from that TIE fighter.

"Let's give them what they want," Rae says. "Let's give them this ship. Let's give them Pandion. Let's give them a show."

Morna nods.

She begins the detachment sequence while Rae punches the self-destruct codes into the hyperdrive matrix.

It all happens so slow, and yet so fast. Norra fires the TIE's cannons at the engines of the shuttle. She wears the shields down like a kid scratching the paint off one of his toys—and then she scores a direct hit. The engines flare bright blue and she expects them to go dark.

But they don't. They do the opposite.

They erupt in crepuscular rays and Norra has to shield her eyes. The shuttle suddenly lists left, drifting not like a ship but rather like a piece of space debris—and she realizes late, too late, *It's going to blow.*

And blow, it does. The entire shuttle shudders and detonates. Fire blossoms into open space. Norra tries to move the TIE out of the way, jerking on the controls to maneuver hard and fast to starboard—but fire fills her window and everything shakes. Sparks hiss up out of the console and down on her head and she thinks, *This is it, it's over—*

At least I went doing what I wanted to do.

At least I went down fighting.

At least Temmin knows I love him.

I love you, Temmin—

And then she's gone.

INTERLUDE:

JAKKU

THIS IS A DEAD PLACE, Corwin Ballast thinks.

Out there—it's nothing. Nowhere, stretched wide and made infinite. The dry crust of desert. The whipping tails of dust. Past that: dunes. Mounds of sand, red as fire. They seem to run on forever underneath the cloudless sky.

Behind him: raggedy, ratty tents. Propped up by scraps of rusted pole and rebar, some of it kinked with an arthritic bent. The wind threatens to pick it all up and carry it away, but it never does. These tents have been here for so long they're a part of the world. Just like the people.

Corwin steps out of his speeder—a limping junker he bought from a couple of anchorites outside of Tuanul. (He gave them more than he owed. Charity. What does it matter now, anyway?) Then he descends among the scavengers, the castoffs, the dregs of the galaxy's populace. All of them dust-cheeked. Scarred, too—branded by the roughness of this place. A round-faced brute with a crown of wispy black hair and a fat body wreathed in rags steps in front of him, licking his chapped lips and chuckling. "What have we here—"

But Corwin knows the play. He's no fool. Not any-more. He hooks his thumb around the button loop of his jacket and tugs it back, showing off a lean, mean, vent-barreled HyCor laser repeater.

Seeing it, the rag-man grunts and wanders off in search of prey that doesn't sting or bite. Corwin, for his part, searches out the bar.

It's not much to look at. The bar has been welded together out of scrap, the whole thing warped and crooked and shaped into a rough half circle, all of it underneath the cap-top of a 323 Rakhmann concussion-miner. Dust and sand hiss against the can-opy of thin metal.

Corwin pulls up a rusted stool next to a socket-eyed skull-face: one of the Uthuthma, with swaddles of chain forming a scarf and obscuring its toothy maw. The alien chatters at him in its language: "*Matheen wa-sha wa-sho tah*." A statement or a question, Corwin doesn't know. All he does is wink and give the stranger a thumbs-up. The Uthuthma keeps staring with those dead empty holes it report-edly calls *eyes*. A loud, gurgling throat-clear from be-hind the bar, and Corwin turns to see the tender—

Big fella. Muscle gone to fat. Nose like a fallen tree. Whole right side of his face is peppered with scars, some of them lumpy with bits of scree and stone. One bit of gravel is bigger than the pad on Corwin's thumb and sticks in the man's cheek the way a rock pokes up out of dry, dead ground. "Whaddya having?"

"Whaddya got?"

"Nothing but one thing: Knockback Nectar, they call it."

"If you only have one thing, then why ask me what I'm having?"

The bartender shrugs and snorts. "People like the illusion of choice. Gives them comfort in these strange times."

"Then I will have that, my good man."

"Good man," the bartender mutters, then pours from an old oil can into a smaller oil can and plonks it down in front of Corwin. The so-called nectar is the color of hydraulic fluid. And bits float in it. Spongy, bobbing bits.

"What is this?"

"Knockback Nectar, I told you already."

"No, I mean, what *is* it?"

"Ugh. Huh. You know, I don't ask. They just bring it to me. Something about scraping the lichen rocks from the dead buttes down in the south. I hear tell they pickle it in fuel barrels or some such."

"It'll get me drunk?"

"It'll get a space slug drunk."

Corwin tips it back. It tastes like sour spit with a motor oil aftertaste. Doesn't take long before his gums start to feel numb and his teeth buzz.

All righty, then.

The Uthuthma babbles at him again: *"Matheen bachee. Iss-ta ta-hwhiss."*

"May the Force be with you, too," Corwin says. His voice is stripped raw after one sip of the Knockback. The words wheeze out. He laughs: It's a mad, desolate, empty sound. Like this little enclave. Like this whole planet.

"You're not from here," the tender says.

"What gave it away?"

"Not many folks *from* here. Most folks . . . just end up here. Jettisoned like so much worthless cargo. Dropped like waste."

Corwin shrugs and chuckles and sips his poison.

"You're a strange fella. You looking for work?"

"Could be. What's around?"

"Haw. *Pfft.* Not much. Most of the mining is on the far side, and even that's pretty meager. We do get magnite here, and bezorite, and there's talk of some new kesium gas wells going up near Cratertown, but that might just be rumor. You got the scavenger packs. You got the Wheel Races north of here. You could say your vows and be an anchorite but, naw, not you. And I'd say you could be a bartender, but turns out that job's taken."

"I'll think about it, thanks."

The tender keeps on him: "So how'd you end up here?"

"I didn't 'end up here.'"

"Not from here. Didn't end up here. How'd you come to be sitting at Ergel's Bar, then?"

"You Ergel?"

"I'm Ergel."

"Well, Ergel, I came here."

"You came here? Of your own free will and such?"

"Of my own free will and such."

Ergel stands there and stares for a good ten seconds, then bursts out laughing. A big, booming, gurgling laugh like he's choking on his own lung-meats in the process. His jowls shake and his belly bounces back and forth. "Galaxy's a big place, fella. Wide open as a nexu's fang-lined maw. The stars are endless. The worlds are countable, but not by one hand and not by a hundred. You got planets and outposts and stations and spaceships and—" More laughing. "You came *here?*"

Corwin nods. "I did."

"Why? I have to know. I have to know what drives a man to this."

"*Matheen vis-vis tho hwa-seen,*" the Uthuthma says.

"Shut up, Gazwin," Ergel grumbles. "Let the man finish." Then to Corwin: "Ignore the skull-face. I gotta know."

Here, Corwin blinks a few times. And every time he does, he sees it happen again right there in his hometown, right in Maborn on Mordal:

His little girl lying there in the open street.

The shallow rise and fall of her chest.

The Imperials entrenched at one end of town. The rebels on the other.

Corwin's there, off to the side, hiding behind crates of vittles with his wife, Lynnta, and suddenly she's up and running for the little girl, and then he's running after her, hard-charging, screaming, reaching—

Laserfire. Crossing both directions.

Lynnta's head snapping hard the one way—

Then she's down.

Corwin leaps—

But something burns into his side. Cuts through him. He hears the sizzle of it. Feels his system go through shock: like a bomb detonating underwater. *Boom.*

Then he's out.

When he wakes up weeks later on a bacta drip on a crawler outside of town, his family is gone. Already buried. And neither side won its war, and both sides went home licking their wounds.

"War," Corwin says. "I'm tired of war."

"You don't look like an Imperial. You were a rebel, I bet."

"No, no rebel, either. Just a man trying to make do with his family."

"You brought your family here?"

"I did," Corwin says, but he doesn't explain that he brought them only in his heart—and in the picture he's got stuffed in his boot. "Wanted to take them as far away from the fighting as I could. A place where the war will never find us. The farthest-flung nowhere rock I could find on a star map."

"Well, you found it, buddy. You don't get more nowhere than here. War ain't got no reason to roll up on this rock."

"You promise?"

"If the war comes here, I'll buy you all the Knockback Nectars you want."

"Deal."

"This is a dead place, you know."

"I know."

That works for Corwin. A dead place for him: a man gone dead.

PART FOUR

PART FOUR

CHAPTER THIRTY-EIGHT

AND THEN, she's back.

Norra cries out in the darkness, and then light rushes in. Everything feels electric. Her body is bright, too bright, everything vibrating and burning and she's scrambling up and something's on her arm—she starts to yank at it, and something in her nose and mouth and she pulls at that, too. Gagging. Coughing. Suddenly someone is there. Holding her. Pinning her arms. *Let me go,* she wants to say. She tries to say it but her voice is a scratchy, gargling mess. All she hears is a voice:

"Shh. Mom. Shhh. It's okay. It's okay." Temmin. Oh, by all the gods of all the stars, it's her son. He holds her close. She holds him back.

She sees now: She's in a white room. Blue skies outside. A medical droid standing off to the side, ready to act.

Temmin kisses her cheek. She kisses his brow with chapped lips.

Norra cries.

Days later, when she has her voice back, she sits in the lounge of the medical building here in Hanna City. Out of the glass she can see the city there—and beyond it, the windswept meadows. Chandrila has been a peaceful place, long separate from the war. It seems an artifact out of time—a souvenir from some other era.

She sits there with two others:

Admiral Ackbar.

And Captain Wedge Antilles.

Wedge looks better than she does, though maybe not by much. He's walking with a cane right now, though he says that should change soon.

Ackbar, for his part, looks tired.

But he looks happy to see her, too.

"You're quite something, Norra," Ackbar says.

"I don't know about that, sir," she says. Her voice is still scratchy. She still feels edgy, touchy. Ever since the droid woke her up out of that coma with whatever that chemical concoction was—she feels like an overcharged battery. Like she wants to get up and run, leap, dance. But her body can't do those things: She feels raw, sore, as tired as an old musk-hound.

Ackbar and Wedge share a look. Wedge nods. Ackbar produces a small box. "This is for you."

She gives a quizzical look and takes it. Norra hesitates but Wedge urges her on: "Open it, Norra."

Inside: a medal.

"I already have mine," she says, "this must be a mistake."

"One can earn more than a single medal," Ackbar says, somewhat gruffly. But his lips twist into a strange smile. "Your efforts on Akiva have had tremendous effect."

"I . . . hardly see how . . ."

"Humility is well and good but facts persevere beyond the shadow of one's own feelings," Ackbar says. "You saved Captain Antilles. You helped us capture two high-value Imperial targets—General Jylia Shale, and Palpatine's adviser Yupe Tashu—and confirm the deaths of two others: Moff Valco Pandion and slaver Arsin Crassus." The way Ackbar says that word *slaver*—it drips with rage and condescension.

"Admiral Sloane," Norra says. "What of her?"

Wedge sighs. "We got her attaché, Adea Rite. But the admiral herself got away. It's why you've been here for the last month, in a coma. She blew the shuttle and got away in an escape pod." Norra realizes: *Of course.* The front cockpit of those *Lambda*-class shuttles becomes the escape craft. She finishes the story for him:

"Let me guess. She took that escape craft right to the Star Destroyer—"

"And they took that ship to lightspeed. Yes."

She scowls. Disappointment stabs her in the gut.

Wedge reaches out and clasps her hands. "We'll find her. We still took down two Star Destroyers. It was a victory for the New Republic."

She nods and forces a smile. "Thank you, Captain."

"There's something else," Ackbar says.

"Sir?"

"I have more work for you if you want it."

"I . . . I don't know, sir. My son. I . . ."

"Just hear me out, will you?"

She nods. She listens.

And in the end, she says yes.

Akiva. Still hot. Still muggy. A storm came through the night before, and now the landing pad is littered with palm fronds and the fat, broad leaves and crinkly blue blossoms of the asuka trees. The flowers lie matted against the ground, still pretty in their way, but drowned looking, too.

Norra stands there, a sack over her shoulder.

Temmin stands with her. He has a bag with him, too.

A New Republic flag flies over this landing pad, and a Corellian corvette roars overhead. Akiva: the first Outer Rim planet to officially have joined the contingent of worlds pledging themselves to the New Republic. The satraps saw the Empire's betrayal—and the rage of the people of Myrra—and decided that the only way to save their skins and their rule was to give it over, in part, to the Republic. (And Norra thanks the stars that the first order of business was routing out corruption and crime—Surat fled, but the rest of his gang went down. Many in prison. The rest went out in what they probably thought was a blaze of glory but what instead will likely end up as a bloody and brutal footnote in Akiva's history books.)

"Are you sure about this?" she asks.

"Yeah. I'm sure."

"You can stay here. I understand."

"I don't want to stay here. I thought this place was home. It's not."

She smiles. "It still could be."

"You're my home. Wherever you go, that's where I live." She pulls him close.

He says: "Do you think we'll find Dad still?"

"It's possible. Those data cubes you stole from Surat had a lot of information about the Empire's criminal dealings." Jas was the one who translated them. Looks like Surat may have been collecting that information in case he ever had to bargain his way to freedom with the burgeoning New Republic. Temmin stealing that from him bought him the only chip he had to play. The archive offered a bounty of information connecting the Empire with several crime syndicates across the galaxy. "The Hutts and other syndicates operated black-site prisons for the Empire. I'm hoping our journeys will take us there." The holocrons will in part inform their new mission. "But I also don't want to promise anything. Not like I did before. I don't know what's going to happen out there. You have to know that, Temmin. But we'll try. Okay? We'll try."

"I know." He looks up. "Hey, here's our ride."

A ship drifts down, its twin engines pivoting and firing against the ground to slow its ascent. It's an SS-54 assault ship. On the side is the scratched-up painting of a little tooka doll holding a sharp knife. The words that were above it are mostly gone, except for two:

PLAY NICE.

It settles down, and once it does, three people step off. Jas is first off the ship, craning her neck and cracking her knuckles. Sinjir follows after. He's still got that rough-hewn edge. His scruff has grown out a bit more. Though that Imperial *vibe* still hangs about him like a miasma.

Last off, a man with thick muttonchops that connect to a bushy mustache. Arm in a cast, blaster at his side. Helmet palmed in his hand.

He steps off and heads right for Norra, hand out.

"Norra Wexley, I'm guessing?" he asks.

"Jom Barell," she says, shaking his hand. "A pleasure to meet you finally. I just want to say again I appreciate you fighting the fight on Myrra. I had thought all of you SpecForce guys and girls died that day. I'm happy I was wrong and thanks for taking the initiative."

Temmin walks past and mutters: "Though you almost killed us."

"Your boy?" he asks.

"My boy," she says.

Temmin gives Jas a hug. Then gives Sinjir a punch to the arm.

Norra calls after: "Temmin, I think you're forgetting something."

"Oh! Yeah." He sticks both fingers in his mouth and whistles. "Yo. Bones! Let's roll."

From far off the field, Mister Bones jerks his head up. The droid, which Temmin and Norra rebuilt together from scrap in Esmelle and Shirene's basement over the last week—a "family project," she said— waves. In one hand, a flower. In the other, a blaster.

"ROGER-ROGER!"

The battle droid jogs past, leaving small craters in the landing field. Which tells Norra they still have a little work to do on his pneumatics.

Jas and Sinjir come up to her.

Jas says: "So, we ready to hunt some Imperial war criminals?"

"Oh, I *guess*," Sinjir says, pouting. "I like to pretend we're going to be hunting down dangerous prey, but most likely we're going to be chasing a bunch of pudgy Imperial accountants across backwater worlds."

"Duty calls," Norra says. "I'm glad you all answered it with me. I didn't think you'd go for it. Ackbar suggested we all work together again and . . . I thought he was crazy."

"There's money," Jas says with a shrug.

"And there's drink," Sinjir adds.

Jom frowns. "Oh, this is going to be fun. Come on. The job awaits."

Norra smiles.

Temmin stands on the ramp of Jas's ship. He waves. She waves back and heads aboard, ready to see where the next adventure takes them.

INTERLUDE:

CHANDRILA

"WHAT'S YOUR NAME? Your rank?" Olia asks.

The man at the head of the prisoner procession seems taken aback. "I'm Corporal Argell. Camerand Argell. M . . . ma'am. You are?"

But she doesn't answer. Instead she demands:

"What is this?" She gestures to the lineup of prisoners. Imperials still in uniform, partly: stormtroopers in their underclothes, officers in their grays and blacks. Not a big group: just a dozen or so.

"I feel like . . . that's obvious. Prisoners." He continues, looking nervously over to Lug the Trandoshan, standing there with the camera. "We captured a small holdout garrison down on Coruscant. They're going to be stationed here at one of the camps and Commander Rohr thought it prudent to parade this lot about a bit given the . . . the, ahhh, the triumph of the day and all that." He blinks. "Am I on camera?"

"You *are*," she says, "and this isn't right. Take these men to where they belong. They're not cattle. They're not a prize!"

"But we should be proud of winning this war . . ."

"Nobody should be proud of war, Corporal. Nobody. This isn't a thing we do because we like winning. Because of what glory it is to subjugate anybody. We do it because we want to be on the right side of things. This . . ." She fritters her hands in the air, trying (and failing, somewhat) to contain her anger. "This kind of thing is what the Empire would do. March their prisoners around—a display to rile the blood of the faithful. We don't do that. We have to be better than that. Nod if you understand me."

Hesitantly, he nods. "Of course. Ma'am."

"Good. Good. Go on now. Tell your commander plans changed."

Argell swallows visibly and gives an awkward wave to the camera. Then he snakes back the way he came, bringing the line of prisoners with him. Olia stands there, fuming.

Tracene approaches. The camera is still on.

She puts a hand on the Pantoran's shoulder. A small gesture, but enough: Olia lets out a captive breath.

"That was something, too. You're actually good at this."

Olia smiles stiffly. "We just need to do better. All of us. If we're going to keep this up, we need to do it right."

"Are you worried that the New Republic will get it wrong? That these things—the protester, the orphans, the parade of prisoners—are warning signs? Will the New Republic survive?"

Olia turns. She lifts her chin. She speaks with authority.

"This is democracy," she says. "It is strange. And it is messy. It's not about getting it right. It's about trying to get it right. Yes, it's a bit chaotic. Certainly we will get some things wrong. The Empire? They cared nothing for democracy. They valued order above everything else. They wanted to be right so badly that anybody who even hinted at getting it wrong or doing it differently was branded the enemy and thrown in a dark prison somewhere. They destroyed other voices so that only their own remained. That is not us. We will not always get it right. We will never have it perfect. But we will listen. To the countless voices crying out across the galaxy, we have opened our ears, and we will always listen. That is how democracy survives. That is how it *thrives*. Look. There."

She points.

And now, a new procession:

Senators. A hundred of them, maybe more. From systems all across the galaxy—even a few from the Outer Rim now. Marching toward the old Chandrila Senate house. Small crowds of citizens gathering, applauding, whistling. It's just a start. A humble new beginning. But there it is.

Olia smiles.

"That is democracy. That is the New Republic. And if you'll excuse me, we have a great deal of work to do. May the Force be with you, Tracene."

The newswoman smiles. "Knock 'em dead, Olia."

EPILOGUE

RAE STANDS on the bridge of the *Ravager*. There, staring out the window at the glowing Vulpinus Nebula, is the fleet admiral.

His hands behind his back. Humming a little. Something classical. Something from the Old Republic days. She listens a little: the Sestina of Imperator Vex, maybe.

"Sir," she says.

He holds up his finger. A sign for patience. He continues humming, his head swaying, until it reaches a small crescendo. Then, without turning toward her, he lowers his finger and says:

"Yes, Admiral Sloane?"

"Something I've been wanting to ask you."

"You may always speak frankly with me." He turns to face her. His countenance is cold. His stare, scrutinizing. Like she's wet, fresh meat and he's picking her apart to look for the tastiest bits. "Please."

"The summit. On Akiva."

"Dreadful thing."

"It did not go as planned." She hesitates. "Though

now I'm not so sure. Did you . . . plan for it to go that way?"

He smiles. "Explain."

"I've . . . been thinking. Everything happened so fast. Faster than it should have. Faster than any timeline predicted. And I wondered: Did we have someone in our midst who summoned the rebels? I went and I looked and I found . . . communications. From an encrypted channel on this very ship. Sent out to what appears to be a rebel frequency."

"Enlighten me. Why would I have cause to do that?"

She hesitates. "I've been thinking about that. I would guess . . . to eliminate competition."

"An interesting theory."

"I'm more interested if it's an accurate one, Admiral."

He takes her hand and gives it a squeeze. "It was a test."

"I could have died there. On Akiva. Or been taken captive."

"But that did not happen. You were not captured. And you remain alive. You are my best and my brightest, and that is why you passed this test. I need people like you."

This, a question she hates to ask: "And if I hadn't survived?"

"Then my assessment of you would've been wrong. You would not have been my best and my brightest. It's like the others. Pandion, Shale, and so forth. They were weak. Sick animals that had to be culled from the herd. They did not pass the test and now they are no burden to us."

She tries to repress a shiver.

"Here," he continues, pointing out at the glowing red bands of the Vulpinus Nebula—the swooping whorls of crimson clouds and the stars beyond them. "Look out there. That is no longer our galaxy."

"Admiral, we have not lost yet."

"Oh, but we have. I see the dismay in your eyes, but this is no cause for despair, Admiral Sloane. This is how it must be. The Empire became this . . . ugly, inelegant machine. Crude and inefficient. We needed to be broken into pieces. We needed to get rid of those who want to see that old machine churning ineluctably forward. It's time for something better. Something new. An Empire worthy of the galaxy it will rule."

Sloane doesn't know what to feel. Right now it's some strange mix of terror, disgust, but also? Hope.

Did he try to betray her?

Or was it truly a test he expected her to pass?

All she manages to say right now is: "Of course, Admiral."

"Now, if you will excuse me? I have thinking to do."

He gently touches her shoulder—a seemingly warm gesture, until he uses it to turn her around and send Sloane on her way.

Read on for an excerpt from

Star Wars: Bloodline
by Claudia Gray

Published by Century

An entire generation has prospered during an era of peace. The New Republic, governed by the Galactic Senate on Hosnian Prime, has held power for more than two decades. The wars that divided the galaxy are fading into legend.

Yet conflict has begun to take shape within the Senate. Two unofficial but powerful factions have formed—the Populists, who believe individual planets should retain almost all authority, and the Centrists, who favor a stronger galactic government and a more powerful military.

As the political gridlock threatens to cripple the fledgling democracy, Centrist leaders have called for the election of a "First Senator." It is their hope that this powerful position will bring order to the divided Senate. But Populists like Senator Leia Organa Solo know all too well the price of such order. Even as the election nears, the divisions between the worlds of the galaxy are growing wider. . . .

The conference building of the New Republic senatorial complex contained multiple rooms appropriate for every kind of auxiliary function imaginable, from memorial concerts to awards ceremonies. Leia and Tai-Lin Garr headed toward one of the smallest banquet rooms. The breakfast meeting had been organized by Varish Vicly, who couldn't imagine a bad time for a party.

Varish came loping toward them now on all fours. "There you are! I was worried you'd be late."

"We're still early," Leia protested as both she and Tai-Lin were wrapped in quick, long-limbed hugs.

"Yes, but I worry. You know how these guys get."

"These guys" meant prominent representatives of both the far-left and far-right branches of the Populist faction. The far-right branches wanted to dissolve the Senate so each world would again become a totally separate entity; the far left hoped to open voting to the general populace, so that instead of thousands of senators refusing to agree, they could have trillions of citizens refusing to agree. The only thing these senators had in common was, it seemed, a willingness to support Leia's candidacy for First Senator.

"Now come along and be introduced to everyone," Varish insisted. Soon Leia found herself shaking hands and paws, murmuring greetings; thanks to some review holos Korr Sella had prepared for her, she recognized each senator in attendance and could even ask a few pertinent questions about their families and worlds.

In other words, Leia thought as she listened to someone cheerfully talk about his grandchildren, *this is going wonderfully for everyone but me.*

They entered the banquet hall together, the entire group walking two by two. Leia knew the seat at the far end of the table would be hers, guest of honor as counterpart to the host. So she walked the length of the room, attentive to the senator at her side, before glancing down at the arrangements—sumptuous even by Varish's standards, with a velvet runner stretching along the table and delicate paper streamers lying across the tables, beneath elaborately folded napkins. Leia had to laugh. "Honestly, Varish. For breakfast?"

This won good-natured chuckles from the room; Varish Vicly's lavish tastes were well known, a foible she herself joked about. Today, however, she shrugged. "I didn't request this. Maybe the serving staff heard my name and assumed that meant to go all out." Varish smiled as she took her seat. "If that's my reputation . . . you know, I can live with it."

Leia settled into her chair, picked up her napkin— and stopped.

Something was written on the paper streamer on her plate. Actual writing. Virtually nobody wrote any longer; it had been years since Leia had seen actual words handwritten in ink on anything but historical documents.

But today, someone had left this message on her plate, only one word long:

RUN.

Leia shoved her chair back, instantly leaping to her feet. "We have to get out of here," she said to the startled senators at the table. "Now. Go!"

But they didn't move, even as she dashed toward the door. Varish said, "Leia? What in the worlds—"

"Didn't you hear me?" Damn fools who had never been in the war, who didn't know an urgent warning when they got one. Leia held up the paper so they could see it. "Run! Everyone get up and run!"

With that, she took off, running as fast as she could, finally hearing the others stir behind her. Maybe they thought the note was only a prank, but Leia knew better. The inchoate dread that had swirled inside her all morning had solidified; *this* was what her feelings had been warning her about.

As they dashed through the hallways of the conference building, Leia glimpsed an alert box and swerved sideways to hit it. A robotic voice said, "No detected hazards at this—"

"Override! Evacuation alert *now*!" Leia resumed running just as the warning lights began to blink and the siren's wail sounded. Immediately people began filing out of various other rooms, mostly grumbling but at least moving toward the exits—and when they saw her, they, too, started to run. The sense of urgency built behind her like a wave cresting, preparing to crash.

Leia's breath caught in her throat as she pushed herself harder, running full out toward the doors, so fast they almost didn't have time to open for her. In the square beyond, security droids had begun herding people away from the building, but too many continued to mill around, staring in consternation at the scene. The others evacuating flooded through the doors behind and around her, but once they were clear of the structure, half of them stopped, remaining stupidly within range.

Within range of what? She still didn't know. But every instinct within her—the Force itself—told her disaster was near.

Leia didn't stop. She kept running as hard as she could, never looking back, until . . .

Brilliant light. A roar so loud it resonated in her skull. And hot air and debris slamming into her, knocking her down, rolling her over, erasing the world.

READ THE REST OF
THE AFTERMATH TRILOGY
BY CHUCK WENDIG

LIFE DEBT
BOOK 2 · OUT NOW

EMPIRE'S END
BOOK 3 · OUT NOW

CENTURY